A Scheme Created by Extraordinary People . . .

Dr. Jan Szukalski—whose research into typhus struck the spark of ingenuity that could save a town from extinction.

Father Wajda—who broke his sacred vow as a Catholic priest after a guilt-ridden Nazi soldier confessed to the horror that was Auschwitz.

Dr. Maria Duszynska—the beautiful woman whose skills as a doctor equaled her amazing courage as a spy.

. . . Thwarted by an Extraordinary Enemy

Maximilian Hartung—whose love for Hitler and ruthless personal ambition were hidden behind a handsome face, a charming manner—and an unerring eye for resistors of the Reich.

NIGHT TRAINS

BARBARA WOOD & GARETH WOOTTON

BALLANTINE BOOKS • NEW YORK

Library of Congress Catalog Card Number: 79-14286

ISBN 0-345-28806-8

This edition published by arrangement with
William Morrow and Company, Inc.

Manufactured in the United States of America

First Ballantine Books Edition: August 1980

This book is dedicated to Alfons Lewandowski,
who was there when it happened
and whose experiences gave us
what no history books could;

To Pope John Paul II;

And to the nameless thousands who, like him,
fought in the Polish Resistance.

This is their memorial.

Author's Note

For the names of all people and places in Poland, we have chosen to use Polish spelling throughout. Below is an alphabetical list of key names found in this book and their correct pronunciation.

PEOPLE

Moisze Bromberg	MOYsheh BROMberg
Leokadja Ciechowska	layoKAHdya cheKHOVska
Djapa	DYAHpah
Edmund Dolata	EDmund doLAHtah
Maria Duszynska	maREEah dooSHINska
Ben Jakoby	ben yahKOHbee
Anna Krasinska	AHnah kraSHINska
Jerzy Krasinski	YEHRzhee kraSHINski
Alfons Lewandowski	ALfons levanDOVski
Brunek Matuszek	BROOnek mahTOOshek
Stanisław Poniatowski	STANyiswav ponyahTOVski
David Ryż	DAHvid rish
Każik Skowron	KAHzhik SKOVron
Jan Szukalski	yahn shooKALski
Abraham Vogel	AHbraham FOHgel
Piotr Wajda	pYOTr VIda
Antek Wozniak	AHNtek VOZnyak
Żaba	ZHAbah

PLACES

Krakow (Cracow)	KRAHkov
Majdanek	MIdanek
Oświęcim (Auschwitz)	oshVYEHchim
Saint Ambroż	Saint AHMbrozh
Sofia	ZOHfya

vii

Warszawa (Warsaw)	varSHAHvah
Wisła (Vistula River)	VEESwah

* NOTE: In pronouncing Polish words, the following should be kept in mind.

j = y
ż = zh or sh
ł = w
w = v
sz = sh

BUENOS AIRES—
THE PRESENT

Adrian Hartman opened the side door to his palatial home at 3600 Avenida del Libertador and stepped out into the crisp morning air. He was an avid jogging enthusiast and physical fitness aficionado with a rigid routine that meant starting his exercising at a specific time, and then competing against himself with a stopwatch. He grew restless to begin.

"My God, Ortega," he called to his bodyguard valet. "What's keeping you?"

He bounced on the balls of his feet and stretched his arms overhead, breathing deeply of the fresh air. What a lovely morning! And where was Ortega? He called again inside the half-open door.

"What's keeping you, man?" Disgusting, thought Hartman. Ten years ago Ortega had been one of the finest *fútbol* players in all of Argentina. Now he had to be practically dragged from bed to keep up with his sixty-four-year-old employer on his morning exercise run.

Adrian Hartman continued his warm-ups. He toyed with the idea of taking off ahead of the bodyguard, but there had been some terrorist kidnappings in Buenos Aires recently, and he was one of the wealthiest jewelry manufacturers in South America. The thought of abduction did not appeal to him.

Finally Ortega appeared at the door, holding his running shoes in his hands, and he sat on the threshold to put them on.

Seeing the bodyguard overweight and already straining to put on his shoes made Hartman impatient. He reached down, closed the ankle zippers on his jogging suit, and then turned to Ortega.

"I'm going to start now. The usual course through

1

the park and around the lake. Five kilometers." He checked his watch. Five forty-five A.M. Pushing the stopwatch button, he jogged down the winding drive to Avenida del Libertador and turned right. Hartman was about three hundred meters down the street before Ortega reached the driveway gate. He adjusted his shoulder holster and seated the nine millimeter Hi-Power in firmly so that it would not jar loose while he was running. "Crazy old fool," muttered Ortega, seeing that there was no way he could catch up with Hartman unless he cut across the park. But he dared not do that, for then he would lose sight of him.

Hartman jogged along with a certain tension to his gait that only those driven by impatience and insensitivity have.

The sun was lighting the eastern sky but was still below the horizon. Hartman noted that the eucalyptus trees were getting new leaves. As long as he had lived in Buenos Aires he had never gotten used to the idea that October was springtime.

Turning left at Avenida Sarmiento, Hartman entered the beautiful green Parque 3 de Febrero. He picked up his pace a bit as he went into the park and could see in the distance on the shore of the lake the clubhouse, a building that had just recently been reopened since the military junta. It had been closed during the Perón regime soon after the Jockey Club had been burned. Hartman seethed and thought: The dirty Communist bastards almost ruined things for everyone.

Placing his hand on his neck as he ran, Hartman brought the stopwatch up to his eyes so that he could count his pulse. He counted for ten seconds. "Twenty-two," he muttered as he exhaled. Not bad. That multiplied out to a hundred and thirty-two beats per minute. With a heart that good he could live to be a hundred. Maybe a hundred and fifty like some of those Russian peasants he had heard about. *Bullshit*, said his mind as he ran. Their secret to living to a hundred and fifty is that they count by twos!

Hartman turned left when he reached the Avenida Infanta Isabel, a small dirt road that led more deeply into the park. He glanced back up Avenida Sarmiento and saw Ortega still a good three hundred meters behind him, puffing and pumping his arms as he jogged like some little potbellied steam engine pulling against a grade.

The sun broke above the horizon and lit the sky with the promise of an unseasonably hot day. Hartman glanced about the park as he approached the lake and was satisfied that it was still nearly empty. He could see only one other person in the park, another man jogging with his dog, and he was going in the opposite direction on the other side of the lake. No cars were on the road except for a single parked car way across on Avenida del Libertador—actually outside the park—and it appeared to be empty.

As he reached the lake he went to the right, taking a quick look at the street sign as he continued along Avenida Infanta Isabel and maintained his steady pace along the lake shore.

The man with the dog had rounded the lake and was now on Avenida Infanta Isabel, about a hundred meters separating him from Ortega.

The dog, a large Doberman pinscher, pranced alongside his master, straining at the leash, now and then yanking him forward.

"Easy, Drum," murmured the man, tightening his hold on the lead. "Take it easy, boy."

The road was now heavily lined with eucalyptus trees and it curved as it reached the opposite end of the lake. As Hartman reached the curve, the runner with the dog closed the gap to fifty meters. Hartman looked over to his right and saw the Hipodrómo de Palermo. He could see the horses going through their morning workout. The air was so still he could hear the hoof beats as they ran around the first turn.

As the man with the dog rounded the curve behind Hartman, he looked back. Ortega was out of view. Raising his arm over his head as if to signal someone, and without missing the rhythm of his step, he unsnapped the leash. "Sic him, Drum!"

The Doberman leaped away from his master and took off toward Hartman. As the dog made his run, the car parked on Avenida del Libertador moved away from the curb and accelerated toward the entrance of the park. It squealed as it made the sharp right turn.

Hartman heard the padding of the animal's feet on the pavement but did not for the moment distinguish it from the distant sound of the horses' hooves.

By the time he was aware of it, however, it was too late, for the dog had already reached its full speed and flew through the air, striking Hartman with its thirty kilograms of weight directly at shoulder level and at the same time closing its massive jaws on the back of Hartman's neck.

The combination of the tremendous blow from the dog and Hartman's own forward momentum staggered, then felled him spread-eagle with the side of his face smashing into the lightly graveled road.

The dog's master was now upon Hartman and the dog. He held a .357 magnum in his right hand and snapped to the dog, "Hold him, Drum, hold!"

Feeling more anger than fear, Adrian Hartman lay still beneath the Doberman and sputtered, *"Get this animal off me before he kills me!"*

In the next split second Hartman realized that this was no accident, for the stranger had commanded the dog to act.

By now the car had reached the bend about seventy-five meters from where Hartman lay. Ortega, still jogging, was taken by surprise and, in a quick smooth gesture, stopped short and reached for his gun. Breathing heavily, Ortega tried to take careful aim and managed to get one shot away before a man from the car with a rifle put two shots into his chest, killing him instantly.

The moment the rifle fired the dog released its grip, and at that instant Hartman's right hand went for the snub-nosed .38 he carried in a holster at the small of his back. He fired recklessly between the two men who ran toward him, and into the knee of the man who handled the dog. The man with the rifle was upon him at once, firing directly at Hartman's head. The blasts created a splash of red and gray in the dirt.

Looking quickly around the silent park, the three men scrambled to the car, the wounded one holding his knee and being helped by the others. The Doberman clambered in behind. Before the doors were even slammed shut the car pulled away from the curb and sped out of the park.

"Here!" The man who had wielded the rifle reached under the seat and, pulling out a rag, handed it back to the man clutching his leg. "Tie it up with this. Be a long time before you see a doctor."

"You blew it, man!" said one of the others, snatching at the rag. "Why'd you have to kill him? You could have just wounded him!"

The man with the rifle wiped a hand across his sweating forehead. Early morning Buenos Aires, still sleeping and peaceful, sped past. "I had to do something. His next shot and one of us could have been dead. Look at it this way. We've saved everyone the trouble of a trial. Hell, he would have been executed in six months anyway."

"Yeh," growled the other man, doing his best to bandage his friend's knee. "Only now we don't have anything to show the world. We had to show everyone what a swine he was. We need the publicity."

"At least," said the driver of the car in a deep voice, "the police will most likely suspect leftist terrorism here. Hartman was a conservative. They'll never think of us."

"And is that so good?"

The question went unanswered, for the men were intent upon their final destination.

Screaming to a halt on the apron of the Aeroparque Ciudad de Buenos Aires, the three men piled out of the car and hurried toward the waiting DC-3 freighter. Letting the dog run up first, the men followed, climbing the stairway into the plane.

When the door was closed, the airplane taxied away from the apron, opened full throttle and rolled down the runway.

Before stepping into his office to see the last patient of the day, Dr. John Sukhov paused at the window of his little laboratory and glanced out at the late afternoon scene. It was a lovely day—too nice to be indoors—with the sun shining and children playing in Central Park. It was nice for October; trees were still green and the day was warm. New York City seemed to be enjoying a lingering summer.

There was a faint knock at the door. A gray-haired woman wearing a white uniform and a smile said, "You know there is someone in your office, don't you, Dr. Sukhov?"

He turned around, returning the smile. "Yes, thank you, Natasha. I had not forgotten. But it is such a lovely day outside. Come and look at the park. All the people are enjoying themselves."

As his nurse came into the laboratory where John Sukhov did blood and urine tests, the doctor pushed his way out and into the hall. He looked at his watch. Nearly four o'clock. Perhaps this one wouldn't take too long and he could go for a walk down in that park. How often did the opportunity arise?

With a slight limp and straightening out the lapels of his lab coat, Dr. Sukhov made his way to his office and stopped before entering to read the chart that Natasha had placed in the box.

It contained nothing more than an information sheet, only sparsely filled out, with the lines reserved for the patient's reason for coming to see him left blank. Mary Dunn. Marital status not filled in. Birthdate: February 22, 1916. Address: Americana Hotel. Occupation: hospital administrator. And birthplace: Poland.

He lingered over this last, allowing a fleeting, brief memory to flash in his mind; then he closed the chart and went into the office.

"Good day, Miss Dunn," he said, holding out his hand.

A well-dressed woman in her sixties took his hand and shook it firmly. "Hello, Doctor."

"Have a seat, please." Sukhov took the chair behind his desk opposite the woman and folded his hands in his lap. "What can I do for you?"

"I am a little hesitant to say, Doctor. Pardon me a moment." She spoke with a faint accent. "May I lay these here?" She held a clutch purse and folded newspaper.

"Of course."

Placing the purse and paper on the edge of the desk, Mary Dunn drew her hand away, and the newspaper accidentally fell open, revealing the front page. "I am not sure if you can help me at all, Dr. Sukhov," she said quietly, keeping her eyes on his face. "My problem is an unusual one and I have been to so many doctors."

John Sukhov nodded. He had heard the same introduction from countless patients in the past. "I shall see what I can do. Please go on." As he said this, his eye caught sight of something on the newspaper, something which made him sit up slightly.

"Someone recommended you to me, Dr. Sukhov," she went on in the same tone.

"Yes . . ." He could not take his eyes off the photo on the front page.

"And I don't really know where to begin."

John Sukhov brought his eyes back to the face of the woman and felt himself frown. "Excuse me, may I look at this for just a moment?"

"Certainly."

He picked up the paper and narrowed his eyes at the picture. Then he read the caption beneath. "Adrian Hartman, well-known jewelry manufacturer in Buenos Aires, was shot and killed by unknown assailants early this morning."

"I beg your pardon," said Dr. Sukhov. "For a moment there I thought I . . ." His eyes drifted back to the paper, scanning the article that accompanied the photograph.

It was fairly long, describing mostly Hartman's dealings and connections in South America and a history of his twenty-odd years in Buenos Aires, and ended with the statement that his death had most likely been the result of a recent wave of terrorism in Argentina and that Hartman had been a well-known arch conservative.

"Interesting. . . ." murmured John Sukhov, his eyes still on the face in the photo.

"I beg your pardon?"

He turned to Miss Dunn. "Oh, excuse me. One

rarely sees a copy of the *Buenos Aires Herald* in New York City. Have you just come from there?"

"Well," she chose her words carefully. "It is related to my problem. You see . . . I am looking for someone. . . ."

John Sukhov rested back in his chair, and studied the face of the woman before him. How strange. It had that same vague, haunting familiarity that the face in the newspaper had. Familiar, and yet not. . . .

He looked again at the picture. And as he stared, his eyes taking in every detail of Hartman's face, John Sukhov felt himself shudder involuntarily. No! he thought wildly. It couldn't be! Not after all these years!

Finally he laid the newspaper down and leaned across the desk, clasping his fingers as he did so. "Miss Dunn," he said flatly. *"Do I know you?"*

CHAPTER 1

POLAND, DECEMBER, 1941

SS-Rottenführer Hans Kepler stood on the platform of the railway station at Oświęcim waiting for the train. It was six o'clock on a sharp, biting cold morning, and to the young corporal who stared down at the snow-flakes melting on the damp wood as fast as they fell, the wait was interminable. Three hours he had waited now, squinting down the track in the gently falling snow, watching for the headlamps of the engine, straining his ear for a distant whistle.

Tomorrow was Christmas, but there was no festivity in the young soldier's heart; his soul was as bereft of holiday cheer as was this half-dead railway station, the only evidence of the Yuletide season being a pathetic clump of pine boughs clustered over each Nazi flag. The other solemn travelers who milled silently about the station, accustomed now to the irregular schedule for the trains, gazed in saturnine detachment into the pale morning.

His cheeks and nose red with cold, Hans Kepler stamped his feet on the platform in an effort to warm them. Surely this was the worst winter he had ever known; not even his heavy greatcoat could keep out the cold. Although possibly, Kepler conceded as he craned his neck down the track once again, it was not so much the raw morning air that was chilling him as the cold winds which blew through his soul. Poland had known worse winters than this one. But *SS-Rottenführer* Hans Kepler had not known a worse day.

A whistle sounded in the distance, and after some moments there could be discerned the chugging hiss of an engine as it drew close to the station. As its lights appeared through the lacy veil of falling snow, Kepler speculated on the reason for its lateness: that the train had been forced onto a siding in order to let other trains, coming from the north, pass. He had seen three such special trains move through the station during his wait; sealed boxcars from the direction of Krakow that had not stopped at this station, but which had rumbled through in a desperation that had sounded in the lonely echo of their whistles; the only trace of their passing being the powdery mounds of snow the powerful wheels had plowed out of their way.

Of the few silent passengers who waited on the freezing platform by the tracks, only Kepler knew what cargo the dark trains carried.

As his own train drew into the station, *SS-Rottenführer* Kepler picked up his duffel bag and walked briskly to the boarding doorway of one of the passenger cars, and showed his papers to the guard who, after careful inspection, motioned him aboard. As he maneuvered his unruly bag along the narrow corridor, Kepler glanced briefly into each compartment, praying he would find an empty one, although he was not certain that the company of others would be worse than the company of his own thoughts.

He paused at the second to the last compartment and dropped his bag to switch hands. Inside, facing one another along the two wooden benches, were four soldiers of the Wehrmacht, comfortably arranged in the compartment, murmuring quietly among themselves as they passed around a bottle of schnapps.

Noticing Kepler hesitate outside the doorway, a soldier who was polishing his boots jerked up his arm and said, *"Heil Hitler."*

Kepler gazed back at the soldier, stared at the smooth face that was as young as his and murmured, "Hitler," returning the salute.

"Will you join us, *Herr Rottenführer?*"

Kepler shook his head. "No, thank you, I have friends up ahead. . . ."

"Are you going to the front with us?"

Picking up his heavy bag and taking a step back, he

said in a vague voice, "No, I'm on leave. In Krakow I'll be taking the train to Sofia." As he started to back away, he could not take his eyes off the young soldier's face. To the front, he had said. To the *Front*. Spoken with such pride in his voice and the glint of glory in his eyes. And Hans Kepler saw there the reflection of his own face as it must have appeared eighteen months before. The idealism. The bravado.

He turned and stumbled to the next compartment which, to his infinite relief, was unoccupied.

Dropping his duffel bag onto the bench next to him, he sat down and pressed his forehead against the window. There was the hiss of air brakes and then the train suddenly jolted forward. The stop had been a surprisingly short one. But then, so few passengers had gotten on. No need to travel these days; where to go?

As the train gathered speed, Kepler kept his face pressed to the cold glass and continued to gaze out the window into the pre-dawn light. He tried to concentrate on Sofia. It was the town of his birth, of his boyhood, of the most pleasant years of his life. He tried to conjure visions of the Wisła in the summer, when he had swum in it with other boys. Of the Wisła in the spring when the yearly flood was an exciting event. Of the Wisła in the winter, as it must appear now, frozen over with a layer of ice thick enough for skating. Then he thought of his grandmother, a kindly Polish lady who owned a little bakery and who had a special place in her heart for her only grandson—no matter what the color of his uniform.

Hans heaved a great sigh. How ironical, he thought, that a bare two years ago he had thought the achieving of this uniform to be the pinnacle of his life; only to realize now that all the Death's Head insignia earned for him were fearful looks, derision behind his back, and an impermeable wall that kept all friendship out.

His eyes screwed tightly against the memories he carried from his post, and yet he knew nothing would keep them away. In his struggle, Kepler felt his mind run around in circles like a tethered animal, going over and over the same ground he had covered these last harsh months, with the solution no closer at hand; and always, the predominant question: How did it come to this?

Always he went back to the very beginning, as if by retracing the two years every step of the way, he would be able to find the exact moment when it had all started to go wrong.

Born twenty-two years before to a German father and a Polish mother in the town of Sofia, which was exactly halfway between Warszawa and the Czecho-slovakian border, Hans had lived his first twelve years in this farming region on the Wisła River. Then his father, an engineer in metallurgy, had moved his family to Essen in Germany where, having a prominent position with the Krupp plants, he had been able to raise his only son in upper-middle-class comfort. Hans, having joined the Hitler Youth, had expressed a desire to enlist in the Wehrmacht, with visions of the Iron Cross and other lofty honors firing him with patriotic idealism. But his father, wishing something more for his son, had insisted the youth continue with his education and hold out for something better.

That "something better" had come along a short while later in the form of conscription into the *Waffen SS*.

Not the elitist *Schutzstaffel* of the smart black uniform that caused people to both shudder and gaze admiringly, but the recently formed *Verfügungstruppe*, the military formations of the SS. Known these days as the *Waffen*, this branch of the SS had been supplied of late by conscripted troops to fill the ever growing demand for fighters on Hitler's newest front: Russia. While his uniform was not the coveted black one, Hans Kepler still had had the honor of wearing the skull and crossbones insignia and was, albeit a long way down the line, ultimately under the command of *Reichsführer* Himmler.

How proud he had been upon receiving his orders to report for basic training; a cocky, self-assured young man in high-stepping boots and driven by ideals and an inflated eagerness to serve the Führer. He saw before him the beaming smiles of his parents, seeing him off at the train station eighteen months ago, the embraces and words of encouragement. Hans had assured his mother and father on that sunny day that he would return bearing the Iron Cross, and that it would go in a place of honor over the fireplace for friends and future generations to admire.

Rocking gently with the clickety-clack of the train and staring blankly at the snow which fell against the window like a drape of lace, Hans felt his heart fill with sadness and remorse.

He closed his eyes. No . . . not an Iron Cross . . . From Oświęcim, his "reward" had been a gold watch taken from a dead Jew.

"Oh God!" he whispered and pushed himself away from the window. Running a hand over his forehead he found that he was sweating heavily. The memories were starting to come back; they were too strong for him. If only he could talk to someone! But who? Who in all the Reich would give a confident and understanding ear to the formidable secret he harbored? And even if there were such a person, how could he, *SS-Rottenführer* Hans Kepler, reveal what he knew without making himself a traitor to the Reich?

"Oh God. . . ." he moaned again.

The train plunged forward into the snowy morning, and Kepler, alone in his cold compartment, sweated and shivered in the folds of his gray uniform. Two weeks, he thought bleakly. A two-week leave from that place; two weeks in which to think it all out, to find himself again.

The train screeched inhumanly and it reminded the young corporal of another screech, also inhuman, back there. Back in Oświęcim. Auschwitz. . . .

The snow was falling with equal density in Sofia, blanketing the quiet streets in a soporific whiteness, and creating a mood of tranquility on this day before Christmas. Yet this was deceiving, for not everyone on this holy morning was lighting Christmas tree candles or roasting a goose, for a wheat farmer named Milewski was impatiently urging his horse along the slippery cobblestone street. There was need to hurry on this ostensibly peaceful dawn, and its cause lay in the oozing

wounds of the man who lay unconscious in the back
of Milewski's wagon.

When he drew up to the side door of the massive
gray stone edifice that was Sofia's hospital, he swung
down to the snow and tried to steady his horse. The
animal, smelling the fresh blood of the cargo it carried,
danced nervously in its harness. A moment later two
old men in white orderly's smocks appeared from the
doorway and began at once to wordlessly transfer
the victim to a stretcher. White-faced and fumbling
for a cigarette, Milewski watched in silence as the
naked man, wrapped in a blood-stained canvas, was
lifted from the back of his wagon and onto the
stretcher. He watched as the two orderlies hurried
with their burden back through the bright light of the
doorway, their shoes crunching the snow, and disappeared inside. He continued to draw on the cigarette,
gazing philosophically at the place where the wounded
man had lain, and thought that some of those blood
stains would never be washed off.

He glanced up to find himself in the presence of
another man, dressed in a white lab coat, who was the
first to break the silence.

"The boy you sent ahead to prepare us," he said
with a detached, professional voice. "Your son?"

"Yes, Doctor."

"It was good you sent him. We have the operating
room ready. You acted wisely."

"Yes, Doctor."

Both men continued to stare at the blood-soaked
wagon. After another moment of silence the physician
said, "Your son had an interesting tale to tell. Most unusual. About that man."

The farmer, for the first time, brought his old eyes
up to the tall and straight doctor. Then he shook his
craggy head, saying, "It's an unusual story, Doctor, but
it is true. And there is more."

The doctor's impassive face twitched slightly. "Tell
me what happened."

Upon arriving in Krakow two hours later, Hans
Kepler was relieved to learn that the train to Sofia

would be along shortly. It was still snowing and the gray and metallic morning light promised nothing more than continuous snow all day. The young SS man who stood with the few other travelers on this Christmas Eve gave evidence of his impatience to be moving on.

A few meters away from where Kepler stood, holding his vigil over the track, a young woman eyed him furtively. There was something about the young soldier's appearance that caught her attention. His eyes never remaining in one place for long, his hands toying with one another in nervous agitation. And yet even more unusual than this, the girl noticed, was the way his shoulders slumped slightly, as though he were extremely tired, and it struck her as oddly out of character in a man whose back should be ramrod straight. She had seen many of them in this area of Poland; the self-assured, swaggering members of the Black Order. In pairs or groups they always struck her as being prancing show dogs, and even alone, an SS man always maintained an arrogant bearing. But not this one. His whole body seemed somehow deflated.

A whistle in the distance alerted the waiting passengers that the train was arriving. The girl gathered up her many parcels, trying to balance them all in her arms, and Hans quickly seized his duffel bag.

When the locomotive thundered into the station and hissed to a halt, Kepler noticed with dismay that the train was horribly crowded, mostly with Wehrmacht troops on their way to the Russian front. Suddenly, a handful of German privates inside the station dashed forward to join their comrades on the train, knocking the Polish girl out of the way and causing her bundles to fly.

When she cried out, Kepler turned around. Seeing her on her knees and frantically grabbing for the packages, he dropped his duffel bag and went to help her.

"The brutes!" she muttered in Polish as she tried to gather all the scattered articles again into her arms.

"They just didn't see you," said Kepler in Polish, retrieving a wrapped parcel off the concrete and noticing that a stain was spreading over the brown wrapper.

"They saw me!" she retorted. "The dogs! They're all alike!"

Hans held the wet package at arms length and wrinkled his nose at the smell. "I'm afraid something broke in this one."

She looked at it and cried out again. "Oh no! A whole half liter! And it was so difficult to get! Just leave it, it can't be salvaged."

They rose to their feet at the same time, she brushing off her knees and pushing her hair out of her face, Kepler silently holding the rest of the packages.

"Thank you," she said breathlessly, tossing strands of hair out of her eyes. "I would have missed the train—" She stopped short suddenly, staring at his uniform.

Kepler quickly turned away and walked to where his duffel bag lay. Picking it up with his free hand, he headed for the train.

Before stepping up, he paused and looked back. The girl was still rooted to the spot. "Come on!" he called. "Hurry!"

The whistle blew and the train jerked forward. The girl suddenly dashed to where Kepler stood and managed, with both arms full, to struggle aboard.

To catch his breath and get his footing, Hans fell against the wall and, keeping his eyes on the bewildered girl, thought: I've seen you before.

The girl also leaned against the wall. She was able to turn away from his gaze now and force her eyes to look out at the passing scene.

Kepler continued to stare at her. He watched her thick brown hair, parted in the middle and falling to her shoulders in a gentle page-boy, lift up in the cold breeze. He took in her large brown eyes, the thinly arched eyebrows, the small round nose and full mouth. Yes, he had seen her before, a hundred times before. She was of Polish peasant stock, cast from the same mold as those he had left behind at Oświęcim. The only difference was, back there, those girls had been only the haunting shadows of this one, their eyes hollow, their mouths thin and lifeless. This one was probably just what they had been like once. Those back there. . . .

He abruptly turned away.

When she murmured, "Thank you for helping me," he brought his head back and tried to force a smile.

Kepler pushed away from the wall. "Let's find somewhere to sit."

Fighting against the motion of the train, he led the way through the second-class car. Most of the compartments were taken by the German troops, singing, reading magazines, and filling the air with cigarette smoke. Finally, at the end of the car, and not wanting to struggle farther with his duffel bag and the girl's bundles, Kepler stopped in the doorway of the last compartment. In it was an old Polish couple; a withered old man and his corpulent wife, both of whom, upon seeing the soldier in the doorway, snapped nervous smiles and hastily removed their possessions from the bench.

He slid in, fell onto the seat next to the window, and dropped the parcels next to him. He motioned the girl inside. She took a seat opposite him and continued to cradle the bundles against her breast.

"Put them up there," said Kepler, jerking his head toward the overhead rack.

But the girl shook her head.

He shrugged and settled himself into the hard seat. The others in the compartment stared at him suspiciously.

"What was in the package that broke?" he asked the girl suddenly. "I've never before smelled anything like that."

She answered him in an uncertain voice. "It was ether."

"Ether!"

"It was for the hospital in Sofia."

"And the rest of these packages?"

"All supplies for the hospital. Sulfa tablets mostly, a few half-liters of ether, and bandages. Things are difficult to get."

He nodded, watching her face. On the surface he

saw apprehension, a little fear, and some curiosity. But there was something else there also on the girl's attractive peasant features, something underlying, as if she were trying to hide it. Rebellion? Hatred?

"You speak Polish very well," she ventured.

"I was born in Sofia and grew up there. My name is Kepler. Hans Kepler."

"How do you do. I'm Anna Krasinska. Is that where you're going now, to Sofia?"

He nodded.

"I thought you must be on your way to the front, with the others on this train."

Kepler smiled grimly. "The *Waffen* has other duties besides fighting the Red Army. I am on a two-week leave from my post. Do you live in Sofia?"

"With my parents. My father is a schoolmaster there, and I am a nurse at the hospital."

While Anna Krasinska spoke, Kepler chanced a quick glance at the old couple. With the commencement of ordinary conversation they had relaxed, and now sat back with their eyes closed.

It was the same everywhere. The look in Anna's eyes when he had held out the dripping bottle of ether, when she had realized who—rather, *what*—he was, he had seen in countless other eyes. The fear, the wariness, the mistrust. And he felt like shouting: This uniform is not my skin! Strip it away and you will find *me*, Hans Kepler!

Just as in the station, Anna Krasinska could not keep herself from staring at the soldier who had now fallen to gazing out at the wintry countryside. He seemed too young for the uniform, the trace of innocence on his face clashing with the skull and crossbones on his cap. Kepler had loose blond hair which fell in a boyish, haphazard way, and she noticed his eyes were the color of corn flowers on a summer day. Yet even here she saw the inconsistencies; the restlessness behind his eyes, a vagueness to his stare.

The train rocked and swayed, plunging through the snow-covered valley of the Wisła River. Again, their progress was delayed by the passage of trains from the north, each time forcing the Lublin-bound train to pull onto a siding; each time, the sealed boxcars rumbling past in a desperate urgency. They had a deadline to meet, these mysterious trains. They had to make their grim appointments.

Hans Kepler closed his eyes against the sight. Why couldn't this train move faster? It would take forever to get to Sofia. Forever. . . .

The tall doctor stood on the other side of the glass window that separated the operating room from the scrub area. He wore a white gown and mask over his regular clothes, but he was not part of the surgical team. He was a spectator, standing on the sidelines watching the team get ready to operate.

The patient on the table, whose blood had spilled in Milewski's wagon and who had not once regained consciousness since being brought here, lay like a corpse beneath the white sterile sheets. He was barely alive.

Sweet and Holy Mary, thought the doctor behind the glass as he watched every precise move of the surgeon. Let him live. Let him live just long enough to tell me what happened.

Fighting the unbearable craving for a cigarette, the doctor chewed anxiously on his lower lip. The story that the farmer had told him, the incredible tale that the bleeding man had managed to sputter out before slipping into unconsciousness, was the most astounding thing he had ever heard.

He watched without blinking as the scalpel glinted in the glare of the operating lights. And he repeated to himself again: Sweet and Holy Mary, let him live. The story can't be true. *It just can't be.*

"Would you like something to eat?"

Kepler snapped his head up. He narrowed his eyes at the old Polish woman who had a lunch spread out in her generous lap. She was proffering a piece of hard cheese.

"No, thank you."

Kepler looked again out the window; it was lighter

outside. The day was wearing on. What time was it? Had he slept?

In sudden alarm he turned his eyes to the girl opposite him. Her face was impassive and the distance in her eyes assured him that all was well. If he had cried out, if he had said anything at all in his sleep—even one word about the awful burden he carried with him—the shock would be evident on her face.

"I have my own—" he began as he reached down to the duffel bag which lay between his feet. After fumbling about inside for a moment, he produced a large blood sausage and a wedge of chocolate. Three pairs of eyes immediately grew wide.

Drawing also a knife out of his bag, Kepler sliced off several thick slabs of the black sausage, and offered them to the incredulous old couple. The man, timid but eager, took them with a murmured, *"Dziękuje,"* and then with an apologetic lift of his shoulders, cut the pieces into yet thinner slices.

When Anna was offered a piece, she accepted it wordlessly but with a smile, and started at once to nibble on it.

The chocolate was next carved up, and when morsels of it were handed to the couple, real cries of appreciation erupted. "It has been a long time, *mein Herr,* since we have tasted chocolate. This will be for the grandchildren on Christmas morning."

Wrapping her own piece in a handkerchief and stuffing it into her coat pocket, Anna said, "It has been two years since I've had chocolate. One works hard for ten *groszy.*"

"Then here." Kepler placed the rest of the chocolate, a large hunk, in her lap, and returned to slicing the blood sausage for himself.

Anna gazed at him in bewilderment. "I couldn't! Why should you give me all your chocolate?"

Kepler avoided her eyes, popping a slice of the crumbling black sausage into his mouth. "I told you I have plenty. And in two weeks, when I return to my post, I shall have more."

Squirreling the rest of the candy into her coat pocket,

the girl asked off-handedly, "Is your post near here, *Herr* Kepler?"

Yes, he thought bitterly, I am a guard at a concentration camp. But aloud he said, "Thirty kilometers from Krakow. I sit at a desk and move papers around."

She smiled again, and it was the first gesture of warmth Kepler had received in eighteen months.

The blood sausage suddenly caught halfway to his stomach, a painful mass that could not be coaxed down as he remembered the incalculable expense of the food he now devoured. Part of the inmates' rations this was, just as the gold watch belonged to them, and the silk stockings he was bringing to his grandmother.

Letting the lump stick here, he turned his face to the window. He caught only brief glimpses of his reflection, but it was enough to enable him to see the beads of sweat.

He stood up suddenly, startling everyone, and tossed the rest of the sausage into Anna's lap. "Take this to your schoolmaster father. I have plenty more and am not hungry." This he said in a forced, tight voice. Then he stumbled over their legs, hurried down the hall, and fell into the lavatory which, thankfully, was empty.

Holding himself over the toilet, he waited patiently until the swaying of the train helped deliver the sausage. It finally came up, tumbled without a sound out of his mouth and scattered on the track below.

He straightened up and emerged into the space at the end of the car, where open windows sent in blasts of biting air and a few snowflakes, and, standing there, thought: Why will it be different in Sofia? I shall be just as sick there. I shall still have the nightmares. And then I shall have to *go back* after two weeks.

Back in the compartment he slumped again into his seat and avoided the curious eyes of his companions. He looked out at the snow, and he could feel Sofia drawing closer and closer, and with it the inevitability of having to tell someone what he knew. It was becoming obvious to him now that, if he were to maintain a final hold on sanity, he would have to unburden himself of his awful knowledge. In his heart, Hans Kepler knew he was a traitor, and this, coupled with the awesome secret he carried, was making him a tormented man.

"Cigarette, *Herr* Kepler?" asked Anna Krasinska.

He looked at the cigarettes. *Damske* brand, made originally for women, with only half tobacco and half cotton filter, but these days the only cigarettes anyone could afford. Kepler thought of the ones in his bag, the coveted *Płaske* brand, refined and oval, coming in a flip-top carton and found now among only the very privileged. But he took one of hers, touched by the gesture of sharing her last two.

They smoked and spent the last few kilometers of the journey in silence. The train finally pulled into the station of Sofia.

Gathering up all her packages and managing to balance them in her arms, Anna thanked Hans Kepler for his help and for the food, and made a hasty exit from the train. While he slowly buttoned his greatcoat, Kepler watched through the window as the pretty young girl ran into the embrace of a man standing on the snow-covered platform.

When Kepler himself was finally off the train and walking toward the station, he was glad that no one had been here to meet him. It was Christmas Eve; before he could appear on his grandmother's doorstep, he had a place to visit and a task to perform, something that had come to him in the final moments of his train ride home.

The church of Saint Ambroż was in the center of town, standing on the far border of the large cobblestone square, opposite Nazi Headquarters. It was an impressive Gothic structure with matching spires that loomed up into the falling snow, covered with statues of medieval saints and protected by rings of gargoyles.

Hans Kepler looked up at the ornate oak doors. It had been many years since he had been inside a church, although before that, in all the years of his boyhood, he had been a devout Roman Catholic. As a Hitler Youth he had had to forsake that Polish part of him and had even, of recent years, embraced the fashionable SS paganism. But now, standing once again on the steps of the church that had baptized him, that had given him his first Holy Communion, he felt a surge of peace he hadn't known in months.

Removing his hat and mounting the steps, he pulled the door open and slipped in. At once the warmth and the fragrance of incense swept over him, causing him to drop his duffel bag in the shadows and stand, for the moment, transfixed.

Kepler looked down the length of the nave and saw, in the distance on the left, the little wooden boxes with their curtained doorways, behind which sat the confessing priests. A few parishioners stood quietly in line while a handful of others murmured their penance at the altar.

Kepler dropped his fingers into the bowl of holy water at his right, touched his forehead, heart and either shoulder, and then, before crossing to the arcade which would take him to the confessionals, dropped to one knee in the direction of the altar. As he stared up at the dying Jesus on the crucifix that hung above the Tabernacle, he felt his palms grow moist and his face break out again in a profuse sweat, quickly soaking the collar of his coat. He got up and felt his knees tremble as he saw that one confessional stood empty.

He parted the velvet curtain and stepped inside. Falling to his knees, Kepler crossed himself and touched a finger to the crucifix which hung over the small window, now shuttered, on the other side of which sat the faceless priest.

As a boy, he had made his first confession in this very box.

His heart was pounding so loudly that he barely heard the grating sound of the shutter sliding to one side as the priest leaned in his direction. Through the closely knit lattice of the screen which separated them, Hans could vaguely make out the outline of the man's head. The priest was whispering something.

When an interminable period had gone by, the sweat running down onto his clenched hands, Kepler heard the priest murmur, "Yes?"

Hans made a strangled sound.

"Is something wrong, my son?" whispered the priest.

"Father, I—"

Kepler wiped his hands down his coat. He trembled so badly that he was afraid he might send the whole confessional over on its side. *Give me absolution, Father, without making me tell you why!*

"Are you ill?" came the priest's gentle voice. "Would you prefer we spoke in my office?"

"Father!" he blurted. "Father . . . it's been many years since my last confession. Bless me. . . ."

The priest went back to whispering his incantation and Kepler, having finally started, felt the words come more easily.

"Father, I have something to tell you. . . ."

CHAPTER 2

Dr. Jan Szukalski walked slowly down the stairs from the second floor of the hospital. He walked alone, listening to his own heavy footfall as he took each step. The limp from a leg injury in childhood that had left him with a slightly crooked leg was more noticeable at times like this, when he was particularly tired or weighed with concern, and it made him appear older than his thirty years.

He paused at the bottom of the stairs and looked down the long, dim hall to where his office was. The hospital was ominously quiet on this Christmas Eve of 1941, despite the fact that all fifty beds were filled. Jan Szukalski wanted to be home right now with his wife and son. But he couldn't leave. Not yet. And possibly not for a long while yet. The gypsy had not yet regained consciousness.

He looked at his watch. Six-thirty. He made the long walk down the hall, entered the office, and flicked on the light.

A single overhead bulb illuminated the sparse furnishings which consisted of a plain wooden desk, a lattice-backed swivel chair, two other lattice-backed chairs, and a wooden file cabinet in one corner. A marble fireplace was built into one wall, but this was now boarded over and a modern steam radiator had been installed on the hearth.

He sat wearily behind the plain wooden desk and rubbed his eyes. Here was the crux of what was disturbing him: the gypsy. . . . He stared up at the water-stained ceiling. It just didn't make sense. The bizarre tale the farmer Milewski had pieced together from the wounded man's ravings couldn't possibly be true. And yet, how to account for his condition and for the way

25

Milewski had found him? And that most aggravating puzzle, why had the man been alone?

In all his experience, Szukalski had never known gypsies to travel alone. Always, regardless of the situation, they traveled together—at the very least in pairs, *but never alone.* And yet this one had been just that, all by himself, sprawled in the snow at the edge of Milewski's farm, his head pierced with a single bullet wound, and the most incredible words coming from his feverish lips.

Something about a massacre. . . .

Szukalski shook his head as if to dispel those thoughts and turned for the moment toward the radio which stood at the far edge of his desk. He considered turning it on, to send this oppressive silence into the shadows, to bring some cheer to this room, but then he recalled that his favorite radio programs, Polish tangos composed and conducted by the great contemporary musicians Gold and Petersburg, were no longer to be heard. It seemed that Gold and Petersburg were Jews.

As he drew his hand back from the radio, he heard a knock at the door. "Yes?" he called out.

The door opened slightly, and the familiar face of his assistant, Dr. Duszynska, peered in. "Am I disturbing you?"

"No, not at all. Come in."

"Jan, I've just come from upstairs. The gypsy came to a minute ago."

Szukalski shot to his feet. "What? Why wasn't I called?"

"There wasn't time," said Duszynska. "I only happened to be looking at a patient in the next bed when he opened his eyes and started talking. It was only a few seconds later that he slipped back into coma."

"And?"

Szukalski's assistant stared back at him through the frail light of the room, seeing the furrow between his brows deepen, and said in a solemn voice, "Everything the farmer said was true."

Szukalski sat back down and indicated that Duszynska do the same. "How are his vital signs?"

"Not very good, I'm afraid. The bleeding from the head wound has stopped, but I'm certain he has pneumonia."

"You did your best for him in surgery," said Jan. "There was nothing more you could do. After all, he had been lying naked in the snow for how long?"

"From the moment of the massacre to the time when Milewski found him, the gypsy had been in the snow for nearly twelve hours. Jan, is all of it really possible?"

Dr. Duszynska, not receiving a reply, sat back in the wooden chair and took a moment to study the director's face.

"Let's go over this incredible thing, this gypsy's story, once again," said Szukalski suddenly. "He and his clan—about a hundred of them altogether, men, women, and children—were camped in the forest when a troop of German soldiers came upon them. There was no fighting, he said. The Germans simply came up to them, held their rifles at them, forced them to group together and then marched them to the edge of the wood. Here, in the snow, the gypsies were forced to dig a long and deep pit, like a trench, after which the Germans lined them up along the rim of this pit, had them strip off all their clothes and leave them in neat piles in the snow. Then the Germans shot them, one by one, in the back of the head—men, women and children—making sure they fell forward into the pit. Our gypsy was one of the last to be shot. If we can believe him, he says that he was still alive when the Germans started filling in the trench with dirt and snow to make a mass grave of it, but that when it came to the end where our gypsy lay, the Germans did a sloppy job and only half covered him. He tells us that he lay motionless beneath the body of a woman so as not to give away the fact that he yet lived, and waiting for a long time after the Germans had left, he managed to crawl out from beneath the bodies, and proceeded to drag himself through the snow away from the area. Eventually, somehow, he ended up at the Milewski farm. Is that how you understand the story?"

Duszynska whispered, "Yes," then said in a stronger

voice, "but why? Why would the Germans do this? Soldiers fight soldiers, that's what war is. But this senseless massacre of innocent people?"

Jan Szukalski's face filled with fury. "I didn't believe it myself, my dear Duszynska, but there's no reason to doubt the man."

A heavy silence again fell between them, as tangible as a brick wall, and when it was breached by Szukalski, it was for him to say, "I think we are facing only the very beginning of something we will never be able to fight."

The shadows in the dreary office took on a sinister aspect, as though the words uttered there had somehow altered the very physical structure of the room. What neither Szukalski nor his assistant knew was that he was right.

"I want to go home," said Szukalski wearily, staring at his hands.

Szukalski's assistant stood, and quietly left the room. For a few more minutes Szukalski remained in his chair, thinking about the irony of life, about how circumstance had robbed him of the assistant he had had for several years, about how the Nazis had removed that man and had replaced him with Dr. Duszynska just over a year ago, and about how he, Jan Szukalski, still had reservations about accepting his new assistant; old prejudices died hard.

Szukalski made his way back to the gypsy's bed and stared at the body. He had seen this face many times before on autopsy tables. It was a curious mixture of white and gray and yellow with purple lips and cheeks sunken so low that surely this must be a corpse. And yet a quick feel of the radial pulse told him that the gypsy still clung tenaciously to life. Pulse a little thready, but only eighty beats a minute. He stared down at the unconscious man, ruing the limitations of mortal doctors.

Carefully tucking the gypsy's hand back under the covers, Szukalski left the ward. In the corridor, Szukalski found Dr. Duszynska hurrying down the hall toward him. This time, he saw his assistant was not alone, for a stranger followed close behind.

Trying to smile when they joined him, he was not in the mood to meet someone new and was anxious to be alone for a while. But for Duszynska's sake, he put on a good show.

"Jan!" said his assistant breathlessly. "Such a surprise! I didn't know Max was even coming to Sofia, and when I went down the front steps of the hospital, there he was!"

Szukalski turned his smile to the stranger. "How do you do," he said, and they shook hands.

"Maximilian Hartung," said Dr. Duszynska excitedly. "We were college friends. This is Jan Szukalski. He's director of this hospital. Oh Jan, we haven't seen one another—well, for nearly two years, I guess!"

Szukalski felt his smile become strained. He also noticed the two were holding hands. It disturbed him. Szukalski slowly took in the face of Duszynska's friend. Hartung had an aristocratically chiseled look, with features a bit too harsh to be considered refined, yet he was tall and attractive, with obsidian eyes and a smile that seemed genuinely friendly. When he looked down at his old college friend, a head shorter than he, his eyes sparkled almost mischievously.

"I have a room at the White Eagle," said Hartung in a deep voice. "And before I left this evening I paid the owner a *zloty* to hold a table for us tonight. Would you care to join us, Doctor?"

Szukalski politely refused. Then he said, "How long will you be in Sofia, *Panie* Hartung?" He was trying to be amiable, forcing interest while trying at the same time to think of a convenient exit. Whatever his assistant did after hours and with whatever choice of companion, male or female, Szukalski did not care to know.

"I am stealing time from my company," said Hartung with a sly grin. "At the last minute I had to accompany a shipment of bearings to a factory in Lublin, and I have to be on my way back to Danzig day after tomorrow."

"Jan," said Duszynska, glancing at the door which led to the main ward, "how is he?"

"Stable. You two go on. You must have a lot to . . . to talk about."

Wishes of a Merry Christmas and good nights were exchanged, and Dr. Jan Szukalski stood to watch the pair hurry down the hall. Before they reached the entrance, he saw Hartung and Duszynska embrace, kiss one another boldly on the lips, and then push their way out into the snowy night.

Szukalski continued to stare after them for a moment; then, with other, more important things troubling his mind, he slowly limped back to his office.

Hans Kepler, turning his collar against the wind, was uncertain of which way to go. He stood at the bottom step of the church and stared blankly ahead.

Deep inside the pit of his soul, where there had once been the light and hope and courage of a proud soldier, there was now only a barren wasteland. He had betrayed the Reich.

Unable to continue just yet to the little bakery shop of his grandmother, where he knew she awaited him with the treats he had known as a boy, *SS-Rottenführer* Hans Kepler felt the need to walk.

On the other side of the town square, just opposite the church, stood the foreboding building of Nazi Headquarters, festooned with swastika flags and guarded at the entrance by two heavily armed soldiers. The Nazis owned Sofia now, and they governed it with relentless militarism. Even though it was not yet the curfew hour, the pairs of patrolling soldiers gave evening pedestrians no peace. Anyone out on a sidewalk after dark was invariably stopped and questioned. Yet Kepler would not be, and he knew this. A Nazi salute from his comrades would be their total exchange so that he, *SS-Rottenführer* Kepler, unlike any one of Sofia's other ten thousand citizens, had the sole privilege of walking the streets with the privacy of his thoughts.

Shouldering his duffel bag, the young soldier wondered if it would be this cold in hell.

Szukalski savored his weak cup of coffee, knowing that the supply was getting low and that no one knew when more coffee would be coming into Sofia.

He thought first of Duszynska, a doctor from Warszawa who had come to him just a year ago, newly graduated from medical school, and who now shared intimacies with Maximilian Hartung. It disturbed Szukalski that he let his prejudices interfere with his judgment, and yet the fact was unavoidable. All his life he had thought that someone of Duszynska's type could never make a good physician, but just the opposite had proven true. Duszynska had proven to be a surprisingly intelligent, competent and efficient medical doctor. But despite the fact that he was aware of such qualities, Jan Szukalski still found it difficult to accept Duszynska as a peer.

Maybe it was because she was so beautiful.

Szukalski thought back to the day she had arrived at the hospital, and how disappointed he had been to discover she was a woman. All he had been able to think was: How can such a young woman of this grace and beauty fill the demanding shoes of a man? And among his colleagues in the hospital, from the nursing staff to the other two doctors, the beautiful young woman had been received with mixed emotions. At twenty-six, with cornsilk hair and milky skin, Maria Duszynska had had to prove herself against all odds.

And she's done it, conceded Jan as he sat in the dim light of his office. Still, it would be a lot better if she were a man. . . .

His thoughts rambled about. Everything started to collide. There was not enough space in his mind for everything that had to be thought. There was the gypsy, his frightening story, and the feeling deep down in Szukalski's gut that what he had feared and dreaded these past two years might actually come to pass.

And then there was his own insufferable mixture of patriotism and frustration, for surely the two must go hand in hand. Especially for a man who, when he had applied to go into the Polish military four years before, had been refused because of his deformity. In 1939, when the Nazis marched into Poland, Szukalski had had to sit by and watch the slaughter.

He rose up from his chair and started pacing the floor. His thoughts grew stormier. As if the slaughter hadn't been enough, they send in sadistic swine to be our overlords, to invent their own laws, to keep us living in constant fear, watching us, badgering us, making slaves of us in our own town! Pompous bastards like Dieter Schmidt, ruling by terror and telling me how to run my hospital! And how does he expect me to run a hospital when they take away my best doctor just because he is a Jew and replace him with a woman? And what about supplies? Sending nurses off to the cities with shopping lists—so much ether, so many bandages—for the vital commodities that even the poorest hospital should have in stock!

Jan Szukalski, thirty and frustrated and limping, decided to shed the confinement of his office, and gave in to the sudden need to be out and walking in the snow.

Maria Duszynska and Maximilian Hartung laughed quietly as they strolled down the street arm in arm. They aimed their steps toward the Wisła, where the town's only hotel, the White Eagle, sat upon the river bank, and they spoke very little in order to savor this brittle, precious moment.

Twice they had been stopped and questioned by the soldiers of Dieter Schmidt, the Gestapo commandant; twice they had had to show their papers to the soldiers and explain their presence on the streets at that dark hour; and had twice been sternly reminded of the ten o'clock curfew hour. But neither interruption had spoiled their mood.

"One month," she murmured to him as the wind off the river cut their faces. "You said you would be back in a month. And that was two years ago. What happened, Max?"

Hartung squinted against the wind, as if trying to see something, and his lips grew thin and white. In the moment it took for him to find words to reply, Maria studied his face.

He had not changed in these past two years. Still brutally handsome. Still severe in the line of his jaw and nose. Still those penetrating eyes that had always reminded her of a bird of prey. How ironic it was that this man of imposing stature and with eyes the color of cold blue slate should harbor a personality that was almost the antithesis of the portrait he struck. Maximilian Hartung, twenty-eight years old and awesomely severe, was a man who laughed his way through life. And this was just what she had so loved him for, back in their days together at Warszawa University: the carefree way he had of mitigating life's harsh realities.

"Do you remember, Maria, that my father owned a foundry in Danzig?" He was talking now into the wind. "We manufactured, among other things, bearings for heavy machinery. And, quite often, for German tanks. I left school that summer, Maria, to visit my parents in Danzig, and had every intention of coming back to you in a month."

He looked down and smiled. "I haven't forgotten. We spoke of marriage then."

"Yes. . . ."

"Anyway, *kochana* Maria, I had returned home to a funeral. My father had died of a heart attack, leaving the foundry in my care. In the midst of my grief, I had to learn the business as quickly as I could, and at the same time, the Germans invaded Poland. The foundry was busier than ever before. We had to speed up production to day and night work. There was no way, Maria, I could have returned to school. And of course, that's also why you don't see me in a uniform." He grinned again, this time not bothering to hide the edge of cynicism. "I guess the Nazis need bearings for their tanks more than they need one more soldier."

Maria glanced down at his heavy overcoat, at the leather gloves, the knitted scarf around his neck. She hadn't even noticed. In the initial excitement of finding him on the steps, she had forgotten there was a war going on.

"I'm glad you're not a soldier. I couldn't have stood

to see you in a German uniform, not after all those good times together in Warszawa."

Max turned to face her, his lupine eyes suddenly serious. "Does it bother you, about my foundry? The bearings I manufacture were in the tanks that rolled into Poland. But you see, I have no choice! Either I comply with the Nazis or they will take my family and me away to one of their mysterious camps, and put the foundry in the hands of other Germans. It was for survival that I did it, you must understand that! Anyone who is not a willing worker for the Reich is removed. What good would it have done my family had I resisted? Someone will be made to produce those bearings, Maria; it might as well be me. I only want to survive and to live in peace. And if that means helping the Nazis build their tanks—"

She put a gloved hand to his lips. "Please, Max, no more talk of war."

Max and Maria entered the White Eagle, their seriousness eclipsed by the atmosphere of cheer and merriment, band music, and bright lights. The Nazi banners which hung over the entrance and exits failed to cast the slightest gloom.

The hotel owner himself, dressed in his best suit and grinning like a polished apple, showed the young couple to the one empty table in the dining room. They removed their coats and hung them on a nearby rack. Max smiled broadly at Maria and took a moment, before sitting down, to fill his eyes with the sight of her.

Wasn't that the same navy-blue skirt she had worn in her freshman year? And that blouse—he recalled when it had been new, a brazen fashion several years ago with the masculine Schiaparelli padded shoulders, but seen today on every woman. The mannish look, so deplorably popular now, did nothing to detract from Maria's femininity; indeed, the square shoulders and calf-length skirt only enhanced her long legs, her tiny waist, the gentle curve of her breasts beneath the thin fabric of the blouse. She was just as he remembered her. She hadn't changed.

Imported wine was impossible to obtain at any price, so they had to settle for a local Polish wine which, though made from plums and a little coarse, went very well with the dinner the owner's wife was cooking in her kitchen. First a heavy potato soup laced with leeks, followed by a steaming plate of *kapusta* and pork hocks.

"Tell me what you've done since I last saw you, Maria."

Maria murmured softly to the background accompaniment of the violin soloist who was playing *"Ostatnia Niedziela."* "I finished my last year of medical school at the university, then I went to the Institute of Hygiene in Warszawa. It's a good place to study, the Americans helped build it. I was there for six months, going to lectures and doing a great deal of lab work, most of which had to do with health research and disease control. I guess it's because of the good training I had there with serums and vaccines that I was sent here. Our biggest problem in these rural parts of Poland is trying to convince the peasants that unclean living causes disease."

"You don't sound happy."

She sipped the wine and shrugged. "In an age when I have no choice of where to practice, Sofia isn't all bad. It's a nice-sized town and the hospital is decent."

"How about the guy you just introduced me to, Szukalski? He seems a dour sort."

"Jan isn't so bad. He's just quiet. And takes life very seriously. With him, it's professionalism before anything. But the patients like him. He's a very good doctor and has quite a reputation." As she spoke, Maria's eyes trailed over to the violinist who had subdued the noisy dining room with his song, and she was reminded for a moment of the Polonia Hotel in Warszawa where she and Max had spent some sweet nights. "Jan is . . . well, I don't think he likes female doctors. In fact, it's hard to find a man who does. Which can make for a lonely life, I suppose. But our work keeps us busy, so I guess I'm happy most of the time."

Max's hand slipped across the table cloth until it found her fingers. "So what do you assist him in?"

"Oh, running the hospital. And his research, of course."

"What kind of research?"

The violinist had stopped playing and the whole band struck up a tango. Several couples were on the floor swaying to *"Bajka."*

"What kind of research? Oh, mainly infectious diseases. Things like typhoid, typhus, hepatitis. He has a rather well-supplied lab."

"Any great discoveries yet?"

She looked down at the hand cradling hers, at the size of it, the smooth palms, the long powerful fingers, the fine blond hair. And it made her suddenly melancholy. "No. He thought he had developed a new vaccine for typhus a while back, but he only found himself on the wrong track. If there's one thing Jan Szukalski is determined to do, it's keep diseases like typhus out of Sofia."

She fell silent for a moment and stared at the man opposite her, losing herself, as she had done so many times in the past, in his remarkable eyes. "Max, tell me something."

"What?"

"If your father hadn't died, if the war hadn't broken out, if . . . if a lot of things, tell me, would you have married me?"

He squeezed her hand and grinned playfully. "And who's to say it won't still happen?"

Maria sat back in her chair and looked around the room. It was animated now. People had finished eating; they were drinking vodka, singing, dancing. "Now it really feels like Christmas. I'm so glad you came, Max."

"And if I hadn't? Then what? A dreary night spent at the hospital feeling feverish brows?"

She smiled, tapping her foot to the music.

"Why is Szukalski hanging around there instead of going home? It's Christmas Eve for him, too."

"We've a pretty serious case we're watching."

"Is it the gypsy I heard him mention?"

She nodded, keeping her eyes on the dancers. A lively polka was now spurring everyone around the dance floor, causing the room to shake and reverberate with the thunder of stamping feet.

"What happened to him?"

"It's not really a pleasant subject."

"My God, he doesn't have a contagious disease!"

"Oh Max." She turned back to him and smiled. "Jan takes care of other kinds of patients, too. This case is —well, it's different." Leaning forward, Maria quietly recounted to Max the gypsy's strange tale. As she ended, she paused and said, "I hope he survives. We want all the details we can get of what happened out there in the forest."

"My God," whispered Max. "What are the Nazis up to! I've never heard of such a thing!"

At that moment, the polka ended, and the band immediately struck up a lively and familiar beat. At once the couples on the floor spread out and positioned themselves, clapping their hands to the quick triple meter.

"Mazurka!" exclaimed Max. He seized her hands. "Maria, do you remember?"

Her eyes grew wide. "Oh, I don't—"

Before Maria could draw another breath, Max pulled her to her feet and twirled her onto the floor.

Father Piotr Wajda wearily lifted the heavy silk cope from his shoulders and gently slung it over a wooden coat hanger in the clothes wardrobe. He moved slowly, his joints and muscles aching with fatigue.

The sacristy was exceptionally cold tonight, but Piotr Wajda did not feel it. The onus of a troubled conscience so preoccupied him that he was oblivious to all else. Mechanically he undressed, pulling the white cotta over his head and folding it neatly into its drawer. Then, he locked the cupboards which contained the few valuable holy objects that were stored in the sacristy between services. The other priest who had helped him to celebrate the midnight mass had had to hurry off to an outlying farm to give last rites to a dying parishioner, so Father Wajda was completely alone.

And this, more than the penetrating cold, the dampness of the small room off the altar, did he feel most poignantly; that he was alone. Totally and absolutely alone.

Father Wajda took a few minutes to look around to be sure nothing had been left undone. From the doorway that led to the altar, he emerged far enough to see deep into the church, and to see that it was empty. In the dim shadows he heard the peculiar scraping sound that his deformed old caretaker, Żaba, created as he moved awkwardly among the pews. Żaba was making his faithful rounds to see that the church was secure.

Then Father Wajda glanced up at the altar. He scanned the white lace cover, the candles, the Tabernacle containing the Body of Christ, and he wondered where that young German soldier had gone.

This gave him a sharp pang. Turning away, the priest started to hurry. The duty of going to the hospital and giving Communion to the patients had fallen to him. As the early hours of Christmas morning were rapidly approaching, he knew he would have to hurry.

Still, it was difficult, for the pallor of gloom that had hung over him since hearing that incredible confession slowed him down, caused him to pay scant attention to what he did, and made Father Piotr Wajda feel like the loneliest man in God's Universe.

With his equipment gathered together in his bag, Piotr donned his four-cornered hat with its black pom-pom and pushed his way into the snow.

His footsteps fell heavily; the profound responsibility of the secret he now carried seemed to push him down into the slush. Forty-year-old Piotr Wajda, in his twenty years as a parish priest, had never before known such fear.

So entrenched in his troubled thoughts was Piotr that he did not see the casual approach of a shadowy figure on the dark street. And it was not until the other person was almost upon him and murmuring, "Merry Christmas, Father," that he snapped his gaze up from the sidewalk, startled.

"Jan," he said quietly. It was highly unusual to encounter anyone on the streets after midnight. Gestapo *Hauptsturmführer* Dieter Schmidt was unfailing in his strictness about his curfew law, and saw to it that his soldiers enforced it ruthlessly. Two exceptions, which he grudgingly gave, were doctors and priests who, by the nature of their professions, often had to be called out during the night.

The turmoil of the priest's soul was evident on his face, and it did not escape the keen eye of Dr. Szukalski. "You don't look well, Father."

"I'm fine. I'm fine. Where are you off to at this hour, Jan? It's past midnight."

"Well . . ." he heaved a sigh, sending a cloud of mist into the falling snow. "I had just been out walking to give myself a chance to think, but I've decided to go home and be with my wife and son. If my special patient wakes up, the hospital will call me."

Father Wajda nodded. Szukalski was not the only one making a keen scrutiny of faces, for the priest saw in his friend a peculiar mask of distraction. "And are *you* well, Jan?"

The doctor laughed softly. "You worry about my soul, Piotr, and I'll worry about my body."

But the priest remained grave. "It was your soul I was asking about, Jan."

The smile faded from Szukalski's face.

"Jan," said Piotr in a gentle voice. "Will you be awake in a little while? I have to first see to my parishioners in the hospital, but after that—"

"I won't be sleeping for a while, Piotr. But there's no need to come by. I'm all right, really I am. I guess I'm just tired. . . ."

"No, Jan. It's not for you. It's for me."

Szukalski's eyebrows rose. Again he scanned his friend's face and the look he saw in the wide gray eyes mildly alarmed him. "What is it, Piotr?"

"Not here, Jan, not now. Later. If . . . if I come by at all, which I might not do . . ." His voice drifted off.

"You know you're welcome at my house any time, Piotr."

"Yes, yes. It will be later then. Now I must hurry. Good night, Jan."

Szukalski stood in the snow and watched the priest

hurry off down the street. Father Piotr Wajda had not even wished him a Merry Christmas.

They had had to dodge in and out of doorways to avoid being caught by the patrolling Nazis, and so had arrived at her flat unseen.

"You shouldn't have gotten that room at the White Eagle," muttered Maria as she fumbled in her purse. "You have a place to stay right here."

Maximilian held her against him, his face buried in her neck. "I didn't know what I would find, *kochana* Maria. It was all I could manage to find out where you'd been assigned. I had visions of you being married and with six children and terribly fat."

"In two years?" She giggled. "Ah!" She brought out the key.

Taking it from her, after a few drunken attempts Max unlocked the door.

They stumbled in together, arms about one another. When Maria reached out to flick on the overhead light, Max caught her arm, pulled her to him, and pressed his mouth against hers. Drawing back from her, he murmured in the darkness, "I should never have left Warszawa."

"Forget the past," she whispered.

"Very well, *moja kochana*. We'll think only of the moment, of you and me, of Christmas, of drinking champagne and making love."

"We don't have any champagne."

"What? But we must have it! It's traditional. What do you have then?"

"Beer."

"Beer! That's blasphemy. We need champagne. I'll see if I can get us some."

"At this hour? Max, don't be silly."

"Ah . . ." He laid a hand gently against her cheek. "I think maybe the owner of the White Eagle can be persuaded to part with a bottle. If he has any."

"But it's so late!"

"Don't worry," he murmured, moving toward the door. "I'll be careful. I just want everything to be perfect tonight. After all, it's been two years. Now, light the fire, okay?"

In the darkness he felt her nod, so Max quickly turned and hurried out the door.

The ward was dark and silent at this hour, with the patients sleeping peacefully, and the one nurse on duty sitting on the other side of a glass partition at the far end.

A dark figure stole through the exit at the opposite end of the ward, through a doorway that led to a corridor which in turn went to the street, and stood unmoving in the shadow. It was easy to see, from this point, all the beds and their occupants, and easy also to see that the nurse had her head bent over a book. The only illumination in the long room came from a single light at the end.

The dark figure looked to either side, down each row of beds, and saw the bandaged head and still form of the unconscious gypsy. The darkness and the heavy silence were an excellent subterfuge, so that the intruder was able to hide in a natural cover. Concealed thus, it was possible to dart swiftly and noiselessly from bed to bed until the gypsy was reached.

The silhouette looked down the length of the ward. The nurse was still reading.

The man in the bed lay in gentle repose, his face smooth and untroubled. The dark figure hovered over him, curiously studying his face, listening to the whisper of snow against the nearby window panes. Bending slowly with exquisite grace, the intruder managed to artfully draw the pillow out from under the man's head.

With breath held and body rigidly tense, the figure glanced up once more at the nursing station. The nurse continued to read quietly. Looking down, however, the stranger saw that the slight disturbance had awakened the gypsy, who now lay blinking up into the darkness.

The black visitor hesitated over him, poised and ready, waiting for the exact moment to—

"You!" blurted the gypsy hoarsely, his eyes flying open.

"Yes," whispered the figure, who then brought the pillow down firmly and precisely onto the bewildered man's face.

CHAPTER 3

David Ryż nudged the large gray horse with his heels, urging her forward into the driving snowfall. They had ridden all day and late into the night, their progress impeded by the necessity to avoid the roads and country lanes, so that now, as they neared the Wisła, both horse and rider were on the brink of exhaustion.

As the mare's legs plunged into the snow drifts, David leaned forward and patted her neck, murmuring quietly in Yiddish, coaxing her with endearments he had used with her on the farm when they had plowed fields together. They were close to home now, he promised her, and a blanket and hay awaited her. Just a little while longer. . . .

David Ryż straightened up and squinted into the cold wind that blew against his face. He had to duck now and then to avoid low-slung branches as he plodded through the trees, his strong legs hugging the massive body of the horse, for he rode without a saddle. Although it was past midnight and the snow was falling heavily, and although the young Jew wore only a shepherd's sheepskin jacket over his shirt, David was not cold.

A fire burned deep within his soul that flamed his body in a warmth of anger and fury.

Skirting the broad fields and pastures that swept away from the Wisła and off to the distant farms, he slowed the plow horse until they were picking their way through the thick woodland that bordered the river's banks.

He drew the mare to a complete halt and sat for some moments to listen. His ears, red and bitten with the cold, heard the howling winter wind shaking the

43

skeletal trees. But what he listened for, he did not hear. The crunch of a footfall.

Finally David bent forward on the horse and, leaning against her neck, whistled—three long, low notes.

He was immediately answered with a short, high whistle.

David released a heavy sigh and kicked the horse forward again. They moved quietly through the trees, the young Jew listening and watching the hollow night about him, until they came to a parting in the trees and saw the beginning of a narrow trail.

Knowing he was being watched, and taking comfort from it, David urged the horse down the path that led from the top of a steep granite bluff down to the frozen bed of the Wisła. The bluff was not very high, but it was sheer and impregnable, rising straight up from the gravelly bank of the river and crowned with a thick growth of birch and aspen trees. The cave at the bottom, its opening small and unseen on the face of the cliff, was unreachable except by this one trail.

David stopped again, halfway down, whistled three times, and heard once more the single, sharp reply.

He reached the mouth of the cave a few seconds later and, dismounting, gave a quick look around at the desolate river before slipping inside.

"David!" came an anxious cry from the deep shadows of the cave. In an instant, the smiling, excited face of Abraham glowed in the firelight, tears in his eyes. "David," he said, embracing his friend and drawing him into the comfort of the cave.

Others now rose to greet him: Ester Bromberg, hurrying over with a towel for his hair which was getting wet with the melting snowflakes; two men pushing past him to take care of the horse; and all the rest, all twenty-three faces turning toward him, anxious and hopeful.

"I was so afraid!" said Abraham Vogel, pulling David close to the fire. The light from the flames filled the large cave with a reassuring glow, casting tall shadows on the craggy walls. High overhead, several meters above them, smoke from the fire dissipated slowly through crevices in the top of the cliff. "You were gone so long! Sit, David, sit! And eat!"

But David waved a hand. "I have no stomach now. I must tell you what I have seen."

"David," came a deep, rich voice. This was Moisze Bromberg, a Polish Jew of forty-five years and once the kosher butcher of Sofia. He was a square, heavyset man with large hands and a resonant voice. In the year that these twenty-three refugees had made the cave their home, Moisze Bromberg had gradually become their leader. He stepped forward with a cup of steaming chicory and placed it in David's frozen hands. "David, eat first. Rest yourself. You are nearly frozen through!"

David lifted the cup of chicory to let the steam warm his face. Eighteen years old and a student at the outbreak of the war, David Ryż was a handsome and passionate youth with dark stormy eyes and a head of thick black curls. He was known for his zeal and impatience, qualities he had acquired the day the Nazis had taken his parents away.

"Moisze, I must talk. I have to tell you what I saw!"

Abraham took a seat next to David by the open fire and leaned forward apprehensively. "We hadn't thought you would be gone so long, David. You had us all so worried."

"I'm sorry for that, my friend, but I had to find out something."

Moisze raised his bushy eyebrows. "Find out? Find out what? You went to see how close the Germans have come to the river. What else had you to find out?"

David lifted his dark, fiery eyes and said in a low voice, "I had to find out where the dark trains go."

"Oh David. . . ." said Abraham sadly. He was David's best friend, this Abraham Vogel, a Polish Jew like the others; twenty years old and by profession a violinist. Abraham Vogel, gentle and slender with a dreamer's face.

"And did you find out where the dark trains go?" asked Moisze.

"Yes, I did. And I also found out what they carry."

Ester Bromberg, a slight woman who was now

spooning out some hot stew from the bubbling pot over the fire and handing the bowl to the youth, said, "Where did you go, David?"

He kept his eyes on Moisze. "I went to Oświęcim."

"Oświęcim!" chorused several voices at once. "But why there?"

"That's where the trains go, Moisze. That's where they unload their cargo."

"What do they carry, David?" asked Abraham softly.

"People, Abraham. The trains carry people. Of all ages and types. Most of them Jews. Children, Abraham, and pregnant women, and old men."

"Of course," said Moisze Bromberg, running his thick fingers through his graying hair. "There is a work camp at Oświęcim. It's also a relocation center. Jews are being given new homes."

David snapped his head about. "It's a death camp, Moisze! They are either executing or starving everyone to death! And at Birkenau it is strictly extermination. There are gas chambers and crematoria—"

"It can't be!" whispered Ester Bromberg.

"David," said Moisze in the same controlled voice. "How can you be sure?"

The youth looked down at his hands and scowled. "I was close enough to see. The railroad divides the camp. At the one called Auschwitz there are several factories and a number of large buildings that look like barracks." David's voice grew quiet, solemn. "It was difficult to tell exactly what was going on there, but I saw a lot of prisoners in striped uniforms out in the snow and many of them were lying on the ground, apparently dead."

"How close did you get?" asked Moisze.

"Within about three hundred meters. Close enough to get a good look through these field glasses. I didn't dare get much closer. SS men with dogs were patrolling the fences."

A heavy silence followed which lasted for several moments until it was broken by a soft voice from the edge of the circle of light. "Did you see my husband, David?"

He looked up and saw the elderly woman who had

spoken, crouched on a rock with her arms wrapped about herself. David couldn't recall exactly why she had joined their group; all the stories were so similar —to hide from the Nazis.

"No, *Pani* Duda," he said gently. "I didn't see your husband." David turned back to the former butcher. "I didn't see anyone I recognized, Moisze. But at that distance and in those striped uniforms I'm not sure I could have recognized anyone. Moisze, we have to do something about it!"

The older man shook his head uncertainly. "I can hardly believe it, David. A death camp! It doesn't seem possible. I think you are mistaken—"

"What he says is correct."

The three by the fire turned to the one who had spoken. He was a tall bear of a man whose stature seemed to fill the cave.

Moisze got to his feet at once. "Ah David, in my excitement to see you I had forgotten our guests. Come over and meet them."

David glowered in distrust at the stranger. "Let them come here and meet me. They are the guests, let them show manners."

In Yiddish, Moisze said, "The *goyim* are our friends, my hot-headed Zionist. They are as much the victims as are we."

"He's right," said the stranger approaching the fire. "We should show our manners." He held out a strong, calloused hand. "Brunek Matuszek. Captain, army of Poland."

David eyed him suspiciously, not letting go of the cup and bowl in his hands. But the stranger smiled. "And it is true about Oświęcim, I'm afraid." He took a seat opposite the youth, the campfire glowing brightly between them. "It is a death camp."

Two other strangers came to stand behind the one called Brunek. One was a younger man who introduced himself as Antek Wozniak, soldier of the Polish Army, to whom David gave scant attention. But the third of the trio caused him to sit up and take notice.

She was a young woman of twenty-five, dressed in men's working clothes, her white skin reflecting the firelight. When Moisze introduced her as Leokadja Ciechowska, David nodded slowly, taking in the unkempt beauty of her raven hair and the astonishing green of her eyes. She returned his stare boldly, almost defiantly, then sat on a stool next to Brunek.

"They came to us a while ago, David," said Moisze, who was the spokesman of the group in all matters. "They were told by friends in Lublin to contact Dolata in Sofia, who directed them here."

"What do they want?" he asked bitterly. "To hide with us?"

"To fight," said Leokadja.

David studied her again. Then he said, "Let me make something clear. I am not fighting the Nazis because I love Poland. I am fighting them because they are imprisoning and slaughtering my people. My people belong in Zion and God has called for a gathering of Israel. That is why I fight."

"David," said Moisze patiently, "the dissident voice of the zealot student is often not realistic. We are too small a group and our weapons too few not to accept the hand of any who would help us. These people have come to fight with us. Welcome them, David!"

The youth nodded again and murmured, "For Moisze's sake I welcome you," but the tethered hostility remained in his eyes.

The butcher turned to the three newcomers and said, "David was away at school when his parents were taken. He came home one day to find their farm burned to the ground, and news from the neighbors that his mother and father had been loaded onto a cattle train. That was a year and a half ago. He never found out where they were taken. David has no fight with you and your friends, Brunek. He has little love in his heart for anyone these days."

"We understand," replied the Captain, staring into the flames of the fire. "Antek and I have been on our own since our unit was broken up. That was two years ago. We too have lost our families. We don't know what happened to our comrades; many of them escaped through Rumania, we are told. Antek and I have been one step ahead of the Nazis ever since."

"Running."

The Polish Captain smiled sadly at David. "You might think so. But we are fighting as well. There is a large, organized Resistance in Poland and we fight for them where we can. Perhaps you think we are cowards, but our aim is to stay alive and help fight for our country."

David took a longer, closer look at the face of the man opposite, taking in the large hawk-nose, the high forehead, the straight black hair combed back over his head. He said quietly, "You are right, Brunek Matuszek. I suppose whoever fights the Nazis is an ally of the Jew. At least for the present."

The Captain smiled again. "If we can help here, we will. And we will stay for as long as we can. But the Nazis are always on the lookout for us. Any man who was in the Polish military is being conscripted into the Wehrmacht and being forced to fight the Russians." Brunek turned and looked at the young woman sitting next to him. "Leokadja's husband was not as lucky as we. The Germans took him and put one of their own uniforms on him."

David held his gaze on her startling beauty.

Brunek turned to Moisze. "Where do you get your food from?"

"From the people in Sofia. You know Dolata. He was the Mayor. He and several others are aware of us and bring us what they can. But it's dangerous, as you know. The Nazis patrol this whole area quite heavily."

"Are you all Jews?"

Moisze shook his head. "Eight of us are. We escaped to this cave when the Nazis came to take the Jews out of Sofia eighteen months ago. Some of us were able to escape. The rest of these people have joined us since then, all with reasons to hide from the Nazis."

Brunek looked slowly around the cave. The twenty-three faces, looking pale and bewildered in the flickering firelight, ranged from very young to very old, men and women. Some of them smiled weakly at him.

"You see that we haven't much strength," said Moisze. "We haven't the manpower or the weaponry to effectively fight the Nazis. We do what we can, small acts of sabotage here and there to make life inconvenient for them, but. . . ." He spread out his hands.

"We want to fight," interjected Abraham Vogel who had, so far, said little. He had a slender, delicate face and large, soft eyes. But there was passion in his voice. "But we cannot fight unless we become an army."

"An army," said Moisze, "an army without weapons is called a crowd. And a crowd against weapons is called cannon fodder. So, the larger our group, the more cannon fodder we become."

Abraham opened his mouth to retort, but Brunek was quicker. "Your leader is right. No matter how many numbers you recruit, you will still be a helpless mob. What you need are weapons. Can Sofia help us?"

Moisze shook his head. "Sofia is mainly an agricultural town."

"But there *is* something," came David's solemn voice.

All faces turned to him.

"The munitions storage depot."

Brunek's eyebrows shot up. He looked at Moisze. "Is this true?"

"We cannot go near it," protested the older man. "It is heavily guarded! We would be fools—"

"Weapons!" cried David. "A warehouse full of German artillery!" He spoke hurriedly. "This is a main staging area for Nazi troops going to the east. They come here and are outfitted from the munitions installation outside Sofia. It's an enormous place, Brunek. They have gasoline tanks, storage bunkers, trucks and tanks—everything! If we were to blow it up, that would give the Germans something to think about."

"No, David," came Moisze's steadying voice. "It is too dangerous. Our purpose is to stay alive, not commit suicide."

Now the youth rose to his feet and towered over the group. His eyes flashed as he spoke. "Listen, my friends, for the past year we have done little more than save our own skins. We have harassed the Nazis but little—if at all—and we have done nothing much more than kill a few sentries and wreck a supply truck or two. You mark my words, if the Nazis win this war, there won't be a live Jew left on this continent. I'm telling you that if we don't start fighting we will all surely die. We may live a few weeks longer by hiding this way, but in the end we will die. And isn't that also suicide?"

He glared at the silent faces turned up to him. "Anything we can do to slow down the Nazis will be a help to their enemies. And we can help ourselves. Dear God!" he cried, shaking a fist. "You didn't see what I saw at Oświęcim! Little children being herded into a gas chamber! Even from where I stood I could hear their pathetic cries to be released—"

"David!"

He looked down at Moisze, then added more quietly, "Why make the conquest easy for the Nazis? Why are we *here* if not to fight?"

"I agree with David," said Brunek. "However, I think it would be foolish to try to blow up the Nazis' precious supply depot without sufficient arms. If we are to do anything effective against the Nazis the first thing we must do is get weapons. What do you have?"

Ester Bromberg, coming back to the fire after having handed out a few bowls of stew, said, "We have some rifles—not many—five shotguns, and less than two hundred rounds of ammunition, not counting your two rifles and shells."

Brunek considered this. "Not much to work with. We need more weapons. And even more than that, we need explosives. Moisze, are there any mines around here that might have dynamite stored in them?"

"No, I'm afraid not. Most of the mines are east of here. This area is all agriculture with some very light manufacturing. But then, as David said, there is the storage depot. The Nazis have all the gasoline and ammunition and spare parts and repair shops they need for this area of Poland in that installation. It is quite large and, as I said, heavily guarded."

"Then," said Brunek, "we will let the Germans supply us with weapons."

"And what good will that do," rejoined David bitterly, "without the manpower to use them? We need people! We need an army!"

Abraham spoke again, softly. "Where do we get them, David, these people?"

"From the dark trains."

Moisze's bushy eyebrows arched. "You're not serious!"

"There are hundreds of people on those trains, Moisze! If we stop one and free them, we will have our army."

The butcher looked over to the Polish Captain and saw Brunek frown. "That would not be wise," said the latter. "The risk is much too great. We must first work on getting the weapons, then we will tackle the problem of manpower."

David opened his mouth to speak, but changed his mind and remained silent. Despite his feelings of enmity toward the newcomer, he had to admit that Brunek Matuszek was a man of action. For the moment, David was willing to go along.

A stray draft found its way through the narrow cave opening, and blew through the large stone chamber, causing everyone to shiver. The flames danced in the campfire and the shadows wavered on the rocky walls.

Moisze Bromberg broke the silence by saying, "What do you suggest we do, Brunek?"

"I think we should watch for a chance to blow up a bridge under a supply train, one carrying guns and ammunition. If we watch the trains loading at Sofia's supply depot we will know which one to hit and when."

"And then?"

"Then we will have the weapons we need. After that, we will worry about recruiting more people, and then consider what to do about the supply depot. If it is as valuable to the Nazis as you say, then I think we should consider it a prime target."

Another whisper of icy wind flew through the cave, reminding a few of the partisans that it was Christmas Eve. But there was nothing they could do about it. There would be no tree, no presents, no goose for dinner, no mass at the church. This night would have to pass like any other. Their only thought must be to fight and survive.

Another man joined the group now, one who had been sitting in one of the corners, feeding Ester Bromberg's stew to an old man who could not feed himself. This was Ben Jakoby, old himself but vigorous enough to fare the harsh winter and the Spartan life of the cave. Also a Jew, he was sixty-five years old, short and frail, had a shock of white hair atop his head, and had once been Sofia's pharmacist.

He came now to warm his hands by the fire and force some of the pale chicory down his throat. "I have been listening," he said. "And I would like to know, Captain, how you propose to stop a train. Especially one that is guarded as heavily as the Germans guard their precious supply trains."

Brunek, who had met with Ben Jakoby earlier and had had a few words with the pharmacist, said with a smile, "I have a plan. But I will need your help."

Ben Jakoby looked surprised. "My help?"

"To stop a train we will need some high explosives. And the best one for our purpose, I believe, is nitroglycerine."

"Nitroglycerine!" said Moisze. "You can't be serious! It's dangerous! And besides, where would you get it from?"

Brunek kept his eyes on Jakoby, who had already guessed what the Captain was going to say. "We will make it ourselves."

"We will blow ourselves up," whispered Vogel.

"It's the only way," continued Brunek, growing serious. "It is easy enough to make, if we have the ingredients. I was a chemical engineer in Warszawa and have, in the past two years, had practice in its use and manufacture. With *Pan* Jakoby's help, it should not be too difficult."

"But how—"

"First we will have to go into Sofia and take a look at what is left of his pharmacy. If it is like what I have encountered in other towns, the Germans will have taken only what they need and destroyed the rest.

There is a possibility that some supplies remain. Chemicals that we require."

"Go into Sofia!" For the first time Moisze Bromberg lost his composure. "You can't take a chance like that!"

"This is war, Moisze. Men are taking chances everywhere."

David found himself suddenly smiling at Matuszek. "I will help you, Captain," he said evenly. "What is your plan?"

Brunek's voice fell to a whisper and everyone in the circle leaned forward. "There is a large bridge over the Wisła to the west of Lublin. A very important bridge for the Nazis. I propose to blow up the bridge with a munitions train on it."

"A munitions train?"

"Yes."

"Then we will all be blown to hell."

"No, Moisze. Not the way I have it planned. Now listen, these trains are very heavily guarded, and the Germans always check the bridge before the trains are allowed to cross. I myself have watched how the guards walk across a bridge and check for planted explosives. The train must sit there for five or ten minutes before it moves across."

"Then," said Moisze, "we cannot hope to blow up the bridge."

"I don't intend to put the explosive on the bridge itself. I intend to put it on the train."

"What!" blurted David. "That's impossible! Those trains are crawling with soldiers. There is no way anyone can get near the trains, let alone load one with nitroglycerine! You would be seen!"

"Ah, but you are wrong, my young friend." Brunek smiled around the circle. "We cannot fail. I have a plan that will make me invisible."

CHAPTER 4

Jan Szukalski sat in a high wing-backed chair staring into the fireplace and watching the flames dance. His hands were clasped beneath his chin. The rest of the house was silent; Kataryna and the boy were safely asleep upstairs. They had been asleep when he had come home, and Jan had not, upon looking in on them, disturbed their slumber.

For how long, wondered his troubled mind, will they be able to enjoy such peace and tranquility?

The fire cracked suddenly, sending a cloud of sparks upward, and bringing Jan out of his thoughts. He dropped his hands and shook his head. He would not think of his wife or child now. Or of his brother, a sweet and gentle youth of nineteen who had been in the Polish Cavalry during the invasion of 1939.

When the smiling face of Ryszard threatened to materialize, Jan abruptly rose out of the chair and strode to the fireplace. Here he stood before the two paintings over the mantelpiece; one, the kneeling figure of Jesus in Gethsemane, and the other a portrait of Poland's national poet, Adam Mickiewicz. The two had equal status in the Szukalski household.

A soft knocking at the front door brought his mental focus back to the room and he limped slowly to answer it.

Piotr Wajda stood shivering on the threshold and blowing on his hands. He gave an apologetic smile for the lateness of his arrival and quickly slipped into the warmth of the small entryway. "Good evening, Jan," he murmured, shaking like a dog to shed his layer of snow. "Or should I say good morning?"

"Come in, come in, Father. In my medical opinion, I'd say you need a drink."

The priest was ushered into the cozy living room. On the way over from the hospital he had been stopped by the brutal henchmen of Dieter Schmidt, pinch-faced men in black leather coats who had detained him in the snow to ask their interminable questions. Always the same interrogation, always the same response. And just when he had thought his feet would freeze right to the icy sheet, they had let him go.

Piotr Wajda removed his berretta, knocked the snow off the pom-pom, and took the glass proffered by Szukalski. The drink was a strong brew of honey and vodka spiced with cinnamon and cloves and steamed with a hot poker from the fireplace. His host also poured himself one, and then fell back into the wing-backed chair. The priest sat opposite the doctor in front of the fire and took a long draw on the drink.

The two men sat in silence for a while, saying nothing, staring into the fireplace and letting the effects of the alcohol start to work. At last the priest spoke. "Jan . . . I am troubled tonight."

Szukalski studied his friend in concern, seeing how burdened the huge frame seemed with fatigue, how uncharacteristically the broad back curved beneath an invisible weight.

"I don't know where to begin," he said quietly. "Or even if I *should* begin. In my twenty years as a parish priest I have never before violated the sanctity of the confessional, nor have I even *considered* doing such a thing. But Jan . . ." Piotr took another long drink from the glass and returned his stare to the fire. "I have learned something tonight. . . ."

Szukalski reached for the pitcher which held the hot brew and refilled his friend's glass. As he did so he said, "I think I know what you're saying, Piotr. Doctors have the same privileged communication between them and their patients. I am morally and ethically required to keep such information private, just as you are with what you hear in the confessional."

"True!" rejoined the priest with sudden strength. "But it's not the same, Jan. If you were told by a patient what I have heard tonight, you would readily repeat the tale. *I* cannot."

The doctor released a sigh and emptied his glass. "Drink your drink, Piotr. You and I share the burden of this town as no other men do."

The priest gave a short, dry laugh. "Yes, I know. You take care of their bodies and I take care of their souls." Emptying his own glass, Piotr Wajda finally leaned back in his chair and rested his head. "I know that I can talk to you, Jan; indeed, you are the only one I can talk to. But you have to realize how difficult it is for me. It means breaking my holy oath. I can be excommunicated for this. And yet I must, for I must share with you what I have learned tonight, and I do it only because it involves the safety of countless others. It is a life-and-death matter, Jan."

Szukalski nodded, his face becoming grave. Father Wajda, with his jet-black hair and youthful strong body seemed old tonight, Jan Szukalski noted uneasily.

"Somehow, Jan," continued the priest in a quieter tone, "I feel I can tell you what I have learned in the confessional without thinking I am committing a sin." Then he straightened up and the whiteness of his face shocked Szukalski. "The concentration camp at Oświęcim," said the priest, "is a death camp."

Jan sat unmoving in his chair, conscious only of the crackling fire and the intense gray eyes of the man opposite him. Slowly, carefully, he said, "I understand that people must die there because of deplorable conditions. Is that what you mean, Piotr?"

"I mean," said the priest thickly, "they are being *exterminated* there. By the trainloads, Jan. As many as six thousand a day."

"Holy Virgin," whispered Szukalski. "You can't mean that!"

The walls of the room seemed to move in; the air grew hotter as the two men stared at one another. Szukalski went on. "It's impossible, Piotr, just the logistics of it. It isn't possible to kill that many people in one day and hide it. And *why?*" His voice started to rise. *"Why, Piotr?* Who are they killing?"

"As for your logistics, my sadly idealistic friend, I can tell you that the Nazis have built giant gas chambers at Oświęcim that resemble showers into which the prisoners are herded under the pretext of being washed and deloused. Afterwards, after the gold is extracted from their teeth, the bodies are cremated in huge ovens—"

"No! I don't believe it!"

"And as to *who* these poor wretches are, they are mostly Jews, gypsies, Czechs, Poles, children, old people, cripples, anyone who doesn't fit into Hitler's twisted notion of human perfection. If they aren't able to work at slave labor, they are executed immediately. Those who do work only delay their entry into the gas chamber, for they are quickly starved and weakened."

"Oh God. . . ."

"And I haven't even mentioned the medical experiments—"

"Piotr!" Szukalski shot to his feet, visibly shaken. "It isn't true! I just don't believe it! You say you heard this in confession?"

"Yes, just tonight." Father Wajda looked up at his friend with despair in his gaze. "A young man from Sofia who worked there, he saw some people that he knew from this town go to their deaths in just such a fashion."

As if his knees were going to give away, Jan Szukalski folded his arms on the mantelpiece and then laid his forehead on them. "Oświęcim is just a concentration camp for political rebels, and a relocation camp for war refugees," he murmured into the crook of his elbow.

"It isn't that at all, Jan. It is a death camp."

Piotr Wajda had thought that by sharing it with his closest friend the pain might somehow be mitigated. And yet that was not the case.

Sadly, the priest continued, "Hitler has an ultimate plan to reduce Poland to a country of slaves for his Reich, to kill off all of the intelligentsia, all of the clergy, and anyone who has less than a strong back. And I think, Jan," Piotr's voice became tight at this point, "that if the Nazis weren't so busy fighting the Russians, they would probably have gotten to us all by now."

Dr. Szukalski straightened up and stared at the painting of Christ kneeling in prayer. "Can it be a fabrication, Piotr?"

"If you could have heard it, Jan, you would know that the boy had spoken from his troubled heart."

"Boy?"

"A young soldier in the *Waffen SS*. I can't reveal his identity, but one young enough and sensitive enough to have seen the crime in his work. Not a volunteer, Jan, but a draftee. He has been a guard at Oświęcim for over a year and told me the most . . . incredible things."

"Yes . . . he's telling the truth." Szukalski's voice grew distant. "You know . . . a friend of mine passed through Oświęcim only three weeks ago, and commented to me about the awful stench that hangs over the town, and that the townspeople are complaining of it. He said it had smelled like burning flesh. At the time I gave little consideration to what he said. But now . . ." Jan brought his hands up to his face and rubbed his eyes. "Jews and gypsies, you say. . . ." He finally turned to regard the priest. "Piotr, I have a patient in the hospital right now. . . ."

Szukalski related to Father Wajda the story of the gypsy found at the edge of the Milewski farm and added at the end, "The last thing the man told the farmer before he slipped into unconsciousness was that the men who had committed this slaughter had worn the Death's Head."

"The SS? But why, for the love of God, why?"

Jan Szukalski wrung his hands. "I don't know, Piotr. I don't know what's happening." And as he stared down in horror at his friend's face, Jan heard muted scratching sounds pathetically touching the periphery of his mind. And then, recognizing if for what it was, he slowly moved away from the fire and limped to the kitchen door. Opening it a crack, he saw the anxious little button face of the dog Djapa peer up at him. Jan stared down at it, at the moist brown eyes and the wet nose, and thought: How innocent it is. Then he pushed the door all the way open and the little dog scampered out of the kitchen, ran across the floor, and leaped into the priest's lap.

"Djapa, Djapa," murmured Father Wajda, allowing the sloppy tongue to cover his cheeks.

When Jan returned to the fireplace he said, "I think I have felt it coming. It takes a blind man to look at the dark clouds gathering on the horizon and not suspect a storm."

Wajda nodded thoughtfully as he stroked the ragged dog in his lap. "That's why I had to tell you what I learned in the confessional, Jan. I wanted you to know what possible future lay before us. But I also told you for another reason." He lifted his head and gazed up at his friend. "The soldier who told me all this is going to commit suicide."

Hans Kepler found himself standing next to a doorway with a rifle in his hand. For some reason, the blue sky had gone and was replaced now by a metallic pall which hung over the camp like an inverted pewter bowl. The wait was interminable. From the other side of the building he could hear the fruitless efforts of an SS Sergeant as he tried to start the engine of the diesel truck. Over and over again, grinding, whirring, while subliminally, from inside the concrete chambers at Kepler's side, could be faintly heard the sobbing and crying of people begging to be let out.

He knew what the delay was. The exhaust fumes from the truck were to be piped into the rooms in this building in order to stop the people from creating a disturbance. They were waiting just as impatiently as he, for they had been crammed in there for more than an hour already, packed so tightly together that not one more person could have been fitted in, and there was not even enough room to turn around or to bend one's leg. And they were all of them—men, women, and children—stark naked, a few of them clutching bars of soap.

Kepler dug the toe of his boot into the dirt.

Finally, after two and a half hours of standing by that door and trying to ignore the muffled cries of those inside, he heard the diesel engine start up. At first

Kepler could hear the distant shrieks of panic coming over the cold wind as if from very far away, although he knew that they came only from the other side of the concrete wall. There were moans and shouts, a curious blend of anger and shock, indignation and fear, an eerie chorus of human wailing that sounded to Kepler like the whistling pipes of an ill-tuned organ. And then, like a dying breeze, the bizarre chorus slowly faded away.

It had taken thirty-two minutes.

Now came the part that Kepler disliked, even though it was his duty.

While some Jewish inmates stood by the wooden doors, ready to open them, Kepler was joined by other soldiers, their rifles ready. When the doors came open, an uncommon stench wafted out, a putrid odor which stung his eyes and caused them to water before he could actually see the cause of it.

Eight hundred people—men, women, and children —of all types and shapes stood erect like marble pillars, frozen in a queer attitude of death, colored the deep cherry-red of carbon monoxide poisoning, their bodies dripping with sweat and urine and feces and menstrual blood. The Jewish slaves who stood at hand now fell into this unearthly crowd and tossed the corpses out, where more workers waited to tear open the mouths with iron hooks in search of gold. Still others roughly inspected anuses and genitals for hidden money or diamonds.

All the while, Hans Kepler stood to one side with his rifle at the ready.

Indifferently, as if he had willed his mind elsewhere, and had other scenes than this before his eyes, the young *SS-Rottenführer* stared without emotion at the grisly display. Body after body went past him, some almost sadly beautiful in their death state, others with mouths twisted in strange rictus smiles, and it appeared from the insouciant way he stood that the *Waffen* corporal was unmoved by what he saw.

But then, after a few minutes, after the air over the camp was filled with this acrid stink, after the piles had grown so high that the corpses were being dragged off to the ovens for cremation, Hans Kepler's eyes focused on the face of an old woman who had been thrown close to his feet.

He stared down, his head tipped to one side in curiosity.

The features of the old woman were strangely familiar; the plumpness of her cheeks, the short nose with the wide nostrils, the way one side of her mouth curved down lower than the other.

Then, in the curious reflex that sometimes occurs after death, the eyes snapped open and stared up at the Corporal. The irises were the color of lettuce.

Hans Kepler heard himself scream.

He screamed again.

Shooting bolt upright in bed, the young soldier found himself shivering and trembling, his teeth chattering, and he saw that he had sweated so profusely that the bed clothes were soaked.

As he cradled himself in his perspiring arms, trying to control the shuddering which shook his bed, he heard footsteps on the other side of his door, then the light burst on and a silhouette stood before him.

"Hansy!" she whispered.

He opened his mouth to speak, but the only sound that would come out was a choking, gutteral bark.

In the next instant, his grandmother was sitting on the bed and reaching for his hands. Her lettuce-colored eyes anxiously surveyed his face. Her mouth, with one corner drooping lower than the other, began to murmur soothing endearments as one plump hand wiped the sweat from his face.

"Hansy," she cooed. "A bad dream?"

With a stifled sob, Hans Kepler threw himself into his grandmother's comforting embrace, crying, *"Babka!"* and wept uncontrollably.

"Why should he do that?" asked Szukalski, reaching once again for the pitcher. The vodka mixture was going lukewarm so he picked up the poker out of the fire and thrust it for a second into the drink. Then he poured himself another hot glass. "Why should he want to kill himself?"

"Rather than go back to the camp," said Wajda sadly.

"So what do I care if an SS man kills himself? Just one less of the bastards. If he feels so damned guilty, then why doesn't he just desert and flee the country?"

The priest's voice was quiet. "You know that would be tantamount to suicide, Jan. He'd be shot on sight. Where can he run to?"

"To hell." Szukalski brought the glass to his lips and tossed his head back. "Then let him go back to the death camp and live with his goddamned guilt or kill himself if he wants to. If I thought I could do it myself and get away with it—"

"Jan," said Piotr gently.

Dr. Szukalski stared down into the gray eyes of his friend. "If I know the Nazis, were I to kill one of their men they would come back and raze this town to rubble as retaliation. And, now that I think of it, so would they do if an SS man were to commit suicide here, because the Nazis would just assume we murdered him. They'd kill us all for punishment. Hasn't the High Command issued some kind of order to the effect that for every German killed by civilian resistance, one hundred people will die? *Psiakrew!*"

"I think we should try to help him," came the priest's quiet voice. His massive hands were still gently stroking Djapa's fur.

"Help him! So he can go back and butcher more innocent people? *Gas chambers,* Piotr!" He slammed his glass down on the mantel, causing Djapa to snap his head up. "Six thousand a day! Sweet crucified Jesus! What kind of madness is this!"

"He couldn't help it, Jan. It wasn't his fault."

"Of course not. No snowflake ever feels responsible for the avalanche. So you feel sorry for him."

Father Wajda looked down at the little mutt curled up in his lap and said softly, "I absolved him."

Another silence fell over the room, and this time it was filled with a mingling of bitterness and uneasiness.

"I'd like to be able to help him, Jan. I don't want to see him go back there."

"What? Aid an SS man? You're mad, my holy friend. And besides, what could you do? Or even I? Anything we could come up with would only be temporary. Maybe I could find some medical excuse to prolong his stay here in Sofia, but eventually he would have to go back. Piotr," Jan straightened up and faced the priest squarely. "Are there other death camps?"

"I've heard of one at Majdanek near Lublin. I believe there are many others. It's time we fought, Jan."

"And you think I wouldn't like to!" boomed Szukalski, nearly shouting. "Don't you think I tried my damndest to get into the military only to have been rejected because of my twisted leg? So, while Poland falls helplessly before the Nazis, I have to stand by and watch. And now you come along and accuse me—"

"I am not accusing, Jan."

"One bastard Nazi soldier suddenly has all your concern—"

"Jan," said the priest in a gentle voice, "I am only thinking of the others, those back at Oświęcim. I haven't been able to fight in the war either, Jan, but if God has granted me this one small part to play—to keep that soldier from killing more people—then I shall not turn my back on it."

"Sweet Holy Mother of God, Piotr, face reality! Lift one finger to fight the Nazis and you'll cause the destruction of Sofia."

Under the cover of the dark hour just before dawn, David Ryż and Abraham Vogel crept like shadows through the town of Sofia. Keeping a careful watch for the patrolling Nazis and avoiding the streets with lamps, the two young Zionists drew up to the small brick building on the outskirts of town that housed a paint-and-lacquer-manufacturing plant.

It had been taken over by the Nazis who were using it for maintenance of their military vehicles. David and Abraham worked swiftly and quietly to get inside and to locate the two things they had come for.

Finding them almost immediately, the two young Jews hurried out of the plant and blended back into the night, having left no evidence of their visit. They hastened back to their cave by the river with two valuable prizes.

Nitric and sulfuric acids.

Gestapo *Hauptsturmführer* Dieter Schmidt took a last look at himself in the mirror. The reflection that stared arrogantly back at him was an awe-inspiring sight to Dieter who, lacking all traces of modesty, was always insufferably impressed with his image. He loved to see himself in mirrors.

The uniform was impeccable. A most formidable black, it was exquisitely tailored to emphasize the elite Gestapo image, and trimmed with the savage subtleties of skull and crossbones on the peaked hat, the lightning bolt insignia of the SS on the collar patches, and gleaming belt buckle proclaiming the proud motto of the SS: *Honor For Us Means Loyalty*. Then there were the shining black jackboots, the swastika armband on the left arm, the polished buttons, the immaculate white shirt and black tie. Top all of this off with a knee-length black leather overcoat and black leather gloves, and you have the most breathtaking sight known to Dieter Schmidt.

What he failed to notice, however, as he turned this way and that before the full-length glass, was that neither his face nor his body went with the uniform.

Although tall in his own mind, thirty-eight-year-old Dieter Schmidt fell miserably short of the statuesque Teutonic image the Reich had of its Gestapo leaders. In fact, Schmidt was a short, beefy man with a blunt square face, a coarse complexion, and small, slippery eyes the color of mucus. His proudest facial feature was the jagged scar that ran the length of his left cheek, a wound which he was quick to boast about as being the trophy of a Heidelberg fencing duel, but which he had in truth received from a broken beer bottle in a barroom brawl.

He searched around his room for his swagger stick.

Dieter's were modest quarters. Having taken up residence in the Town Hall of Sofia in November 1939, Gestapo *Hauptsturmführer* Schmidt had established himself in what had once been the town's Council Chambers, and had had a bed and table and washstand brought in. He was not a man to live extravagantly, at least not in the last few years, ever since he had learned that his superior, *Reichsführer* Himmler, despite his power and influence, still lived privately a Spartan life. Ever one to emulate his superiors, Schmidt saw to it that he lived in comparable style.

In the same fashion, he ran his headquarters after the manner of Gestapo Headquarters in Berlin where he had been able to prove himself to those over him, and thus earn for himself the command of this rich, rural area of Southeast Poland. It had been a simple thing, really, that had earned the praise of his superiors and a rise in rank, just a routine interrogation and the good luck of "persuading" a certain political prisoner to divulge secret information. Standard work at Gestapo Headquarters at Number Eight Prinz Albrechtstrasse, and yet Schmidt had proven himself in one small matter. He had been the only one to get the prisoner to talk.

And this was, without doubt, Schmidt's one priceless gift to the Reich: his ability to get information out of the most tenacious resister.

Of course, now that he was such an important man with a full staff under him, and with a sizable town to govern and a major military installation to guard, the daily mundane interrogations were no longer his personal duty. He left such routine matters to his subordinates, having taught them the finer techniques of torture and perseverance.

In fact, they were at it now, his special team, working this delightful Christmas morning on a man who was showing every sign of breaking down. A farmer named Milewski.

Finding his swagger stick on the table by his bed, Schmidt returned to the mirror for a lingering look. Without a doubt, the leather-covered willow stick with its stag's-horn handle added just that special touch to his imposing portrait.

A knock at the door brought him to swing about and

bark permission to enter. An SS Sergeant, bringing his heels together and giving the Hitler salute, informed his commander that the Polish farmer had finally broken down under interrogation. The Sergeant went on to disclose exactly what the farmer had confessed about his suspicious movements of the day before, and the story behind his blood-soaked wagon.

Dieter Schmidt listened in grim satisfaction. A fat story, this one, with enough ammunition in it to hang someone for sure.

He dismissed the man and turned again to the mirror. Unsheathing a double-edged smile and silently commending himself, Dieter assured himself that there was certain to be some sort of punishment in order for what had happened during the night. After all, a crime had been committed and he, Dieter Schmidt, was the supreme law-giver and judge in the area.

There had been too few executions lately. Last year, ninety-six partisans had swung from his gallows in the town square, but this year the number had been embarrassingly small. The people were well behaved, *too* well behaved. And too damned careful. These sporadic acts of sabotage around the outlying areas and occasionally in the town itself were being committed by *someone,* but Schmidt had so far been unable to find out who. There was an active Resistance in this area, yet he had not been able to get a lead on their identities.

But now, he thought happily as he struck his thigh with the swagger stick, now it seemed a door had been opened. And what better method to strike fear into the hearts of the Resistance fighters than to make an example of an esteemed citizen of Sofia?

The respectable Dr. Szukalski. . . .

CHAPTER 5

When Alexander scampered down the stairs in his own inimitable fashion of coming down on his belly feet first, the living room was bright with lights, a fresh fire roared on the hearth, and the candles on the Christmas tree were lit. Seeing the gaily wrapped presents under the tree, Alexander squealed with delight, and waddled over as fast as his plump legs could carry him. For a two-year-old, he was very fast.

Close behind, taking the stairs slowly and trying to dismiss from his mind the thoughts that weighed heavily upon him, came Jan Szukalski, tying the belt of his dressing gown. At the foot of the stairway he paused and watched his little boy with pride. Golden-haired, blue-eyed and robust, the sturdy little Alexander was the fulfilling of Jan Szukalski's most pressing want out of life. He was a handsome little imp, this cherub, with the Nordic features of his mother and none of his father's ancestral swarthiness. But in character and temperament he was very much like his father; a quiet child with a gentle introspective nature. He would probably grow up to be a poet or a philosopher.

Under the Christmas tree were some toys that Szukalski had been lucky enough to get from a carpenter friend, items that were otherwise unobtainable and very costly and which enabled the Szukalskis to enact the ritual of Christmas as if, for this one morning, no other purpose existed in the world. There was a little wooden sled and a rocking horse with a long braided mane and enameled blue eyes, and a regiment of toy soldiers that Jan had been able to muster up from various sources and repaint. It was upon the painted saddle of the rocking horse that little Alexander now slapped his plump bottom, whereupon he proceeded to gallop with wild abandon.

As he did so, his squeals ringing through the house, the elder Szukalski remained on the last step of the stairs and felt his face darken. Piotr Wajda's words of just a few hours before came echoing back: "And the children they exterminate at once, being of no use to the Nazis."

By the time Kataryna, also wrapped in a dressing gown, came down from the bedroom, Jan was seated on the floor next to his son, trying to keep the excited little body of Djapa from getting caught under the rockers. He heard Kataryna moving about the room, lighting votive candles before the painting of the Madonna that sat in its own niche, giving the fire a few pokes to liven it up, and lastly coming to join her two men at the foot of the Christmas tree. A quiet woman, she held out to her husband, with a hand roughened from housework, a gift wrapped in colorful paper, and as he took it, he gave in return a kiss and a little cameo brooch that had belonged to his grandmother. Hearing the tinkling laughter of Alexander and the little yaps and growls of Djapa, Jan Szukalski wished he had the power to make this moment go on forever.

But he had not. The placid hour quickly passed, the morning breakfast was eaten, and the moment for reality came all too soon. Dressing warmly and promising not to be too long at the hospital, he left the tranquility of his hearth and plunged into the biting day.

At the hospital he met a shock.

The head nurse, a thick-waisted woman in a crisp white smock, approached him halfway down the hall, her face severely set, a clipboard full of papers in her arms.

"It's the gypsy, Dr. Szukalski; he died during the night."

"What? But he was stable when I left! Who has seen him?"

"Dr. Duszynska. She was in early this morning."

"And what did she say?"

"That it was either pneumonia or intracranial bleeding. Whatever, he died without regaining consciousness, Doctor. I know that for a fact from the night nurse who was on duty. She said she was in the ward the entire night, and never once heard a sound out of him."

Szukalski rubbed his chin thoughtfully. His disappointment did not surprise him, for he had been counting heavily on further information from the gypsy regarding the circumstances of the massacre.

"His body is in the morgue, Doctor. Will you be doing an autopsy?"

Szukalski considered this. Then he said, "I think not. In all probability Dr. Duszynska was right, pneumonia or bleeding. Or. . . ." he shook his head slightly. "Maybe the poor man just didn't want to wake up. Not after what he had been through. Call the mortician and have him make arrangements for burial. I doubt anyone will be coming to claim the body."

She nodded curtly and turned on her heel, leaving the clipboard with the doctor. He stood for a moment to flip through the small stack of papers, then continued on his way to the first ward.

Halfway down the hall he was stopped by Dieter Schmidt.

Szukalski came to an abrupt halt. It was not common to see the Gestapo commandant in the hospital, a territory Schmidt usually relegated to his subordinates. Seeing the chunky man in black, his feet spread apart as if to block the passage, startled Szukalski greatly.

"*Guten Morgen, Herr Doktor,*" said Schmidt smoothly, spitting out the last word as if it were derisive.

"Good morning." Szukalski glanced at the three men who stood behind Schmidt, Gestapo guards who carried Erma submachine guns and whose faces looked as if they had been stamped out of rough metal. "What can I do for you, *Herr Hauptmann?*"

"*Hauptsturmführer,*" corrected Schmidt through a narrow mouth.

"Of course, my apologies. What can I do for you, *Herr Hauptsturmführer?*"

Dieter Schmidt raised his eyebrows and stretched a

finely honed smile across his heavy face. "Why, my good *Doktor*, this is merely a social visit. It is, after all, Christmas, is it not?"

They spoke in German, for Schmidt deplored the Slavic tongues, feeling they soiled his mouth. And besides, he had never been able to master any language other than his own. Jan Szukalski was admirably proficient in German, having had to study medicine from texts in that language, so that the sly subtleties of what the commandant said were not lost on him.

"How is your family?" asked Schmidt. "Your beautiful wife and that handsome little boy? They are well? Unharmed?"

Szukalski felt the corner of his mouth jerk up. "They're fine, thank you."

"Good, good. And the hospital? Is everything going well? Nothing too hard for you to handle, *Herr Doktor?*"

"Everything is fine, *Herr Hauptsturmführer.*"

Dieter Schmidt's eyes flashed. "Nothing out of the ordinary?"

"No, *Herr Hauptsturmführer.*"

"Good, good." Schmidt shifted his weight a little and, in so doing, brought his hands from behind his back and produced the willow swagger stick. He slapped it in his open palm, curled his fingers around the shaft, and drew it in and out of his fist a few times, thoughtfully. But he kept his eyes fast on Szukalski.

Presently, the Gestapo officer said, "Tell me, *Herr Doktor*, have you ever heard of *Nacht und Nebel?* Of course you have, you are not an ignorant man."

Szukalski nodded darkly, feeling an uncomfortable tautness creep up his legs. The term "night and fog" was a well-known cliché to connote the midnight arrest of someone and his subsequent disappearance, never to be heard from again. It had happened to his former assistant two years before.

"A few weeks ago, our Führer made it an official decree, this *Nacht und Nebel,* making it legal that anyone . . . *Herr Doktor* . . . at any time can be visited by the Gestapo and *removed* in the night and fog without the usual bothersome trials and hearings. Think of it, *Herr Doktor,* think of your precious little family being awakened in the middle of the night and roused out of their warm beds. And you being dragged out of the house, in only your night shirt, to be driven off in a Gestapo car." He drew back an oily smile. "Never to be heard from again."

Szukalski's face remained impassive. When he felt his fingers close tightly on the clipboard in his arm, he forced himself to relax them. And when he felt his jaw similarly draw up and knew that the cords of his neck must be standing out, he called upon an inner reservoir of strength to smooth out these signs of tension so that Dieter Schmidt couldn't see them.

Schmidt was not an exceptionally bright man, nor had he above-average intelligence or cunning. But he was an artist when it came to instilling fear into someone. And it was for this reason alone that Szukalski did not take him lightly. While under other circumstances, in another age and another setting, Dieter Schmidt might almost be a pathetic man, here he was the most powerful man in the land and therefore one to be feared.

Schmidt ran the swagger stick through his fingers and said, "Oh by the way, *Herr Doktor,* I believe you will be called out today to a nearby farm. It seems a man there has been injured terribly."

Szukalski's blood ran to ice.

"His name is Milewski. Poor swine. It seems he met with a horrible accident. Oh, it was awful. Isn't it ironical how so simple a thing as his mouth can save a man's life? But poor stupid Milewski, Polish donkey that he is, kept his mouth closed too long. And when he did open it, well. . . ." Dieter Schmidt sighed, and Szukalski could hear the faint crackling of the black leather coat. "Lost an eye, he did. Came right out of his head, you know, like a little red onion dangling on a string. And the most peculiar marks all over his body. Especially his groin. Poor man. Still, I suppose he has enough children to satisfy him. You Poles do breed like street dogs, don't you?" His grin flashed like a blade of cold steel. "Anyway, *Herr Doktor,*" he continued, sneering the word, "it distresses me that you people still continue to commit crimes against the Reich. You still fight, as if you had a chance. But don't you know, *Herr Doktor,* how futile it is? And we ask so little, *so little.* Like your daily morning report to me, for instance." He shook his head and made a clucking sound. "Such a simple thing. Everyone must turn one in to me, everyone in Sofia who is in any position of authority. Even the fireman, who really has nothing to say, even he sees to it that his reports are to my satisfaction. No one is above the law. It is essential that I be kept apprised of what is going on in this area, and your reports, above all, are crucial, since they come from the hospital. Being hospital director, you more than anyone should know the importance of *complete* records."

Szukalski swallowed hard and said as casually as he could, "You can be assured, *Herr Hauptsturmführer,* that I do." His voice came out even, controlled. His handsome face betrayed nothing of what he was thinking. "Am I to gather from this visit, *Herr Hauptsturmführer,* that you will be collecting the morning reports in person from now on?"

For the most fleeting instant a tiny explosion took place behind the SS officer's eyes, and his square blunt face, for one passing second, seemed to flare with wrath. But then it quickly subsided and Dieter Schmidt was as equally recovered and composed as his adversary. "I am here to remind you, *Herr Doktor,* that any man who omits information of any kind from his reports to me is considered an enemy."

Szukalski stared calmly at the little hard balls of steel Schmidt used for eyes, and said quietly, "Have I omitted information, *Herr Hauptsturmführer?*"

Now they had arrived at Schmidt's favorite part of the game, so he savored it, tried to draw it out a little longer. Much as he hated him, he had to admit that Jan Szukalski was a good opponent. This man did not squirm, there was no sweat on his upper lip, he did not twitch nervously. Victory would be uncommonly delicious.

"I am talking about the gypsy, *Herr Doktor.*"

"Yes?"

Schmidt held Szukalski's gaze with a deadly steadiness. "He was not on yesterday's report."

"Of course not, *Herr Hauptsturmführer,* the man arrived after the report had been sent to your office."

The two men faced one another in the quiet hallway as if they were physically bound to one another. Schmidt tried to fight down an irritation that had started to grow, an impatience with this stubborn Pole that also started to stir his anger. His voice continued to be staid. "Where is the gypsy?"

While Szukalski had been able to control his body, there was nothing he could do about the savage pounding of his heart, and he was almost afraid the Nazi could hear it. "In the morgue, *Herr Hauptsturmführer.*"

"He's dead?"

"Yes."

"How convenient for you."

"How so, *Herr Hauptsturmführer?*"

"I shall not be able to question the man. Tell me, *Herr Doktor,*" now Schmidt's voice started to rise. "Did you really think you could get away with keeping it a secret? And did you really think that by leaving him off your report I would never find out about him? It was foolish of you, Szukalski, to think that by not reporting the incident I would never find out about it."

"I don't know what you're talking about, *Herr Hauptsturmführer.*" Szukalski wanted desperately to lick his lips but didn't. "The man's death is not convenient for us. In fact, we tried our best to save him."

"Don't lie to me, Szukalski! You silenced the gypsy because you didn't want me to question him!"

"But that—"

"How fortunate it is for me that Milewski has no balls! It didn't take much for him to tell me the whole story. So your little plan to keep the gypsy a secret has failed, *Herr Doktor!*"

"Excuse me, *Herr Hauptsturmführer,* but I really don't know what you're talking about." With steady fingers, Szukalski methodically shuffled through the papers on his clipboard and eventually said, "Ah, here it is," drawing out a sheet of paper. "I believe this is what you're looking for, *Herr Hauptsturmführer.*"

Holding it out to Schmidt and thankful that his hand didn't shake, Szukalski said, "You can see that the report is dated for today, December twenty-fifth. I was just about to send an orderly over to your office with it."

Dieter Schmidt slowly took the paper and rested his eyes on it. They seemed not to move, not to go back and forth across the lines, but stared instead at one spot. Nonetheless, Szukalski knew that the Nazi commander was reading. That Milewski had found the gypsy at the edge of his farm, that he had brought him to Sofia's hospital, that the gypsy had been able to tell his story to the farmer, that his wound had been caused by the attack of a group of SS soldiers, that a hundred other people had been shot with him, that Dr. Duszynska had operated on him and had removed the bullet, and that the gypsy had died during the night without regaining consciousness.

Not one single fact had been left out of the report; everything that Jan Szukalski knew of the affair, Dieter Schmidt now knew. And he read it all in the meticulous, floral handwriting of Dr. Maria Duszynska.

Long after the Nazi had finished reading, his eyes remained on the paper. And like Szukalski, he was able to control himself phenomenally. But to a trained physician like Jan, the tell-tale signs were evident. The throbbing pulse in the carotid arteries. The dilated pupils. The peculiar ashen color of the skin.

When he finally looked up, Schmidt's eyes were cold and piercing, his face calculating. Then, nodding slowly, he said quietly, "The report is complete, *Herr Doktor.* As usual you have excelled yourself."

"Thank you, *Herr Hauptsturmführer.*"

"Yes. . . ." said Schmidt, still nodding thoughtfully. "A very interesting report." Then, as if suddenly remembering himself, the Gestapo commandant straightened himself up and slapped the stick against his thigh. "From now on, *Herr Doktor,* I want *two* reports from you. Morning *and* evening. Is that understood?"

"Yes, *Herr Hauptsturmführer.*"

"And if anything unusual comes to your attention, it is to be reported to me at once. Is that also understood? *At once*, Szukalski."

"Yes, *Herr Hauptsturmführer*."

Thrusting the sheet of paper at one of the guards, *Hauptsturmführer* Dieter Schmidt spun about and strode off down the hall.

For a Christmas day the town was ominously silent. Or was it just his imagination? Were the priest's words of the night before making his mind believe things that were not really there?

No, decided Szukalski as he mounted the steps of his house, it was not his imagination. Perhaps the spirit of Christmas still existed somewhere, but the war had managed to subdue it.

Alexander was anxious to go outside and try out his new sled and, as Kataryna was still working on the Christmas goose, Jan decided to spend some time in the snow with his son. Bundling up the boy so that only his little eyes showed and depositing him on the sled with Djapa curled in his lap, Jan Szukalski took hold of the slender rope and struck off down the street.

He was thankful for the brief spell to forget about the dead gypsy and Dieter Schmidt, and Piotr Wajda's grim revelations. Jan found himself running down the street, the little boy screeching with delight, the little dog running at his heels and yapping.

Presently he had to slow down, breathing heavily, and he entered upon the white-blanketed town square where a statue of Kosciuszko stood beneath epaulets of snow. Djapa raced around, burrowing under drifts, while Jan gave himself up to the freedom of the moment.

The idyll was quickly shattered, however, by the tiny high-pitched cry of Alexander who, thrusting his overstuffed arm toward the other end of the square, shouted, *"Tatuś! Tatuś!"*

Jan spun around. At the far side of the square, emerging along the main street between the tall buildings of the business district, was a convoy of German trucks, tanks and armored troop carriers, all marked with the white "G" of the *Panzer Group Guderian*. They formed a macabre procession, moving slowly and silently down the street, their grim militarism starkly contrasting with the winter wonderland atmosphere of the square.

Although these past two years Szukalski had hardened himself to the sight of occupying troops, to see them in such force and with such armament jolted him into swooping down and gathering Alexander into his arms. Instinctively, Djapa ran up and pressed himself between his master's legs, sensing the sudden change of mood and the intrusion of something unwelcome.

Keeping his eyes on the gray tanks as they rolled by, Jan squeezed little Alexander to him until the child had to squirm uncomfortably. Many of the soldiers, Jan noticed, were smooth-faced young men whose eyes had a sort of bewildered wonder and who held themselves stiffly with practiced determination. Handsome young men with milky skin and cheeks like roses and frosty blue eyes and the Nordic coloring of their ancestors.

Unwittingly Jan Szukalski fell back into the protection of the doorway. Once again, like the melody of an unwelcome song, the words of Piotr Wajda whispered in his mind. And they said: "He told me something else, too, this young soldier in the confessional. He told me about something called *Lebensborn*."

Jan Szukalski screwed his eyes tight. But still the priest's voice echoed in his mind, uttering again the last thing he had said last night before leaving. "It's a plan perpetrated by the SS to populate Germany with only pure Teutonic stock. They kidnap the blond-haired and blue-eyed children of conquered people, and place them in German homes to be raised as Germans. It doesn't matter if they're Polish or Dutch or Czech. If a child fits the perfection of Hitler's ideal, it is stolen away from its natural parents and—"

"*Tatuś!*" came Alexander's muffled voice.

Szukalski looked down. He had embraced the child so tightly that the boy's face was buried in his coat.

"Alex. . . ." he whispered.

Then he looked up. The convoy was gone, having passed through the town and continuing on its way toward the Russian front.

Szukalski wasted no time. Before returning home for his Christmas dinner, there was one thing he had to do. And it would take only a few extra minutes. Picking up the rope of the sled and calling to Djapa, he hurried off in the direction of the church.

"Piotr," he murmured, placing Alexander gently on the floor.

The priest swung around and at once broke into a smile. "Jan! And little Alex!" Piotr bent over and dropped a heavy hand on the child's head. "Merry Christmas and God bless you, Alexander." When he straightened up, he saw the gravity on the doctor's face. "This is not a social visit then?"

Jan tried his best to smile, but failed.

"Come inside and have a seat. Mass isn't for a while yet. I'm just moving around to keep warm."

Piotr thrust his hands into the pockets of his long black cassock and leaned against a table. "What is it, Jan?"

"Piotr, I've been thinking. And while I can't promise you anything, you understand, I will try. I'll try to think of some way to get that German soldier a medical excuse for not going back to the camp."

Father Wajda closed his eyes and nodded with relief. "Thank you," he murmured.

"I want you to understand, Piotr, that I don't do it for altruistic reasons. My motive is not the same as yours. I only want to save this town from destruction."

"Your motive does not concern me."

"You must know, Piotr, that I really don't care if he rots. I just don't want him to commit suicide and have his death bring destruction to this town. All I'll do is try to help extend his leave from duty so he can come up with a plan of escape."

The priest sought Szukalski's hand and squeezed it. "Thank you for what you're doing, Jan. In the end, our motives *are the same,* for we are both fighting for Poland. Now, what do you plan to do?"

"Send the soldier to see me tomorrow at the hospital, and I'll see what I can come up with."

Turning quickly on his heel, Dr. Jan Szukalski hurried out of the sacristy, pulling little Alexander behind him, and went into the early afternoon sunshine.

CHAPTER 6

A light snowfall late Christmas night helped to camouflage the furtive movements of two dark figures that crept through the deserted streets of Sofia's Jewish quarter. As they stole past dark doorways and broken windows, Ben Jakoby had to swallow down his fear. There was some comfort in the mass and courage of Brunek Matuszek, so that the old pharmacist remained close behind him, but it was not enough to keep the terrifying memories from the old Jew's mind.

The ghetto was still and empty now, but eighteen months before it had been alive with screams and cries. On that day, a few months after the Blitz, Nazi soldiers had marched into the Jewish quarter, gathered all the Jews in the streets, and then systematically ravaged all the buildings and property. Ben Jakoby, who had been at an outlying farm delivering medicine at the time, had come back late at night to see fires light up the spring sky and had heard, from a distance, the frightened cries of his people as they had been taken away.

Ben Jakoby remembered that night well, for he had managed to sneak his way back to his pharmacy and had found the body of his wife amid the rubble. What had happened after that was mercifully blank. Moisze and Ester Bromberg had found him and taken him with them in the flight from the Nazis. And in the eighteen months that had passed since then, Jakoby had not been back.

But he was back now, creeping through the town in the middle of the night, and although Sofia was silent at this hour, in the old man's ears there still rang the noise of carnage and destruction.

David Ryż had wanted to accompany Brunek on this

mission, but Ben had insisted on going along. Only he knew where certain supplies had been stored, and only he could help with the manufacture of the nitro-glycerine. And only he had the determination in his heart to go back to the scene of his fears and draw strength from it.

So Matuszek and the old but determined Jakoby had struck off on foot after sunset, and had come to the edge of the Jewish ghetto just after midnight.

A few Christmas lights burned in distant windows, but no other signs of life shone. And no one but these two conspirators and the usual patrolling Nazi soldiers were abroad at this cold hour.

When they reached the pharmacy, dark and gutted, Jakoby had to stop and lean against a wall. "To catch my breath," he whispered.

"Are you all right?"

He nodded. The cold sweat on his face and neck had turned into a lacy frost, but he made no attempt to wipe it off. His exhaustion came not from the physical exertion but from the terror that had gripped his soul. While it had given him courage and the will to accompany Brunek, it was nonetheless a draining power. He had to gulp the sharp, wintry air.

"All right," he whispered at last. "Let's go in."

The pharmacy itself was totally ruined with little more than a few bare shelves still standing. The two men picked their way over the debris and made it to the back. Here was where Ben Jakoby had stored most of his supplies and it was here that the Nazis had been more meticulous about their destruction. Lighting a match and searching the cupboards, Brunek saw that all the best supplies had been taken long ago.

"They've left some things, though," he whispered, motioning to the old man who seemed to be moving in a dream. "What's this?"

The pharmacist struck his own match and peered closely into the storage chest. A few dusty bottles and tins glimmered back at him. "Laxatives," he whispered. "And stomach tonics. But here—" He reached in with a shaking hand. Holding the jar up before their eyes, he said triumphantly, "Glycerine!"

Brunek took it from Ben and gave a quick look around. Against one wall stood a long wooden work bench which was littered with the glassy remains of laboratory equipment.

The two men went over to it and quickly searched through the debris. They found a beaker, a few unbroken bottles, and a dusty thermometer.

"We can begin," whispered Matuszek.

Jakoby used the woolen scarf about his neck to wipe out the beaker while Brunek produced two sealed jars from under his coat. He said, "It would be best if we mixed up a small amount of the explosive here and take it out and test it. That way we know we have the right formula. We'll take some of these things back with us and mix up a larger amount when we need it. That way we won't have to worry about storage or deterioration."

Brunek opened the two jars which contained small amounts of the chemicals David and Abraham had stolen from the small paint- and lacquer-manufacturing plant. They were labeled: nitric acid, sulfuric acid.

"We were lucky to get these," whispered the Captain. "Now, we'll need some kind of ice bath. Does this thermometer still work?"

Jakoby examined it by match light. "Yes. We'll put the water in here," he said, pointing to the sink.

As the pharmacist took care of filling the sink, Matuszek proceeded to fill the beaker with measured amounts of the two acids. "When I add the glycerine, we have to be careful not to allow the temperature to come above ten degrees centigrade."

Jakoby looked up at the soldier in the darkness. "I think we're ready," he whispered.

Beads of sweat appeared on the big man's forehead as he started to slowly add the glycerine to the acids. "Be careful," he whispered hoarsely, "not to stir or strike the side of the beaker with the thermometer. You know how unstable nitroglycerine is."

"Yes, I know. Don't worry, Captain. I no more want my head blown off than you do."

The two men continued in tense silence until the chemicals were all mixed and stabilized. The clear, thick, oily liquid sat innocently in the beaker like a sugar syrup before it crystallizes.

Brunek touched his fingertip to the syrup, then licked it off. The sweet burning taste was familiar to him and the immediate headache that followed confirmed the presence of a strong nitrate.

"It tastes like nitroglycerine to me," he whispered, trying to keep his large hands from shaking. "But we have to test it to be sure. We'll set it off on the way back to the cave. Here, help me pour it into one of these bottles. Oh God, steady now. . . ."

Placing the rest of the supplies and empty bottles into the knapsack they had brought along, the two men stole out the rear of the pharmacy and joined the snowfall. Matuszek carried the small bottle of nitroglycerine in his gloved hands.

Knowing it would soon be daylight, they hurried smoothly through the sleeping town, watching all the while for Nazis, trying very hard not to jolt the fluid in Brunek's hands. They were hoping to make it to the woods before being seen.

When an open field stretched before them at the edge of the town, Brunek and Ben hurried for the cover of the pine trees that bordered this stretch of the river. Because of the nitroglycerine they carried, running was impossible, so that they had to walk as smoothly and rapidly over the low brush as they could.

Their footsteps crunched and snapped and seemed magnified in the stark night, causing both men to perspire heavily. Matuszek, the deadly mixture in his hands, felt his bowels creep with terror.

As they were about to reach the trees, a voice pierced the night. "Halt! You two there! Halt!"

Brunek and Ben froze.

"Do not move or I will shoot you on the spot." The voice spoke in German, a language both men understood, and it came closer to them. "Fritz, bring up the motorcycle."

Daring to move his head ever so slightly, old Ben chanced a glance over his shoulder and saw two German soldiers approach them with their guns ready.

"Well, well," said one of them, coming around and

stopping several feet away from the two partisans. "What have we here? Are you two gentlemen out for an evening stroll? Or should I say an early morning stroll? Put your hands over your heads where I can see them." The soldier motioned menacingly with his rifle.

Now the other soldier came before them and said in a steely voice, "You know you two are violating the curfew, don't you? What's in the knapsack?"

"Supplies," said Ben in a feeble voice. "We have some sick people—"

"And what's this?" barked the first soldier, jerking his head toward the bottle in Brunek's hand.

"Medicine," replied Matuszek calmly and in perfect German. "We have some sick children at our farm. We needed the medicine right away and couldn't wait until—"

"Silence! I'm not interested in your drivel! Nor do I care if your brats die! What kind of medicine is it?"

Brunek Matuszek eyed the two soldiers who stood several feet away from him and rapidly evaluated the situation. Beside him, he could feel fear begin to crumble Ben. "It's for the cough," he said quietly. "Cough medicine is all."

"I don't believe you! What is it? Vodka? Rat poison? Same thing! Let me see it!"

A whimper escaped Ben Jakoby's lips. The second soldier brandished his rifle, ready to shoot.

Brunek held out the bottle and took a step forward.

"Stay where you are!" shouted the first soldier. "I don't like pigs near me. Toss the bottle."

Brunek glanced quickly at Ben Jakoby. Then he said softly, "Very well. . . ."

The large Pole suddenly lobbed the bottle high in the air, hoping his rapid calculation to have it fall just behind the soldiers was accurate. But the Germans, seeing that the toss was going to overshoot them, fell backward and one of them caught the bottle smoothly.

Ben Jakoby whimpered again and Brunek felt himself sway with tension.

The soldier brought the bottle up before his eyes and squinted at it in the darkness. "Cough medicine? That's not what it looks like to me. Looks more like vodka. Are you two planning a party?"

"Please," said Brunek quietly. "It really is medicine and we have sick children who need it at once."

The German soldier stretched his lips into an evil grin and bent forward, placing the bottle on a large flat rock. "This is what I think of your medicine!"

The two Poles stared in horror as the German raised his foot over the bottle, and as the jackboot came down on it, Brunek threw himself on Jakoby, hitting the ground as the night tore apart with the explosion.

They lay still for some moments, then shakily got to their feet and found a crater in the snow before them, surrounded by a corona of dirt and rock and bits of bloody flesh.

Jakoby's hands flew to his mouth as he lurched forward, but Brunek caught him and held him fast. "Well. . . ." sighed the Captain, fighting down his own nausea. "Our formula works. . . ."

They stood quietly for another moment, gathering their strength and letting the shock subside. Their eyes remained fixed on the large hole that was splattered with blood and pieces of gray uniform. "I cannot believe so little nitroglycerine did that much," said Jakoby.

"Wait till you see what it does to a bridge. Come now, we'll take their motorcycle. It won't be long before the Nazis are all over this spot. I'm sure the explosion was heard by someone."

He started the engine and warmed it up while the pharmacist clambered into the sidecar, cradling the knapsack on his lap. Then the two partisans ground over the snow away from the red crater where two German soldiers had stood.

CHAPTER 7

As Jan Szukalski plodded through the slushy snow early the next morning, he kept his head huddled down in the collar of his greatcoat and walked with one shoulder thrust forward. The snow was falling unusually hard this morning, coming down at a treacherous slant and attacking his face with little pricks of ice. It had been difficult to pull himself out from under the eider-down of his bed, or away from the rich brew of coffee and chicory and barley Kataryna had made. But there was work to be done. There were the usual patients; and then there was the young German soldier that Father Wajda was going to send by . . .

On his way to the hospital, Szukalski went over the events of the evening before.

After dinner, Maria Duszynska had shown up unexpectedly with her friend from Warszawa, Max Hartung. They had brought with them a bottle of genuine French wine and a parcel of whipped pastries. There had also been, from Maria, a little gift for Alexander.

Watching his son try to fit his pudgy little hand into the terry-cloth puppet that Maria had sewn, Jan Szukalski had laughed until the tears had rolled down his cheeks, and when he had said thank you to Maria for the present, he had meant it more for the gift of laughter she had given him than for the toy itself.

"It was so kind of you," Jan had said to her, wishing now he had thought to give her something for Christmas. While Maria had worked with him as his assistant, the two had maintained little in the way of a social relationship. Indeed, this evening was only the third time Maria had ever been in the Szukalski household.

Kataryna had served the pastries on a platter and Jan had refilled the wine glasses. Maximilian Hartung,

86

relaxing in his chair before the fire as if he were an old friend of the family, had entertained everyone with jokes and funny stories.

As the evening had worn on, however, and as the wine bottle had been emptied and the mood grown mellow, the laughter had subsided and everyone had fallen to staring into the fire. The long silence had been broken by Maximilian who, having glanced up at the two paintings over the fireplace, suddenly had said in a somber voice, " 'Now is my soul incarnate in my country, and in my body dwells her soul; my fatherland and I are one great whole. My name is million, for I love as millions, their pain and suffering I feel. . . .' "

Both Maria and Kataryna had turned to stare at Maximilian, their eyes filled with wonder and sentiment, while Jan Szukalski, to whom the words were painfully familiar, had remained glaring into the fire. And it was then he who spoke up first, saying, *"Konrad. . . ."*

"I see, Dr. Szukalski, that you are familiar with Mickiewicz."

Jan finally tore his eyes away from the flames. "I am not only familiar with him, *Panie* Hartung, you see that he shares equal space with Jesus Christ. In my life as well as over my fireplace. 'My name is million, for I love as millions. . . .' Adam Mickiewicz was the greatest poet who ever lived."

"I don't argue with that, Dr. Szukalski. Today, I would say he is Poland's true symbol of patriotism. And with the rape of our beautiful country, who can—"

"I had thought by your name, *Panie* Hartung, that you were German."

But Max had taken no offense. "I am German on my father's side. But what's in a name? Can you be certain of a man's loyalties merely by the sound of his name?"

"You mentioned a factory in Danzig."

"Quite right. But when my father owned it, Danzig was neutral; a little German, a little Polish." He flashed a disarming grin. "And please, no more *Panie*. Just plain Max will do."

Szukalski had nodded thoughtfully. The stirring

words of Adam Mickiewicz coming from the mouth of
this stranger had caused him to lower his usual defenses. Generally a man to adhere to formal terms of
address and to shy away from the more intimate rela-
tionships, Szukalski had said to Hartung, "I'd prefer
it if you just called me Jan," and surprised even himself in the process.

"Against a common enemy we are no longer Mister
and Doctor, not man or woman, but simply Poles. And
it is for Poland that we must cleave together in friendship. It is to my great regret, Jan Szukalski, that I have
to leave Sofia tomorrow. You see, I have made friends
here now, and. . . ." He reached for Maria's hand.
"Maria is here. I don't want to leave her again. But I
have to."

"To go back and make bearings for the Nazis?"
asked Jan sharply.

But Max had only grinned sheepishly. "They're not
very good bearings."

Everyone had laughed, and when the chuckling had
subsided, Max had said in all seriousness, "I am just
as sad as you to see what is happening to this country.
And now the same thing is happening to Russia. Can't
the Nazis be stopped?"

Szukalski had raised his eyebrows, startled. He had
glanced quickly at the two women, and said, "You
speak too openly, Max. I think people have been shot
for a lot less in the past two years."

But Max had been unruffled. "And who is my execu-
tioner? You?"

"Partisans are watched for, Max; how do you know
you can trust me?"

He had smiled flippantly. "Any man who has the
portrait of Adam Mickiewicz over his fireplace—"

"I'm serious, Max. To speak as you did, like a partisan, like a revolutionary, is dangerous. We have to be
careful in these times."

Maximilian had shrugged. "Careful people don't win
wars. I don't mind saying that I have many friends
who are working hard to subvert the Nazi plan. The
Resistance is everywhere, Jan. Even here in Sofia, I'll
wager there is such a movement."

Szukalski had sat back in his chair and eyed Maria's friend warily. This talk made him uneasy; in the two years since the Blitz he had not encountered such explosive words. Although in his heart a patriotic man, Jan Szukalski nonetheless believed that the answer to survival—of himself and his family—was peaceful co-existence with the occupying forces. Resistance only meant suicide. And though Jan would dearly have loved to see Poland freed from this tyranny, he was not prepared to pay so high a price.

He had said with a sigh, "Sometimes I think I'd rather have an epidemic on my hands than this war. At least that way we could keep the Nazis out. And as for the Jews, well, as far as I know, they have all been restricted to the ghettos or shipped out of the country." As he had spoken he had tried to ignore the picture Father Wajda had planted in his mind of the camp at Oświęcim. "We want only peace here in Sofia."

Maximilian Hartung had continued to hold his obsidian gaze on the doctor, his mouth fixed in a wry smile, and then, raising his glass, said, "To peace then, Doctor."

When he came to the steps of the hospital, Jan stopped and stared up at the entrance.

"To peace," they had all echoed, draining the last of their wine. But while the conversation had moved on to lighter, more relaxed topics, the tension in the air had nonetheless remained. And for the rest of the evening, the chilling thought that now plagued him on the hospital steps had echoed in his mind: If the Nazi threat is as real as Piotr believes and if our worst fears do come to pass, then what chance have I, a cripple, or my little boy with his crown of Nordic curls, remaining as we are?

Footsteps whispered up the stone stairs and a form blurred past. The hasty murmur of "Good morning, Doctor," brought Jan to shake his head and blink up at the person who hurried past. Recognizing the slender form of Lehman Bruckner, a laboratory technician, Szukalski forced the gloomy preoccupation from his mind and hurried up the steps.

He was pleased to find the radiators were working

on this raw morning and that, as a consequence, the hospital was comfortingly warm. As he made his way down the hall toward his office, a nurse walked alongside and gave him a running commentary on the status of his patients. At the door of his office she ended with, "The farm boy who lost his hand was taken away early this morning by his father who has lost faith in our medicine and thinks he can cure his son with recipes from his pantry."

Szukalski smiled defeatedly. "It'll take a long time for the peasants to learn. I know what'll happen to the boy. For a while he'll find relief from his family's folk medicine, but it won't last, and then he'll be back to have the entire arm removed." Jan shook his head sorrowfully.

"One last thing, Doctor. Father Wajda came by a while ago with a new patient. I've let him wait in your office."

Jan looked up at the door. "That's fine, Nurse, thank you."

He hesitated before going in, taking a moment to remind himself of his promise of yesterday to the priest.

Jan Szukalski stepped quietly in and silently closed the door behind him. At once the young man jumped to his feet, saying, "I apologize for this intrusion, Doctor. Father Wajda said—"

"It's quite all right. Please sit down."

They kept an eye on one another as the tall doctor, trying suddenly to keep from limping, walked over to his desk and sat down. He was surprised to see just how young the boy really was. The priest had already told him of this fact, but somehow in his mind Szukalski had pictured someone sturdier than this, someone crueller and older. Instead, here was a round, smooth face, wide, questioning blue eyes, and a mouth that seemed to pout a little in innocence.

Dr. Szukalski felt his guard drop a little. This was not the adversary he had been prepared for.

"*SS-Rottenführer* Hans Kepler," said the young man nervously.

It was not difficult to sense the young man's discomfort, his loss for a way to begin, so Jan said, "Father Wajda and I had a long talk the night before last."

Kepler nodded.

Szukalski took another moment to scrutinize the boy; the severe cut of his blond hair, the immaculate press of his gray uniform (exactly the type Hitler had worn when he had declared war on Poland), the Luger in a holster on his belt, and the gleaming black jackboots. He cut a fine portrait. The only inconsistency was the face. And the anxious, darting eyes.

"Did he tell you about the camp?"

"Yes, he did, although there were some unbelievable things—"

"They were true! All of them, Dr. Szukalski—" Kepler slid to the edge of his chair. "I know I've betrayed the Reich and that I have soiled the honor of my family, but it came to be more than I could bear. Some of them—most of them, I think—enjoy what they do at the camp. The cruelties, the sadism . . . but I cannot. I stood it for a year and then . . . and then. . . ."

"You were given a two-week leave."

"The camp doctor said I needed a rest. I've been having horrible nightmares. I cry out in my sleep. And I can't eat, Doctor; there is a sickness deep inside me."

The first words came out in a rush, jumbled, halting, as they had in the confessional, but as he talked on, it became easier. "I'm sure you don't believe it. No one would. Even I didn't at first. But then, six months ago, there came a direct order from—" Kepler stopped suddenly and looked at the door.

"It's all right," said Szukalski in a quiet voice. "No one can hear us. You're free to talk."

Kepler licked his lips and continued more quietly. "Six months ago there came an order direct from Himmler himself to Camp Commander Hoess, ordering him to construct the gas chambers and ovens and to begin a massive full-scale system of extermination. It had been my job to assure these new arrivals, stripped down and prodded along like cattle, that nothing was going to hurt them, that they were only going in for a shower, to be deloused, and that new clothes would be given them afterward. There they stood, the whimpering old people, the crying children, the angry, helpless men, the innocent young women. . . . *Oh God!"*

Suddenly, Hans buried his face in his hands. His fingers slid over the sweat that now started to pour copiously from his forehead. His stomach rose up to his throat, filling him with the familiar acrid taste of bile, causing his heart to thump wildly against his rib cage. And through the fog he heard a gentle voice say, "Are you all right?"

With great effort, Hans Kepler sat upright and ran his moist hands through his hair. "Yes," he whispered. "It passes. It always does."

"If it helps," said Szukalski quietly, "I do believe you."

Kepler nodded.

"Tell me," said Jan carefully, measuring his words. "Are there other camps like that one?"

"Oh yes. Auschwitz is not alone. There is a plan." Kepler looked quickly at the door again and once more dropped his voice. "Before I went to Auschwitz I was given a pamphlet called 'The Subhuman,' and in it Slavs are referred to as 'the afterbirth of humanity.' On Hitler's scale of subhumanity, the Slavs are considered but one degree above gypsies and Jews, and they're considered only good for slaves to serve their German masters."

"God help us," murmured Szukalski.

"They intend to make Poland a slave nation. Not just the Jews, *everyone,* Doctor. And they also plan to get rid of the useless ones like cripples, simpletons, the aged, children. . . . You cannot imagine what it is like at Auschwitz. Do you know what an inmate's life is worth? The guards are told not to shoot one because each bullet costs the Reich three pfennigs. Three pfennigs, Doctor! So we gas them. They arrive on the trains, many of them dead already because they've been traveling for days standing up like cattle without food or water. And then the ones that will work at slave labor are chosen by a camp doctor. Pregnant women or women with children automatically go to the gas chamber because they have proven to be fighters and have caused the guards no end of trouble. Families are broken up, husbands and wives are separated, only to be told that they will be united again on the other side of the showers." As he spoke, Kepler's voice drifted lower and lower, as if the life were seeping out of him. "We gas them by the thousands, Doctor, every day. At first we used carbon monoxide which came from the exhaust of diesel trucks. But this was inefficient and it took a long time to get the engines started. The prisoners were packed in so tightly that none of them fell when they died. We on the outside could hear their weeping and their cries for mercy. Sometimes it took more than an hour before they were silent. And then we would open the doors—"

"Corporal Kepler."

"But then we changed to a gas called Zyklon B which you must know is prussic acid. Have you ever seen anyone killed by that means?"

"Corporal, please!"

"Yes, you can shut me up and it goes away. How do I shut up my mind? How do I stop the memories? I am half Polish, Doctor, I was born here, and yet I have been helping the Germans to exterminate my mother's people. I can't go back! The thought of returning sickens me. Once I thought of joining the Polish Resistance, but who would trust me? It is hopeless . . ."

"Is there no way you can request a transfer?"

"Then I shall be sent to the eastern front."

"So you want a medical excuse from me."

"If that's not possible, then give me enough sleeping pills to let me sleep forever, and I'll take them far away from Sofia in a place where no one will find me. Don't worry, Doctor, your town will be safe from reprisal."

"I don't know if I'll be able to come up with anything plausible. If we tell the Germans that you have anything wrong with you, they'll want you transferred back to one of their own hospitals. Anything, that is, unless it's a horribly contagious disease. That would be the only way we could get them to leave you here."

"What sort of disease?"

"I really don't know. They can all be checked by blood analysis, and there is no way we can falsify that."

"It is hopeless then?"

Szukalski looked long into Kepler's wide blue eyes and felt the conflict within his own heart. "Give me a day or two to think about this; perhaps I will be able to come up with something."

As Kepler stood, ready to leave, Szukalski added, "I think it would be best, Corporal, if you were to wear civilian clothes from now on. Is that permissible while you're on leave?"

"Yes. I have some other clothes at my grandmother's house. I will change before I come to see you again. Two days, Doctor?"

Sofia's hospital, small but well equipped, served the town and surrounding area of farms and villages totaling thirty thousand people. Jan Szukalski had been its director since 1936 when, twenty-five years old and with two years of supervisory and research experience behind him from a hospital at Krakow, he filled a vacancy left by the previous medical director upon his death at eighty-three.

The nursing staff enjoyed working under Szukalski, for he was a man known for his fairness and compassion and his medical acuity. Although possibly too austere and aloof to win him any friends, Jan was nonetheless known to be kindhearted and generous beyond bounds. And as his temperament was generally one of professional distance and detachment, no one noticed that on this particular morning the hospital's director was unusually preoccupied.

No one, that is, except his assistant.

Making rounds with him, changing dressings, writing orders for the nurses, prescribing medications and discharging the well patients, Maria Duszynska was acutely aware of his mood of uneasiness.

So it was no surprise to her when, after they were through, he asked Maria to come to his office with him.

Locking the door to be sure they would not be disturbed, Jan prefaced his speech with a warning of caution and words that emphasized the need for absolute secrecy. "No one, Maria, not one of the other doctors, none of the nurses, not your friend Max, *no one* must know anything of what I am about to tell you."

She had been surprised at the gravity of his tone and had even taken it skeptically, but when she heard the entire story of Hans Kepler and the problem of a false medical excuse that Szukalski now faced, Maria understood the extremity of his concern.

She had sat listening for nearly an hour, her face blending from one shade of gray into another until it came out at the end a stark white.

After a period of silence, he leaned forward over his desk and looked at her intently. "If I can't come up with a foolproof excuse for Kepler, then I won't attempt it. But please think about it, Maria. I trust you and I need all the help I can get."

She stared pensively at him, her beautiful face drawn tight. "There are a lot of diseases that would make someone sick enough to exempt him from military duty, but every one I can think of can be verified by a laboratory test. We could always fake the disease, but there is no way to falsify lab tests."

"That was my feeling."

When Maria stood she discovered how deeply his strange tale had affected her, for her legs had gone weak and she had to hold on to the desk for support. Studying Szukalski's impassive face, realizing that even after a year of working with him he still remained a mystery to her, she said, "Of course I'll try to help."

And yet it was difficult to concentrate. This was her last night with Maximilian who was leaving on tomorrow's train, so that as they finished their supper at the White Eagle, the dilemma of Hans Kepler was disconnected from her mind.

And as always when one tries one's best to make the time drag and last forever, the evening flew by more quickly than any other time she had known, bringing them ultimately into one another's final, desperate embrace beneath the warm eiderdown of Maria's bed.

Old promises had been renewed tonight, and new ones had been made, but the uncertainty of the times and the war that had already once shattered her hopes now caused Maria to lie restlessly in Max's arms, unable to share his peaceful slumber. And as she lay looking up at the dark ceiling, reliving briefly their days together at Warszawa University, lingering forlornly over the sweet words he had uttered to her tonight, Maria felt the nagging problem of Hans Kepler gently tug at her mind.

It swirled through her brain like a mist. The haunting tale of the concentration camp, the tragedy of the boy's disillusionment, his shame of himself, his promise to commit suicide rather than face the nightmare again. And her responsibility to try to help him. Yet it seemed an impossible task. How could they fool the German-controlled laboratories? How could they fake a serious illness and get away with it? What possible course could they—

Suddenly it hit her.

"Typhus," she said aloud, and as she heard her own voice fill the night, she quickly put a hand to her mouth to cover the sound that had already gone.

"What?" mumbled Max sleepily. "What did you say?"

"Oh, I. . . ." Her eyes raced in the darkness. "I said typhus. I must have been dreaming about a case I saw today. I was just drifting off . . . I'm sorry. Did I wake you?"

Max opened one eye, and in the obscurity she could see his playful grin. "Did you really expect me to sleep, lying next to you like this?"

He reached up and drew her down onto him, capturing her mouth in a deep kiss. Beneath his hand, which now gently explored the contour of her breasts, he felt the rapid fluttering of her heart and believed himself to be the cause of it. He was only half right.

Edmund Dolata was a small, thin man with a balding head and round shoulders. He had at one time been the most powerful and influential man in Sofia. He had been the Mayor. But now, Edmund Dolata was an ordinary citizen.

He hardly recognized his old office as he stood before the familiar desk nervously awaiting the arrival of the commandant. This room had once been his private chambers in the Town Hall, but now it was the office of Dieter Schmidt.

All of the furniture was gone except for the desk and chair behind it. No other chairs for visitors. Dolata's photographs and paintings had all been taken down to be replaced by a single, giant photograph of Adolf Hitler hanging behind the desk, flanked by two large red Nazi flags.

Dolata took out his handkerchief and wiped the sweat off his head. He had an idea of why Schmidt had summoned him. Dolata had, as many other townspeople, been awakened just before dawn by the muffled sound of a distant explosion.

The former Mayor jumped and dropped his handkerchief when Schmidt suddenly entered the room, slapping his thigh with his ever-present swagger stick.

"Dolata, I have warned you before," said the commandant without introduction. "I told you when I first came to this miserable town that I would tolerate no resistance from the people. Cooperation, that is all I ask for, and what do I get?"

Dolata stretched his eyes wide.

"Mines!" barked Schmidt. "The fields outside of town have been mined!"

Dolata's mouth dropped open. "I don't under—"

"Two of my men were killed this morning by an exploding mine!"

"Oh my G—"

"Who do you suppose planted it, Dolata?"

"Oh, *Herr Hauptsturmführer,* surely you don't think anyone in Sofia did it. Where on earth would they get such mines? And even if they could, they wouldn't want to, I assure you!"

"Liar! Your people are going to pay for this, Dolata."

"Oh please, *Herr*—"

"What do you suggest I do?" Schmidt's face contorted into a sneer.

Edmund Dolata tried to think fast. If Dieter Schmidt was telling the truth, then the mine could only have been planted by someone who was bent on fighting the

Nazis at any cost. And the former Mayor had an idea of who that might be.

"There is only one way to correct such subversion, Dolata. Your people are going to feel what it is like to step on a land mine."

"Wait, please—" The frightened little man was thinking about the people hiding in the cave. And he weighed, for an instant, the value of their twenty-six lives against the thousands of lives in Sofia. Then he considered what Schmidt would do to him if he revealed now that he had known of their existence for some time, and quickly dismissed any idea of mentioning the cave.

"What are you going to do, *Herr Hauptsturmführer?*"

"I want you and your council to assemble the townspeople at the field on the northeast edge of the town. Get everyone there, Dolata. Children, too. I am going to make them walk across that field."

"But why?"

Schmidt smiled an oily smile. "Can you think of a better way to find out if there are any other mines hidden there? Now listen! I want every inch of that field walked, do you hear me? So if there are any more mines buried there, they will be exploded by the people who put them there!"

"But, *Herr Hauptsturmführer*—"

"By noon, Dolata! Every man, woman and child in this town at that field by noon. And you, *Herr Burgermeister*, will lead them across."

Maria and Max parted early in the morning at the train station. Promising to return in a few months and to write letters in between, Maximilian sadly climbed aboard the train bound for Lublin and watched Maria as the platform drew away from him. She remained a little while staring down the empty track until the last vestige of the train's smoke had faded, then she struck off resolutely through the snow.

As her steps drew her nearer to the hospital she remembered the revelation that had come to her during the night, and Dr. Maria Duszynska felt her heart race once more.

Typhus.

Her step picked up, gained speed until she could hardly keep from running. She had to see Szukalski. Before all else, she had to see Szukalski.

It was far fetched, and the risks were immeasurable, but it might work. It just might work. . . .

CHAPTER 8

By the time Maria reached the hospital, Jan had already started rounds. Quickly changing into her white smock and joining him at the chart rack on the first floor, Maria barely gave him the opportunity to say good morning. She startled him by grasping his arm, saying with controlled excitement, "I have something to tell you. Can I see you in your office right now?"

He was even further surprised when, as they entered the office and she closed the door behind her, Maria said suddenly, "Typhus!"

He looked at her quizzically. "What?"

"Typhus," she said again breathlessly.

"What do you mean, has a patient got—"

"No, no, Jan. Your young soldier. He can have typhus. That will be his excuse for not going back to the camp. Typhus, Jan!"

He pondered uncertainly for a minute, and then said slowly, "Well, they certainly wouldn't want him back on duty if he has something as contagious and deadly as typhus. But the diagnosis of typhus can be verified by the Weil-Felix test. It would be impossible to invent the disease where it doesn't exist."

Maria smiled cryptically. "Let me ask you something, Jan. Didn't you tell me that two years ago you were performing experiments with a typhus vaccine you had made out of Proteus bacteria?"

"Yes," he said slowly. "I did."

"What were the results of that research?"

"It didn't work at all to protect against typhus."

"But what else did it do, Jan?"

"What else?" Szukalski frowned. "Well, it confused the Weil-Felix test by . . ." His voice trailed off and a look of astonishment came over his face. "Maria," his voice grew excited. "My experimental vaccine *confused the Weil-Felix test by showing a false positive!*"

"Did you ever report the results of your research to anyone?"

Szukalski was speaking faster now. "No, I never reported it. It didn't seem important to me at the time that I had accidentally discovered something that gave a false positive test for a serious illness with a vaccine that didn't work." He made a wry smile. "And besides, the Germans invaded us at the same time. My research came to an abrupt halt. Maria, this is incredible!"

"One more thing, Jan," she went hurriedly on. "Do I have this right? If we were to make up a vaccine using Proteus bacteria and administer it to someone, in a week or so his blood would show that he had typhus when in fact he did not. Is that right?"

"Psiakrew!" he murmured, turning away from her and driving a hand through his hair. "Yes, that's right!"

"And no one else knows this can be done? Jan?"

Szukalski dropped heavily into his chair and spread his hands squarely on the desk. "No. No one else knows this can be done. Unless it was discovered somewhere else coincidentally. Which I doubt. But you forget one thing."

Maria sat opposite him and twisted her hands. "What?"

"This has never been tried on a human being. All of my results are based on laboratory animal studies."

"Is there anything that makes you think the results wouldn't be the same in humans?"

"No. I'm almost certain that the antigen-antibody response would be the same. I just never bothered to test it on humans once my results with animals told me I had not found the vaccine I was looking for."

"I think you should try it, Jan."

He ran his hands over his face. "God, it's an idea, Maria! And I'm tempted."

"Then do it. It's our only hope. If the Proteus vaccine will give the false positive you say it does."

"Oh it does, all right. In fact," he smiled crookedly, "at the time I recall being very annoyed by the false positives I was receiving."

"When will the soldier be back?"

"Tomorrow morning."

Maria nodded, relaxing now by visible degrees. Now, there were other things to consider. "Jan, can you trust this soldier? How do you know he isn't a spy sent here to see if he can stir us up so that Dieter Schmidt will have an excuse to liquidate us?"

"You know, I said the same thing to Father Wajda when he first told me about the boy. But if you saw him, Maria, and heard him tell his own story . . ." Jan got up from his chair and went over to the mantelpiece, leaning on it. "Anyway, it's worth a try. Surely there's every reason it will work. Only. . . ."

"What?"

"I might have trouble isolating the right bacteria again. I lost all of my specimens when the Nazis sacked the hospital two years ago. They smashed all the tubes I had specimens in to prevent my poisoning the water supply, they said."

"Which Proteus strain was it?"

"X-19."

"How would you isolate it?"

"The way I did it before, by growing it from the urine of someone who had typhus. Proteus, for reasons not really understood, is found in the urine of those with typhus, but does not cause it. So our plan will be to get a vaccine made from Proteus into Kepler without having to give him the disease itself."

"There's a typhus case on a dairy farm not far from here."

"Yes, I know about that one. We'll send someone out there today for a sample of the man's urine. With luck, it will contain Proteus."

"You can send Lehman Bruckner; the lab isn't busy today. And he won't think it odd. We can make it look like a routine urinalysis."

Szukalski nodded. "While you're at it, have him collect a blood sample as well. We'd better make sure it is typhus that the old man has. In the meantime, I'll get some broth media and some agar ready to start the cultures."

She rose and took a few steps toward the door, but

then stopped and turned to say, "Jan, tell me something."

"What?"

"Let's say we go ahead with it. Let's say you can remember how you made up the vaccine and we inject it into Kepler."

"Yes?"

"What if it doesn't work?"

Lehman Bruckner returned in the early afternoon with the urine and blood samples of the old dairy farmer and reported that the old man was seriously ill.

"I'll stop by and see him this evening then," said Szukalski as he prepared the samples for routine analysis. "I don't give him much of a chance. Typhus is almost a hundred percent fatal in anyone over the age of sixty. Be sure you change your clothes and have the ones you wore out there cleaned well. Any lice from the old man or his house could have gotten on you, and lice carry the disease."

"I'll take care, Doctor," said Bruckner. A lean young man with a narrow face and shrewd eyes, Bruckner had disdained the task of collecting blood and urine from the Polish peasant. Although born in Poland, he was the son of pure German parents and considered himself part of Sofia's "better" class.

"Oh, and Lehman, I'll take care of the urine specimen, but I want you to send the blood off to the communicable disease center in Warszawa with a request for the Weil-Felix test."

"Yes, Doctor." The young lab assistant turned stiffly on his heel and walked out. Szukalski was glad to have such an efficient young laboratory man sent to him, although it occasionally struck him as odd that Bruckner had not been conscripted into military duty.

A short while later, after the lab had been closed and Szukalski was confident Bruckner would not be returning, he called Maria to join him. She stood by while he inoculated the urine specimen into the broth medium he had prepared and then onto an agar plate. Then he placed both cultures into the incubator.

"We'll set it at thirty-seven degrees centigrade. We should have enough bacterial growth by tomorrow night to determine whether Proteus is one of them."

After supper Jan Szukalski drove in his 1929 Chevrolet to Piotr Wajda's house. It was a small, free-standing cottage set not far from the edge of the church graveyard, and although his housekeeper as a rule answered the door, this evening the priest himself opened it.

"Jan," he said quietly.

"I'm going out to the Wilk farm, Piotr; the old man is dying. Will you come with me? I need to talk to you about . . . that problem."

"Yes, yes. The Wilks. I had been planning to go out there anyway to administer the Holy Sacrament. Typhus, I think you said the other day. Let me just get my things."

Szukalski waited in the doorway while Father Wajda gathered up the items necessary for extreme unction, and after only a minute the two of them were in the car.

"I'm glad you came by when you did, Jan," said the priest as the car coughed to a start and lurched off down the street. "This has been a bad day."

"I heard about that business at the field."

"You and Maria were lucky, being allowed to continue your duties at the hospital instead of having to take part in it. At least Schmidt isn't insane enough to risk killing the only two doctors in town."

"Nazis get sick, too."

"I had to walk with Dolata at the head of the crowd, traipsing through the snow and thinking that each step might be my last. I must have said a hundred Hail Marys, crossing that field."

Szukalski nodded gravely. "And there were no mines."

"None. Whoever blew up those two soldiers left no trace of how they did it."

"Resistance fighters," said Jan. "And they are getting bolder each day."

"Who are they, Jan? Where are they hiding?"

Szukalski shook his head and gripped the steering wheel until his knuckles were white. "I don't know, Piotr. I wish I did, for I would tell them they're going about it in the wrong way. They can't win this way; they will only make the Nazis angrier."

Both men were silent and pensive during the drive. At this dark hour the scenery was cold and mystical, like some strange planetary landscape, with its skeletal trees, undulating hills of snow, and running shadows. By the time Dr. Szukalski pulled up before the Wilks' farmhouse, neither man had said a word.

The Wilk residence, with its thatched-roof cottage of straw and limestone sitting at the edge of a long narrow strip of farmland, was typical of farms in this region of Poland. Inside the modest house, which was filled with the aroma of caraway and where the dirt floors were sprinkled with fine white sand, dwelt seven people in one room and a loft.

Szukalski could remember, as they knocked on the heavy door, a time when the Wilks had been respectable farmers, healthy and robust, living off their land and selling their surplus for a few luxuries in life. But then the war had come and in September of 1939 the Nazis had taken possession of all property, reducing the Wilks and all others like them to serfs on the land they had owned for generations. Now the Nazis exacted a specific quota each harvest, and carted away all they produced, leaving the Wilks to subsist on a level somewhere below abject poverty.

The priest and the doctor were taken to the far corner of the cramped room. A makeshift altar had been fashioned over the flagstone fireplace with many candles burning before a blue-and-gold plaster statue of the Virgin. And in the dark corner, lying on the floor with only a blanket between him and the bare dirt, was old man Wilk.

Dr. Szukalski knelt down first while the rest of the family, the son Wadek and his wife and their four gaping children, looked on. Jan stood up immediately and backed away. "My skill is no longer needed here, Father. This is your department now."

Piotr nodded and gently urged the family to wait in

the loft overhead. He then began the last rite. Applying sacred oil to the old man's eyelids, nose, mouth, ears, hands, and feet, he murmured, "Go forth, Christian soul," and made the sign of the cross.

When he stood, as if on signal Wadek Wilk descended from the loft. From among the beds of hay overhead came the sound of weeping. Seeing the tears in the big man's eyes, Jan Szukalski had to steel himself for what he was about to say.

He explained as simply as he could to the uneducated man that the disease which took his father could also claim his family. It was caused by a germ, he said, transmitted by lice. All the bedding and clothing of the deceased, as well as all other bedding and clothing in the house, should be treated at once.

"Take a barrel, *Panie* Wilk, and drill holes in the bottom. Place all your clothing in it and put a lid on top. Then put this barrel on top of a tank of boiling water. Steam it for an hour. Do you understand?"

The peasant nodded dumbly, tears streaming down his thick face. Jan glanced around the room. Of course. There were no clocks. What need had a dairy farmer of any timepiece other than the rising and setting of the sun?

"Steam them for a *very long time, Panie* Wilk. You must kill all the lice. Check your hair and your children's hair. If you are to avoid the sickness that took your father you must be clean. Do you understand?"

Again the man nodded.

Jan gave his condolences, and assured the farmer that he would come at once if one of the others fell ill.

The priest and the doctor crunched over the snow toward the old Chevrolet, their duties accomplished, and climbed into the car. As the motor warmed up, Father Wajda said, "Is there any chance of an epidemic?"

"No. They're isolated. No one will go into or come out of that farm for the winter. It won't spread from there. Just be sure you steam or boil that cassock you're wearing and clean the contents of your bag thoroughly."

"What about the rest of the family?"

Jan pictured the skinny children: the hollow eyes, the blank stares. "They'll probably get it. If they're lucky, they'll die from it."

"Jan!"

Szukalski took one last look at the little cottage sitting peacefully in the ghostly moonlight. He was thinking of Auschwitz.

On their way back, Szukalski explained to his friend the plan he and Maria had devised for Kepler. The priest became excited at the prospect, but Jan cautioned him. "I did those experiments two years ago and only came across the false positive by accident. I can't be sure I'll be able to reconstruct the experiment. Nor had I tried it on humans. I have no idea of the results."

"But . . . if you *do* succeed, then this false vaccine will somehow make Kepler's blood look like he has typhus where in fact he doesn't?"

"I'm hoping that an injection of the harmless Proteus into Kepler will, after a week's time, produce a reaction in his blood that will make the Weil-Felix test at the German-controlled lab read him as positive for typhus. In that way, Piotr, it'll be the Germans themselves who are officially relieving Kepler from duty."

"Why, that's—"

"Right now I'm not even sure we have Proteus to begin with. It all depends on what we can grow from the old man's urine."

Szukalski dropped the priest off at his home and then returned to the hospital, entering by a rear door and going directly to his office. He rapidly changed his clothes, depositing the garments he had worn to the Wilk farm into a laundry bag which he sealed tight, and passed on to an orderly, with instructions that it be sterilized thoroughly apart from other laundry.

Then Jan Szukalski struck out once again into the winter's night. Halfway home he stopped short and looked down the dimly lit street. Coming toward him, a rifle slung over one shoulder and blowing on his cold hands, was a German soldier. In his comings and goings at odd hours due to his profession, Szukalski was used

to these soldiers and gave them scant thought after
two years. Rather it was something else which had
caused him to pause now.

Something the priest had said, something he was
unable to recall but which, for some unknown reason,
kept prickling his mind like a bothersome burr. He
couldn't seize upon it. And yet, though he could not
grasp it, Jan had the strong notion that it was important.

The Nazi soldier recognized the director of Sofia's
hospital and gave a polite nod. Szukalski, barely
acknowledging him, slowly turned about and began to
retrace his steps. He did not want to go home just yet.

He walked for half an hour and still it wouldn't
come. He found himself in front of one of the town's
two movie theaters. As it was not yet the evening curfew hour, the theater was still brightly lit and running
its feature.

Jan gazed at the colorful billboard. *"Biała Snie-
gowica i Siedem Karzelków."* He felt himself smile. It
was not a new film; he himself had first seen it three
years before in Krakow when he had stood in the rain
for two hours to get in. The theater was running it this
week for the Christmas holiday; a special treat for
families. Jan Szukalski took out a *zloty* and bought
a ticket.

Inside there were surprisingly few empty seats. The
people of Sofia sought an hour or two of escape and
pleasure in this warm, dark movie house, listening to
a language they did not understand.

Jan sank into a hard wooden seat on the aisle and
stared at the screen. The movie was already half over,
but that didn't matter. He had come in here to think, to
try to trick his mischievous memory into revealing the
nagging thought that teased his mind. He looked up at
the bright splashes of crimson, magenta, lemon-yellow,
and the deepest ocean-blue, and marveled again, as
he had three years before, at the genius, artistry, and
magic of an American named Walt Disney.

And when, after a few minutes, the seven dwarfs
were marching single file back to their cottage, singing,
the words of Father Wajda of just a short while ago

now sprang up again. "Is there any chance of an epidemic?"

Jan Szukalski's eyes grew wide.

Is there any chance of an epidemic?

An epidemic of typhus.

He kept his eyes fixed on the screen, but they did not see the Polish subtitles written at the bottom, nor did he now see the brilliant colors anymore or hear the lilting music. Instead he saw before him the Wilk farm being mercifully spared from the Nazis because of their disease. He had said they were lucky. Better to have typhus than become slaves of the Reich. And he saw Hans Kepler. Getting his medical reprieve from the German laboratories themselves.

And Jan Szukalski felt himself tremble suddenly, uncontrollably.

"This is the bridge I think we should take out," said Brunek Matuszek, pointing with a stick at the crude map he had scratched in the dirt. Four faces peered down at it: Moisze Bromberg, Antek Wozniak, David Ryż, and Leokadja Ciechowska.

"This bridge across the Wisła is on the main rail line from Krakow to Lublin. If we can spot a munitions train coming from Krakow that doesn't offload at Sofia's supply depot, or a train loading at the depot and heading north, then we will know it is bound for Lublin. And will cross the river here."

David Ryż looked intently at the map, envisioning the terrain in that area. He knew it well. With his plow horse, David had been the main scout for the group in the past year. He also knew trains.

"We will need someone to watch the supply depot at Sofia and spot our target for us. David?"

The youth looked up. "Are you ordering me, Captain?"

Brunek shook his head patiently. "I am ordering no one, David. I don't assume command of you or anyone else. This is a project we must all cooperate in or it will not work."

"I'll watch the depot," said David. He returned his gaze to the map, wishing he could warm up to the robust Pole. Loyalty to his cause for Zionism kept David from finding it in his heart to consider the *goy* Captain a friend; but the youth did admit that Brunek was finally persuading the group into action, which was what he himself had for a long time failed to do. David hungered for action. He wanted immediate victories, he wanted to see the Resistance an instant success and had little patience for long-term plans.

"If we pull this one off," continued Brunek, "then we will have guns and ammunition for a thousand."

"And no one to handle them," said David sullenly.

Now Moisze spoke. "First things first, David. Weapons first, then maybe an army."

David scowled darkly into his hands. He was impatient. He wanted that army and he wanted it now. And he knew where to get it.

"Unfortunately," he heard Brunek say further, "there will be no chance to rehearse. We will have to make this one chance work, for I doubt we'll have another. Now then, as we look at the bridge which stands right here," he pointed with the stick, "just below Sandomierz, the train stops here while the soldiers go across the bridge and inspect for explosives or any kind of sabotage work. There are armed men on top of the train as well as in the engine and the caboose, so that all avenues to the stopped train are closely watched. Except one."

The four faces looked up.

Brunek grinned. "I told you I had a plan to make myself invisible. I plan to come from a direction that the Germans aren't watching.

"I will come from *beneath* the train."

CHAPTER 9

Dr. Jan Szukalski arrived at the hospital at six o'clock in the morning and went straight to his office. It took only a moment to decide to leave his work and go down to the lab to check his specimens in the incubator.

In the lab, Jan snapped on the fluorescent lights which flickered momentarily before settling into a steady glow. Szukalski headed right for the incubator, opened its door and removed the test tube containing the inoculum in the liquid broth. He held it up to the light. It was quite turbid.

Good, he thought with satisfaction. At least there is some bacterial growth. Now let's hope the old man simply didn't have chronic prostatitis.

He removed the stopper carefully and sniffed the contents of the tube. Dr. Szukalski smiled ever so slightly at the faint trace of ammonia, which is a breakdown product of Proteus metabolism.

He replaced the tube in the incubator and removed the petri dish containing the nutrient agar medium. He lifted the lid and studied the surface of the smooth gelatin-like medium. Several small colonies of bacteria were growing in the path where they had been inoculated by the streaking loop the day before. The colonies looked like small white beads half buried in the caramel-colored glistening surface of the agar. At first his brow furrowed as the thought went through his mind that all of the colonies looked like either Coliform or Staphylococcus. He held the plate up toward the light and turned it back and forth in his hand, trying to study the reflection of the light on the surface of the plate.

With few exceptions the colonies all looked alike. It could be that almost all of the growth was Proteus.

There was no film, so if it was Proteus it was a non-motile strain. And X-19 was a non-motile strain. He placed the dish back in the incubator.

When Jan returned a few minutes later to his office, he found Hans Kepler waiting for him.

"Good morning," said Szukalski. He passed a hand over the radiator and felt no heat coming from it.

Kepler, standing by the window in a fisherman's sweater, a heavy wool jacket and dark pants, and twisting a stocking cap in his hands, swung around and said abruptly, "Are you going to be able to help me, Doctor?"

Szukalski hesitated before sitting down. In the watery light of morning and without his uniform, Hans Kepler, Jan noticed, seemed so vulnerable.

"Please sit down, *Herr Rotten*—" Szukalski stopped himself and cleared his throat. "*Panie* Kepler. Yes, I am going to try to help you."

The young man stared at the doctor.

"Please sit down," repeated Szukalski. "Now then, I must tell you right off that there are no guarantees. And more importantly, I cannot emphasize enough the need for utmost secrecy. What I am going to attempt with you is highly risky, for both of us. One word of this—"

"I will tell no one, I swear."

"Who is your family here in Sofia?"

"I'm staying with my grandmother."

"She must not know."

"Very well."

"Now then, *Panie* Kepler, this is what I propose to do. I am going to send a report to the German Public Health Authority that you are very ill and that I suspect you have typhus."

"Typhus! But how can—"

"I am going to give you an injection of a vaccine that will act upon your body's immune system in such a way that when I draw a blood sample from you seven days after the injection there will be a factor in your blood that will give a false positive result for typhus when the German-controlled lab tests it. Do you understand what I am telling you?"

"I think so, Doctor. But how will they be fooled? Won't they check for this particular vaccine you're going to give me?"

Szukalski shook his head and reached in his pocket for a pack of cigarettes. Offering one to Kepler and lighting both of them, the doctor said, "I have reason to believe that I am the only one who knows such a false positive can be arranged. This vaccine I spoke of, it is of my own invention."

"I see. . . ."

"Now this vaccine has never been used on human beings and I don't know for certain what will happen when it is. The vaccine, which I must make up myself, is very similar to the vaccine used to prevent typhoid fever but uses a different strain of bacteria. I've used it on animals but always small ones like guinea pigs. I've never tried it on any kind of large animal. Now, the least serious complication is that the vaccine will not work the way I want it to and the most serious would be some type of allergic reaction and your dying from the injection."

"I see. . . ." murmured Kepler again, his face etched in thought. "The way I understand it then, Doctor, is I have nothing to lose. If it fails, then I am back where I started. If I die from it, then . . ." He shrugged. "It will save me the trouble. When can we start this?"

"The vaccine must still be made up. I hope to have it in six days. How long is your leave? Two weeks? Then we have time. Come back in four days and I'll let you know how I'm progressing."

Kepler stood stiffly and jerked the wool cap over his head. Thrusting out a hand and shaking Szukalski's, he said rigidly, "I can't thank you enough, Doctor."

"Thank me next week, Kepler. Good day."

Kepler was so preoccupied with the possibility of being saved by the Polish doctor that he barely noticed the young girl who passed him on the icy steps of the hospital's entrance.

He stopped quickly and turned around. "Hello!" he called.

Anna Krasinska looked behind her and, seeing him wave a hand, came back down the stairs until she was even with him. Her comely peasant face was set in a puzzled frown. Then it cleared with recognition as she said, "Oh, it's you."

Kepler grinned at the girl, enjoying the loveliness of her face, the soft brown hair that fell to her shoulders and curled under. He would have known her anywhere, the large brown eyes and thinly arched eyebrows. She came to just a head shorter than he as he smiled down at her.

"Didn't you recognize me?"

"Not without your uniform," she said hesitantly. Anna tried to force a smile. "In fact, I'm glad I ran into you. I wanted to thank you for the chocolate and sausage you gave me on the train. It really was such a treat for my family. I'm afraid Christmas dinner would have been quite bland without it."

"I was quite glad to give it to you." Kepler continued to smile at her, feeling freer than he had for a long while. "Would you like to have dinner with me to-night?" he said in a rush. "At my grandmother's house?"

"Oh—" she fell back a step. "I don't think—"

"Please forget that I'm a soldier of the Reich. I know that would be hard, but I am on leave, and for now I'm simply a citizen of Sofia. After all, I *was* born here."

"I usually have dinner at the hospital during the week."

"Come on. I'll meet you when you get off work. What time?"

"I really don't know. . . ."

"What time?" he said in a softer voice.

"Eight o'clock."

"On these very steps then."

"All right," she conceded, tipping her head to one side. "After all, I guess we are old friends."

"To old friendships," he said, raising his cap and feigning a toast. "Until this evening. Good-by."

Maria Duszynska arrived at the hospital a little while later and found Szukalski sitting with his elbows on his desk and his fingers forming the steeple of a country church.

"I saw the German boy leaving as I was coming into the hospital," she said. "I assume you had your talk with him about the idea of making it appear as if he had typhus."

"I explained it all to him, Maria, plus the possible consequences. He seemed to take it all very well. Considering what he's up against, the punishment he would receive at the hands of the Gestapo, I think he's being good about it. I think Hans Kepler is a strong person. He has courage; he's not a coward."

"But you don't like him."

Szukalski lifted his eyebrows at his assistant and was surprised that she would make such an accurate observation. "No, I don't. Does it show?"

She nodded. "I would be surprised if you liked him. After everything he's been involved in, I don't like him either. But we have to help him."

"Don't get me wrong, Maria. It's not Kepler I'm helping. It's the Poles he might go back to Oświęcim to kill. Come on, let's make rounds."

The two doctors completed their regular hospital duties by ten o'clock and went to the laboratory where Lehman Bruckner was busily working on the morning lab specimens. He bade them both good morning with his usual crisp, indifferent air and continued his work with the reagents and test tubes.

Dr. Duszynska examined the agar plate in the incubator and was at once convinced that the dense round hemispherical colonies at the edge of the plate were Proteus bacilli.

Taking the plate from her, Szukalski lit the bunsen burner on the laboratory counter. Then he took a fresh agar plate from the refrigerator and laid it on the counter next to the burner. Picking up a thin wire streaking loop and heating the tiny circular tip until it glowed yellow, he then allowed it to cool, knowing that any residual bacteria on the loop were now incinerated. When this was done, Szukalski opened the petri dish containing the bacteria and carefully touched the loop to the area he and Maria suspected was covered with

Proteus bacilli. He then streaked the new agar plate with the inoculating loop. Satisfied, he covered the petri dish and placed it in the incubator.

"Must be a pretty important patient for both of you to be in here doing his lab work."

They both looked up at Lehman Bruckner.

"Nobody important, Bruckner," said Szukalski casually, suddenly realizing their carelessness. "Just scientific curiosity." His mouth snapped a quick smile. "You know how doctors are."

Bruckner's pinched face remained impassive and he went back to work.

Turning her back to the technician to shield her actions, Dr. Duszynska spread her bacteria specimen onto the center of a microscope slide and passed it through the flame of the bunsen burner to fix it.

As she did so, Szukalski walked over to where Bruckner worked, took a look at what the technician was doing, and discussed with him briefly the patient Bruckner's test pertained to.

Maria placed the slide under the microscope. She looked through the eye piece, adjusted the illuminating mirror and finally the focus. As the microbes on the slide came sharply into view, a look of excitement washed over her face.

"Dr. Szukalski," she said with great control. "Will you look at this, please?"

"Yes, of course."

When he peered into the microscope and saw the red-stained, slightly bent, rod-like organisms his heart gave a leap.

"They certainly appear to be what we suspected," he murmured.

The two doctors took a moment to tidy the area they had worked in and, replacing their specimens in the incubator, they bid Bruckner good day and left the lab.

The pair arrived at Szukalski's office and maintained their silence until he closed the door behind them.

Jan cleared his voice and said, "I'm afraid my curiosity got the better of my judgment on this. We'll have to be infinitely more careful from now on."

Maria nodded, and an introspective silence fell over

the room. Szukalski realized that the seed planted in his mind by Father Wajda had been germinating all night and all morning, growing until it now occupied his entire brain. And no matter how much Szukalski tried to discard the fantastic notion, it only took a firmer roothold.

A typhus epidemic.

"Jan," said Maria suddenly, stepping away from the window and facing him squarely. "I've been thinking."

"Yes?"

"This thing might really work for Kepler. It's possible, it's *really possible* that you can make the Nazis think he has typhus. And the Germans, being what they are, wouldn't want anything to do with him if they really believe it. So I was wondering. . . ."

"Go on."

"It came to me early this morning. As I was walking to the hospital actually. I was thinking about how easy it might be to save Kepler. And then I thought: Mightn't we do the same thing for others?"

Szukalski could not mask his amazement. "Others!"

"I know it sounds wild, but what if we inoculated other people in Sofia, got confirmed positive results from Warszawa? We could almost have an epidemic."

"Maria—"

"I know it sounds crazy, Jan, and I've been debating all morning about whether or not to even bother telling you about it. But think. If the vaccine works for Kepler, then it *could* work for others, too."

"For God's sake, Maria, that's just what's been on my mind since last night!"

Szukalski's relief was matched only by his excitement. Relief that Maria had solved the dilemma of whether or not to bring up the idea, and excited that, farfetched as the idea was, now that it had been voiced and was out in the open, it seemed suddenly, chillingly credible.

"And why wouldn't it work?" he went on. "With enough positive results, a hundred or three hundred— as many as we want—the Germans *themselves* would declare this an infected area. And, Maria, might that not keep them away?" Kepler's grim picture of Oświęcim flashed in his mind. "You know how fastidious the Germans are, Maria, how much more pampered, more *civilized* than we Poles. As a race, they haven't been exposed to as much typhus as we have and as a result their natural immunity is lower, so that when they do contract the disease it is usually much more severe and with a higher mortality rate."

As he spoke, Maria could not help but notice a side of Szukalski that she had never seen before. The man that surfaced now was emotional, excited, and burning with a vision.

"You yourself know that at this moment the Nazis on the Russian front are facing a situation very similar to what Napoleon faced. Their supply lines are strung out. They are crowded together in bunkers. Their clothing is filthy and you know they must be getting lice from the Ukrainians. So with the lice and the filth, the only missing factor is the typhus microbe which, if they get it, will give them an epidemic as severe as the one that decimated Napoleon's army. And as a consequence, the Wehrmacht is scared to death of a typhus threat. They wouldn't be able to withstand it, Maria."

He came around the desk, visibly restraining himself, and said more quietly, "Typhus is a dreaded disease to us, but to the Germans it is a disaster. If an area were to be declared epidemic, *quarantined*, they would want nothing to do with it."

Her lips formed the words, "I know," but no voice came out.

"The Nazis would avoid us like the plague, and I mean that literally, and the ones that are already here would most likely leave—at least the majority of them would. They'd be scared, especially if their own labs in Warszawa confirmed our supposed findings. They wouldn't even want to take food out of the area. Our farmers would cease to suffer from the Nazi pillage that has left them near starvation."

When his words fell off, he and Maria looked intently at one another, her eyes of ice-blue held by his own dark, turbulent gaze. The moment stretched interminably, and then quietly, Szukalski said, "But then we could merely be dreaming. A few microbes on a slide and we are saving the whole town from the Nazis. We don't even know yet if we can make up the vaccine, or what its result will be in a human. And then to speak of an all-out epidemic is just madness. On paper it would look realistic, but in actuality. . . . How to make an entire town look sick? And how to keep it a secret? Everyone would have to know. And if the Germans came to inspect, what would they find but normal, healthy. . . ." He released a heavy sigh. "I seem to have become carried away with . . . with. . . ."

"A need to fight for your country," she said softly.

"Your friend Hartung was right, Maria, we have to fight some way, in a way each of us knows best. We've been sheep. I want to live. And I want my wife and son to live. Since the invasion I have been concerned only with survival, even if it means leading the life the Nazis want me to lead. But maybe that's not enough anymore."

He pulled back his sleeve and looked at his watch. "I'm going to see Father Wajda now. Will you meet me in the lab this evening?"

After meeting at the priest's home, the two men walked back through the snow to the church where they found Żaba the caretaker lighting a little brazier in the sacristy. A man without a name, of an age not even he could recall, Żaba was the homely, clumsy image of his namesake, Żaba—which meant Froggy. Speaking in a twisted Carpathian Polish and reeking of vodka fumes, the derelict had presented himself at the back door of the church fifteen years before, fearing that one more bitter winter was going to be his death. Coincidentally in need, at that time, of a gravedigger, Piotr Wajda had taken on the misshapen little man whom the children made fun of, provided him with food, a few *zloty,* and the shelter of a shed that crouched in the shadow of the church's buttresses. And in those fifteen years, old Żaba had repaid the priest with the undying devotion of a dog and the diligent work of several men. He also still reeked of vodka.

"Thank you, Żaba," said the priest and waited until

the caretaker had ambled out of the room before turning to the doctor.

Szukalski took a seat and signaled to Piotr that he would prefer to wait another minute before speaking. So Father Wajda said, "I'd offer you some wine, my friend, but the altar boys have run off with it again. If one of us fails to lock the sacramental wine securely, those little devils in angels' guise will take it. And I don't think the wine is even reaching their homes. Last summer, Żaba found an empty bottle in *Pani* Kowalski's pumpkin field."

Szukalski laughed politely. He had heard the story before. After a few more minutes he got up, went to the door that entered upon the altar, and gave a long, careful look around the church. Cold and gray, it was utterly, dismally silent.

"We have to be careful."

"Żaba can be trusted."

"No, Piotr, it's something else this time. I have something new to tell you, and while you will wish to give me your reaction right away, please sit patiently and hear me out. And remember, at this point it is only an idea."

So in the frail light of the sacristy, amid the hazy smoke from the brazier mingled with traces of holy incense, Jan Szukalski briefly outlined his theory about the possibility of extending the Kepler experiment to attempt the staging of an epidemic.

When the doctor was through, the priest sat silently studying his massive hands, his misty gray eyes turned inward, his large head bent slightly forward. After a short spell, he spoke. "It's foolhardy, Jan."

"I know."

"And yet you plan to attempt it?"

"I don't know yet. It all depends on Kepler's results. I only came to you now with it because I need to know something from you. Something I must know before I even consider such a fantastic plan."

"And that is?"

"Will you help us?"

"Oh Jan. . . ." Father Wajda placed his hands firmly

on his knees and rose up to his towering height. "Jan, I can't. It's too . . . too. . . ."

"What, Piotr?"

"You can't possibly expect to get away with it."

"I'm not saying we will. All I want to know from you now, Piotr, is *will you help us?*"

The priest swung away, driving his hands deep into the pockets of his long black cassock. Szukalski saw the brawny shoulders rise and fall with indecision, heard the breath come sharply.

"You know what's coming, Piotr, as well as I. Cripples, priests, gypsies, all *subhumans*. And for my little Alex? *Lebensborn* if we're lucky! And my sweet wife? Into the gas chambers at Oświęcim? And those mischievous little altar boys of yours? What sport will the Gestapo make of them? And poor Żaba! Last night, Piotr, I told you that the Wilks were the lucky ones, because their disease will keep the Nazis away. Better to have typhus than to suffer the tortures Kepler has witnessed, or the fate of that gypsy! If my experiment works on Kepler, then it can work on another man. And another, and another. Until we have somehow managed to convince the Nazis that we're all so disease-ridden that they wouldn't want anything to do with us!"

Szukalski took a step closer. "Piotr," he said slowly, "right now Maria and I are isolating the bacteria in the laboratory at the hospital, and we plan to work on the preparation of the culture tonight."

"It can't work, Jan!" said the priest, swinging around.

"Why not? There are other towns in Poland right now that are quarantined off because of typhus. Only those are real cases. I am mandated to send all blood samples of possible typhus to the German-controlled Central Laboratory in Warszawa. After I've sent them a few—"

"No, Jan."

"Why not?"

"Because we have a duty to keep this town alive. You and I are responsible for the survival of Sofia. We can risk it with Kepler because if we should happen to fail and Dieter Schmidt finds out, then there is a hope that he'll punish only us. But, for the love of God, Jan, if we involve the whole town and then fail, *the whole town will perish!"*

Jan Szukalski stared up at the tower of strength that was Piotr Wajda and said slowly, "And what do you think will be this town's fate when the Nazis come here to execute their Final Solution?"

Father Wajda reeled back as if he had been struck in the face. "Jan, I don't know what to tell you."

"I'll tell you one thing, Piotr. If Kepler receives a medical leave because of my vaccine, then I plan to go ahead and vaccinate others. All I know is, if the Nazis will leave Kepler alone because of the disease, then they'll leave others alone. And that is worth a risk. You speak of fates, Father, but which would you prefer? Annihilation at the hands of the Nazis when they come to butcher us like sheep, or running the risk of possibly being found out as a partisan and dying for your efforts?"

The heavy air descended upon them, gradually lowering like a doomsday pall, driving all else from the room except for that last unspoken answer.

When Father Wajda regarded his friend once more, there were tears in his eyes. "If you do it, Jan, I will help you. But you must involve no others. The other priest, Żaba, my housekeeper, all must remain ignorant of this. You and I alone must suffer the consequences."

"I'm prepared to do that."

"What will you need of me?"

"Two things, Father. If my experiment with Kepler works, we will need a hiding place where we can set up a small laboratory since the one at the hospital is not safe. Just think about it for now, Father; the decision will not have to be made for a few days yet. And then, maybe, not at all."

Piotr nodded gravely. "And the other thing?"

"I need a kilo of veal. And I'll need it by eight o'clock tonight."

"Veal?"

"I'll explain later."

*   *   *

Matuszek regarded his friends and said, "Now here is the plan."

The group gathered closely around him, twenty of the cave inhabitants, those physically able to take part in the mission. David Ryż, standing next to the towering Pole and feeling himself grow tense with excitement, looked across the circle at Leokadja Ciechowska, and found himself once more wondering about her.

In the three days she had stayed in the cave, she had said little and had kept mostly to herself. How she had come to team up with the wandering Brunek and Antek was something no one had explained, and since she kept her thoughts to herself, David was beginning to find her an intriguing mystery.

But when his mind started to wander from the matter at hand, he sharply reminded himself that she was *goy* and that she was seven years older than he and that she had a husband fighting in the Wehrmacht somewhere. But even so, forcing his eyes from her painfully beautiful face, David had difficulty concentrating.

"We have just enough guns," Brunek was saying in a low voice, "for each of us to carry one. The women as well as the men. It will be necessary for all of us to take part in this if it is to be successful." He then held up a strange apparatus. "This is a canteen like the ones that will be filled with nitroglycerine, which will be mixed up at the bridge site. You see that it is attached to a cord and a cycler's legging clip. I will be beneath the train and will attach the clip over the axle of the car. I will also try to put one under the engine."

"You will be blown up the instant the train starts. There is always a jolt before the train moves and you will be directly beneath."

"Yes, Moisze, I know that. And that is why I must attach these canisters after the train has started moving. There is a brief period between the starting jolt and when the train picks up speed. It runs smoothly in this moment, almost glides, and this is when I will try to attach the nitro. Once the train is in full motion, these things will swing like pendulums from the wheel axles and then, when the train comes to an abrupt stop, they will swing up and strike the bottom of their respective cars. And . . . *boom!*"

"What will make the train come to an abrupt stop?"

"I am coming to that. There is something we must first do tonight. Moisze, you and Antek and a few others will go with me to the bridge and do some preliminary work. First, we must cut a section of a railroad tie up about where the engine will be when the train stops before crossing, and we will dig a hole and slip in this oil drum."

The men in question looked over at the large metal drum and eyed it dubiously.

"Then we will cover it back over with the tie on top. You can see that the top lifts off and that it is easily big enough for a man to get inside. I intend to wait in here until the train starts rolling, after the inspection of the bridge, and as it passes slowly over me I will attach the canisters of nitroglycerine to the axles."

"And the abrupt stop afterward?"

"On the day of the attack we will also dig a hole beneath a tie about fifty meters from the opposite end of the bridge and put a small canister of nitro in it, then pull a spike out so that there should be more than enough vibration on the rail to make it explode. The train will screech to a stop, causing these others to go off. The bridge will collapse, and the train will fall into the Wisła. I am praying that the ice is thick enough so that we won't lose everything in the water. If we have picked the right train, we will have enough guns and ammunitions to supply an army."

David glanced over at Abraham, his sensitive young friend, and nodded with him. Abraham Vogel, who had worked most of his twenty years to become a concert violinist, did not seem part of this revolutionary bunch. He was a shy, quiet youth with heavy brooding eyes and a dreamer's smile. But David Ryż knew what was secretly in Abraham's heart, for the two were best friends, as close as brothers, and Abraham had shared his deepest thoughts with David.

Abraham also had a dream of an army rising up against the Nazis. And his vision was no less idealistic

than David's. Between the two of them, they knew it
was only a matter of time before they stopped one of
the dark trains and created an army of its prisoners.

But first, they needed weapons.

Brunek Matuszek continued. "I spoke with Edmund
Dolata in the woods early this morning. He was afraid,
because of what happened in the field, but he has
agreed to supply us with five horse-drawn wagons and
trustworthy men to help us. All we have to do is get
word to him in time. Ester, I think that would be a
good job for you."

She made a face of displeasure. "I would rather
blow up the train."

"Ester—" said Moisze, but she silenced him with a
wave of her hands.

"You will have to do your best to see to it that the
Germans don't get away. If any of you are afraid to
shoot, or don't know how. . . ." Brunek looked around
the crowd. No one spoke.

"This is a dangerous job we do," he said solemnly.
"I can't guarantee you'll get out of it alive. I am proud
of all of you. All over Poland, groups such as this are
making life miserable for the Nazis. But not miserable
enough. The Wehrmacht troops are still getting to the
eastern front and we still have Nazis for overlords."

"But not for long," murmured Leokadja, and David
saw, in the dim light of the cave, a fire burn in her
eyes.

CHAPTER 10

By the time Father Wajda arrived at the laboratory, Doctors Szukalski and Duszynska were already at work cleaning and sterilizing glassware in preparation for making the vaccine.

"I have that thing you wanted me to get," said the priest, looking warily about.

"Thank you, thank you, Father. Don't worry. We're completely alone. After six o'clock the laboratory is empty. Lehman Bruckner, the technician, has gone home, so we have it all to ourselves. Come over here and see what we're doing."

The priest removed his berretta and hung it on the hat rack. He followed Jan to where Maria was working.

"Good evening, Father," she said with a bright smile.

"Dr. Duszynska."

Szukalski reached for the package the priest had brought and placed it on the counter. Unwrapping it, he said, "Excellent. Father, I would like you to take the meat and cut away all of the fat and any of this kind of tissue you see." He pointed to the fibrous threads connecting the sections of flesh. "Then I want you to run the meat through the grinder."

Father Wajda stared in wonder at the mysterious apparatus all about him and said, "Jan, what is all this for?"

Maria, who had been busily working at the laboratory sink washing out test tubes and Kolle flasks, turned toward the priest and gave him an explanation. "Tonight we're going to make a veal infusion which is the basic ingredient of the culture medium we will use to grow the Proteus bacteria on. If we work efficiently we will be able to inoculate our medium tomorrow night and harvest the growth the following night and prepare the vaccine." She pointed to a large kitchen knife for the priest to use in preparing the meat. "Tonight we are preparing the glassware and the gauze and cotton plugs for the Kolle flasks," she said, holding up a small flask shaped like a flat-bottomed pear with a short neck.

While the priest got to work carving up his veal, Szukalski was intently studying the nutrient agar plate that he and Maria had inoculated earlier in the day.

"I am always amazed at how rapidly certain bacteria grow. It is no wonder some diseases progress so quickly. . . . I don't think there is any question but that this is Proteus we are growing here." He handed the plate to Maria.

She held the petri dish in her hand and scrutinized the growth on the surface of the medium. A pure culture of dense round hemispheres. "You're right, Jan. But. . . ." she raised her eyes. "Do we have the X-19 strain?"

"We won't know until we have tried our vaccine on Kepler and sent the blood specimen off to the Central lab for the Weil-Felix test. Anyway," Szukalski turned to the priest, pleased with the neat work he was doing with the veal, "tell me, Piotr, have you given any thought to a place where we can work in secret?"

Father Wajda laid down his knife and looked up. "I thought of only one place, and it is the best place in all of Sofia. No other will serve us as well."

"Great! Where is it?"

"The burial crypt beneath the church."

Szukalski's face fell. "Oh, I don't—"

"Now let *me* explain something to *you* two," said the priest with a smile. "You need a place where you would be able to work totally unnoticed and in no danger of being detected. There truly is no such place in all of Sofia, except for this one."

"But Żaba, the altar boys—"

Wajda shook his head. "Żaba is Poland's most superstitious old man. In the fifteen years he has been with me, he has never once gone down into the crypt. And once, when I asked him to go down and inspect it when I had suspected rain damage to the foundation, he refused. Jan, that was the first and only time Żaba had ever refused an order from me. And the boys? They are frightened of the place. Old priests are buried there; medieval sarcophagi and the mummified corpses of my predecessors occupy the crypt. It's a taboo place, Jan, not because of any rules or laws, but by man's own fears and superstitions. No one has been down there for many years, and no one ever will. You are a regular churchgoer; so is Dr. Duszynska. It is not unusual to see you around the church. The Nazis would never know. And even if they did suspect something, the crypt is well hidden. I don't think many people know of its existence."

"We'll need lights, though."

"I've thought of that already. Electrical wires can be run down from the sacristy. Believe me, Jan, it is the safest place."

Jan Szukalski looked at Maria and, when she shrugged, he matched her gesture. "Very well then, Piotr. Now listen, there is an old incubator in the laboratory storeroom. It's been buried so long that no one will notice its absence. Can we take it over to the church tonight and get it going so it will be functioning by tomorrow night?"

"I see no reason why not."

"We'll need refrigeration," said Maria.

"I have a spare ice box," said the priest. "My housekeeper will be glad to see it go."

"Excellent. We can move that in tonight also. For once, Father, I'm glad you're a bigger man than I am."

Wajda smiled sadly. "The Lord's work requires broad shoulders."

Szukalski laughed and helped his friend put the veal through the meat grinder. When it was all done, the priest said, "Now if we had some cabbage we could make stuffed cabbages!"

A quiet fell over the room as Maria took the meat, placed it in a beaker and poured a liter of distilled water in with it. She then stirred the contents into a thin meat gruel. After this was completed, she poured the gruel into a large Erlenmeyer flask and closed it with a rubber stopper.

Szukalski spoke to her. "I think you had better take the veal infusion home with you for refrigeration. I wouldn't want to have to explain it to Bruckner. I want everything to continue to appear as though this is normal hospital procedure."

After the glassware was carefully stored away, Maria wrapped the flask of veal infusion in a pillow case and hid it under her coat. Then she left by way of the front of the hospital.

Szukalski and Father Wajda cautiously removed the incubator from the storeroom. It was slow going and Saint Ambroż was ten blocks from the hospital. They were fortunate to pass through the stretch unseen by the patrolling Nazi soldiers, and to slip through the rear of the church out of sight of Dieter Schmidt's headquarters, which stood opposite the church across the town square.

The grating sound of the ancient iron gate, which stood at the foot of a steep spiral stairway, rang throughout the whole building, rebounding off the vaulted ceilings and the Gothic pillars. But the church was empty.

The smell of dust and decay that assailed Szukalski's nose as they descended yet another spiral stairway gave him the sensation of stepping back in time. The stone coffins were no comfort either, with their archaic effigies of former Sofia prelates carved on the cold marble lids.

"The practice of burying the priestly dead down here ended many years ago," whispered Wajda, aware of Szukalski's unease. "I think the last one was in 1887. Now, of course, we are put in the graveyard along with everyone else."

"Don't complain about that," whispered Szukalski.

It took Father Wajda no time to run electrical wires down into the crypt from the sacristy, concealing them above by rugs. They plugged in the incubator.

"We'll set the thermostat for thirty-seven point five degrees centigrade," said Szukalski, still whispering.

The slightest footfall was many times multiplied in

this hollow, echoey chamber. They left the crypt, ascending to the relatively fresh air of the church, and went straight to the priest's home where they undertook to remove the little ice box.

By 1:00 A.M. they were finished and Szukalski was climbing into bed next to his sleeping Kataryna, pulling the eiderdown up to his chin, grateful for the glowing tiles of the ceramic oven that stood in the corner of the room. He stared up at the dark ceiling, thinking about the strange turn his life was taking, and wondering, as he drifted off into sleep, if when he awoke in the morning he would find it had all been a dream.

"Will your parents be angry with you?" asked Hans Kepler as he sheltered Anna with an arm.

"They're very understanding. I haven't been out in such a long time. Most of the young men left Sofia long ago, as you know, and they either died in Blitz or they escaped from Poland somehow. I had a boyfriend in the air force. Three weeks after the invasion he was given a false passport, a new name, he grew a beard, and he escaped through Rumania. Someone has told me that he is now in the British Air Force."

They stood beneath the glow of a solitary street lamp on the sidewalk before Anna's house. The night had passed all too quickly, since eight o'clock when they had arrived at the home of Hans' grandmother, and had enjoyed the sweet hot chocolate and the delicate pastries that were the specialty of her little shop. The young couple had laughed and talked together, and had ended, in this frigid hour after midnight, by standing in the snow, she protected in his arms, trying to think of a way to make the moment last just a little bit longer.

At this point, Anna Krasinska knew as much about Hans Kepler as he wanted her to know. That he was a member of the *Waffen SS,* that he had been drafted, and that his duty lay somewhere in the region of Oświęcim. More than that, of his betrayal to the Reich, of his mental anguish, and of what he secretly planned with the director of the hospital, he did not tell her.

Anna's face was so round and innocent, so sweetly

young and naive, that nothing in the world could have compelled Hans to reveal to her the harsh realities of his life.

"Babka liked you," he said, looking down at the gentle, doe-like face.

"Your grandmother is very sweet. I love the way she calls you Hansy."

Kepler laughed. With Anna Krasinska beneath his arm and with the snow delicately drifting around them, and with his future looking brighter because of Jan Szukalski, the young German-Pole felt more generous toward life than he had felt in a long time.

"I would like you to meet my family, but . . ." she said quietly.

"I know, Anna. It's all right. What could you tell them? Only the truth. I am an SS man and they would at once be frightened of me. And then they would probably try to forbid you to see me."

He peered through the lacy fabric of the falling snow and added ruefully, "By the time they'll expect to meet me, I shall have to return to duty."

When Anna smiled, it was so honest, so gentle a gesture that it made his heart race. "You know," she said, not looking up at him, "I don't want to think of the end of your leave. So many people have gone out of my life already. The war has taken all of them. And if my father weren't too old, he would have gone into the Polish Army and probably would have died, like everyone else. The future is gone for me, Hans, I live now from day to day. I think that's best."

"All right," he murmured, bending his head so that his cheek rested against her hair. "Now that today is done, we shall have to think about tomorrow."

"Tomorrow. . . ." she whispered. "Only four days ago I saw you on the train and I was afraid of you. And now look at us."

He tightened his hold on her shoulders. He wondered at the miracle that had happened to him, this finding of Anna Krasinska, and wondered also if it would last, if he were worthy. "There will be a Flip and Flap film at the theater starting tomorrow. Will you go with me?"

"Oh yes," she said, giggling. "It's been so long since

I've seen one of their movies. I should like that very much."

"Tomorrow night?"

"I can't tomorrow. But the day after I'll be free. That would be very nice. Hans . . ."

"Yes?"

"I've been wondering about something all evening. And perhaps I shouldn't ask. But still, I'm curious."

"What about?"

"It's unusual for a German soldier to . . . *fraternize* with us. Usually the Nazis treat us like dirt. I am curious—"

"But I was born in Sofia, Anna. I'm more than half Polish."

"That's not what I was going to say. I was wondering . . . how do your comrades feel about it? Surely the other soldiers must have opinions."

Despite the glare of the street lamp, Hans Kepler's face darkened and he pictured his "comrades" back at the camp. Three of them, in need of a slow afternoon's diversion, had taken an inmate at random, a Jew with his head shaved and wearing the degrading striped "pajamas" of the camp, had tied up the cuffs and waist of his pants and then had dropped a rat down the trousers. And they had laughed hysterically at his torture. Or that other one, Helmut Schneider, now there was a sadistic one. He had used an inmate as target practice one afternoon, setting a bottle on the poor man's head and making him stand still while he, Helmut, stood fifty yards back and took shots at the bottle, William Tell style. The inmate, an old man, had died of heart failure and had spoiled Helmut's fun.

So much for Kepler's comrades.

"I'm in civilian clothes, Anna; I don't think any of them in this town know I'm a soldier. If they ask, I have my identification with me."

Now the young girl turned around to face him, her head tipped to one side quizzically. "You know," she said quietly, "you're not like the others. You're different somehow."

He inclined his head a little so that their lips were nearly touching, and he said, "You're different, too,

Anna. Night after tomorrow we'll go to see Flip and Flap. I want to laugh with you again, like we did tonight. Can we do that?"

She gave him a barely perceptible nod.

When he released her abruptly and turned to leave, Anna Krasinska stood for some time, despite the curfew, and watched him dissolve into the glacial night.

Dr. Duszynska had already started work in the hospital laboratory when Dr. Szukalski and Father Wajda joined her at eight o'clock the next evening. She had brought the veal infusion from her refrigerator and placed it on the bunsen burner to begin the slow heat to boiling. Under the instruction of Dr. Szukalski, the priest retrieved the glassware from the storage room and placed it all in the sterilizer. After that, Jan carefully measured out the ingredients to be used in turning the liquid veal infusion into the gelatinous infusion agar that the Proteus bacteria would be grown on to facilitate easier harvesting.

Peptone, ten grams.

Sodium chloride, five grams.

Agar powder, eighteen grams.

Szukalski measured and poured all of these ingredients into a two liter flask.

Maria continued stirring the infusion as it began to boil.

"It needs to boil forty-five minutes," said Szukalski, "then we can pour the broth into the flask with the chemicals and mix them together." This he explained to Father Wajda, who was looking on.

As they watched Maria, each with his own special thoughts, Father Wajda said, "Jan, what do you suppose Dieter Schmidt would do to us if he discovered what we are doing?"

"We would first of all tell him that we are preparing a typhoid vaccine. However, in a few hours, it would be a little difficult to explain what we're using the Proteus bacteria for. As to what he would do to us. . . ."

Maria called over her shoulder, "Is the incubator set up?"

"Yes, Piotr and I did it last night. Also the ice box." Szukalski grinned despite himself. "You're going to love our new laboratory, Maria."

When the timer rang, indicating that forty-five minutes had passed, Maria turned off the bunsen burner. Dr. Szukalski placed a layer of cheesecloth over a large funnel that he had thrust into the flask containing the chemicals, and held it while Maria poured in the hot liquid.

"The Kolle flasks are ready," said Father Wajda, whose job it had been to oversee their sterilization.

"Good. Set them up in four rows and we will pour this soup into them. Remember that we have to re-sterilize again tonight before we can inoculate our bacteria."

Watching the clear brown liquid fall into the flasks, Father Wajda said, "Do you suppose they would execute us if they caught us pulling a hoax on them?"

Szukalski kept his eyes on the operation. "We should pray, Father, that that is all they do. Only a few weeks ago we had a woman brought in here for treatment; she was suffering from malnutrition and exposure to the elements. And she, like that poor gypsy, had a story to tell. And what she said was this: About a month ago, the Nazis came into her village—not far from here, Piotr, you understand—and made all of the Jews assemble in the village square. They loaded all of the able-bodied men into a truck and drove off —God knows to where. And when it was out of sight, amid all the screaming and crying and begging for mercy, the Nazis took all the women and threw them down the town well, twenty-seven in all, and then poured gravel over them until all of those who didn't drown were buried alive beneath the gravel. I don't think there is any question, my friend, as to what the Nazis would do to us if they found us out. It is only a question of how they would do it."

Maria looked up from her work and Jan saw how blanched her face was. And he thought: Now we, too, are in the war.

"We should be able to inoculate our media in one

hour," said Maria, "and by this time tomorrow we will have our vaccine."

Szukalski looked at his assistant thoughtfully. When it came to laboratory work and the training she had received at the State Institute of Hygiene in Warszawa, Jan recognized his assistant's expertise in this area.

Szukalski took the covered petri dish from the incubator and ran his eyes over it. "I have heard of germ warfare before, but I must say that I feel a bit uneasy when I think that our lives actually depend on the microbes in this dish. If the experiment with Kepler fails . . ."

Maria turned off the heat and exhausted the steam. The Kolle flasks were removed from the sterilizer and placed on the table to cool and allow the agar to harden. Then Maria took a sterile pipette and, with Szukalski flaming the top of each Kolle flask, she dropped a single cc of the Proteus suspension onto the gelatinous medium and it swirled out over the surface.

After all the flasks were stoppered, Father Wajda gathered them into a cardboard carton for transfer to the incubator in the basement crypt of the church.

"Be sure it is set at thirty-seven point five degrees," said Maria, "and keep them in it all night and tomorrow. Then you'll have to bring them back here again tomorrow night."

"It's awfully risky," said the priest, cradling the box as though it contained a precious holy relic.

"There's no other way," said Jan. "Unfortunately we need all the equipment in this lab. Anyway, till tomorrow night, Piotr."

When he had left, the two doctors stayed behind to clean up the laboratory. They threw all of the remaining Proteus on the petri dish and the original broth culture into a large earthenware refuse jar that stood beneath one of the sinks. Then they hastily left the hospital.

From his position on the stairway which overlooked the transom of the laboratory door, the crouching figure of Lehman Bruckner, hidden in the shadows, watched until all three of the conspirators had left the hospital.

The curiosity of Lehman Bruckner drew him into the laboratory five minutes after the doctors and the priest had been gone. Just after he had closed up the lab, he had been surprised to hear voices as he had come down the stairs about to leave for the night. He had ducked down to eavesdrop. Unfortunately, the voices had been too muffled for him to hear anything. While it was not unusual for the doctors to work in the lab after hours, it *was* odd that the priest should have been there and that he should have emerged carrying a box.

Bruckner crept into the lab and waited for a moment before turning on the light. He took a slow look around.

Everything was clean and in order. Nothing to indicate what they had been up to. Lifting up the lid of the large earthenware jar, he spotted the discarded petri dish and test tube. The dish lay unopened and intact atop some broken glass. This he gingerly drew out and tilted this way and that in the light, studying the raked surface of the agar, curious that nothing had been labeled.

Bruckner knew an easy way to discern what it had been. He lit the bunsen burner with his lighter, flamed a streaking loop and, after finding a remnant of Proteus bacteria on the agar, inoculated it onto a fresh nutrient plate. Then he labeled the lid: "L.B. December 29, 1941" and placed it in the back of the incubator.

He flicked out the light, saw to it that the door was securely locked, and made a mental note to check on the plate in a day or two.

CHAPTER 11

David rode ahead on his gray plow horse while Brunek followed closely behind on the German motorcycle. Far behind them, walking all the way and following the river, were eighteen men and women, all of them armed. One of them—Antek Wozniak—carried the chemicals that would be mixed at the bridge site to create the explosive.

It was a bitter cold day, this fifth day after Christmas, with savage winds whistling down the frozen river. A metallic-gray sky rolled overhead, and occasional flurries swirled around the trudging column of partisans. Each man and woman had come willingly, full of the conviction that action was the only answer.

David set his face against the brutal wind. He was elated at the thought of finally *doing something*. Once the weapons from this train were harvested, there would be no end to what the group could accomplish. They had even talked, just the night before, of how to go about destroying the Nazis' precious storage depot. Without it, Sofia was nothing to the Nazis.

Unfortunately, Brunek had said, they would need artillery and men to overpower the installation, for it was large and heavily guarded. Once again David had expressed his desire to stop one of the dark trains on its way to Auschwitz and turn the passengers into an army. And once again, both Brunek and Moisze had cautioned David against such a folly. "Where would we hide so many people?" "How would we feed and take care of them all?" But David remained adamant. The time would come, he knew, when they would have to turn to the dark trains for their army. And he and Abraham would be ready.

The bridge was nestled in a deceptively peaceful and

serene setting, spanning the white ribbon of river and laced with freshly fallen snow. All around, the pine trees were heavy with white powder, their boughs hanging low to the ground.

Within minutes the partisans were situated in their assigned positions, David, Brunek, and Antek having placed them all and given them last-minute encouragement, so that it was not long before the Wisła was at peace once again, with no evidence of the twenty people who stood armed and ready in the forest.

Also hidden were five wagons and horses, camouflaged down by the river bank, with Edmund Dolata once more going over their instructions. The eight men from Sofia who had been able to slip unseen out of the town were to transport the train's cargo to a pre-arranged cache at the cave. They were reliable, trustworthy men and faced their task with determination.

David Ryż, having ridden on his horse down to the town of Dabrowa and having watched a partial unloading of the train a short while before, had raced back to the cave to let his comrades know what was coming. Two boxcars full of rifles, submachine guns and ammunition; another full of bazookas and mortars. The rest were flatcars loaded with tanks going to the Russian front. And approximately fifty soldiers were guarding the train. He had then notified Dolata who had mustered his wagons and who had been able to get them to the river without Dieter Schmidt's knowledge.

So now they waited, this handful of Resistance fighters, watching hopefully and fearfully through the falling snow.

Leokadja Ciechowska, her thick black hair bound up under a knitted cap, fingered the trigger of her rifle as she stood patiently at her position on a rise above the train tracks. Twenty meters away she could see Abraham Vogel, the young violinist, absently pointing his rifle at his toe.

Leokadja felt herself smile. He was no soldier, that one, always dreaming, talking like a poet, as though he existed somewhere on the edge of reality. Yet he had courage and she admired him for that. Still, he had no real place in all of this, nor, for that matter, did the rest of this makeshift company. She watched them through the trees and thought that they might almost be ludicrous if this mission weren't so deadly.

It was for this reason that the twenty-five-year-old Resistance fighter was boundlessly proud of her comrades. Look at Ester Bromberg, shivering in a snow drift wearing a man's overcoat that came down to her toes. A little woman, it seemed that if she were to raise the rifle up just slightly, she would topple over backwards. And old Ben Jakoby, playing soldier and obeying Brunek's orders with a salute, but standing in the pine trees with his knees knocking together.

Leokadja respected and pitied and loved them all, admiring their eagerness to fight with so little advantage on their side. Just like the rest of the Resistance in Poland.

Ever since losing her husband to the Wehrmacht, the young woman from Torun had been an active part of the Underground, fighting like a man, running dangers at the sides of her compatriots, burning with the determination to keep the Nazis from ever totally conquering Poland.

She never lost faith that her husband was still alive somewhere; she carried his memory and love in her heart like a banner, drawing courage from it. Leokadja had fought in the Polish Resistance for almost two years; moving from one area to another, fighting battles and then escaping to join the next fight. In some places she had joined up with organized remnants of the Polish military; air force pilots, sailors, infantrymen and cavalrymen, mobile and efficient and striking with awesome force. And in other places she had come across groups like this one, a hodge-podge of civilians, old and young, none of them trained for combat but all of them driven by the same blazing love of country.

A wind arose, causing Leokadja to shiver. In the distance, the wail of a lone timber wolf echoed through the trees. The temperature seemed to be dropping, and it appeared a blizzard might be building up.

And still, all along the railroad tracks, the same undisturbed forest peace.

Leokadja looked across the tracks and saw, about thirty meters distant from her, the fiery young Jew, David Ryż.

His stormy black eyes were watching her as they often did, and a scowl distorted his handsome face. He stood spread-legged in the snow, a challenging stance, the rifle hefted under his arm. He looked at the girl across from him with a deep, unreadable expression, causing Leokadja once again to wonder about him.

They had said little to one another in the five days since she had come to the cave, but she had often looked up to find him staring at her. Leokadja knew the tempest that raged in his heart; it matched the one in hers. The girl felt she understood David perhaps better than anyone did, and she also sensed that he knew this. But David Ryż was an angry young man, mistrustful of Gentiles, and bitter toward life in general. Perhaps at another time, under different circumstances, she could have loved someone like David. . . .

Leokadja shook her head to dispel such thoughts. Since the day she had parted with her husband, this young woman had allowed no man to touch her. There was no time now, no *room* for love and tenderness, not in these days of war and bloodshed. Brunek and Antek had been kind to her, protected her, and shared their food with her, but they had known from the very first that there was nothing Leokadja could offer a man. So they had learned to accept her as just another soldier. And this was how she wanted it. Until the war was over and her husband restored to her.

Leokadja turned away from David and continued to watch down the tracks.

Matuszek, sweating with fear and tension, tried not to move around in the cramped confines of his oil drum. He needed to constantly remind himself of the three canisters of nitroglycerine he was keeping warm against his body; knowing that if he made a sudden, abrupt move the whole mission would turn instantly into nothing more than a large hole in the railroad tracks and he would be a mere cloud of vapor.

The wait seemed interminable, but finally the metered pulsation of the approaching train in the far distance could be heard.

The engine and its twenty cars thundered to a stop just before the bridge, and the partisans hidden in the trees could see that the engine had stopped directly over Brunek Matuszek.

Listening to the crunch of Nazi boots as they plodded through the snow toward the bridge, Brunek cautiously raised the lid of the oil drum and silently pushed it up and out of the way. He surveyed the undercarriage of the train. Its massive push rods and firebox looked strange to him from this angle. He inspected the huge wheel axle and hoped that it wasn't too large for the spring clip to fit over.

The Nazis slowly walked across the bridge, carefully checking for any sign of sabotage. And as they did, twenty pairs of eyes watched them through the trees.

Ten long minutes later, the soldiers turned around and signaled to the engineer to bring the train across. He backed the train up enough to close the space in the couplings, then moved forward. Matuszek waited as the percussion of the jolting train cars stretched into a smooth roll. Moving swiftly and expertly, he barely had time to attach the explosive to the engine before it passed over him.

The next canister he attached to a large flatcar loaded with heavy artillery, and the final canister went under another car toward the end of the train. His hands flew with seeming ease as the massive machinery thundered over his head. As soon as the last canister was set, he ducked back into the barrel and closed the lid. Crouched in the absolute darkness of the oil drum, Matuszek waited with sweat pouring down his face.

Spewing black smoke into the pristine wilderness, the engine chugged across the bridge and cleared the other side. In another few seconds, but which seemed like an eternity, the mammoth wheels of the engine struck the loose rail over the buried nitroglycerine and jarred the shock-sensitive liquid beyond its exploding point.

The discharge beneath the rail was followed a split

second later by an explosion of the engine itself, which then triggered off the remaining two charges along the rest of the cars. An impressive pyrotechnic display briefly filled the winter scene, sending sparks and clouds and flying bits of metal up to the sky; then the bridge collapsed in two places and the unsupported center swayed precariously to one side. A second later, the bridge gave way completely, buckling the train and pitching the cars and tanks down to the river. The sound of ice breaking and tearing filled the forest with a deafening roar until the train settled, half in the water, and everything was quiet again.

The partisans, rushing out from the trees, began firing on anything that moved, killing the soldiers who had survived the crash and were trying to save themselves. Within ten minutes all the Nazis were dead.

Brunek led the descent to the river, waving a rifle over his head and screaming to his comrades. They swarmed down the snowy banks and dashed onto the churning ice floes.

Brunek paused to fire a flare gun, signaling to Edmund Dolata to bring his wagons out of hiding.

The next few minutes were fast and furious, a brutal pillage of the train, loading crates of guns and ammunition into the wagons. The horses reared and bucked, their eyes rolling back in fear. The partisans slipped and struggled on the ice, many of them getting soaked with freezing water. And all the while, a savage wind building up into a snowstorm blew around the nightmare scene with fury.

Once the wagons were loaded and all salvageable weapons removed from the wreckage, Dolata gave the order to move out. With astonishing precision the Sofians who had come to help swiftly led their horses back to the river bank and headed toward their destination.

The rest of the partisans scattered, as preplanned, each taking a different route back to the cave, while Brunek Matuszek and Antek Wozniak climbed onto the motorcycle.

David Ryż, soaking wet and turning blue from the cold, seized Leokadja, pulled her away from the frozen river that was starting to break up, and led her quickly to where he had tethered his horse. Wordlessly, she climbed on behind him and wrapped her arms about his waist as the mare galloped off.

The snowstorm turned into a blizzard just moments later and soon, as if part of the plan, covered the departing tracks of the partisans. The smoldering wreck of the train gradually froze where it was; a snow-covered monument to the anger and bravery of the ragtag citizen soldiers.

CHAPTER 12

The final preparation for the production of the vaccine got under way at nine o'clock that evening. Maria arrived first and was just hanging up her coat when Father Wajda came in, carrying his carton of Kolle flasks.

"It wasn't easy this time," he said a little breathlessly, placing the box on the counter top. "I had two very close calls getting over here from the church. A bridge and train were blown up today near Sandomierz and Dieter Schmidt is like a wild man. His men are out in full force tonight, and they are questioning *everyone* and taking many to Nazi headquarters. It took me nearly half an hour to get here." He removed his hat and ran his hands through his hair. "Twice, Dr. Duszynska, I came very close to being caught."

Maria nodded thoughtfully. "Dieter's men stopped me several times on my way over here from my home. That explosion was the boldest move the Underground has made yet." Shivering, she rubbed her arms roughly. "If they keep that up, the partisans are going to have the entire town of Sofia executed."

"Luckily," said Wajda, going to the door, "that bridge was just out of his territory, or else I think he would have punished the whole town for it."

At that moment, the door burst open and a white-faced Jan Szukalski hurried in. Seeing his startling color, both Maria and Piotr stared at Jan without speaking.

As if his arms and hands were made of lead, Szukalski very slowly and laboriously removed his overcoat, shook the snow flakes from it, and methodically hung it on the coat rack by the door. He ran fingers through his hair and took a deep breath before turning to his friends. "They killed the dog. It happened just an hour ago. Little Djapa, he—"

"Jan," said the priest, taking a step forward.

But Szukalski waved him to silence. "I had gone home for dinner and was getting ready to come back to the hospital. Two of Dieter Schmidt's men met me on the steps of my house. Kataryna was still saying good-by to me at the door, and Alexander was standing between her legs. The soldiers pushed in front of me and demanded to know where I was going. Before I had a chance to reply, one of them reached out and took hold of my arm. Just as he did so, little Djapa suddenly darted out from nowhere and attacked the man's leg. He. . . ."

Szukalski ran his hands over his face. "The soldier drew his gun and fired point blank. It was all so confusing. I was stunned; I just stood there. Alexander started to cry, and the other soldier simply laughed. With his other foot, the one who had killed Djapa booted him down the stairs and out onto the street. And the one who was laughing, he . . . he asked me if Alexander was crying because they had just killed his brother. It was . . . like a nightmare."

"Jan, sit down. Come on."

Father Wajda straightened up and looked gravely at Maria. In the pasty fluorescent light of the laboratory her face was unearthly pale, unnatural shadows filling the hollows of her eyes and cheeks. There was fear on her face, and something else. He recognized it as the patina of horror.

"He knows we're up to something!" she whispered. *"Dieter Schmidt knows!"*

"No, he doesn't," said the priest quickly, trying to fight down his own panic. "He wants us to think he knows. But look around you, Doctor, look around you!"

She stiffly rotated her head, her wide bewildered eyes taking in the twisted, writhing coils of the laboratory apparatus, twining and interlacing in and out of the pools of shadow and light. Somehow, it wasn't familiar anymore; the room had taken on a sinister, almost menacing aspect.

"We're alone," whispered the priest. "And we sit here undisturbed. No one knows we're here. If Schmidt had any idea, he would have been in here by now, smashing the lab apart for a little diversion and carting us off to his special basement. We're still safe, Doctor. For now. But we won't be for long."

Jan brought his hands together and squeezed them until his fingers were white. "I must confess to you both that I had been harboring doubts about this epidemic, about our chances of being able to pull it off. Now I don't think we have any choice. In fact, I'm beginning to think we should have started this long ago."

The three gazed at one another in the eerie light of the laboratory and nodded agreement. Maria said, "Who are they? Who is the Resistance in Sofia, Jan?"

"I don't know. They keep themselves well hidden. I don't think they're headquartered in the town, but I don't know."

The priest's voice was heavy as he said, "Maybe we should help them, Jan."

Szukalski looked at his friend in surprise. "What?"

"They're fighting, Jan, risking their lives and actually accomplishing something. Maybe it's time we started fighting the Nazis, too, in the only way they understand."

Szukalski considered this a moment, then shook his head. "It cannot be the better way, Piotr. They accomplish something, yes, but their results are only immediate ones. In the end they will end up losing as many of their own as they kill Nazis. Our way is best, Piotr. *We* will succeed, the three of us and our passive resistance. We'll save many lives and not shed a drop of blood."

"He's right," said Maria. "Blowing up bridges may inconvenience the Nazis but it won't stop them. Our way has to be better."

Father Wajda nodded in resignation.

The two doctors took up their work and as the minutes ticked away, Father Wajda kept a careful watch of the street below. On the sidewalk, Nazi soldiers strolled in pairs, rifles slung over their shoulders.

He turned and looked at the two doctors, bent over their labors, and thought: Their fight is no less brave and no less dangerous than the one being waged on the Wisła. They're right; the only way to defeat the Nazis is to outsmart them. "Are we about ready?" he asked quietly.

Jan nodded.

Father Wajda shook his large head. "I still don't see how you're going to do it, Jan. It's not possible to stage an epidemic. Someone would be bound to let the secret out."

"Who? Certainly not one of the three of us. Not Kepler; he has as much at stake in this as we. Who would tell?"

"One of the other people you inoculate!"

Jan Szukalski let a sly smile cross his face. "You underestimate me, my friend. I have no intention of letting one single other person in on our secret."

The priest's eyebrows shot up. "Then how do you propose to inoculate a thousand people without telling them what you're doing?"

"That, surprisingly enough, is the easiest part of all. It's what happens afterward that will take a lot of work. To answer your question, Piotr, I plan to have Maria and myself administer the vaccine as protein therapy to anyone who comes into this hospital with even the remotest symptom of typhus. By that I mean anyone who comes to us with any kind of malaise, chills, fever, backache or pains in the legs will be given a shot of protein therapy—or so they will think."

"Why just those people?"

"So that later on, when I send blood samples to the Central Lab in Warszawa, I can show proof that the patient came to me originally with symptoms of typhus. Do you follow me? Let's say a man comes to me complaining of a headache. I will tell him he has typhus and give him our injection, telling him it's protein therapy. In seven days I will ask him for a routine blood sample, which I will then send to the Central Lab. Now, if our vaccine works, the man's lab test will come back as positive for typhus. Although the patient himself will not be aware of it, the authorities in

Warszawa will have him on record as a typhus victim.
And I will be able to show on my own records that
he did indeed come to me with a symptom for that
disease."

Father Wajda wrinkled his face in thought. "But he
won't really have typhus."

"No, but his blood will say that he does. And with
enough positive results like that, the Germans themselves will declare this area quarantined. They won't
come in to investigate because they have such a dread
of the disease, and besides, their own labs will give
them proof enough that there really is an epidemic
here. I also intend to fill out as many death certificates
as I can with the cause of death as typhus."

"What about Dieter Schmidt?"

Now Szukalski's smile drifted away and his face
clouded. "He could be a problem. What we will have
to gamble on is the man's own personal fear of the
disease. If he is as fastidious as I think he is, Dieter
Schmidt will not be one to come to the isolation ward
of this hospital to see if the reports are true, nor do
I think he will care to investigate the farms and villages that the German authorities will themselves be
declaring quarantined. You see, Piotr, it won't be
me or Maria who will be coming up with these findings,
but the *German Health Authority,* so why should he
question them?"

"But he won't see any sick people."

"He won't go looking for them. They'll all be in the
hospital or in their homes. Or so he'll think."

The priest looked at the two faces before him. He
realized that Szukalski's plan had begun to find a home
in his rational mind.

"We also have to hope, Jan, that the partisans who
blew up the bridge won't do something foolhardy and
end up having every Nazi in Poland sweep down on us.
We'd be annihilated before we even started."

Szukalski smiled grimly. "That's why we must hurry.
It seems, at the moment, that we are not only racing
against time but against our fellow countrymen as
well."

Father Wajda shook his head again. "And all of

this predicates upon the success of Kepler's lab test," he said, picking up the equipment and preparing to leave.

"That," said Szukalski, "and that alone. If Kepler's lab result comes back negative, then we will have to abandon the whole idea."

"For this I will say a special mass tonight. I think we can use one more Hand to help us."

"And while you're at it, Piotr, would you have Kepler meet us at the church in the crypt tomorrow morning?"

Their final act was to transfer all of the vaccine into neat little vials and pack them for storage in the ice box beneath the church.

True to his scientific nature, Szukalski placed a final label on the lid of the carton.

Proteus Factor
Batch Number: I
Volume: 1,000 cc's
Date: December 30, 1941

There was undisguised contempt on the face of the Gestapo man who stopped Hans and Anna and questioned them about their destination. Demanding to see their papers, it was not until he learned the rank and status of Kepler that he forced a begrudging protocol and let them go.

Kepler kept his manner light and carefree as they continued their way down the street.

"They can't imagine what you're doing with me," said Anna sadly. "They think you have degraded yourself."

Hans forced a smile and seized her gloved hand. "Not on your life, *kochana* Anna! They were jealous, that's all. Wondering who the hell I am that gets the prettiest girl in town!"

She blushed, "You're very sweet, Hans Kepler."

"Is that what you've told your parents about me?"

"I've told them very little, and they're not pushing me. They haven't even asked why I don't introduce you to them. In these times, they seem to sense these things."

Despite the unusual number of Nazis patrolling the streets, the evening was delightful and exhilarating, with sharp clear air that was like glass and a rich plum sky beginning to fill with stars. Hans was trying desperately to hold on to the moment, tramping through the snow with Anna's hand in his. But it was difficult. There was something on his mind.

"There is a reality we have to face, Anna. My leave is over in seven days and there is no way I can extend it. Nor can I tell you when—or even if—I will ever be back to Sofia. With this war, who knows—"

"I won't have you speaking of it. Not tonight. You promised me we would spend this evening laughing."

He looked down at her face and felt his heart move in his chest. Falling in love with her had been so simple to accept, but this other thing, this not being able to share his secrets with her, that was the difficult part to bear. It was only when Hans assured himself that it was for her own good, for her *safety,* that he was able to refrain from rash confidence, from telling her everything.

They trudged down the street to the theater.

"There's a line!" said Anna, giving a little cry.

"There always is for Flip and Flap."

They took their places at the end and slowly filed in with the rest of the people, buying tickets, and taking seats down near the screen. Tonight's was a silent film so the organist had uncovered his instrument and was preparing the selections for his impromptu soundtrack. As they watched the rest of the audience fill all the seats and then find places to stand around the walls and sit in the aisles, Hans Kepler inclined himself to Anna and murmured, "There will be a New Year's Eve party at the White Eagle tomorrow night. The curfew will be lifted. Will you go with me?"

He saw her nod vigorously as the house lights dimmed.

Kepler focused on the screen, settling back as the title and credits rolled before his eyes. He tried to fight back the ponderous thoughts of his mind: the rapidly approaching end of his two-week leave, the mysterious injection Szukalski was going to give him, and the days of waiting afterward. . . .

Just when it seemed more than he could withstand, just when he thought he must jump up and run out of the crowded movie theater, the opening scene of the film flared onto the screen. And as Hans Kepler felt himself starting to chuckle with the rest of the audience at the mere sight of the fat man and the skinny man in derby hats, he also felt the weight of his conscience slowly dissipate. And for the rest of the evening, he was able to deliver himself up to the zany world of the lovable, slender, insouciant Laurel, and his fat, dyspeptic companion, Hardy.

It was eight o'clock exactly the next morning when Hans climbed the medieval steps of Saint Ambroż. Uncertain of where exactly to go, he slid quietly into the church, removed his woolen hat from his head, and made a good genuflection toward the distant altar. Then he waited.

Kepler heard soft footsteps draw close, and soon saw Father Wajda emerge from the shadows.

"Good morning," said the priest congenially, as if this were any ordinary day.

"Good morning, Father. Tell me something."

"Yes?"

"Do you suppose I will always feel nervous in a church?"

Wajda's face took on a forlorn aspect as he said in a comforting tone, "As you gradually make peace with yourself, my son, so will you make peace with God. Now come with me."

When Father Wajda opened a small gate at the end of the church, Hans found himself in the center of a towering, cavernous and richly carved apse.

"It's been stripped, of course," whispered the priest as he led the way past the altar steps and to a recessed doorway sunk deep in shadow. "When the Nazis came two years ago, they ravished the church, taking away most of the gold and precious objects. But the icons of Saint Ambroż that you see in the polyptych behind the altar are genuine and were first placed in here in 1407. Here we are."

He produced a key from the pocket of his cassock and slipped it into the iron lock of the door leading to the crypt. The hinges made no sound as the door swung smoothly open, not as they had when Wajda had first come down here with Szukalski and the incubator. They had since been oiled. He closed the door behind him and locked it. "Be careful now," he whispered, "these stairs have been worn smooth over the centuries and are slippery."

They made a slow descent into the subterranean chamber that was sunk directly beneath the altar, and Kepler felt his eyes straining in the obscure light.

Eventually they reached the bottom and Kepler wrinkled his nose at the unpleasant odor. It was thick and loamy, like moist soil, mingled with another, almost rancid stink. He imagined they were breathing the same air as the medieval priests who had long ago buried their dead down here.

In one corner he saw Dr. Szukalski and Dr. Duszynska working at a small table.

"Don't be nervous, Kepler," said Szukalski, who recognized that some of the youth's loss of confidence had been caused by the startling surroundings. "We have selected this particular place to do our work not because of you but because we might be extending our experiment a little." Jan Szukalski offered his most reassuring smile. "Believe me, all of this is not just for your sake. If it were only you we could have risked it in the hospital."

"Extend the experiment?" Kepler's eyes were still wide and staring.

"Yes, to other people. If we can rescue you from the Nazis, then why can't we do it for other people?"

Although he whispered, the doctor's voice took on a queer resonance in this burial crypt.

"Sit down, please," said Jan, motioning to one of the folding chairs which made up part of the Spartan furnishings. "We have prepared the vaccine I told you about, but there are a few things I want to discuss with you before we go ahead with the injection."

"You told me there might be some hazards to the injection."

"Yes, there is that possibility. I think that probably what will happen is that you will get a sore arm at the site of the injection and that you will run a low-grade fever for a day or two. Nothing very serious. At least, that's what we're hoping for. But as I told you before the worst complication I can conceive of is that your body will have some kind of completely unexpected response, one that we cannot possibly anticipate beforehand, and that the reaction will be fatal."

"You're right, Doctor; that would be a serious complication. But at least it would get me out of going back to the camp."

Szukalski did not smile at this but said grimly, "It could also get us all executed. Dieter Schmidt would like nothing more than to pin the death of an SS man on us."

"Doctor, exactly what are your plans if your vaccine does make it appear that I have typhus?"

"If it works, Kepler, then we are going to try to make it appear as though others in this area have the disease as well, and that we have an epidemic situation. We hope for a quarantine."

Kepler nodded. He looked at Maria Duszynska, her face a spectral white, as if she had just risen from one of the sarcophagi, then at Father Wajda. The priest's heavy face was grave. "It's an interesting idea. Quarantine. But to fool the Nazis?" Hans shook his head. "For a week maybe, or even a month. But eventually they would learn the truth and then everyone in this town would be shot. Sofia is important to the Nazis, Doctor, but the people of Sofia are not."

"We have to try," said Jan softly, "just as you have to try what you're doing. We also must be assured that we will have your full cooperation if we decide to execute that plan. We will need your help."

"Of course you will have my help. I will do whatever you say."

"Let's get on with it then. Now remember, Kepler, I am going to have to contact the German authorities in five or six days and tell them that you are ill and that I suspect you have typhus. In seven days I will draw blood from you and we will send it to the German-controlled Central Laboratory in Warszawa. They will then let me know if your Weil-Felix is positive, confirming my typhus diagnosis, or negative, in which case I will have to assume that either the Proteus bacteria is not the X-19 strain or that the reaction I observed in the guinea pigs is not the same in humans. In order to avoid any suspicion, you should know what the symptoms of typhus are so that you can start feigning at least enough of them to require our hospitalizing you as if you really did have the disease."

Szukalski turned away and said to Maria, "Will you explain to him what typhus is like and what symptoms would be expected to appear?" He then turned to the table and opened the first vial of vaccine and withdrew one cc into a syringe, held it upright and expressed the small air bubbles out through the needle.

Kepler removed his coat and rolled up his shirt sleeve to expose the upper arm. Szukalski cleansed the skin with an alcohol-dampened cotton ball, then injected the vaccine deep into the lateral head of the triceps muscle. Kepler winced slightly.

"There we are," said Szukalski as he withdrew the needle and massaged the injection site with the cotton. "We have taken our first step."

"Dr. Duszynska, you were going to explain to me—"

"Oh yes." She snapped her head up, her eyes breaking away from the injection needle. "A typical case of typhus begins rather abruptly with a succession of chilly sensations followed by a fever. The fever mounts fairly quickly to between a hundred and two and a hundred and four degrees. Headache, dizziness, muscular aches and pains and insomnia accompany the fever. You will have to feign these symptoms and we will want to hospitalize you, probably by tomorrow. Your grandmother will be the one to convince that you are getting sick so that she will call a doctor. If you can, keep a very hot towel on your head for a little while before telling her you don't feel well; that way, when she places a hand on your forehead, which she is bound to do, she will think you are burning up."

"Must this be done tonight?"

The two doctors nodded.

"I'll try. I'm going to the White Eagle for the New Year's dance."

"All the better. Start complaining to whoever you are with. Now then," Szukalski cleared his throat and the sound rebounded off the ancient walls. "There is one more thing we have to make clear. If the Weil-Felix test comes back negative, we simply change our diagnosis on you to influenza and you will be on your own. We won't have enough time to try another vaccine on you before your leave is up."

"Then I'll celebrate properly tonight, Doctor. Tomorrow is the new year and possibly a new life for me. I shall make this evening worthwhile." He managed a feeble smile. "New Year's Eve and I have a date with one of your nurses."

Szukalski, who had been leaning against the table, shot up, startled. "What? Who is she?"

"Anna Krasinska."

"You haven't. . . ."

"No, Doctor, I have told her nothing. Believe me, I am as aware of the need for secrecy as you are." He rolled down his sleeve and put his coat back on. "You will hear from me tomorrow."

As he turned to go, *SS-Rottenführer* Hans Kepler paused to regard Piotr Wajda in the medieval light. And as if he were acting out a part in some bizarre play, the young SS man said solemnly, "Father, pray for me. . . ."

CHAPTER 13

They worked quietly and relentlessly to hide the weapons they had taken from the train. Their storerooms were the little chambers and niches that riddled the giant cavern; each limestone room was filled with guns and ammunition and then concealed by a wall of rocks and debris. The stowing was so meticulously done that only the closest inspection would detect the hidden chambers behind their stone walls.

The partisans then relaxed in the warmth of the main cave, some of them eating, many of them sleeping. The old ones that had remained behind had cooked a hearty stew that the fatigued partisans now devoured.

"I can't get over it!" said Moisze with a heavy sigh. "We actually did it. And we got away with it!"

Ester nodded vigorously and pointed her spoon across the campfire. "We owe it to Brunek. Without him we never could have attempted something so great."

"We have well over a thousand guns and rifles of all types," said Antek, running a crust of bread around his bowl. "Enough for an army."

"An army of twenty," came a dark voice.

They looked at David. He hadn't touched his food.

Moisze Bromberg started to speak, but David continued. "Now is the time we should gather our forces! With an army at the backs of the Germans and with the Russians in front of them, we could crush them! We could drive them out of Poland! And our army will grow. We will amass more and more weapons, draw more and more numbers to our cause."

Moisze shook his head. "It would not work, David. Those Jews on the trains have been told by the Nazis

156

that they are being taken to a place to work, to new homes. Do you think they would gladly follow you off the train?"

"But if we *told* them!" David's voice rose. The veins in his neck bulged. "They would believe us, they would believe fellow Jews. We would tell them what awaits them at Auschwitz and then they would swarm off the train and take up arms to fight with us!"

"You are right," said Brunek Matuszek in a calm voice. "We do need an army. But not one such as you speak of. We need to muster what is left of the Polish military and organize them. They're scattered all over the country, all of them in hiding and doing Resistance work. That's what we need. And then we should systematically destroy the Nazi strongholds. Like that munitions storage depot outside of Sofia."

"In fact," said Antek, speaking up before David could, "we should make another large hit and soon. Make the Nazis think we *are* a large and powerful group. Did you see the mortars that are in those crates? They are the perfect weapons against the supply depot. One more big strike, then abandon this cave and hide in the mountains before they can find us."

Brunek nodded thoughtfully. "What is better than one large army, my friends, is to have several small, highly efficient sabotage groups, striking hard and fast and then disappearing before the Germans can get their trail. This is how it is done in the north, around Warszawa. This is the way to be truly effective against the Nazis."

David spoke up. "All right then, you can still use the people on the trains. They would gladly follow your orders. Give them weapons and tell them what to do. Organize them into small bands, with each of us leading. They would fight if they knew where the Nazis were taking them."

Moisze sadly shook his head. "They would never believe you, David. The Germans are such excellent liars. The people calmly and peacefully climb aboard those trains. I don't think you could convince them to get off and pick up a gun."

The eighteen-year-old ran his eyes around the circle,

stopping first at Abraham whose face, he saw, mirrored his own passion, and resting at last upon the beauty of Leokadja. Her eyes, like polished malachite, looked intently into the fire. And David thought: She knows what I am feeling. She agrees with me.

Brunek, saddened by the desperation in the youth's voice, said gently, "We know that Jews are not afraid to fight. But what we need is a strong core of trained men. You are suggesting a rambling, disorganized—"

David shot to his feet. "You are wrong," he said in a tight voice. "You are all wrong." He turned on his heel and headed for the entrance, snatching up his sheepskin jacket on the way.

"David!" said Moisze, starting to rise.

But Brunek laid a hand on the butcher's arm and shook his head. He said, "You were young once, my friend. Have you forgotten the fires that burned in you then? He's a good fighter. And he has the courage of a hundred men. Let him think about our words. He'll come around. Don't fight with him, Moisze. We have to stick together."

As soon as the youth had slipped through the small opening in the face of the cliff, Leokadja impulsively stood up and hurried after him.

The others around the fire watched her go and said nothing. They all, every one of them, knew that these were special times.

David yanked on his coat and gloves as he marched away through the snow and up the narrow trail. The two hidden sentries, keeping watch over the cave from a secret lookout point, watched as Leokadja hurried to catch up with David and then fall into pace at his side.

When they reached the top, David paused and looked around at the pure snowscape. The serenity was almost a mockery. He turned to the girl and heard her ask softly, "Where are you going?"

"When I worked on my father's farm," he said distantly, "and when I wanted to think, I always took the mare and rode into the country."

"Do you want to be alone?"

He looked into her green eyes, the color of spring moss, thought a moment, then said, "No."

Without another word, the two continued walking through the trees. When they came upon the mare, grazing on a bit of exposed grass, David and Leokadja mounted her the way they had the day before at the bridge site and, with Leokadja's arms tightly around his waist, they rode off into the woods.

Lehman Bruckner hurried down the slushy street with his shoulders hunched against the cold, stopping every few meters to stamp his feet and stimulate circulation. His coat collar was pulled up around his ears and his gloved hands were shoved deep into his pockets. Bruckner hated the cold; he could never seem to get warm in the winter.

As he came to the two-story brick house where he had a two-room flat over a dry goods store, the narrow-faced technician could see by the tracks in the snow that his roommate had arrived home ahead of him. He also noticed in irritation, as he stepped through the door and into the little foyer he shared with the store, that Sergei had tracked snow upstairs again. Lehman pounded his feet angrily on the little mat just inside the door and muttered invectives against his thoughtless and lazy roommate.

Mounting the stairs, Bruckner was further angered to see that the door to their flat stood wide open. "It'll be freezing!" he muttered as he entered the tiny living room and slammed the door hard into the jamb. "Freeze my ass off all day in that lab and then come home to the same thing!" he said through his teeth.

Without taking his coat off, Lehman Bruckner dropped his lean body onto the couch and glowered petulantly into the fire.

"Lehman, is that you?" called a voice from the little room that served as kitchen and dining room.

Bruckner did not reply.

Presently, a muscular young man, naked from the waist up, appeared in the doorway. He was a large youth with broad shoulders, well-toned bulging muscles and a heavy square jaw. He spoke Polish with a faint, unidentifiable accent. "Lehman?"

"You swine," growled his friend, not looking up.

"You are the most inconsiderate pig I have ever encountered. *Psiakrew!* I work my fingers to the bone trying to keep this place clean and you track your goddamn wet feet in here and don't even close the door behind you so that this drafty hole will stay warm. You know how sensitive I am to the cold."

"Lehman, Lehman." Sergei approached the couch and was unruffled. "The room was so warm when I came in that I opened the door for a little fresh air. Come now, it's not as ghastly as that now, is it?"

He dropped a large, well-developed arm around Bruckner's shoulder and patted him softly. "Now tell me, how was your day?"

Bruckner sank back into the couch and rested his head against a cushion. "The same crap, that's how it was. What a stinking, Godforsaken, thankless job that is! I'm sick of the lab, Sergei. I'd give anything to get out of it."

"There are days when you love it."

"Yes, my crazy days. But those doctors get on my nerves. Who knows what they're up to! Who can figure them out?"

"What happened?"

"Oh, nothing really. A couple of nights ago I found the two of them working over something in the laboratory, and after they left I decided to check it out. Hell, the way they were acting you'd think it was a secret or something."

"What was it?"

"Nothing. Just a worthless growth of Proteus bacteria. Who knows what they want it for! To hell with them. I don't care."

"Let me fix you a drink."

Lehman Bruckner continued to pout. "There must be something better for me. There's got to be an out somewhere."

"Talk like that frightens me and you know it. Here." Sergei handed his friend a tumbler of vodka and took a seat next to him on the couch.

Bruckner grunted and took a sip.

"I got some pork chops today," Sergei went on,

searching for the magic word that would bring his friend around. "Fresh ones. And they were easy to take; no one saw me. And we still have three potatoes. Help me cook dinner, Lehman, you'll enjoy it. And then after that I'll give you a massage. You know how much you like a massage."

Bruckner said nothing as he took another draw on the vodka.

There was something else troubling him, something besides the irritating behavior of Sofia's doctors. But he could not voice this to his roommate, for what was disturbing the lab technician was something he could speak to no one about, not even his only friend.

Lehman Bruckner had a secret. He was in reality a member of the SD—the SS Intelligence Service—and his true position in Sofia was not as a lab technician but as a spy.

He had been sent here a few months after the Blitz when the Resistance in Poland started gaining ground, and it had been Bruckner's job for the past year and a half to ferret out partisans and inform on them to the local Nazi commander, Dieter Schmidt.

Unfortunately, during his time as a spy, Bruckner had had few successes because of one simple fact: he could not make friends.

A good spy, he knew, had to be able to ingratiate himself among the ranks of those he was sent to spy on; he had to gain their confidence and, in time, their secrets. For this particular mission, however, Bruckner had been a poor choice. While he had the education and training and the sharpness of wit to work as an undercover man for the Intelligence Service, the lab technician lacked the humanity to be successful.

And what was worse, Lehman knew this.

He simmered over this fact now, tuning out Sergei's cooing, and dwelling upon a shortcoming he had no way of compensating for.

These acts of sabotage around the area were obviously the work of a secret Resistance group. They had to be nearby, maybe even headquartered in Sofia. But how to infiltrate them? How to gain their trust and learn their secrets? The pressure was on Lehman from his superiors to find these partisans and turn them over to Schmidt.

Bruckner glowered darkly into his drink. The fact was that he had so far been unable to uncover any information regarding the Sofian Resistance activities. And if he didn't make progress soon, he might fall into disfavor with the High Command.

He thought of the doctors and their peculiar movements. He thought of the priest that had been with them in the lab, and he decided to keep a closer watch on them.

They had ridden quite a distance, stopping now and then to listen for German scouts, when they came to the edge of the wood and saw before them a vast expanse of white fields.

"Where are we?" whispered Leokadja, speaking for the first time since leaving the cave.

David gazed out over the gentle undulation of snowy fields and pastures, turning cold and lavender in the dusk, and said quietly, "We are near my father's farm." His voice was heavy and morose. "I have been back several times since it was burned to the ground. There's nothing there really, just a ramshackle old barn that the Nazis didn't bother wrecking. The house is gone, of course."

David scanned the white blanket that stretched to the horizon, slowly taking in the scattered dots that were farm buildings. Some of them had spirals of smoke rising from their rooftops—farms still occupied because the Germans needed the crops.

"They say there's no such thing as a Jewish farmer. That we're all tailors and jewelers. But my father was one. He loved the earth. He loved animals and working the soil. He saved every penny to send me to the University of Krakow. I was going to be a mathematician."

With a gentle prod of his heels, David urged the mare forward. They rode speedily across the white fields, the horse's hooves muted by the powdery snow. Leokadja, holding fast to the youth, kept a keen lookout for patrolling Germans. But the two were able to reach the ruins of the Ryż farm in a few minutes, unseen.

David jumped down, then helped Leokadja slip to the ground, his hands on her slender waist. "I want to look around."

She nodded, understanding.

The twilight was quickly fading into a purple night as the two solemnly trudged through the snow. They stood for some time in silence before the blackened foundation of the house, David with his head bowed and his hands clasped. Leokadja watched him closely, feeling her heart go out to him.

By the time David had paid his homage, night had completely descended, turning the winter scene into a fantasy of white trees and crystal stars. They came to stand by the mare, looking at one another in the darkness and feeling the silence of the farmland move in on them. The horse snorted and pawed the snow; she was growing cold and impatient. Lifting a hand, David affectionately patted her broad belly and murmured something in Yiddish.

"What did you say?" asked Leokadja.

"I told her I wasn't going to force her to ride back tonight. We'll have to stay here. At least for a while."

"All right."

Taking the reins, David led the horse toward the dilapidated barn where a cruel wind whistled through the broken boards. Inside, he found some mouldy hay and a few burlap sacks in one corner. He called to the girl. "We can be sheltered in here, and the horse can eat. There might even be something to build a fire—"

Something white and fast suddenly darted out from under the hay and ran between his feet.

"What is it?" whispered Leokadja, startled.

David stared after the animal and then broke into a grin. "A duck! No, not a duck. A dinner!"

In an instant, he was off and running after the bird, tracing a crazy, zig-zag pattern in the snow. Leokadja laughed as she watched David leap high in the air and come down in an explosion of snow. When he rolled over and sat up, grinning, he had the duck by its neck. "We eat!" he cried.

"Give it to me." Leokadja took the strangled duck from him and unsheathed a knife from her belt. "Build us a fire. I'll take care of this."

David had no trouble digging a pit in the earth floor of the barn and encircling it with rocks he found beneath the snow. The fire was equally as easy to start; he tore off a few planks from one of the barn walls, splintered them, and ignited the driest with a match. Placing a few smaller stones at the bottom of the pit and keeping them hot with some added hay and sticks, David had a good, steady fire ready for Leokadja.

Marveling at the expert job she had done of dressing the bird, David ran a long straight stick through its body and fixed it up on a spit over the flames.

"In a while we eat," he said. Then he turned to her and smiled. "That was a good job you did."

"I was a city girl when the war broke out," she replied, sitting next to him on the burlap sack. "But in the past two years I've learned to do things that I never thought I would be doing."

He gazed at her. A thousand questions stood on his lips, but he remained silent.

Leokadja smiled almost shyly. "It hasn't been easy. It never is for a woman."

"What keeps you going?" he asked softly.

"The hope that I'll find my husband someday. I'm sure he was sent to the eastern front. That's where all the conscripted recruits are going. And there. . . ." she sighed heavily. "Well, who knows what will happen to him there."

"That was two years ago?"

"Yes."

David fiddled with the spit, turning the duck and poking the fire to flame it up. Then he raised his face again to Leokadja. "You know what keeps me going, don't you?"

"Yes," she whispered.

"You know," he said with a mirthless laugh, "war is a funny business. I wasn't really a Zionist until all this happened. And then I saw what the Germans were doing to my people and somehow it changed me. Abraham and I, well, we weren't always like we are now."

"I know that."

"And my fight isn't really with the *goyim,* although that's what Brunek and the others think. I'm not really *against* anyone, Leokadja, I'm just *for* my people. Does that make sense?"

She shrugged. "In the end, it's all the same. No matter what motivates us, we are all simply fighting. My reasons are different from yours, but our means are the same. And that's what matters at the moment."

"I suppose."

"You know, that's the first time."

He frowned at her. "The first time what?"

"The first time you've called me by my name."

He looked long and wonderingly into her eyes. Then he said almost reluctantly, "It wasn't difficult. It's a beautiful name."

"We shouldn't dislike one another, David."

He stared at his hands, his face twisted in uncertainty. And when he spoke, his words came out almost unwillingly. "I have no room in my heart to like anyone, Leokadja. Just as I know there is no room in yours. In a way, you and I are alike. We're alive for one reason. To fight."

"Yes, I know."

He looked up at her, his eyes full of confusion. "You know why I have to stop the dark trains, don't you?"

"Yes."

"My parents were taken away on one of them. I wasn't able to save them, but I can save others."

"I know." Looking at his youthfulness, his innocent bewilderment, Leokadja suddenly felt many more than just seven years older than he. And she also thought: We are from such different worlds. . . .

When the silence became more than he could bear, David quickly stood up and looked around the barn. "We'll have to make up a couple of beds. You can have the burlap sacks and sleep here by the fire. I'll go over there in the corner, there's enough hay left. . . ."

Leokadja was suddenly on her feet and standing close to him, shaking her head.

"What's wrong?" he asked.

"I want to sleep with you."

The bewilderment was there again, on his face, as she reached up and, placing her hands behind his head, put her lips tenderly on his. He responded warmly, taking her in his arms, then fervently. And suddenly the fight was for something else.

CHAPTER 14

Kepler's arm was bothering him when he met Anna at her home that evening. He stood on the bottom step at exactly nine o'clock, blowing on his hands to warm them, and every now and then rubbing the tender spot just below his shoulder. When the door opened, spilling warm light all over the snow, and Anna stood for the moment silhouetted, Kepler at once forgot his discomfort and grinned.

"You're beautiful," he said, watching her carefully descend the icy steps.

When she was level with him, Anna said breathlessly, "I was so afraid the dance would be canceled tonight because of the bridge bombing yesterday—"

He shrugged. "It's out of Schmidt's territory really, but I'll bet there aren't any parties around Sandomierz tonight! Come on, *moja kochana,* let's forget about bridges and bombs!"

They turned and struck off down the snow-blanketed street.

As they drew closer to the White Eagle Hotel, feeling the sharp, raw wind which blew from the Wisła, Anna instinctively took hold of her companion's arm and drew herself close to him for warmth. As she did so, he released a short, reflexive groan.

"What's the matter, Hans?"

"It's nothing. My arm hurts. I must have banged it against something." He gave her a reassuring smile. Yet he quickly noticed with dismay, as they continued their way along the dark frosty avenues, that not only did the pain in his upper arm seem to be steadily increasing, but he was developing a headache as well.

The White Eagle had been converted from the residence of an eighteenth-century Polish count; it stood apart from the town on its own grounds. Surrounded in the summertime by lush green lawns, the two-story country estate now sat upon a counterpane of snow. There were stables to one side and a gravelly area that was now filled with wagons, *droshky,* horses, bicycles, and some automobiles.

As the young couple followed the flagstone walk which lead to the hotel's entrance, they could hear the lively strains of the band and the distant thumping of many feet. Bright lights shone out of every window and doorway, and smoke from two chimney stacks curled up to the night sky. Mixed aromas of stewed cabbage, roasted pork, and hot pumpkin pie were carried on the river's breeze.

There were no empty tables left in the large hall that served as dining room and dance floor, but a few vacant chairs could still be found. Pushing his way through the crowd that lingered by the door and around the bar, Kepler managed to drag two chairs to a table where three other people sat watching the dancers, and fell into his own chair before Anna had even removed her coat.

His head was now aching terribly.

"Hans?" A cool hand fell over his. "Hans?"

He looked up into the concerned eyes of Anna. "I'm all right," he said, having to shout above the clamor of the five-piece band. A mob of revelers were stomping out a polka on the dance floor.

"Are you sure? You look a little flushed."

"I just need some vodka," he said flippantly, trying to force reassurance.

By the time Kepler had managed to worm out of his coat, favoring his sore arm, a waiter bearing a tray laden with pewter tankards happened by. Hans handed up some money and received two mugs of the steaming vodka and spiced honey brew.

The drink would help. It would *have* to help. Tonight was to be a special night of fun and music and holding Anna in his arms. When would such an opportunity arise again? Perhaps not for a very long time. If only his arm didn't hurt so much. And this growing headache. What was that all about. . . .

The music boomed in his ears. The heat of the room seemed to increase with every downbeat, so that Hans repeatedly ran a finger around the collar of his turtleneck sweater. The crowd screamed and roared, abandoning themselves to one night of madness; young people and old alike, here to forget the meaning of the swastikas that hung over every doorway.

And Hans Kepler wanted to join them. To twirl Anna around the dance floor and hear her laugh. And to kiss her for the first time. But he couldn't. As if his arm and pounding head weren't enough, he felt himself start to sweat miserably.

"Hans, what is it?" Anna now turned to face him, her eyes filled with worry. "You don't look well."

"I must be coming down with a cold or flu or something."

She leaned forward and placed a professional hand on his forehead. "You do have a fever. It isn't much, maybe a degree or two. Do you want to leave?"

"No, no. I'm all right, really. Just a little aching in my head. Another drink and I'll feel fine."

When the waiter pushed by again. Hans bought two more vodkas and proceeded to empty his tankard at one go. But when the band struck up a familiar mazurka and Kepler stood up to take Anna onto the dance floor, he was suddenly nauseated.

My God! he thought wildly. Could they actually have given me an injection of typhus!

He fell back down in his chair, Anna wiping his face with a scented handkerchief. She was saying something to him but he didn't hear.

No, Szukalski wouldn't do that to me! Would he? No, it's crazy! *Why would he want to kill me?*

Although it was Anna who spoke close to his ear, it was Szukalski's voice he heard. "The worst complication I can conceive of is that your body will have some kind of completely unexpected response . . . and it could be fatal."

"Anna. . . ." Kepler heard himself say. "Would you mind if we left? I am actually feeling quite ill."

She hurriedly put on her coat, helped Hans with his, and took hold of his hand as they wound their way through the throng. Outside, in the winter air, Kepler breathed a little more easily.

"Would you mind if we went straight to my grandmother's? I need to lie down. . . ."

They hurried back down the same deserted streets they had taken to the dance, and were stopped by only one patrolling soldier who glanced briefly at their papers and, accepting Anna's story that Hans was drunk, waved them on their way.

By the time they reached his grandmother's little bakery, Kepler's legs could barely hold him up. Most of the weakness was due to a chilling fear that had taken hold of him; the fear that Szukalski's vaccine had actually given him typhus.

Hans Kepler's grandmother met them at the door in a frayed dressing gown and long silver braids. She and Anna guided him to the narrow cot he used as a bed in her small living room. Hans lay down on the makeshift bed, welcoming its familiar embrace—for here was where he had slept the past seven nights— and dropped a heavy hand on his forehead.

"Go across the street to *Pan* Dombrowski," said the grandmother to Anna as she helped Hans out of his coat. "He has a telephone and there is still a light in his window."

Anna was able to get hold of Jan Szukalski at once; he had been at the hospital making late rounds.

When the doctor arrived, he signaled to the two women to leave the room, and when Anna and *Pani* Lewandowska went to the kitchen to make tea, Szukalski sat on the edge of the bed and looked searchingly at Kepler.

After a moment he said, "You really don't feel well, do you? This is not just an act."

"Believe me, Doctor, I'm dying."

"Let me see your arm."

The injection site was red and swollen and extremely tender.

"We are getting more of a reaction than I anticipated."

"I feel *terrible*, Doctor."

"This could be a good sign, Kepler." Szukalski

glanced in the direction of the kitchen and lowered his voice. "It might mean we'll get a strong antibody response. Which is exactly what I want. In the meantime, we'll get you into the hospital tonight. And I'm going to tell Anna and your grandmother that I suspect typhus."

Kepler rolled his head up so that his eyes met Szukalski's in a look that was almost angry. "*Do* I have typhus, Doctor?"

Szukalski weighed the question. His dark eyes, like his handsome face, assumed their usual professional detachment so that Kepler had no way of knowing what went on behind them. Then Szukalski said in measured words, "No, you do not. And as soon as we get to the hospital I'll give you some medication that will ease your discomfort."

The Dombrowski telephone was used again to call the hospital's one horse-drawn ambulance, and Szukalski broke the "bad news" to Kepler's grandmother as gently as he could.

Lehman and Sergei relaxed on the bed side by side. The hot food, the vodka, and the bath had rendered them both mellow and warm. The only sound to break the night silence was the steady hiss of the radiator; the heat might have been oppressive except that the two men, in their nakedness, found it quite comfortable.

After a while of staring at the obscure ceiling and reminiscing about the remarkable chain of events that had brought him to this moment, Sergei lifted himself off the bed and went into the little kitchen. Here a pot of water was just coming to a boil, and into it he placed, for a few moments, a bottle of mineral oil. When he returned, he extended a tumbler of vodka to his friend. Lehman drank it down neat and then fell back to feel the pleasurable fire trickle down to his stomach.

Sergei placed a hand on Bruckner's buttock and nudged him to roll over.

Spilling a few drops of the heated oil onto his hands, he proceeded to massage his friend's back.

"I'm lucky to have found you," mumbled Lehman into his pillow. "Life was so dreary before. It's interesting to have a personal slave." He released a short dry laugh. "Even if you are a stinking deserter."

"You shouldn't say things like that. Not even in jest."

"Why not? It's true. And if I ever wanted to, just like that," he snapped his fingers, "I could turn you over to the Gestapo. What do you suppose they would do to you, Sergei? You know the Wehrmacht doesn't keep Red Army prisoners alive. They shoot them or leave them to starve in the snow like dogs."

"And what would they do to you? You have helped me to hide out. You even got me my job at the restaurant, telling everyone I was a Polish refugee from the Ukraine."

"True, true. But I wouldn't turn you in, Sergei, not while you're nice to me. Get the shoulders. Ah yes, that's it. And all that delicious food you manage to steal. As long as we take care of one another, *kochany* Sergei, we'll have a good life. But if anything should ever happen to me. . . ."

The sinewy muscles of the Russian's arms rippled as he kneaded a little harder. Bruckner didn't need to finish the sentence. Sergei was only too well aware of his chances for survival should he ever lose Lehman. Not that they had a happy and loving relationship—with a cold and calculating man like Lehman that was not possible—but at least he kept his identity safe and provided him with a comfortable hiding place. Much better than a concentration camp or slow death in the snow.

When, from far in the distance, they could hear the midnight tolling of the church bells, Sergei sighed wistfully and murmured, "Happy New Year, *moj kochany.*"

When Kepler was finally settled in a bed at the far end of the men's ward, Szukalski came to him with two white tablets and a glass of water.

Kepler, in a panic and almost delirious, eyed the

pills suspiciously. His face glistened with sweat. "Are they poison?"

"Yes," said Szukalski. "Inside of fifteen minutes you will be dead. For God's sake man, of course they're not poison. They're aspirin tablets. Take them and trust me."

With anything but trust in his gaze, the youth took the pills and swallowed them down with a gulp.

"Although you will feel better in the next twenty-four hours," said the doctor in a low, conspiratorial voice, "I want you to pretend that you feel quite ill when any of the nurses comes to check you or give you medication." Szukalski looked around the ward. Half the beds were filled with sleeping patients, the other half were crisply made up for future ones. The nurse on duty at night was, for the moment, out of the ward. Still, Szukalski spoke barely above a whisper. "Day after tomorrow I'm going to put some medication on your abdomen and chest that will give you a rash. Typhus is a disease that characteristically causes a rash and we must carry this charade off as accurately as possible, even if it's only for the benefit of the nurses. I must warn you that any number of people in this hospital could be in the confidence of Dieter Schmidt. I myself am going to have to report your case to him because it falls in the category of contagious, even if it is yet only a possibility and not confirmed. So we will have to tread very carefully at this point. Do you understand?"

Kepler nodded.

Szukalski inclined himself a little closer and murmured, "And if Dieter Schmidt or one of his men should come by, don't let them frighten you. Chances are that they will be just as afraid of you as you are of them, considering the aversion they have to disease. Just be sure to keep up appearances."

Kepler whispered, "I promise," and soon drifted off to sleep.

David and Leokadja awoke the next morning in one another's arms, realizing that they had started the new year together. Saying nothing, for there was nothing left to be said, they hastily broke camp and rode in the early dawn back toward the river.

A few kilometers south of the cave, David drew the mare to a halt in the thick safety of a forest, tethered her, and led Leokadja through the trees. When they came to the edge of the wood, she saw that he had brought her to railroad tracks and that they now crouched not far from them. When she opened her mouth to speak, he motioned her to be silent. Then he listened.

Before long they heard the hissing approach of a train. David stretched himself flat in the snow and Leokadja did likewise, wondering why he had brought her here.

In another minute the black train emerged from around the bend and chugged past the hidden observers. It was a long cattle train, many of the cars sealed and mysterious, but the rest all open with slats, allowing the cargo to be seen.

Instead of cattle, however, this train carried humans, and they were crammed in so tightly that hands and arms were thrust between the slats. An occasional face was pressed against an opening, gasping for air. And as the dark train trundled slowly before their eyes, David and Leokadja heard a scream, a hysterical cry, the wail of the doomed.

The two waited and watched as the tragic cars passed, and continued to lie silently long after the train had gone. When enough time had passed, Leokadja said gently, "We have to go, David. They'll be worried about us."

But he didn't move. "There's our army," he said through clenched teeth. "These trains must be stopped. And if I have to do it alone, I will."

For the next two days Dr. Szukalski attempted to pay no more than routine attention to his new patient in order to avoid arousing suspicion, and found the hardest part having to continue the masquerade with Kepler's poor grandmother. Beside herself with worry and blaming herself for his misfortune, *Pani* Lewandowska closed down her little bakery and held a constant vigil in the barren waiting area outside the ward. Despite his insistence that there was nothing her presence could do for the boy, that he was doing as well as could be expected, Szukalski was unable to persuade the old woman to go home. And much as he would have loved to take her into his confidence and assuage her sorrow with the news that her grandson's illness was only temporary, Szukalski dared not take the chance.

The one other obstacle was Anna Krasinska, who, equally as upset about Kepler's illness, had by virtue of her profession free access to his bedside. Although assigned to the women's ward on the next floor, Anna took every possible opportunity to come down to see how he was doing. And this was dangerous, for she was a nurse and had handled typhus cases before.

It was Kepler himself who saved the situation by telling Anna that he was feeling too ill to withstand her visits and that the thought of her seeing him in this condition only made him feel worse. Difficult though it was for Anna to accept this arrangement, she nonetheless agreed to respect his wishes.

Dieter Schmidt turned out to be the least of their worries. Just as Szukalski's report of typhus out at the Wilk farm had been met by the Gestapo Captain with indifference, so had this second case. The fact that the possible victim was a *Waffen* Corporal did not interest him. All Dieter Schmidt cared about was that Jan Szukalski was isolating these cases and seeing that the disease did not spread. The SS commandant was obsessed with finding out who made up the Resistance in his territory.

On the evening of the fourth night of Kepler's stay in the hospital, Szukalski and Duszynska brought in a bottle of Trichloracetic acid and, with the flat ends of cotton-tipped applicators, proceeded to place small dots of acid all over Kepler's chest, abdomen, and shoulders.

The following morning, the head nurse reported the outbreak of a rash on the suspected typhus patient, and Szukalski reported this to Dieter Schmidt, telling him that the chances of the disease being typhus were increasing.

Szukalski reported the same to *Pani* Lewandowska and to Anna Krasinska who, it seemed, had lost weight in the five days.

As much as he deplored continuing the grief of these two women, Jan Szukalski braced himself for the final and most crucial step of the experiment: the Weil-Felix test.

Three long and agonized days dragged by before Szukalski could approach Kepler for what he made look like a routine blood sample. In those three days the youth had kept up his constant complaining of pains and dizziness and had suffered the discomfort of the burning rash for which there was no relief.

Since New Year's morning, seven days before, Kepler had felt perfectly fine and had had to remind himself constantly to keep up the pretense of being sick. This was all right in front of the other nurses and his grandmother, but when it came to playing the part for Anna, Kepler had to concentrate with a power almost beyond his ability.

She was so lovely and so desirable. Not once had they exchanged a kiss, not once had he taken the chance to tell her how he felt about her, how sustaining her love was to him. As she sat anxiously beside his bed, her face showing the strains of worry, he wanted desperately to gather her in his arms and tell her the truth.

Instead, he lay against the pillow, moaning now and again, and let her do most of the talking. He smiled weakly at her flowers and thanked her for the precious chocolate she had been able to buy, even though he had to say he felt too ill to eat it. And then she would depart, her eyes misty, her face expressing the fear that he might never recover from this dreaded disease. And then, when she was gone, Hans Kepler would weep into his pillow.

Szukalski drew the blood sample from Kepler on the seventh morning, the same day Kepler was supposed to have reported back to Auschwitz.

The specimen was packaged and sent by mail to the

German-controlled State Laboratory in Warszawa. And on January 9, 1942, a telegram arrived for Dr. Szukalski.

The instant he tore open the envelope and read the results, Szukalski's face was drained of all color. And three words escaped his lips: "Sweet crucified Jesus. . . ."

CHAPTER 15

Maria Duszynska carried under her arm the carefully wrapped bundle of beige wool cloth she had received as a Christmas present as she walked briskly down the narrow street to the shop of the old woman who occasionally made clothes for her. The cobblestones were covered with a layer of ice which, despite the clear blue sky and warm sun, had not melted. The street she followed led directly into the town square which she would have to cross to get to the seamstress's house on the other side. Maria emerged from the shadow of the narrow street and was five or six paces into the open before she was aware of the crowd in front of the Town Hall.

And when she saw the newly constructed gallows she came to an abrupt halt.

From out of a doorway somewhere nearby a German soldier suddenly appeared and was brandishing a weapon at her. *"Mach schnell,"* he growled, indicating that she continue walking.

"But what—"

"Over there, with the others!"

Maria gaped down at the Erma submachine gun in disbelief.

"Schnell!" barked the Nazi, stepping closer as if to prod her with the gun. "Over there! Move!"

As she stumbled forward, suddenly recognizing the savor of fear in her mouth, Dr. Duszynska was vaguely aware that other people were being herded in similar fashion to the place where the gallows stood. A force of about thirty SS men was driving in at least four times that number of Sofians. And when she came to the periphery of the mob, the arrogant soldier standing some feet behind her, Maria Duszynska saw what she was supposed to see.

In a little enclave of space cleared by a ring of Gestapo members stood two men and a woman, their hands tied behind their backs, their white faces frozen in a curious attitude of sullen disbelief. The young woman, who wore only a thin blouse and short skirt, had a sign hanging about her neck on a rough rope, and upon the placard was written in both German and Polish:

"We are partisans. We stole gasoline and food from the army of the Reich."

The face of the young woman was unreadable; it looked to have been wiped clean of all emotion, like a white slate, so that she merely stood mesmerized before the crowd.

The older of the two men, although only around thirty years old, half-starved and with a scruffy beard hiding a trembling chin, stared with vacant horror at the gallows from which three nooses were suspended from a large beam.

But the younger of the men, a smooth-faced youth of no more than twenty, and also without heavy clothing to protect him from the cold, was pleading with the Captain of the guard for the life of the woman.

Maria Duszynska heard, with a sickening twist in her stomach, his pathetic pleadings drift over the heads of the strangely silent crowd.

"Please, she stole nothing! She did nothing wrong! He and I are the only ones to blame! She is innocent. She knew nothing about what we were doing. Please, *for the love of God,* we have children at home!"

"Silence!" shouted a voice from the deck of the scaffold. All heads turned in its direction. *SS-Gestapo Hauptsturmführer* Dieter Schmidt stood spread legged before the crowd like a conquering Caesar, his ivory- and silver-tipped swagger stick rhythmically beating one thigh. Even from her distance, Dr. Duszynska could see the dark malevolence in his eyes, a black fire that smouldered threateningly like two tiny volcanic craters. His square blunt face was congealed in anger, although the corners of his thin mouth betrayed his secret pleasure. And as he spoke, the ragged scar which bisected his left cheek glowed unnaturally.

"These people are partisans! They are dirty, filthy, lice-infested swine who are going to be executed for crimes against the Reich!"

Maria Duszynska felt a peculiar paralysis creep up her body, starting at her feet, as though she were, inch by inch, slowly turning to stone. The soldier behind her didn't need to prod her to keep watching, as he did with some others, for there was no way she could tear her horrified gaze from the spectacle. And the hush which blanketed the crowd, a more profound silence than she had ever heard even in a church, was as intimidating as if it were a great roar.

Dieter Schmidt went on: "This is to be an example for anyone who is considering committing any crime against the Reich. And if you are stupid enough to think that because you are innocent this will never happen to you, then remember that even though you might not actively participate in perpetrating a crime, you will be considered just as guilty because you have not actively stopped it. You have grown fat and complacent. This must end. Smugness breeds carelessness. The Reich has been too lenient. If, from this day forward, a man commits a crime against us, *then his neighbors will be executed as well.*"

Although no sound was heard, it was as if the crowd gasped.

Schmidt motioned to the ring of guards to bring the prisoners up to the scaffold. The woman and younger man moved as if transfixed, their faces set in wonder. The older man, too stunned, had to be seized by each arm and dragged up. A trap door was situated under each victim, yet the hanging rope was just long enough to allow for the shortest drop, choking the victim but leaving the body in full view.

Maria watched in dread as the nooses were placed over the three necks by Schmidt, who seemed to take longer than was necessary. The only person spared from the grisly sight which followed was the older man, the first to have the trap door fall beneath him. The other two were forced to look on as, in the final seconds of agonized death, he writhed and convulsed like a fly on a string, his sphincters abandoning him and soiling his legs.

Then the young man was hanged. And lastly the young woman.

She had not uttered one word.

Jan Szukalski was still looking incredulously at the telegram in his hand when he thought he heard a timid scraping at his door. He looked up, frowned, cocked his head to listen, and then went back to the telegram.

The door was scratched again.

This time, when he looked up, he saw it open an inch, and then another inch, as if a breeze were trying to get into the room. Curious, he rose from the desk and strode over to the door.

Drawing it all the way open, he saw Maria Duszynska on the other side. In his initial pleasure to see her, Jan did not notice the queer expression on her face, nor did he notice, as he turned away and asked her to come in, the oddly mechanical way she walked into the room. It was, in fact, only as he was about to deposit the telegram into her hands that he finally saw the look on her face and this, because it was like the face of a stranger, made him stop short.

"Maria, what is it?"

She opened her mouth, and he thought he heard her whisper, "Jan. . . ."

"Maria!" He took hold of her arm and guided her to a chair, but instead of sitting, Dr. Duszynska only continued to stare vacantly at him.

"What's wrong? Maria?" Jan Szukalski did not think it was possible for a person to be so white and yet still be alive. "What happened?"

"Oh Jan," she sighed, her thin shoulders shuddering. "Dieter Schmidt. He—"

"Tell me." Jan placed a hand on her arm, his voice taking on a compelling tone. "Tell me what happened."

"He just hanged three people."

"What!"

"In the town square. Right between the church

and the Town Hall. Two men and a woman. He hanged them!"

"Oh my God—" Szukalski turned away from her.

"He said they were partisans. That they had stolen gasoline and food from the Reich. And he also said that from now on he's even going to execute anyone who's *just a neighbor* of a partisan!"

Jan spun around and before Maria could say another word he brought up his hand that still clutched the telegram, and held it out to her.

Maria held back her tears and looked down at the yellow paper. Gingerly, as if it might burn her, she took the telegram and stared at it a moment before reading it. And when she did, her hands shook so badly that it was some seconds before its message could be read. When she saw that last word, the decisive word, Maria let the tears fall from her eyes.

"Oh Jan," she murmured quietly. "It was positive. . . . *It was positive!*"

"A worthless experiment that I threw out two years ago," Jan said quietly. "And now it has the power to save lives."

Maria looked up, her beautiful face blotched with patches of red, her lips quivering, her eyes touchingly childlike. She could only whisper one word, "Positive. . . ."

"Old man Wilk will never know how he's helped us. It's the X-19 strain, Maria. And with a little luck and a lot of perseverance, I think we might just be able to pull off the greatest typhus epidemic of 1942."

When he finished telling Kepler the news, after an admonition to the youth to contain his elation and to act distressed with the report, Dr. Szukalski said quietly, "We've come to the next stage, Kepler. I'll tell Schmidt that you definitely have typhus, that you are unfit for duty and that your superiors will have to wait until you are well."

Kepler nodded, relieved that the nine days of waiting were over and that the experiment had been a success. "And my grandmother?"

"I've told her that the tests confirmed my diagnosis.

She's not happy, of course, but I told her there is a chance you will survive the disease."

"And Anna?"

"Anna is a nurse. She knows your chances."

"What will you do now, Doctor?"

"There are problems to be worked out. To tell you the truth, Kepler, I hadn't really thought we would get to this stage; it seemed too much like wishful thinking. But we've arrived and now we have to start acting. For one thing, you'll remain in bed a while longer. Dr. Duszynska and I, with the help of Father Wajda, will have to devise a way to start spreading our 'epidemic.' "

Father Wajda looked down at his spatulate hands as Jan Szukalski spoke. They had been down here for an hour so that the stagnant air was almost tolerable. But there was something troubling the priest. Something he regretted having to bring up, but which he knew had to be voiced.

So when the doctor was finished telling him everything that he had said to Maria and Kepler, Piotr Wajda said bluntly, "We can't let the boy back into Nazi hands."

And it didn't surprise him when Szukalski said, "Yes, I've already thought of that."

"Jan, you and I both know that if he were to leave Sofia, to leave our sphere, then we stand a good chance of being exposed. Maybe he won't tell them. Maybe he'll keep the secret. But we both know that Kepler suffers severely from nightmares and that he talks in his sleep. Picture him going back to Auschwitz, or wherever they send him—"

Jan nodded. "Piotr, I said I've already thought of that. To go ahead with our plan, we cannot allow him to leave Sofia. *Ever!*" Jan hesitated a moment, but his voice was strong and firm. "Nothing is going to stop me now. Not now that I can see how my vaccine might keep Sofians from going to the Nazi death camps."

Jan Szukalski stood before the image of the Holy Virgin, gazing down from her niche between the fire-place and the window. While the primitive, superstitious part of his mind turned to the Mother of God for help, the reasoning and pragmatic side sought solace from the pen and intellect of his country's hero, Adam Mickiewicz. The poet's words now filled his brain, stirring Szukalski as no simple prayer ever could. "Now is my soul incarnate in my country. . . ."

He turned to regard the two figures seated on the other side of his desk. He felt his heart swell in gratitude and friendship. It hadn't been easy for them to slink their ways through Sofia's heavily patrolled streets at this late hour. He felt a camaraderie with them, a special bond that made him feel strangely closer to them than he had ever felt toward anyone else in his life.

He realized that even Kataryna, his gentle and perfect wife whom he had loved with a steady devotion, was an outsider; she had no part at all in this burning emotion he now felt for only these two, his long-standing friend of a priest, and his dedicated assistant, whom Jan was beginning to think, at this midnight hour, he had greatly underestimated.

For the first time in the one year he had known Maria Duszynska, Jan not only admired her but he also felt he never wanted to leave her side.

" 'Let us fly away . . .' " Szukalski murmured more to himself than to his companions. " 'God be praised, we still have wings to return. Let us fly, and let us never from now on lower our flight. . . .' "

"What did you say?"

He smiled at Father Wajda. "I was quoting Mickiewicz. He had a way of putting into words the exact thoughts I am thinking."

"I'll tell you what I'm thinking," said the priest, looking at his watch. "I'm wondering where the boy is."

Szukalski was a little disturbed to see Piotr so edgy. That wasn't good. Tonight of all nights—because of what they planned to do—the three of them had to have absolute control of themselves. And yet he could sympathize with the priest. It wasn't going to be pleasant. Not for any of them. "You made the right decision," he said quietly.

But Wajda hadn't heard. He was staring at the effigy of the Madonna.

At precisely midnight there was the expected knock at the door.

Opening the door, Szukalski said softly, "Come in, Hans. You're right on time."

The young man slipped in. He had dressed in his sweater and slacks, twisting the familiar stocking cap in his hands.

"Were you seen?" asked Szukalski softly.

Kepler shook his head and looked around the room. The tension in the air struck him with an uncomfortable note, and the immobile faces of the priest and the woman doctor made him uneasy. It took him only a second to realize that something was wrong.

He glanced quickly around the familiar room until his eyes came to rest on the washstand that stood in one corner. He had seen it before, the porcelain pitcher and matching basin, the stack of neat white towels, the few toilet articles belonging to the doctor. The only thing different was the addition of a straight razor, which now lay on the stand, shiny and clean, and it was wide open.

While Kepler was gazing at this last, Dr. Duszynska got up and went to the door. She bolted it and then turned around to lean against it.

Kepler snapped his eyes to Szukalski. "What's wrong?" he asked.

As always, Szukalski's face was expressionless, unreadable. And his voice was equally as dispassionate. The stance of the professional man. "Hans," he said, "please sit down."

"What's happened? What's gone wrong? The test results were positive, you said—"

"Yes, they were. But there's something else. . . ." Szukalski sighed. "Hans, only the four of us in this room know about the experiment and only the four of us know that the experiment was a success. We have a chance now to make the Nazis believe that we have an epidemic of typhus here in Sofia and possibly its surrounding villages. If we are successful, the German health authorities will themselves declare this an epidemic area and all military traffic will be routed around us. With luck, even the military personnel already posted here will be cut down to an absolute minimum. It is now within our power to save thousands of lives from the hands of the Nazis."

There was a movement in the corner of his eyes. Kepler swung around and saw that Father Wajda had gone to stand by the little washstand.

Kepler gaped again at the large basin and the open razor. For some reason he didn't understand, he began to tremble.

"Hans," continued Szukalski's monotone, "Dieter Schmidt informed me that you are to report to your superiors as soon as you have recovered from this illness."

"Oh no—"

"There is nothing else I can do for you, Kepler."

"But I won't go back! I swear I won't!"

Szukalski shook his head. "Your chances now of running away are far less than they were over two weeks ago. Now you have been brought to Schmidt's attention, he'll ask after you, wonder how you're doing so he can inform your superiors. An escape now will be difficult, if not impossible."

"But I'll try it!"

"Hans, I don't think you understand. We can't risk having you leave Sofia. Don't you see? Thousands of lives are now at stake. We can't risk the possibility of your talking."

"But I won't!"

Kepler looked around at the frozen faces and suddenly felt a curious weakness invade his knees. He fell to the floor, catching himself on the desk. "Let me go. . . ." he whispered.

"We tried to help you, Kepler," said Szukalski grimly. "But now you're right back where you started. Only this time . . . you know too much. It's your one life against thousands."

As Father Wajda, his face set in deadly commitment, took hold of the razor on the washstand, and as Dr. Duszynska kept her back against the door, Jan Szukalski said quietly, "We three have already discussed it, Kepler. Better to sacrifice one life than thousands of others. We could arrive at only one solution, and we are committed to it. For the safety of our plan, Kepler, you will have to die. . . ."

CHAPTER 16

David sat with his face buried in his hands. The others around the campfire could hear him mutter, "I want to kill that murdering swine!"

Moisze gazed at the youth, his eyes heavy with concern, then he said quietly, "David, you shouldn't have gone to Sofia, not in the daytime."

David snapped his head up, his eyes flashing, tears streaking down his cheeks. "And why not!" he cried. "Did you expect me to wait until you said it was all right to go?"

"It wasn't safe——"

"It's never safe, Moisze! I'm tired of sitting around and doing nothing while every day more and more of our people are being slaughtered!" David's voice grew shrill, rebounding off the cavern's walls. *"They were innocent people, Moisze!* Their crime was so small. Stealing food, for the love of God! They looked like they'd been tortured. Probably by Schmidt trying to get information about us from them. Don't you see? Don't any of you see?"

"I do," came a soft voice.

David looked at the gentle face of Abraham and had to keep himself from weeping. Yes, he thought morosely, you do my friend. And so does Leokadja. But the rest of you. . . . David glared accusingly around the circle. "How can you just sit by and let these things continue?"

Matuszek looked down at his large hands and released a troubled sigh. "David is right. We have to act."

But Antek, the Polish soldier who rarely spoke, said, "I disagree, Brunek. I say we should disband and lie low in the mountains for a while."

188

The Captain gazed at him for a moment, then shifted his eyes to Moisze. "What do you think?"

The butcher shrugged wearily. "Ester and I, when we first found this cave, we thought only of hiding. We wanted to save ourselves. We weren't fighters. But," he shook his head uncertainly, "perhaps David is right. We should continue to strike hard and fast at the Nazis while we are able. Occasionally inconveniencing the Nazis is only passive resistance, and that does not seem to be the answer."

David snorted. "There is no such thing as passive resistance!"

Brunek looked back at Antek. "If we disband," said the Captain, "we will do it after we have made Sofia undesirable for the Nazis. We'll blow up their precious installation."

Antek held his superior's eyes for a fleeting moment of indecision, then he nodded. "We fight."

"But with so few people—" began Moisze.

"We either work with what we have," said Brunek, "or try to recruit more help."

"Where from?" someone asked.

The Captain thought a moment, then said, "What about Sofia itself, Moisze? Who there can help us?"

"It's no use, Brunek. Edmund Dolata was our link with the town; he had influence, but now he is being watched every minute of the day by Dieter Schmidt's men. He cannot help us."

"Surely there is someone else? Someone the people respect and will listen to? A priest, perhaps."

Now Ben Jakoby spoke up. "I have known Father Wajda for years. He is a pacifist, Brunek. I know him. His only concern would be to see that his people live through the war. If anything, Father Wajda would counsel against resistance."

"Are there no prominent lawyers, doctors? Towns-people often follow the advice of—"

"Jan Szukalski," said Moisze, "will not fight either. He's so concerned with saving lives that I think he's forgotten what it's like to fight. He'll agree with the priest. He'll go along with the Nazis for as long as is necessary just to keep the town alive."

"Is there no one who will fight? You are describing a town of cowards!"

"No, Brunek, not cowards, just men who believe it is better to be quiet and alive than noisy and hanged. And I sometimes wonder, my friend, if Ester and I would not agree with the priest and the doctor if we had been allowed to stay in Sofia and hadn't had to go into hiding. I sometimes wonder. . . ." Moisze let his eyes stray to the thin, tired face of his wife, her skin unnaturally pale in the fire's glow. "I sometimes wonder what our attitudes would be if we were still living in Sofia. We might not be fighters, Brunek. It seems so easy just to go along with the Nazis and not cause trouble."

"Trouble!" shouted David. "Three innocent people hanged today and all you can call that is trouble?"

"Please!" said Brunek, holding up his hands. "No fighting among ourselves! All right, we are on our own. Sofia cannot help us." He shifted on his stool and scanned the inhabitants of the cave. They sat huddled together in their heavy coats, drinking cups of chicory to keep warm, crouched on the frozen floor of the cave and trying to derive some solace from the campfire. All except one. Leokadja Ciechowska sat upon a rocky outcropping, cleaning her rifle with a detached, cool expression.

"Very well," said Antek. "If you wish to demolish the Nazi munitions dump, I say we get help from other Resistance groups."

With this Brunek agreed. To the others, he explained, "On our way down here from the north we encountered other small bands of independent Resistance fighters, such as you. There is one group not too far from here, east of Sandomierz and south of Lublin. We should contact them and see what help they can give us."

"And then what?" said Moisze. "How can we do it? That installation is like a small town, and it is heavily guarded. We can't even get *near* it. Surely this will call for a little more strategy than was used for the bridge."

"You are quite right, my friend. For a mission such

as this I am afraid we are going to need an ingenious plan. . . ."

"So we gave the vaccine to a total of ten people today," said Dr. Szukalski to Maria as they walked up the dimly lit corridor from the outpatient clinic to Szukalski's office.

"Yes. I was careful to give it only to people who had complaints that could be symptoms of typhus."

"I did the same." Jan glanced over his shoulder, saw that the hallway was deserted, and went on: "We should go cautiously at first and let our epidemic develop with the same pattern that a normal epidemic would follow. A few scattered cases here and there with an accelerating pattern of more and more each month until spring. Then taper down through the summer and fall, accelerating again in winter."

"You know, Jan," said Maria softly, "I didn't realize until today that we had committed ourselves to a project that will have to continue until the end of the war."

"If it ever ends."

"Or until we are caught at our hoax."

"I think we will be safe enough as long as we keep our secret to ourselves. Telling the patients that they have typhus and that the injection is merely protein therapy will give them no information that would be helpful to someone who is suspicious. Like Dieter Schmidt. All of his tortures in the world would get nothing out of those patients other than they had once had typhus and that they were helped by an injection of protein. And then again, why should Dieter even care to ask? Also, there will be enough of the usual number of typhus cases around that our vaccine-induced positives will blend right in."

They arrived at the door of his office and came to a halt. Maria looked around and then said quietly, "Tomorrow when we make rounds we should start injecting the vaccine into anyone who is terminally ill. There are five people in the hospital dying of cancer and three more that I know of at home who will be dead within a month."

Szukalski nodded. "I agree. I would like to have Weil-Felix positive serum tests on all of them. I want to make it look as though most of our dead were victims of typhus. The more virulent we can make this epidemic look, the more likely the Germans will declare us an epidemic area."

It was the ultimate irony that one wall of Dieter Schmidt's office was decorated with a mural of Marshal Pilsudski, hero of Poland, fighting the Bolsheviks. A great red Nazi flag with its taller-than-a-man swastika covered up most of the painting, but around the edges could still be seen glimpses of Poland's past victories.

Seated at his desk, a cup of tea going cold by his hand, the *Hauptsturmführer* finished reading the last of his morning reports. No new information on the secret Resistance. Absolutely nothing. Not even his secret undercover informers, of whom he had many placed in various facets of Sofian life, could find a way into the Underground.

They're sly, he thought scornfully. But I am slyer. Their fighting days are numbered. He emitted a short, self-satisfied laugh that sounded like a bark.

The other annoyance that was irritating Dieter were these increasing reports of possible typhus cases. Oh, nowhere near the number to be concerned about, and they were so far only *possible* since their lab tests had yet to be run, but there had been that death out at the Wilk farm, and then that young *Waffen SS* man who had been here on leave.

Dieter Schmidt made a mental note to admonish Szukalski that if the disease became a threat he would be held responsible, then dropped the reports in the bottom drawer of his desk and removed the cup and saucer. Now it was the way he liked it, the desk top barren except for a single light, a telephone, a copy of *Mein Kampf,* and a Luger P.08. He had seen Himmler's desk like this once and had thought it immensely effective. After all, the man with nothing to hide left everything lying about, all his business was exposed. But a man with a bare desk top, now he was a person whose affairs were concealed, a man who had secrets, and thus a man with power.

It had also been Schmidt's idea to have the desk elevated somewhat, just the barest inch or two, and his chair as well, so that while it was not obvious to the visitor that the commandant looked down from behind his desk, like some lofty judge, the psychological effect was the same.

And Dieter Schmidt liked to use subtle psychological gimmicks to reinforce his power. Like the blood stains on the oaken parquet floor before his desk.

There was a perfunctory knock on his door and a uniformed aide stepped in, clicking his heels and giving the Party salute. This was the hour, he informed his commander, that he had been instructed to remind the *Hauptsturmführer* of the visitor who waited in the anteroom.

Schmidt looked down at his watch and nodded in approval. The aide was phenomenally punctual. And he had a flawless memory. Schmidt made a mental note to reward him. The visitor to whom he referred was an elderly gentleman who had gone to Nazi Headquarters exactly three hours before with a petition of some kind and whom the aide had been instructed to keep waiting for three hours with periodic announcements that the commandant would see him any minute.

Time, Schmidt firmly believed, was his most valuable weapon. He had learned at Gestapo Headquarters in Berlin that the most insidiously effective tool he could use on a stubborn prisoner was the agonized suspense of *waiting*.

Schmidt never saw people in for questioning as soon as they came to his office. Instead he had them sit in the anteroom to wait and wonder, being told frequently that it would be just another minute. He found that letting a man steep for a while in his own suspicion and imagination and anxiety usually reduced him to the state Schmidt wanted him in.

"I'll see him now, thank you."

A withered old man with an amazing shock of white hair shuffled in with the aide and approached the desk in all humility. When he gazed down and saw the blood stains between his feet, his eyes dilated.

Schmidt did not at first look at his visitor, but appeared engrossed in examining his own manicured fingernails. Then he inspected the cuffs of his uniform; at the sign of the slightest fraying he would have a new one made. When sufficient time had passed, he looked up at the old Pole. "What do you want?" he asked slowly in German.

Schmidt was surprised and annoyed when the response came in such natural and accurate German. It was another of his tactics to force the victim to stumble and stammer in a tongue he was not very familiar with. But this wiley old Pole spoke German like a native. "I have come to ask permission, *Herr Hauptmann,* to go—"

"*Herr Hauptsturmführer,*" corrected Dieter in a deadly tone.

"Yes." The old man licked his bluish lips. "*Herr Hauptsturmführer.* I've come to ask permission to go to Warszawa next month."

"Why?"

The homburg in the old man's hands, which three hours before had been a very nice hat, was now reduced to a beret. The gnarled, brown-spotted fingers worked the felt as if it were bread dough. "I am to receive an honor—"

"Your papers!"

"Oh yes, yes, *Herr Hauptsturmführer!*" He fumbled in his coat pocket and produced a battered envelope. This he placed delicately on the desk.

Dieter Schmidt stared coldly at him.

The old man stepped forward at once and pulled open the envelope, spreading its few cards and certificates over the desk top. "I'm Professor Korzonkowski," he said hurriedly. "I used to teach chemistry at the Gymnasium, and next month I am to receive an award in Warszawa. I would like a travel permit."

"An award."

"For meritorius teaching." The professor flushed. "Many of my students over the years have succeeded in becoming doctors, professors, engineers, and . . .

well. . . ." The blush deepened. "The academic community would like to honor me in Warszawa. It's what I have been working for all my life, this achievement. The recognition at last. . . ." Korzonkowski's voice died beneath the cold eyes of Schmidt.

"I see." Schmidt tapped his fingers rhythmically on the desk top, his hard stare fast on the old man. He looked, for the moment, like a steel robot undergoing mental calculations. Finally he said, "I see no reason why you should not go. You are to be congratulated."

Professor Korzonkowski's shoulders slumped as if all the wind had gone out of him. "Thank you, *Herr Hauptsturmführer*," he breathed.

"You've lived a most fruitful life. I grant you your journey." Schmidt rose to his feet and kept his cold, unsmiling face on the old man. "This is a cause for you to celebrate. Someone as brilliant as you, passing on your knowledge to improve your country. A thing to be rewarded indeed." Schmidt's hand slipped down to the top drawer of his desk which he drew open slightly. "Tell me, Professor, do you like chocolate?"

The old man blinked; he was thrown off balance. "I beg your pardon? Oh yes, I do like chocolate."

"And it is so hard to obtain, isn't it? Would you like a piece?" Schmidt's fingers slid down and came against a cardboard box brightly decorated with colored paper. "From Holland it is. Milk chocolate with almonds in it."

The old man's face exploded in a grin. "How kind, *Herr Hauptsturmführer!*"

"I want you to close your eyes and open your mouth. You tell me if you like the chocolate."

The old professor stood in front of the Gestapo commandant with his hands at his sides, his mouth agape as if he were a fledgling about to receive a worm.

Then Dieter Schmidt quietly picked up the Luger P.08, pointed it into the old man's mouth, and blew out the back of his head.

She found Szukalski sitting at his desk and holding a piece of paper in his hand.

"Maria, we've got bad news. The Gestapo took Dr. Zajączkowski away two days ago."

"Oh no." She fell into one of the cane-backed chairs and folded her hands in her lap. In the harsh afternoon light, she noticed that Jan looked older than his thirty years.

"They took him away in the night," he said, "and his family have heard nothing since. Nor do they ever expect to." An older man, unpretentious and simple in his way of life, Ludwig Zajączkowski had lived in a small village twenty kilometers north of Sofia, almost at the fork of the Wisła and San Rivers. His responsibility had been the isolated farms and scattered villages in the Wisła Valley, and he had executed it with love and expertise for nearly thirty years. Now the Gestapo had him.

"But why?" Dr. Duszynska knew Dr. Zajączkowski on a professional level; she had worked with him in surgery and in his district on many occasions.

"Why?" echoed Szukalski. "They claim he was trying to collect and disseminate information about the concentration camps."

"And was he, Jan?"

"I don't know. Ludwig was always outspoken. I'm sure if he got wind of Auschwitz and Treblinka he would raise a cry. Poor old fool!"

"What now?"

"I don't know. The man who brought me the message says he overheard one of the Gestapo men telling Ludwig that if he was that curious about concentration camps, he would have the opportunity to go there and see everything for himself first-hand."

"Oh my God. . . ."

"And I suppose you heard about old Professor Korzonkowski. He used to teach chemistry at the Gymnasium. It seems he went to Schmidt's office yesterday to petition for a travel permit to go to Warszawa."

"And?"

"He never came out again."

"Jan! It's almost as if Dieter Schmidt is goading us into an uprising so he'll have an excuse to kill us."

Szukalski grimly shook his head.

"And another thing, Jan. And this I don't understand. Dieter Schmidt hates you more than all the others, but why hasn't he gotten you yet? Why hasn't he arrested you, humiliated you, executed you? You know how dearly he would love to."

"I guess it's because he needs me." Szukalski coughed a short, dry laugh. "It's rather an interesting paradox. His wanting to liquidate me and yet his wanting me around."

"How so?"

"By the simple fact that I am an available doctor. Schmidt may be an animal, but he's not stupid enough to rid himself and his little army of medical care. For miles around, Maria, you and I are the only medical help available, other than army doctors."

"Then you're safe from him."

"Unfortunately, no. Using Schmidt's warped reasoning, Maria, think of me as a good watchdog that guards the yard. A miserable and unlikable dog, perhaps, but one that at least keeps the house safe. However," Szukalski held up a finger, "just once let me bite my master and he'll quickly dispose of me. And I think Schmidt is even hoping I'll make that slip one day so he can throw the noose over my head. With my wife and son on either side of me."

Maria shuddered and to Szukalski's surprise she took his hand and looked straight into his eyes. "It's all a nightmare," she said quietly. "And there's no way to end it."

"No, but there is a way to mitigate it, and that's exactly what we're going to try to do. The epidemic. But for now we have something else to contend with."

"What's that?"

"How to cover Zajączkowski's territory. It's a broad area with a lot of scattered people and little pockets of population in and out of the hills. They'll need medical care."

"We can't cover all of it, Jan."

"We'll have to try. And at the same time, administer some protein therapy."

She raised her eyebrows. "You mean spread the epidemic that far?"

Szukalski smiled wryly. "Why not? It's certainly reasonable to assume the disease would travel to such limits. And as far as I'm concerned, the wider the perimeter of the quarantine the better."

She thought about this and said, "You're right, of course. And now is the time to do it, with winter still at its peak. The public health authorities will be far more convinced if we spread our epidemic during the winter when epidemics travel their fastest."

"I'd like to think we can turn the arrest of Dr. Zajączkowski to our advantage. Without his being taken away, we wouldn't have this opportunity to broaden our area. Now we can. It eases the pain of his arrest knowing that he has helped us carry out our plan."

They sat in silence for a while, gazing at dust particles that slid down the golden sunlight which poured through the window, each allowing the luxury, for one moment, of the comfort shared in holding hands. But then Jan suddenly let go, and broke the silence. "I'll have to go," he said somberly. "I'll have to go out to Zajączkowski's territory and do what I can."

Maria fixed her wide, frosty eyes on him, knowing what he was going to say next.

"Sofia and the hospital will be yours while I'm gone. Perhaps three or four days, a week at the most. In the meantime, I shall inoculate as many people as I can. Then, after seven or ten days, I'll go back and draw off their blood samples for the Weil-Felix, and while I'm at it, inoculate some more. At that rate, I estimate we will have about a thousand verified cases of typhus by the end of the month."

SS-Hauptsturmführer Dieter Schmidt rode proudly through the streets of Sofia in the back seat of his open-top Mercedes. Although very few people knew it, he had come from a very poor family in Munich, the son, ironically, of a butcher. Raised a Catholic, Schmidt had been only too happy to discard his childhood ideals when he had begun his military training. After receiving his commission in the SS he had readily embraced the new paganism of *Reichsführer* Himmler. Although he had been able to trace his bloodline back to the required year of 1750 and prove that he was pure, untainted German, Dieter Schmidt was nonetheless ashamed of his background.

He savored the rides in the elegant staff car. As it wound slowly through the streets with two soldiers on motorcycles at the rear, Dieter Schmidt was profoundly satisfied with the sight of himself and the reactions from the pedestrians of Sofia who stopped to watch the master pass by.

"Over there," he said sharply to the driver, pointing with his swagger stick to the church. "It has been too long since I have paid a visit to the good Father." The chauffeur grinned and pulled the car up to the steps of Saint Ambrož.

Schmidt ascended the steps and waited at the top while one of the two Corporals who had been driving the motorcycles opened a door for him. Without removing his hat, he stepped inside.

One or two peasants prayed on their knees, but other than that it was vast and echoey and deserted. Schmidt gazed around at the symbols he had come to despise; the marks of liturgy, of hagiolatry, of novenas, rosaries and eucharists. The church stank of popery. It reminded him of the fears of the confessional, of damnations from the pulpit, of cloaked priests and the omnipotence of the Church. And he loathed it.

Dieter Schmidt suffered the continuation of the church and its priests in Sofia for only one reason: they served to keep the people slavish and ignorant.

It was not long before the black form of Father Wajda approached him from a side archway, his huge frame and muscular strength the scorn of short, stocky Dieter.

"Good day, *Herr Hauptsturmführer*," said Father Wajda in excellent German. "To what do I owe this honor?"

Dieter Schmidt hated the priest almost as much as he did Szukalski. This man was slippery. For all his Catholic ignorance he could be a cunning man. "I haven't been around for a while to see you, Wajda. I thought you might be worried about me."

"I do worry about you, *Herr Hauptsturmführer*. I worry about your soul. Are you here to make a confession?"

Schmidt's eyebrows flew up on his forehead and the jagged scar on his cheek flared for a moment. Showing his rage would have been a victory for the priest and yet Schmidt had difficulty checking it. "You priests have always been a condescending lot," he said evenly. "Why must you always think the worst of a man? Why must you look at a man and assume he has a sin to confess? Isn't it more Christian to assume first that a man is all good? You must give mankind more credit, Wajda."

Dieter pushed past the priest and slowly walked down the center aisle of the nave. His booted footfalls were loud and hollow on the stone floor, and the occasional snap of the swagger stick against his thigh echoed behind him. Approaching the altar, he turned around to regard Father Wajda.

The priest responded finally with a faint trace of a smile. "We are simply aware of the frailties of man. And the fact that no one is above fault. We must all answer to a higher Power, *Herr Hauptsturmführer*."

Schmidt's lip curled up in a dog-like sneer. "And how powerful do you think your God would be right now if I chose to have you shot this instant?"

"If you have me shot, *Herr Hauptsturmführer*, who would you have around to convince the Sofians to submit like sheep?"

The sneer turned into a cold smile. "We understand one another, Wajda, that's good. Feed them their holy wafers and clog their brains with incense. In that way the ignorant Sofians would never think to revolt against the Reich. Although. . . ." He struck his thigh several times thoughtfully. "I am sure, Wadja, that if there were any rumblings of resistance in this town you would be the first to know about it, wouldn't you? Catholics tell their priest everything. In those little boxes where you sit like a demi-god. Young women whisper to you their most secret sexual desires. Husbands and wives confess their adultery. Partisans speak of plans to rise up. And if you were to hear such plans, Wajda, I am certain you would pass the information along to me. Isn't that true?"

"The sanctity of the confessional is not mine to break, *Herr Hauptsturmführer*. It is an oath of my office that I never reveal what a parishioner tells me under the aegis of confession."

Schmidt laughed and it was like the short honk of a goose. "It would be interesting to see how well you keep that oath under the *aegis of torture*, Wajda! You're as evasive as you are stubborn, priest, but I won't hold it against you. Keep preaching submission and I'll let you live a little while longer."

A shuffling sound was heard in the shadows and both men turned to see the hooded form of Brother Michał, a Franciscan monk who had arrived just the day before, emerge from behind the pillars. He was carrying a censer to the altar.

"Who's that?" asked Schmidt, motioning to his two guards standing in the back of the church to detain the monk.

"He is the Franciscan I told you about in my report. His monastery near the Czechoslovakian border was destroyed and he came here seeking shelter."

"Oh yes, the deaf mute."

The three Gestapo men scanned the bent, submissive body of Brother Michał, his shoulders hunched forward in fear, the cowl of his robe casting a shadow on the upper part of his face. The lower half was bearded.

"Between him and that caretaker of yours, Wajda, you have a real freak show here."

The Corporals, pressing their machine guns into the trembling body of the monk, laughed.

"Is he useful?" asked Schmidt.

"Yes. He has some talent in caligraphy. And he can restore paintings. The church is badly in need of—"

"My time is too valuable, Wajda, to waste on you and your misshapen pets. Just remember what I said about partisans and take my warning to bed with you tonight. Unless, of course, you have yet another little pet to take to bed with you nights, hm?"

The Corporals laughed again and turned about with their commander, marching back down the aisle behind him. Father Wajda and Brother Michał watched them go, and when the great oaken door had opened and slammed closed and the church was pure again, the two robed men looked at one another.

For the next four days Maria Duszynska had the full burden of the hospital. In all the hours and energy it took to see the patients in the wards, perform emergency surgery, deliver a baby, and continue with the Proteus injections, she had little time to dwell upon her increasing loneliness or the disheartening fact that she still had not, since Christmas, heard from Maximilian Hartung.

The nights were the worst for her, returning home late to find no letters from him, and lying in her cold bed listening to the snow whisper against the window panes. She thought about him during those few moments, and with each passing day of Jan's absence and of silence from Max, her heart grew lonelier.

During the time Szukalski was gone, Maria drew blood specimens from all of the people in the first group they had injected, packaged them, and sent them off to Warszawa. In two days she would know if the Weil-Felix tests would prove to be positive, as they had been for Kepler.

Jan Szukalski returned on the fifth morning looking tired and drawn. He had seen to Zajączkowski's medical practice, had worked almost continuously day and night suturing lacerations, setting broken bones, dispensing medicine, and injecting Proteus. There were even a few legitimate cases of typhus, which was normal for this time of year, and he sent those blood samples in to the German-controlled lab.

He had injected two hundred and thirty people in the broad area twenty kilometers north and planned to vaccinate even more when he returned in a week to draw blood.

Maria had, in that time, given one hundred and twenty injections, and sent them to the lab. When the results of the specimens arrived, she and Szukalski would determine their next move.

"Sergei, I simply don't understand what's going on. I really don't." Lehman Bruckner spoke abruptly.

"Oh, are you on that again?" The muscular Russian was dashing the last spices into a pot of boiling cabbage and paused to wipe sweat and steam from his forehead. "Maybe you're imagining it."

"I am not!" called Lehman from the living room. He was seated in an easy chair before the fire, his feet up on a stool, a glass of vodka in his hand. His narrow face was molded into a frown. This had been bothering him for a few days now. "I tell you, glassware has been disappearing from the laboratory."

"Who'd want it?"

"I don't know, but the doctors have been working late at the lab again. You know, really late. After I've gone. But when I check afterwards, I can't find anything to tell me what it is they're up to."

"Well, they are after all doctors, Lehman."

"Of course they are, but that's why they hired a lab technician. To do that kind of work. Once in a while, maybe, but not so often! I tell you, Sergei, something strange is going on."

Sergei replaced the lid on the pot and wiped his hands on a towel. Coming to the doorway, he said, "You worry too much. You take your job too seriously. Why can't you just forget about it after hours?"

"It's not that simple, Sergei. It just isn't."

No, it isn't, thought Bruckner as his friend went back to the kitchen to slice up the corned beef. You don't know the half of it. You don't know about the reports I have to make to Dieter Schmidt. You don't know just how precarious my position is. And I can't go to him with this business of a few tubes and beakers missing from the lab. He'd laugh right in my face. He'd make fun of me. He does anyway.

Lehman brought the glass to his lips and tossed his head back, feeling the vodka burn a trail down his throat. Dieter Schmidt never missed an opportunity to remind Bruckner that, in the year and a half he had been doing undercover work here in Sofia, Lehman had so far unearthed not a single clue leading to the secret Resistance group working in this area. And because of this, Schmidt found him contemptible.

So Bruckner would not let the stolen lab materials drop. Maybe they were an indication of something. Maybe not. But if they were, and if he could connect them with something more important than the theft of a bit of gasoline, then it was worth pursuing. And he would show Schmidt.

Out loud, for Sergei to hear, he said, "I think I'll do a bit of looking around."

At last the reports of the first group of patients arrived from the Central Laboratory in Warszawa.

All positive.

Everyone who had been injected was on the list; not a single failure in the group.

One week later Szukalski went back to the outlying areas.

CHAPTER 17

Abraham Vogel was standing on the river bank a few hundred meters down the Wisła from the cave entrance when he saw, across the frozen bed, two figures emerge through the trees. Even from this distance he could see that they wore the tattered brown uniform of the Polish Army and that the two men, whoever they were, were in trouble. Abraham watched without moving as they limped, supporting one another, along the river bank.

The snow flurries began to gather strength as dusk drew near, causing the young Jew to shiver beneath his heavy coat and lamb's-wool hat. The two men across the way weren't dressed as warmly as he; they were both bare-headed and only one of them had gloves.

Making a hasty decision, he raised an arm over his head and shouted, "Hello! You there!"

The two soldiers immediately fell behind a tree, fumbled with their rifles and pointed them across the river.

"Don't shoot!" shouted Abraham, cautiously descending the river bank to the ice. He also saw, through the falling snow, that neither man held his gun steadily. "I'm a friend!"

The soldiers remained silent, crouched and pointing their guns. One of them was pale and blue lipped, and leaned against the tree for support.

Abraham picked his way carefully across the thick ice sheet, holding his arms out for balance. With his heavy coat and woolen hat and thick gloves, he looked like a bear lumbering on its hind legs. "I'm a friend! Don't shoot!"

After a moment of silence, one of them called back, "Then throw down your gun!"

Strapped to a belt around his waist was a holster with a pistol. Abraham gave this a second's thought, then did as they requested, standing in the middle of the frozen river, unbuckling the belt and gently lowering it to the ice.

"Now come toward us!" shouted the kneeling soldier.

Abraham did so, his hands held out again to steady himself.

When he was just a few meters from them, plodding up the river bank, the man who had spoken finally stood out from the tree. He looked Abraham up and down, then lowered his rifle. "Who are you?" he asked, speaking the Polish dialect of the north.

"My name is Abraham Vogel."

The man did not mask his surprise. "A Jew? With a gun?"

Abraham ignored him and looked over to the other man who now lay against the tree with his eyes closed. "Your friend doesn't look well."

"He isn't. Stan and I haven't eaten for a long time."

"Where are you from?"

The soldier warily eyed the young Jew. "I would like to ask you that. But I can guess you are in hiding."

"We have a camp not far from here."

"Partisans?"

"We can give you food and a warm place to sleep."

The soldier stared at the delicate, almost beautiful face of Abraham for a moment longer, then he flung his rifle back over his shoulder and thrust out a hand. "Kažik Skowron, Lieutenant, Polish Army."

They shook hands.

Stanisław Poniatowski, struggling to his feet, said weakly, "We are glad to meet you, Abraham Vogel. You are an answer to our prayers."

Kažik grinned and reached out to steady his comrade. "God has a sense of humor. Two Catholics pray for help and He sends a Jew!"

Abraham led them back across the frozen river,

stopping on the way to retrieve his gun, and brought them to the cave. Helping Stanisław through the narrow opening, Każik's eyes widened in amazement. "But . . . we passed right in front of this cliff a while ago! There was no opening here! I know we were across the river, but still. . . ." His voice died when he saw twenty-five faces gazing up at him in the fire's glow. Then his eyes fell upon Ester Bromberg's pot of sauerkraut stew and his tongue ran over his lips.

"Come!" said Moisze, jumping to his feet. "Sit down, eat!"

Brunek Matuszek rushed to assist with Stanisław while Ester set about at once to serve up the food. The two frozen and hungry soldiers were revived by the heady aroma of caraway, dill, and cabbage, and sat down only after they had started to spoon the stew into their mouths.

"Potatoes," murmured Stanisław, eating so fast that some of it slopped down his chest. "When was the last time we tasted potatoes. . . ."

While the strangers ate, Abraham explained to the others how he had found them and who they were.

"We were fighting northeast of here," said Każik with a mouth full of food. He drew a sleeve across his lips. "There was a small pocket of us still holding out after the Blitz. We have been fighting all this time, but we were finally wiped out. Only Stan and I got away, and another comrade who we had to leave not far from here. He was wounded. We built him a shelter and struck out in hopes of finding something. We were told there are farms not far from here."

"There are," said Brunek, "but it would have been unsafe to approach them. The Nazis are very rigorous in their patrolling of this area. The nearest town, Sofia, is valuable to them."

"Tell us where your friend is," said Moisze. "We'll send someone for him."

Każik stopped gulping his food and lowered the bowl. "I don't think I'd be able to give you directions. Stan and I made a lean-to for him and then camouflaged it. You would never see it, even if I tried to describe it to you. And I'm not sure I could tell you how to get there. I memorized landmarks, a tree, a rock. That's how I'll find him. But we left him with a heel of bread and our last drop of vodka. And I gave him my scarf and gloves. Perhaps, if, as you say, the Nazis are thick in this region, we should wait until nightfall to fetch him."

"It's nearly night now," said Brunek. "We'll go in a little while."

The cavern fell silent as the two men finished their soup. They lifted the bowls to their lips and drank down the last drop, then wiped their mouths with the backs of their hands.

Listening to the fire crackle and feeling the outer chill of evening start to penetrate the cave, Brunek Matuszek kept his eye on the strangers. He took in the jagged cut of their hair, the stubble of beard on their chins, the frayed and tattered uniforms, the feet bound up in rags inside rotten boots. They were like a hundred others he had seen. Poland's great military, reduced to this. He turned his head away.

"Where were you going?" asked Moisze, offering them some chicory brew.

"We were going to try for the Rumanian border."

He shook his head. "Too far. And too many Germans."

Każik turned to Stan, his face etched in weariness and hopelessness. "Where will we go now, my friend?" he murmured.

Brunek spoke up. "You may stay with us for as long as you like. We are Resistance fighters and have made this cave our home. We steal food. Sometimes a courageous citizen from Sofia sneaks some to us. We have enough for three more months."

"Bless you," whispered Stanisław.

Każik, holding his hands out to the fire and occasionally rubbing them, looked slowly around the cave. When his eyes fell upon Leokadja and lingered there, he heard Brunek say, "We are all fighters here, the women as well. They are to be treated as comrades."

Każik smiled at Brunek and nodded. "I understand."

"We can use trained soldiers," continued the Captain. "Infantry, did you say? Then you can handle weapons."

Każik lifted his eyebrows. "You have weapons here?"

"Mortar and bazookas. We need to train our people to handle them."

"We are your men."

"Good!" Brunek slapped his knees and stood up, filling the dim cave with his great size. He smiled down at his new comrades. "You will need dry clothes. And those boots!" He looked questioningly at Ester Bromberg. "Surely we have something. . . ."

"Let me look. If they're going to be one of us, they'll have to dress better than that!"

Każik also rose to his feet and gazed solemnly at Brunek. "You are good people. We'll fight by your sides and die with you if we must."

The Captain dropped a heavy hand on the infantryman's shoulder. "We welcome you. Now, to fetch your friend. How much help do you need?"

Każik shrugged. "It's better if I go alone. I can move swiftly and hide myself when necessary. If someone accompanied me, he might slow me down, and two men are twice as easy to spot as one."

"Very well. Does he require medical attention? We have no doctor, but Ben here is a pharmacist and we have a few supplies."

"A flesh wound, Captain, but he lost blood. What he needs is food." Każik paused to look down at Stanisław. "I won't be long," he said quietly. "Rest now. You have earned it." Then he slipped out of the cave.

Dieter Schmidt paced back and forth in front of the three men, compressing his face into an ugly scowl and slapping his thigh with the swagger stick.

The three men stood at rigid attention. Two of them in German uniforms, flanking the one in the middle wearing the tattered Polish uniform, kept a watchful eye on their prisoner.

Finally, Schmidt stopped and spun around. "Pig!" he shouted suddenly, startling the three men. "You call yourself Polish! I call you a pig!"

Każik kept his eyes fixed on a point above Schmidt's

head; he swallowed painfully. The Gestapo commander eyed him with sneering contempt. "Excellent," he murmured in satisfaction. "Just excellent." Then he darted his eyes to the two Nazi soldiers who stood proudly before him. "Truly a moment to congratulate yourselves. Such a prize!"

He stretched his mouth into a bloodless grin. "Say your name again, pig!"

"Każik Skowron," murmured the Lieutenant, still not looking at Schmidt's face.

The commandant threw back his head and burst into shrill, insane laughter. "Każik Skowron! How barbaric! How utterly perfect!"

The laughter ceased as quickly as it had erupted and he brought up his swagger stick, leveling it at Każik's abdomen. "Very well, *Polish soldier,* if your name is Każik, then that is what I'll call you from now on."

Finally the infantryman lowered his gaze and grinned. Każik Skowron, whose real name was Adolf Gasthof—just as Stanisław's real name was Rudolf Fliegel—chuckled with his commanding officer.

Schmidt signaled to the two Nazis to leave, saying as he did, "You are to be commended for your excellent acting job."

"Thank you, *Herr Hauptsturmführer,*" they said and left.

Schmidt returned his attention to his spy. "I cannot believe how well it went. The timing was perfect."

"Your two men played their parts well. Your idea of having me arrested by them in the forest was an excellent one, *Herr Hauptsturmführer.*" Każik/Adolf fingered his side where a soldier had prodded him and winced. "Too well, in fact."

"I know it was an excellent idea. It occurred to me that one of the partisans might follow you, and if he saw you strolling into town and coming to headquarters, he just might get suspicious. This way, if you were seen, they will think you have truly been arrested and they will suspect nothing."

"But I wasn't seen, *Herr Hauptsturmführer.* I made sure of that. So when I go back, I will tell them that I found my friend dead and had to bury him."

"Excellent." Dieter Schmidt strode around his desk and took a seat. "You will go back now and you and Rudolf Fliegel will become part of their group. Gain their confidence! Take part in some of their sabotage. Stay with them until I decide to move in on them."

"Why not arrest them all now?"

Dieter slowly shook his head. "I believe that group is linked with others. I want you two to stay with them and learn what you can. It's not just them I want. I want to know who else in this area is involved. Where do they receive their orders from? Are they linked to Warszawa? Is anyone in Sofia helping them? I want to get as much out of this as I can. And if we are successful, I guarantee there will be high honors for all of us. Keep me informed of their every move."

"*Jawohl, Herr Hauptsturmführer!*" said Każik Skowron. He clicked his heels, gave the Nazi salute, and left.

CHAPTER 18

As late-winter gales kept Southeastern Poland in a merciless grip, there were two separate developments in Sofia.

The people of the cave, though restricted by the blizzards that raged beyond the face of the cliff, slowly and arduously developed their plan to assail and destroy the munitions storage installation at Sofia. It was to be a tremendous undertaking, dangerous and with no guarantee of success, but each and every one of the twenty-eight partisans fell into the plan with full heart and determination. Contact was made with another group in the north, and secret runners, stealing through the cover of snowfall, managed to keep a continuous link between them. A tentative date was set for the major attack, and every day in the cave was spent in training and preparation for it.

Their two new comrades, Kažik and Stanisław, after they had recovered their strength, proved to be of great help, their military training and knowledge of weaponry a boon to these civilians.

The second development was that Dr. Szukalski extended his services into six more villages and hamlets, using up the total volume of the first batch of Proteus vaccine and thereby creating one thousand bogus cases of typhus. The second batch of vaccine was made up in the crypt of the church, for they no longer dared use the hospital lab, and now the ingredients for the third were being collected. Jan Szukalski hoped to have in the neighborhood of five thousand cases of typhus from Sofia and the surrounding villages by late spring.

And, just as they had hoped, the Central Laboratory in Warszawa was reacting accordingly.

Interest flared up and grew quickly as blood samples

which continued to come in from Sofia turned out positive. The physicians in charge were amazed at the high titers the Sofia victims were producing, which was an indication of a highly virulent disease. And the director of the lab, one Fritz Müller, commented dryly to his colleagues, "At this rate we won't have to worry about the Final Solution in Sofia. Typhus will do the job for us!"

But they were far more worried about the contagion for another reason. "To hell with the Poles," the director said, scanning the latest results. "If they can be this dirty then they deserve to die. But Sofia and the region around it is a staging area for our troops and many of our men on the way to the eastern front are outfitted there. We risk having them carry typhus with them and adding that to the deadly Russian winter!"

It was decided, therefore, in the German-controlled Central Laboratory that, with so many cases of typhus coming up in so short a time, and with such virulency, the area should be declared *seuchengebiet,* an infected area .

The director sent a telegram at once to Krakow. It read:

RECOMMEND SOFIA AND SURROUNDING AREA FOR TWENTY KILOMETER RADIUS BE REGARDED AS EPIDEMIC AREA FOR TYPHUS. SUGGEST ALL TROOP MOVEMENT IN THAT AREA BE REROUTED THROUGH LUBLIN AND ALL GARRISONED MILITARY IN THE AREA BE REDUCED TO TWENTY-FIVE PERCENT OF THE PRESENT STRENGTH.

Reichsprotektor Hans Frank himself signed the order to the military commandant in Sofia to reduce his strength and transfer all excess personnel to Krakow. All farm and dairy produce were no longer to be removed from the area but to be confined within the perimeters ordered, and contact with all civilian persons was to be reduced to an absolute minimum.

Dieter Schmidt paled at the order.

Quarantine his area! And ship out seventy-five percent of his men! How did they expect him to continue to control the town *and* maintain a full crew at the munitions depot? And for how long would this be? Sofia was too important, too vital to be quarantined for long. The spring offensive was coming up; all winter, gasoline and artillery had been brought to the storage dump in preparation for moving it all out after the thaw. But now what? And what about the valuable information he was collecting on the partisans? What did High Command expect him to do?

But there was something else even more distressing to the commandant of Sofia. Dieter Schmidt had never been exposed to typhus in his life.

It had been more than two months since Hans Kepler had died, and Anna Krasinska still grieved.

In these nightmarish times of war and Nazi occupation, one guarded emotions and buried feelings. But Anna had made the mistake of dropping her defenses in the presence of the disarming Hans and had, after knowing him only a few days, fallen in love with him. They had never spoken of it, and yet Anna was certain that Hans had felt the same way.

But it was too late now, and in her loneliness and sorrow Anna had made it a practice to visit the church of St. Ambroż twice a day, every morning and every evening, to kneel before the Madonna, light a little candle, and say a rosary for the soul of the one man she had ever loved. For all the years that lay before her, she vowed to the Virgin that she would never again love a man as she had Hans Kepler.

However, of late, as she had knelt peacefully before the Holy Mother, saying her devotions, Anna had felt uneasy. Several times she had suddenly brought her head up from her rosary and looked quickly around, but always she had been completely alone. And yet, still it lingered: that undefinable, scalp-crawling intuition that *someone was watching her*.

She felt it again today.

She knelt with her beads between her fingers, alone in the chapel of the Holy Virgin, whispering/murmuring. "Hail Mary, full of grace, the Lord is with Thee. . . ."

And then it started.

Slowly, eerily. Seeping from the shadows around her as an insidious fog, furling around the pillars and gradually engulfing her until she had to stop her rosary. *Someone was there.* She felt it stronger today than ever before.

Anna stared at her beads. Worn smooth over the years, they had once belonged to her grandmother. They were made of imported mother-of-pearl and the links in between were of pure silver.

She looked up.

A shadow fell back into the inky darkness, but had not been quick enough for Anna to miss the flash of brown robe, the drooping cowl to hide the face, the hands folded into the sleeves.

Anna looked back down at her beads and tried again, somewhat tremulously, to continue where she had left off. "Hallowed be Thy Name. Thy Kingdom come, Thy will be done on earth as it. . . ."

She froze again.

He was there, watching her. It was that peculiar monk, the deaf mute whose sad story was known to almost every churchgoing Sofian. How he had braved the bitter winter to flee from the Nazis after seeing his monastery destroyed and his fellow brothers massacred, coming to Father Wajda for help and shelter.

But why was he spying on her?

Anna turned around a second time and this time, to her great surprise, the monk did not fall back into the shadow.

He stood there unmoving, silent, suspended in the misty light of the candles as mysterious as a medieval apparition, his hidden eyes fixed on hers.

The sight of him, like a spectre from the ancient past, made her stare back in wonder.

She waited for what seemed a long time, and when the monk took a step toward her, she shot to her feet.

"What do you want?" she whispered, clutching the rosary as if it were a shield.

The man said nothing but simply moved—almost glided—toward her. She remained rooted to the spot, wondering if she should cry out, when all of a sudden the silent monk drew his hands out of the sleeves of his long brown robe, raised them up to his head and drew back the cowl.

She gaped in disbelief.

The face was unrecognizable. It was thin and pale; the beard was new, the hair was cut short with a tonsure at the top. But the eyes, those startling blue eyes which were the color of cornflowers in the summer, she knew she had seen before.

After an eternity had passed between them, she with her mouth hanging open, the mute monk gazing at her sadly, Anna Krasinska finally found her voice, to whisper, "Hans. . . ."

Dr. Jan Szukalski was quite startled by the abrupt entry of *Hauptsturmführer* Dieter Schmidt into his office. The man had burst in with an entourage of Erma-carrying henchmen and a fury in his eyes that brought the doctor to his feet.

"Herr Haupt—"

"Shut up! Sit down and listen to what I have to say!"

Szukalski, who had never seen Schmidt with so little command of himself, sat back down in bewilderment.

Without preamble the Gestapo commandant relayed the news of the orders from Krakow.

"If I didn't need you to control the epidemic," he said through clenched teeth, "I would have you shot right now for letting it happen!"

As the Nazi carried on, Szukalski relaxed in his chair. He had never before seen fear on the face of the *Hauptsturmführer*. It was an interesting sight.

"I am holding you personally responsible, Szukalski, for any breach of my restrictions. You understand that no one is to leave this area without my personal permission. All of the trains that normally go through here will be sealed and not allowed to stop. The station will be closed."

He slapped a military map on the desk and pointed with a black-leather-gloved hand to a red circle. "Most transport will skirt this area. Some have to go through. But they will not stop. All farm produce will remain within this area."

Jan Szukalski, incredulous, looked at the map. It was too good to be true. A radius of twenty kilometers had been drawn around Sofia; a red line that was as good as a brick wall. And Dieter Schmidt was actually telling him that the town was going to be left untouched.

"I am posting guards at all roads leaving the area and they have orders to shoot anyone who attempts to leave without my express permission."

Szukalski dropped his hands in his lap. He tried to contain his excitement.

"You will be responsible for posting all of the necessary public health warnings and information as to what the civilian population is to do to clean themselves and rid themselves of their infected lice. I want this epidemic stopped. Is that understood?"

"Yes," said Szukalski quietly.

When Dieter Schmidt was through he straightened up and glared down at the Pole. "You should never have let this happen, Szukalski."

"Yes, *Herr Hauptsturmführer.*"

The two locked eyes for a moment, and then the hospital director said quietly, "Tell me, *Herr Hauptsturmführer,* have you or any of your men ever had typhus?"

Schmidt unwittingly fell back a step. "You must be joking! It's a pig's disease, Szukalski! Only swine get typhus! There hasn't been an epidemic of typhus in Germany for over twenty-five years!"

"That's too bad. I mean, *Herr Hauptsturmführer,* not that there hasn't been an epidemic in Germany, but that none of your men have ever been exposed to the disease. That means, of course, that you and your staff have never built up the immunity that results from exposure to the disease. This strain of typhus appears to be very virulent, *Herr Hauptsturmführer.* We have had several deaths. Someone who has never been exposed to the disease may very well not survive it, if once contracted. And I think I should also warn you, *Herr Hauptsturmführer,* that at this moment there are twenty severe cases of it in this hospital, and at least seven of them appear to be terminal."

"What!" Schmidt fell back another step. "You mean I have been exposed to typhus!"

The four armed men who were with the commandant now exchanged wary looks.

"You are most likely at a safe distance, *Herr Hauptsturmführer*, but I would say that yes, you have definitely been exposed. Be sure to steam all of your clothes when you get back to headquarters. I will send you copies of my public health instructions first thing in the morning. You should try to maintain as little contact with civilians as possible to avoid exposing you and your men. And above all, *Herr Hauptsturmführer*, avoid crowds."

Dieter Schmidt, his flesh crawling, turned a white face to his men. "Have you heard and have you understood?" They nodded vigorously. To Szukalski he said, "I will hear from you tomorrow, *Herr Doktor*."

"Have no fear of that, *Herr Hauptsturmführer*. My oath dictates that I minister to everyone, friend or foe."

They lay in his grandmother's bed staring at the ceiling, Anna's head nestled in the crook of Hans's arm. The house was silent, Kepler's grandmother with the family in Essen ever since the report of his death. Neither had spoken for the longest time, not since Kepler had finished telling her his long and involved tale, filling in the blanks of his background and bringing her up to date to this very moment. He had left nothing out, not even Auschwitz.

He had told her of his confession to Wajda and of his first meeting with Szukalski and of the solution they had come up with. He had told her of their plan to make it appear as though he had died so that he was free from his military obligation, how Szukalski had shaved a bald spot on his head and how Wajda had come up with a new identity and a new costume for him. How they had cremated the body of a pneumonia victim and sent the ashes back to Essen for a full military funeral. And he had told her about the lab in the crypt, about what the doctors were trying to do to save Sofia from the Final Solution. About how he had spied on her in the church every day. About how he couldn't take it anymore.

He had waited until after they had made love to tell her, rather than before. He had been afraid she would reject him once she knew the truth about him, and now he felt guilty. He felt as if he had taken the girl under false pretenses.

Anna, on the other hand, was silent for reasons other than those Kepler imagined. Mostly it was a state of shock that kept her from speaking now, but there was something else, too, which prevented her from being able to talk at the moment.

When he had smoked three cigarettes, when neither of them had spoken for a very long time, when neither had even so much as moved or sighed or disturbed the silence in any way, Hans Kepler could stand it no more. Into the darkness he said gravely, "You despise me now, don't you?"

Anna, startled by the sound of his voice and also by what he said, was silent for a moment longer, blinking up at the ceiling. Then, realizing what he meant, she quickly brought herself up on one elbow and looked down at him. "What?" she whispered in disbelief.

"I don't blame you," he went on, not looking at her.

"Hans! Don't say that! Of course I don't hate you!"

He rolled his head to one side and studied her face in the dim light. She was more beautiful now than ever. The young man was certain he had never known such a perfect moment.

"You mean because of your past," she said in a low voice. "You thought I hated you for that."

He nodded mutely.

Anna gave a little, mirthless laugh. "But that's absurd. What is important is that you left, Hans, and that you were too decent to stand for it anymore. The ones I despise, *moj kochany,* are those back there, the ones who stay and tolerate it. Even . . . *enjoy* it."

"Anna. . . ." he murmured, bringing up his hand and laying it alongside her cheek. "Oh Anna. . . ."

"I love you, Hans," she whispered, the thin light from the outer room catching on the tears welling in her eyes. "Nothing will change it. Not ever, *moj kochany*. In fact, I love you all the more for having had the courage to leave that nightmare and tell what you knew to someone. And then to risk your life for such a cause as saving this town. . . . Oh Hans!" Impetuously Anna bent down and pressed her mouth to his.

Hans reached up and drew her down onto him, feeling the passion in him surge anew, trembling with the ecstasy of holding her in his arms. But when she tried to draw back from him, he released her. It was as important to talk right now as it was to exchange physical gestures of love.

"You were silent for so long," he whispered.

She dropped a fingertip on his lips and shook her head. "For other reasons, *moj kochany* Hans. I was thinking about what you told me. About the camp."

"No—"

"Let me speak. Hans, I had no idea. No idea at all that such things were going on. And yet I do believe that what you tell me is true. It's funny. I both believe you and yet don't believe you at the same time. Is that possible?"

"Anna, when I was at Auschwitz, I both believed my eyes and yet disbelieved them at the same time. I know how you feel."

"But. . . ." her pretty face folded into a frown. "What I don't understand is this thing you called the Final Solution. What is it? And . . . *why* is it?"

Kepler turned his head away and set his gaze on the little night table where his grandmother's personal effects had once stood. He reached for the cigarettes. Lighting one and blowing the smoke up into the darkness he said, "What is the Final Solution? All I know is that part of it which affected me. The concentration camps."

He took another draw on the cigarette, exhaled the smoke and arranged his next words. "In the period before the invasion of Poland, most Jews were cleared out of Germany by the Nazis. Did you know this?"

"I heard stories. Mostly from Jews coming into Sofia."

"The Reich could not tolerate having Jews in its midst and so methodically and expertly eradicated them from Germany. Many Jews went to America or England. But most came this way, into Poland and Russia. That's why we're so crowded, Anna. All of Germany's Jews crammed into our little country. Well, as the plan continued to evolve and as Hitler assimilated new territory into his borders, like Western Poland, he kept meeting the problem of what to do with the Jews. It seemed that, with each step the Reich made toward expansion, it constantly encountered the problem of having Jews within its territory."

He puffed a few more times on the cigarette and then doused it on the little plate he was using for an ashtray. His voice went solemnly on. "Back then, the Nazis were willing to help the Jews get out. Himmler had even at one time entertained an idea of setting up Madagascar as their own personal refuge, like an American Indian reservation. In those days the Gestapo issued travel visas, arranged for transportation and, in some cases, even paid the fare. But then, you see, the borders of the Reich kept moving and more and more Jews were suddenly in the middle of a nation that didn't want them. And so the question arose as to what to do with such a large number of unwanted people. It just wasn't feasible anymore to try to transport them to other countries."

Even in this pale light Anna could see that Hans's face had gone stark white. He continued. "Hitler and his men got together and tried to figure out a solution to the problem. They came up with the Final Solution." Kepler rolled his head back to look squarely at Anna. "Extermination."

"It's too terrible to even imagine," she said in a small voice.

"The SS was given the task of carrying out this plan. In fact, *moja kochana* Anna, the SS regarded this not as a duty but as a *privilege*."

"But how many Jews can there be—"

Now it was his turn to place a finger against her lips. And as he did so, a twisted smile deformed his mouth. "Not just the Jews anymore, Anna, but anyone whom the Reich considers subhuman. The Poles fit into that category, too."

"They wouldn't try to kill all of us!"

"No, the Nazis are not so wasteful. Jews they can do without. Poles they can use as slaves. At least until we all drop dead."

She suddenly collapsed against him and whimpered into the nape of his neck. He draped his arms about her thin, trembling body and waited patiently until she regained her composure. It pained him terribly to have had to tell her such grim news.

"I feel as though I've just awakened from a terrible dream," she said, drawing back from him and wiping her wet face. "Those poor people! And *you*, having to see it all!"

He wrinkled his eyes. No, he hadn't quite told her everything. He couldn't. Not about the medical experiments at Auschwitz, grisly acts performed on the inmates that were more torture than scientific tests. And that popular sport of the officer's mess, to inject Jewish girls with strychnine and then watch their death agonies with amusement. The more gruesome horrors he had kept from her, for nothing could be gained from her knowing of them. It was enough that Anna grasped the essence of the nightmare.

"So now you know, Anna my dearest," he whispered. "The whole story. Forgive me for having hurt you."

Drying away the tears, she gazed down at him tenderly. To have Hans back with her again, alive, was a miracle. "Let me help you," she said quietly, urgingly. "Let me help you and the doctors."

But he said, "No," and he said it firmly. "They must never know that you are aware of what they're doing. Even I, who had sworn my oath to them, had had to 'die' in order to let them carry on with their plan. What would they do with yet another person in on their secret? I'm afraid that, for fear you might give the hoax away, they would stop it altogether. A secret kept by five people isn't much of a secret, is it? And I won't rob them of their security. Not after all they have done for me."

She nodded in agreement, then added, "But if you

do need something, *moj* Hans, from the hospital or wherever, and I can help you, please let me do it."

He didn't answer her. Instead, overcome with the sweetly touching innocence of her round face and the gentleness of her voice, he reached up, took hold of her shoulders, and brought her down onto him once more.

Lehman Bruckner stood with arms akimbo in the center of the lab. His latest discovery was distressing. Most distressing.

Yesterday he had counted his supply of Erlenmeyer flasks. Today there was one less. And it was nowhere to be found.

Maybe he hadn't been able to get a lead on the identities of the Resistance group hiding in the area, but if the medical personnel in Sofia were involved in a subversive plan, Lehman Bruckner was now more than ever determined to find out who they were and what they were up to.

He left the lab and headed down the hallway toward Jan Szukalski's office.

CHAPTER 19

The establishment of a quarantine did not hamper the work of the people in the cave. As they drew close to the day of their full-scale attack, they worked tirelessly to perfect their plan.

Everyone took a turn at watching the depot for a day, each time reporting an increase in gasoline and weaponry being brought in for the spring offensive. Despite the quarantine, the installation remained active with sealed trains moving in and out with the Nazi personnel practicing precautionary measures against the disease.

"However," said Brunek Matuszek one evening, "the Germans cannot move anything out until the quarantine is lifted. It's one thing to bring supplies in, but quite another to ship them out. The Germans aren't going to risk carrying typhus to their already beleaguered front lines."

"How long will the quarantine last?" asked Każik Skowron.

"We have no way of knowing. But we do know one thing. The Germans must be planning a major offensive against the Russians as soon as spring is here. That's why they're stockpiling so much fuel and armament in the depot. This is why we have to move quickly. As soon as the quarantine lifts, everything in the installation will be shipped immediately to the front and there'll be nothing left worth blowing up."

So they spent their days learning how to handle the German weapons they had stolen from the train, trusting that when it came time for the actual firing, the rehearsals would pay off.

They spent their evenings keeping the cave quarters as clean as they could, steaming their clothing and examining themselves for lice. While no one fell ill or even complained of a single typhus symptom, it was the task of Ben Jakoby to interrogate each member every single day and to keep an eye out for the first sign of typhus.

"I know it is a great risk we are taking," said Brunek, "but we cannot disband now merely for our health's sake. We remain together until the depot is taken. Then we can split up."

He stood in the center of the group and pointed to a crude map etched in the dirt. "This shows the approximate layout of the supply depot and the targets we will go after. There are two large gasoline storage tanks here and at night there are two gasoline tank trucks parked nearby. Usually over here," he pointed. "There are several thousand gallons of gasoline also stored in drums over in this area. Now then, their ammunition and artillery shell storage is in those two bunkers that are almost completely underground. I don't think that a mortar shell is going to penetrate through the top, but if we can hit the entrances with bazooka rockets, we will be able to explode the whole works.

"Over here near the repair shops are almost fifty Mark III panzers which are being refitted with new long 50 mm guns. Our targets are clear. The fuel and ammunition are the number one priority."

He straightened up and looked around at everyone. Their faces were tense in the fire's glow. "We will attack," he continued, "in the dark hours before dawn. Everyone but the sentries will be sleeping. We will set up the mortars five hundred meters back and then will commence firing at 0500 hours. We will be positioned in two groups near the main gate. These will be the bazookas and submachine guns. The mortar barrage will be laid down for five minutes into the barracks and gasoline storage area. While this is going on, we will blow the gate open with a bazooka rocket and when the barrage has stopped, we will run like hell inside with the bazookas and submachine guns. Bromberg will take his group and head for the tanks and try to hit as many as he can with bazooka rockets before he runs out of ammunition. Moisze?"

The forty-five-year-old Jew nodded.

Brunek went on. "Antek and I will take our group and get the ammunition bunkers. Każik and Stanisław will be heading a group that will join up with us and hit any remaining gasoline storage and blow up the repair shops.

"We will have ten minutes to carry all this out, then our mortars will start firing again, aiming into the courtyard area of the barracks and the ammunition bunkers. Two riflemen will be positioned to take out the men in the guard towers and blow out their searchlights. We must act rapidly, make our strike, and escape as quickly as we can.

"We will be joined by forty more people here day after tomorrow. All loyal partisans who will fight with us and then disappear afterward."

Brunek took one last look around the circle. "We will strike in three days."

They were sitting at a small table, the only two customers in a little restaurant near the edge of the town. Maria Duszynska sat with her chin in her hands, listening to Jan.

"That makes exactly four thousand cases of typhus we have reported," he was saying quietly, "and since April is upon us, we had better start tapering off the number of cases we report. Maria?" He reached over and tapped her arm. "Maria, are you listening?"

She focused her eyes on him. "Hm? Oh, I'm sorry, Jan."

"Anyway, it's time to start tapering."

"Yes, yes of course." She sat back in her chair and dropped her hands in her lap. She had been thinking of Maximilian Hartung. And of the fact that she still had not heard from him.

The restaurant was a cozy refuge from the strains of hospital work. Simply called *Restaurącja,* it was owned by a family from the province of Swiebodzin who took their time preparing each individual meal. The air was thick with smoke and the rich aroma of onion and garlic and caraway. The dark, foamy beer that was so popular in Poland sat in pewter tankards before Jan and Maria.

"Still haven't heard from him?" asked Szukalski.

Maria shook her head. "I guess he's busy."

Jan nodded.

The main course of the meal arrived, two plates of sausages and tangy sauerkraut. After tasting her food, Maria said, "Yes, the epidemic is working. Do you think that might be why there hasn't been any partisan activity lately?"

He shook his head. "I think the winter held them up, whoever they are, but now that spring is here, you can be sure we'll hear from them again. And considering the weeks they've been quiet, I can imagine they won't start the spring off with something small."

Maria chewed thoughtfully. "It frightens me, Jan."

His shoulders heaved a little as he said, "Yes, me too. I don't trust them. *Psiakrew*, I wish I knew who they were!"

Maria looked around the restaurant. "Because our quarantine *is* precarious," she said in a near whisper, "a major move by the partisans could spoil everything and bring hundreds of Germans down on us. We're not needed, Jan, only that supply and repair depot. If the partisans launched something big, the Nazis would wipe us out, typhus or no."

"Yes, I've thought of that. I wish I could contact them, let them know what we're up to."

"I'm sure they think we're cowards for not fighting with them."

"Cowards. . . ." Jan Szukalski glowered darkly into his sauerkraut.

"Jan," she said, her voice barely audible.

He brought his head up.

"How long do you think we'll be able to keep the hoax going?"

"I guess for as long as the Germans are convinced that we have a truly virulent epidemic on our hands."

"Are you sure there are no other blood tests that can be run to check more specifically for typhus than the Weil-Felix?"

"None that I'm aware of."

"Could there possibly be a cure for typhus that we haven't heard about?"

"Not that I know of. But I will tell you, last year I did read in the proceedings of a conference held in Geneva that the Swiss have developed a new pesticide that they are calling DDT."

"I think I've heard of it."

"It kills body lice and should be very effective against the spread of typhus."

"Do the Nazis have DDT?"

"I'm sure they do. But I doubt they have enough to use on a large scale. Otherwise they wouldn't be so damned scared of our epidemic."

"What if they order us to use it?"

"I think, Maria, we will deal with that problem if and when it arrives."

Despite the fierce cold of the evening, *SS-Hauptsturmführer* Dieter Schmidt stood before his full-length mirror absolutely naked. The lamp from his night table was now on the floor and shining up at him in spotlight fashion while he, with a small pocket mirror in one hand and a comb in the other, meticulously inspected his pubic hair.

This had become a ritual for Schmidt ever since he had begun the twice daily examinations of himself at the onset of the epidemic. Aside from taking punishing hot baths twice a day and a thrice daily change of clothes, he had also had the hair on his head completely shaved off.

Slowly drawing the comb through the short curly hair, *Hauptsturmführer* Dieter Schmidt clinically scrutinized every hill and valley of his genitals and was satisfied, after his search, that no lice were harbored there.

Next he stepped close to the mirror, tossed an arm over his head and raked through the hair of his armpit. First this arm, and then that, concluding the exploration of his body, which left him content that he had made it through yet another day in the battle against typhus.

The battle, yes, but the war still waged. Replacing the lamp on his nightstand, Schmidt next inspected his mattress and bedsprings, as sedulously as with his own person, before making up the bed with freshly cleaned sheets.

Before retiring, he went into the small adjoining bathroom to check on the progress of his makeshift clothes steamer.

With his own hands he had installed a small ceramic coal-burning stove, vented to the outside wall. Upon its short, flat surface sat a large pot filled to the rim with water that was continually at a rolling boil. Suspended above the pot from hooks in the ceiling were his beautiful uniforms hanging limply on wooden coat hangers and wrapped with a cylinder of canvas that kept them in a perpetual cloud of steam.

The steamer had been Dieter's own invention. After reading Szukalski's list of precautions to take against the typhus-carrying louse, Schmidt had painstakingly undertaken to perform as many of these measures on his own as he could. He did not trust any of his aides to safeguard his health.

Of one thing Schmidt felt certain: If he should happen to contract typhus, he was convinced he stood almost no chance of surviving it.

The aide who brought in his meals had also to take precautions. His head was shaved and he was required to wear gloves. Nor could he step very far into his commander's quarters. Even though Schmidt had given strict orders to his men as to their own required rituals of precautions, and even though he was continually assured that they were obeying them religiously, Dieter was still not taking any chances.

He still went down to the office every day, the supreme commander of the area, duty-bound to carry on his job. Although he missed his daily rides in the Mercedes and his surprise visits to various places in town, like the hospital or the church, he was not such a fool as to risk his own health to do it.

Thousands in Sofia and the surrounding area were suffering from the ghastly disease. Many had died already from it, according to Szukalski's daily report, and not a few of them had been German. And it was all that swine's fault! If that pig Szukalski had any sort of competency, the epidemic would never have broken out. Because of him, Dieter Schmidt's life was reduced to farcical rituals.

It infuriated the Gestapo commandant to be so impotent, so utterly helpless. He was getting pressure from his superiors to clear up the epidemic and free the munitions and repair depot for full operation again. But how? Szukalski was doing the best he could, vaccinating the townspeople.

Dieter Schmidt had one consolation. He now knew who the partisans were and where they were hiding. He also knew, through his two spies Każik and Stanisław, about the plan to blow up that installation. Schmidt even knew the day and the hour of the attack.

He assured himself that if he couldn't get rid of the epidemic as the High Command was demanding, Dieter Schmidt was at least soon going to prove himself in a way he had never done before.

Anna Krasinska did not have to turn on the light to find the cupboard she needed. The laboratory was a familiar place to her, even at this dark hour of the night, and she needed only to feel her way about to reach the right spot. It would be in here, what she required, on the second shelf. And she would be able to sneak it out of the lab without anyone knowing.

Anna had gone to Dr. Szukalski for two reasons. The first and most important had been her fear of losing Hans. The typhus hoax meant a great deal to him and he would let nothing get in the way of their effort to save Sofia from the Final Solution. And Anna had feared that if such should come to pass, Hans would choose to give her up rather than jeopardize the project.

The other reason had been the matter of his conscience. It had distressed him to lie to the priest about his nightly whereabouts, and he had grown increasingly nervous about creeping out to his grandmother's house after midnight. The result of this was that Anna felt she was going to lose him altogether.

Unknown to Hans, Anna had decided to seek a

solution on her own. She had been extremely apprehensive at first, sitting in Dr. Szukalski's office and speaking haltingly. But then, to her surprise and relief, the doctor had been most understanding of the situation and had expressed his regret that Hans had not come to him with the problem sooner.

When the four next met in the crypt of the church, Jan Szukalski brought a guest with him.

"We can use her," Szukalski told the others as they sat in a small circle at the center of the sarcophagi. "Maria and I have been risking too much by taking things out of the lab. Anna will be less conspicuous. And she can get other supplies from the hospital as well. I'm transferring her to the typhus ward. It's been a hell of a task to maintain faked symptoms in those patients so that the nurses think they're handling the real thing. With Anna down there to assure them, that's one less worry we'll have."

Szukalski's voice was low and comforting. "Hans, I hope you have more faith in us from now on. Any more problems are to be brought to us at once. I ask you only one thing. When you do go to your grandmother's house again, be sure to tell Father Wajda where you are going and exactly when you will be back."

Having found what she was looking for, Anna secreted it beneath her coat, crept to the door of the lab, opened it a crack, and peered up and down the hall. It was dark and deserted. She slipped out quietly, locked the door behind her, and hurried off down the corridor to the exit.

Lehman Bruckner, hidden once again in the stairwell, rose from his cramped position and followed her.

A light April rain was starting to fall as he emerged from the hospital so that he paused to turn up the collar of his coat and give the girl time to put some distance between them. Sliding his hands into the pockets of his trench coat and feeling the cold metal of the Walther which the SD had issued him, Bruckner struck off down the street a discreet hundred meters behind.

Anna walked briskly and occasionally tossed a glance over her shoulder. The streets were wet and deserted, glistening and slippery. She did not see the man who ducked suddenly into the shadows. Anna headed straight across the town square and hurried toward the church. She threw a quick look behind her at Nazi Headquarters, but saw no guards standing there, and only a few lights on in the front windows. Ever since the beginning of the epidemic three months before, little activity by the occupying troops had been seen.

Lehman Bruckner kept his distance and, instead of plunging through the square as the girl had done, hung back in a doorway to see where she was going.

He was a little surprised to see her run up the stony steps of Saint Ambroż, draw one of its massive doors open and slip inside. Deciding that she must be stopping to light a candle or have a word with the priest, Bruckner remained in his protective shadow and waited, with a cigarette, for the girl to come out.

However, after a few minutes, with the dampness seeping into his clothes and his feet turning numb from standing, Bruckner decided to take a look inside the church and see exactly what it was she was up to. After all, he was certain she had emerged from the lab with an object hidden beneath her coat.

Ever so slowly he drew open the towering oaken door, crept inside and hid at once behind a protective pillar. He strained his ears at the silence and narrowed his eyes down the length of the nave. Except for the flickering of a few candles and the great bouquets of flowers decorating the altar, Bruckner could discern no signs of life in the church.

He slinked over to a side aisle, his hand resting on the handle of the Walther in his pocket, and slowly walked toward the other end of the church. Perspiration sprouted on his upper lip, and, for some reason he could not fathom, his heart started to pound.

A few meters from the door of the sacristy he stopped, stretched his head forward to listen, and kept his body pressed against the cold stone wall. Still silence. No sound. No movement.

Drawing his breath in shallow gulps, Lehman Bruckner inched his way to the sacristy door until he was flush with it, and from here he inclined himself ever so slightly forward and peered in.

Empty.

With his fingers now firmly grasping the gun, he strode into the little room, barely glancing at the hanging vestments which seemed to stare down at him from their clothes trees, and crossed over to another doorway. It was ajar and there was light within.

Tapping the door lightly with his toe so that it swung in just a little, he was able to glance around and see that Father Wajda's office was also empty. A book lay upon the desk, a full fire blazed in the brazier against the wall, and a glass of wine sat next to the book, evidence that the priest would be coming back.

Lehman Bruckner wiped his forehead and tiptoed back to the sacristy. As he was passing through the darkness, his eye happened to catch on a pinprick of light not far from his feet, and, bending close to inspect it, Lehman saw that a small hole had been cut into the floor of the sacristy and that a copper tube passed through it. Following the line with his eyes, he saw that it was connected up to the little sink in the corner.

He knelt down and pressed his ear to the floor. A very faint sound of muffled voices drifted up to him.

Bruckner sat up, puzzled. The sounds, as well as the mysterious copper piping, were obviously coming from some hidden subterranean chamber. But where?

He stood and felt all around the sacristy walls for a doorway of some kind, but found nothing. So he left the small room and, following a hunch, stepped to the rear of the altar and painstakingly made his way along the wall of the apse. Passing behind the towering crucifix and the muted frescoes, he eventually came to a recessed doorway that he pushed open onto a spiral staircase.

Bruckner now withdrew the Walther all the way from his pocket and slowly descended the stairs.

A pungent loamy smell made him wrinkle his nose, and when his hand occasionally came in contact with the damp, slimy growth on the stone wall, he pulled away. He went down carefully into the blackness, one slow step at a time, thinking that this must be what it is like to be blind.

Presently Bruckner was rewarded with the frail dawning of a light. It was accompanied by low murmuring tones, so that he knew his descent was almost at an end. Sweating terribly and fighting the urge to urinate, he finally came to the last step. When his eyes focused on the scene before him, he froze.

Standing under the stone archway of the last step, Bruckner stared in disbelief at the intricate laboratory set-up which covered one long table and took up one fourth of the floor space. He gaped at the stone coffins stacked on the shelves, at the medieval effigies of sleeping bishops, at the electric light bulbs illuminating not only marble tombstones and funerary epitaphs but an ice box and hospital incubator as well.

And if such startling incongruities weren't ludicrous enough, the final touch to the bizarre setting was the brown-robed monk who stood in the center of the chamber embracing a nurse and kissing her on the mouth.

He gasped audibly, startling Brother Michał and Anna, who broke their embrace and whirled toward the sound. Bruckner stepped fully into the chamber, gun at the ready.

"Don't move, either of you," he said smoothly.

Glancing around the room and surveying the laboratory equipment, all of which he recognized as items he was missing, Bruckner growled, "What's going on here?"

Hans Kepler put on his most disarming smile. "It's a burial chamber, as you can see, and this is where we prepare the bodies with a special kind of preparation."

"I see. . . ." Bruckner reached out to the table and picked up a piece of glassware. "What the hell is this? What are you making down here?"

The monk spoke up again, his voice still calm and relaxed. "I told you. It's something we're experimenting with for the preservation of bodies. Now look around you. These medieval—"

"Shut up! It's some sort of vaccine. I don't know exactly what for, but I *am* a lab technician and I can tell you when I'm looking at vials of vaccine."

He studied the faces of the two before him, grading them against this sinister background, and all of a sudden it fell into place. The strange activities of Dr. Szukalski and Dr. Duszynska. The Proteus culture he had found. A typhus epidemic to which no one he knew personally had succumbed.

He squinted at the monk. "Don't I know you from somewhere?"

"I don't believe so. I'm a refugee."

"Oh yes. . . ." Bruckner thought a moment, searching his mind for shreds of the tale he had happened to hear about a monk seeking refuge in the church of Saint Ambroż. He coughed out a reedy laugh. "I remember now. The *deaf mute*."

Anna and Hans exchanged glances.

"Now I know who you are," said Bruckner, drawing his mouth back over his teeth in what he thought was a smile. "You're that SS man who was hanging around here at Christmastime. The one that died of typhus. Well, well. . . ."

He nodded with insufferably smug satisfaction and took a step back toward the stairway. "This is certainly very interesting. Typhus epidemic indeed! How ingenious! I'm sure the *Hauptsturmführer* would love to hear all about it. How he does love a mystery! An SS deserter who has become a monk. And a faked typhus epidemic. I must say, this certainly is my day."

The leer dropped from his face as he jerked the gun toward the stairs. "All right!" he barked. "Now move! We three are going to take a little walk across the town square and pay a visit to the commandant across the way."

Bong . . . bong. . . .

In his sleep, curled up crab-like on his mattress of straw, old Żaba clapped his hands to his ears and groaned. He was having a bad dream.

Bong. . . .

The massive cathedral bells tolled against the night

like a ghostly carillon from hell, reverberating off every spire and finial and buttress of the Gothic masonry. Żaba groaned again and snapped his eyes open. He blinked a few times in his drunken stupor, trying to focus on the low-slung tin roof of his little shack, trying to remember where he was.

When the mournful pealing of the bells finally reached his vodka-soaked consciousness, the old caretaker groaned anew and maneuvered his misshapen form out of bed. Sliding into his one pair of pants and throwing a coat over his flannel shirt, he muttered, "Those kids! I'll give 'em a thrashing this time they'll never forget! Wake up the whole town, they will!" He shoved his bare feet into his crusty old shoes and, without bothering to tie the laces, shuffled out of the tin shack and into the night.

Bending in the only direction his twisted body would go, the caretaker craned his neck to look up at the rear of the church, squinting at the needle spires which stood against the cloudy sky. The bells sounded louder now. They chimed slowly, solemnly with the dignified rhythm Żaba usually reserved for the requiem mass.

"*Psiakrew!*" he muttered angrily. Withdrawing from his shack a kerosene lantern and lighting it with a match, he hurried into the church as fast as his deformed legs would carry him.

Inside, the bells seemed louder, resounding forlornly off every wall and reaching up to fill the high vaulting overhead.

"They'll wake up the town!" he grunted, clambering in his frog-like way down the side aisle toward the front of the church where the bell tower stood. The light from his lantern cast an eerie shadow on the walls, Żaba's grotesque disfigurement dancing over the gray stone like a Halloween phantom. "The things they do to torment me! But this time they've gone too far. Ringing my bells at two o'clock in the morning. *Psiakrew!*"

When he reached the wooden door of the belfry, he found it standing ajar.

The bells continued to knell slowly.

Aha! he thought devilishly. They're still in there! I've

caught them at it, the buggers! By the time I'm through with them the only time they'll show their faces around here will be for confession!

He drew the door open and thrust his lantern into the stairwell. He listened. No sound of footsteps. And still the bells rang.

Moving sideways, dragging his one lame leg, Żaba mounted the ancient steps leading up to the bell tower, holding the lantern before him all the way. Presently he reached the door at the top and this, too, was slightly ajar.

The bells were much louder now. Clamorous, cacophonous. They pounded his ears, clanged about in his brain. He wondered how the pranksters could stand it.

This second door Żaba abruptly yanked open and stuck his head in. Holding the lantern next to his face, he looked up to the tip of the belfry, trying to see the bells. But all was darkness. And in front of him, incredibly, the rope of the bells dangled haphazardly.

He glanced around. In this tiny room where there was barely enough space for another person, it was not possible for anyone to hide. And yet, strangely, it was deserted. Żaba was all alone in the bell tower.

Puzzled, he squinted at the rope moving languidly before his face, trying to figure out what had gotten the bells started, and when the rope started to come down before his bewildered face, Żaba made two fists and rubbed his eyes. Opening them, he blinked at the rope as it made its graceful descent.

Żaba screamed when a nondescript black form slid down into his view and was topped with the bloated, purple face of Lehman Bruckner.

Dieter Schmidt stumbled out of bed and fumbled for the phone. *"Was ist los?"* he grumbled into the receiver. "What is all the racket?"

He listened with his eyes sleepily closed as the officer on duty explained that the bells of Saint Ambroż were ringing.

"Then send someone over to stop them, you idiot!" shouted Dieter Schmidt. "And shoot whoever is doing it! How the hell am I supposed to sleep with that noise!"

Four soldiers were dispatched directly to the church. Arms drawn, they burst through the double oaken doors of the cathedral and stopped short when they saw old Żaba pressed against the wall muttering insensibly.

They rushed up to him and tried questioning him, but to no avail. His warped face distorted by fear, the lopsided old caretaker could only mutter unintelligible words over and over again. So the soldiers made a swift ascent of the bell tower stairs and eventually came upon the rising and falling corpse of Lehman Bruckner. One of them had the presence of mind to reach out and stop him, ceasing at once the bell ringing and allowing the body to gently drift down to the floor. All four men made a gesture of distaste at the sight.

Bruckner's eyes were popped, like those of a putrid fish, and his skin was a peculiar shade of plum. They severed the rope that bound him to the bells overhead and let him drop with a thud.

The four Nazis, their guns ready, were staring in wonder down at the body when they heard hurried footsteps mount the stairs. They turned to see Father Wajda, still buttoning the collar of his cassock, emerge into the cramped tower.

"What's going on?" he demanded, first in Polish. Then, seeing the soldiers, he repeated himself in German. He barely got his sentence out when his eyes fell upon the grisly face of Bruckner and, seeing it, he unwittingly fell back a step.

Father Wajda automatically crossed himself. "Dear Jesus!" he whispered. "What *is* this?"

One of the SS men knelt briefly and slapped his hands perfunctorily over Bruckner's pockets. He produced the lab technician's papers and, crumpled in the pocket of the dead man's trench coat, a piece of paper with only two lines written on it. The soldier, glancing at this last, handed it up to the priest without a word.

Father Wajda, in a state of shock, looked at the note. It was written in German:

"I can no longer live with what I am. May God forgive me."

Looking up at the Nazis, Father Wajda said, "I don't understand. What is going on here? *Who is this?*"

The four men shrugged and shifted their feet uneasily. Only the priest was able to look at that gruesome caricature of a face.

"Apparently," said the leader of the little group, "this man has committed suicide."

"Yes, I can see that. But why? And who is he?"

"I don't know, Father," said the soldier.

The other three men shuffled restlessly in the cramped quarters, displeased with the situation and in a desperate hurry to be out. With an epidemic of typhus raging through this town, none of them enjoyed being in such close company with a Pole.

"But why choose my bell tower?" said Wajda, his voice rising.

The leader shrugged. "I think he was a homosexual."

Father Wajda allowed his eyes to drift once more to that mockery of a human face, letting them travel up and down the body, before he finally said, "Yes, *Herr Unterscharführer,* I think you're right. I remember this man. . . ."

Wajda sadly shook his head. Totally against church dogma, this man had committed suicide. No last rites would be given.

"Will you take care of it, please?" he said to the Sergeant. "I suppose this is in the commandant's hands."

To one of his subordinates the Sergeant snapped an order. "Get this body out of here and prepare a report for the *Hauptsturmführer.*"

CHAPTER 20

All day long, members of the partisan group from the north arrived at the cave; some in twos or threes, many alone. Moisze Bromberg met them at the entrance, briefed them, then passed them along to Ben Jakoby, whose job it was to explain to them that they had voluntarily entered a quarantined area and that they were to report to him immediately should they experience any one of a list of symptoms. After this, the newcomers were directed to their respective groups, outfitted with weapons, and instructed by their group leader as to their specific tasks during the attack. All were experienced fighters and familiar with German ordnance.

Then, shortly before midnight, Brunek gathered them together and surveyed his sixty-five-member force.

"We will begin leaving an hour after midnight in small groups. Rendezvous at your assigned places at 0400 hours. The signal to begin the attack will be the first mortar shot. Now, get some rest if you can. The first groups will move out soon, with the rest following at spaced intervals."

Along with everyone else, Każik and Stanisław picked up one bazooka each, a bag of rockets, and their submachine guns and moved toward the cave entrance, for they would be among the first to move out. They sat quietly and pensively a little way from the rest of the group against the wall where it curved low.

The night passed slowly, agonizingly. A few who could, slept. The rest stared into the darkness, each wondering, each fearful. Finally, Moisze Bromberg got to his feet and spoke. "Time to start moving out. Każik, you and Stanisław go first."

As they rose, gathering their equipment, Stanisław

240

stood abruptly and accidentally banged his head on the low ceiling. *"Verflucht!"* he whispered sharply, rubbing his head.

David Ryż, lying nearby, his head on a pack of bazooka rockets, cocked his ear toward Każik and Stanisław. He watched the two finish collecting their equipment and then slip through the cave opening.

After they had left, David looked thoughtfully at Abraham, then murmured, "Let's go next."

They were on their knees in an instant and hurriedly gathering their arms. Leokadja, who was to be the third member of their group, watched them from a far corner of the cave, her face coming together in a frown. It wasn't their turn to leave yet.

David and Abraham were out of the cave before anyone could see them, and by the time Leokadja could get to her feet and hurry outside, they were gone.

Abraham followed David up the trail until his friend stopped half way and spun around, talking in a hiss. "Abraham, I think there's something wrong!"

Abraham tried to see David's face in the darkness, but could barely do so, for there was a cloud cover over the moon. "What do you mean?"

"Just now, down there, I heard Stanisław curse in German when he struck his head on the ceiling."

"So? Lots of Poles speak German."

"I know. But it didn't seem right. Tell me, Abraham, if you slammed your thumb with a hammer, would you curse in German or in Polish?"

"What do you want to do?"

"Follow them."

"Why? They're only going to the installation."

"Are they?" David turned about quickly and started again up the trail. Abraham followed close behind.

Just as they reached the crest of the cliff, they heard the distant sound of a motorcycle engine through the trees. David and Abraham exchanged glances. "Come on," whispered David.

They had to walk quite a way and along a different track than the one they were supposed to take to Sofia. The sound of the cycle led them through a dense part of the forest, bringing them at last to a small clearing in the wood. Peering through the trees, David and Abraham saw Każik Skowron astride a German motorcycle. He was warming up its engine.

"What shall we do?" whispered Abraham.

"I don't know. I don't see Stanisław." They crouched low, dropping their sacks of rockets to the snow, but holding on to their rifles.

"Perhaps you can see him now," came a voice from behind them.

The two young Jews whipped about and found themselves staring down the barrel of Stan's Erma submachine gun.

"Turn off the cycle!" he shouted to Każik in German. "We have visitors. All right, hero partisans, hands in the air!"

"Oh God. . . ." groaned Abraham, dropping his gun and slowly raising his arms.

"You stinking bastards!" spat David, throwing down his rifle and jumping to his feet. "You're Germans! Spies!"

"How clever of you, Jew. Now turn around. You have a little digging to do."

Stanisław cocked his submachine gun and prodded Abraham with it. Stumbling to his feet, David's friend started to stagger into the little clearing. David marched sullenly behind, hands on his head.

"It's no use expecting help from your friends," said Każik, getting off the motorcycle and coming toward them. "They are in for a little surprise tonight. And they won't hear our gunshots so you can't expect them to come and save you. It's too bad, for you're such nice boys, for Jews."

"Right here!" barked Stan. "Down to your knees. And start digging."

"What are we supposed to be digging?" asked David.

"Your grave, what else? Dig!"

The two German soldiers, their Ermas—which had been part of the partisan supply—pointed at the heads of the youths, watched as David and Abraham started to scoop snow with their hands.

"Faster!" shouted Każik. "We don't have all night. And when the hole is ready, you'll take off your clothes and kneel for us. You will notice that the snow is very painful on bare hands. The faster you dig, the sooner you will be relieved of your discomfort."

His lips in a bloodless line, David Ryż dug frantically, angrily into the snow, while Abraham moved very slowly, almost in a dream.

They had only dug through to frozen hard ground when Każik said, "That's enough! Jews don't need a real grave. Now take off your clothes! *Schnell!*"

David slowly rose to his feet glaring defiantly at the Germans while Abraham remained kneeling, ineffectually fumbling with the buttons of his coat.

In the next instant, a single shot rang through the night, and the head of Stanisław split open like an overripe melon. Każik Skowron, spinning around, received the second and third shots in his face and chest. He teetered for a second, bewildered, then crumpled to the snow.

Leokadja stood at the edge of the clearing with the smoking rifle still at her shoulder.

David grabbed Abraham and pulled his dumbstruck friend to his feet. "It wasn't easy finding you," said the girl, rushing to them. "I had to follow the sound of their voices."

David started to walk away. "That's not the way to the depot," said Leokadja, running after him.

Talking over his shoulder as the other two caught up with him, David said, "Those two pigs said something about our people being surprised tonight."

"Oh God, you don't think—"

"I'll bet they reported everything to Schmidt. And I have a strong feeling he isn't going to bother waiting for us at the depot."

The three staggered and slipped as they ran through the darkness. They were almost two kilometers from the cave.

When they reached the beginning of the trail that led down to the cave entrance, the three were met by an eerie silence. Searching the sheer wall of the cliff and then the trees, and straining to hear the slightest sound, David whispered, "Where are the sentries?"

"I don't like this," murmured Leokadja.

The forest stillness was curiously menacing and the three could not shake the feeling that a thousand unseen eyes watched them.

"David," said Leokadja, stepping close to him. "What has happened?"

Frowning into the darkness, the youth continued to search. When his eyes fell upon a lifeless form in the bushes, he dropped down to one knee. The startled face of old Ben Jakoby stared up at him, his skull crushed. David clasped his hands across his knee and, bowing his head murmured, *"Baruch dayyan ha'emeth."*

Leokadja and Abraham also knelt by the body and all three suddenly had a frightening vision of what they would find in the cave.

Standing up, David said in a choked voice, "Spread out and cover me. I'm going down."

He crept slowly, quietly, trying not to disturb the vast silence. When his foot crunched an occasional twig, he froze and listened. Then he moved forward again. Closer to the entrance he stopped and gave the signal—three long whistles. There was no response.

Painstakingly, he made his way around the sharp corner of the cliff, his body pressed against the wall, his breathing quick and shallow. When he was flush with the entrance, he stood for a moment, listened, then, on an impulse, dashed inside, his gun cocked and aimed, ready to shoot.

Since the fire was out and the cave was filled with a pungent smoke, David could barely make out the grotesque shapes scattered on the floor. He strode solemnly among them and counted ten, strewn about like so much refuse.

Ester Bromberg, her body riddled with bullets. Old *Pani* Duda, one side of her face caved in. The little boy named Icek, his throat slit. And the rest. Lying in the grim and pathetic attitudes of a useless death.

In the center of the cave, the fire had been smothered by a heap of clothes, and as he stared at this, David realized, with dawning horror, what must have happened.

"Oh my God. . . ." whispered someone behind him.

Leokadja stepped delicately among the bodies, pausing at each one to check for possible signs of life, then she came to stand next to David.

"Their clothes," he said in a leaden voice. "The Germans made them take off their clothes before taking them away."

Atop the smoldering fire, David recognized the coats that belonged to Brunek Matuszek and Moisze Bromberg. "They can't be too far; we weren't gone that long," he said.

"The weapons!" cried Leokadja suddenly, sharply.

David looked up quickly and saw the panic in her eyes. Then, without a word, he ran around the pile of burning clothes and hurried to the back of the cave. Abraham and the girl stood for a moment listening to some scuffling and scraping sounds, then they heard David call back, "They're still here!"

When he joined them he was carrying a bazooka. "I don't think Każik and Stanisław, or whatever their real names were, ever knew about our secret cache of armament."

"They only saw what we were going to use on the depot. Otherwise, Schmidt's men would have taken everything." Leokadja reached out and seized his arm. "What are we going to do?"

He thrust the bazooka at Abraham, who took it wordlessly, then strode back to the hidden limestone chamber. There was another scraping sound, and David returned with two bags of rockets. "We're going to try to catch up with them," he said flatly.

Snow had begun to fall again, drifting peacefully down onto the white landscape, but it offered no solace to the three who struck out into the glacial night. They were oblivious to the freezing air and drifts that in places came over their boots, for their attention was concentrated upon a trail that marched away from the cave, a trail created by the tramping of fifty-two pairs of bare feet and countless accompanying jackboots. Along the way, there were occasional splotches of fresh blood.

The trail finally ended at a narrow country road

where, in the slush and newly fallen snow, the fresh imprints of truck tires could be clearly seen.

"Now what?" whispered Leokadja.

David looked up at her. There was a strange light in his eyes, one she had never seen before, and his voice sounded like that of a stranger as he said, "You two wait here. I'll come back for you."

Before they could question him, David was running back the way they had come, his boots frantically crunching the snow. He ran across broad fields, heedless of the fact that he could easily be seen, and then plunged through the forest, thrashing out with his arms, sending branches flailing.

Presently, out of breath and afraid he might drop, he came upon the bodies of Każik and Stanisław. David dashed past them and jumped onto their motorcycle, bringing it to life, the roar of its engine tearing through the night.

Within twenty minutes he was back at the road and found Leokadja and Abraham just as he had left them.

"Get on!" he barked. "There still might be time to save them! If we can catch those trucks—"

David gunned the engine and was swerving off down the road before his two friends were seated. Leokadja, her arms holding him tight, sat behind him, her wind-bitten face pressed into his back. Abraham, cradling the bazooka and rockets in his lap, huddled in the sidecar, holding desperately to its sides.

David shot full throttle down the bumpy road, his eyes always on the tire tracks.

When they reached the outskirts of Sofia, the gray of early dawn was just beginning to diffuse across the eastern sky. David killed the engine of the motorcycle and coasted into some trees near a dark warehouse. Moving quietly, he motioned to his comrades to follow him, taking only their rifles, then he disappeared through the trees.

The three stole silently along deserted streets. Moving in a zig-zag fashion and pausing every so often in doorways to listen, they crept along toward the town square. The trucks, they assumed, would be going to Nazi Headquarters, for it would be there that the prisoners would be interrogated. If the three could come upon the trucks just as they were unloading, it might be possible to launch a surprise attack and, in the confusion, help some of their comrades escape.

But it was as they were sneaking along the stone wall of Saint Ambroż that David and his companions were startled by the sudden explosion of submachine gun fire, followed by the shrieks and cries of its victims.

Frozen in the shadow of the church, the three gaped in horror at the scene before them.

In the center of the town square, among benches and paths and frozen fountains, lay the bloody bodies of their compatriots, heaped in the winter garden like discarded dolls, naked and still. Across the way stood a line of Nazi soldiers, lowering their guns, and, strutting in front of them like a bantam cock, Dieter Schmidt.

David, Abraham, and Leokadja heard his voice toll across the silence. "Get Dolata and his council out here! Tell them they have some clean-up work to do in the town square!"

David looked at his watch through stinging tears— 0600 hours. The attack on the supply depot would have been an hour old. The explosion interrupting the dawn should have been the German ammunition bunkers. And these poor, naked wretches should have been gloriously slaughtering the enemy.

Without looking at one another, without uttering a single word, the three turned away from the sight and moved back through the shadows of Sofia. They climbed once again onto their motorcycle and returned to the forest.

Two days passed, then a third. The weather warmed a little, and what had been snowfall three days before was now a cold spring drizzle. The three lonely partisans labored to remove the hidden weapons that had not been found by the Nazis to a new hiding place beneath a small stone bridge. They also took with them what little food had been left behind and a couple of blankets.

They moved to different hiding places each night, not daring to stay in one place, fearful of the Nazis finding them. And though nothing had been said, all three knew for whom the hidden weapons were intended. These three, their hearts and minds set upon a solitary cause, were going to raise an army.

On the night before their planned attack, they huddled in the meager warmth of a lean-to and listened to David's final words.

"If all goes well we will get a strong group together, attack the Germans for their supplies, and move to the north to the mountains. A mountain stronghold, that's what we must have.

"There is a small trestle that passes over a ravine in the low hills. I have watched trains go over it many times. If we fell a tree across the tracks before the trestle, they will have to stop the train and get out to move it. There are only about ten soldiers guarding these trains, two usually with the engineer, and the rest in the last car.

"As the train rolls to a stop, Leokadja will fire a bazooka rocket at the rear car. This will give you and me, Abraham, a chance to jump in the engineer's compartment. You will hold them captive while I open the boxcars and release the prisoners."

"Can it be that easy?" asked Leokadja.

"It will be if we subdue the guards fast enough. We will have the element of surprise on our side. After that, we will have the people in the cars to help us. We'll have enough weapons stashed nearby to give some of the people guns in case we have to fight our way out."

The following day the clouds were gone and the morning broke clear. A beautiful day, early spring, the warmth of the sun worked on the snow cover and melted it slowly into rivulets.

David, Leokadja, and Abraham waited at their positions near the railroad track. In the distance could be seen the belching smoke and dark profile of the huge decapod pulling its closed boxcars.

"How will we know that this train isn't really carrying cattle or freight instead of people?" asked Abraham.

"I will know," said David grimly. "I will know. . . ."

At the sight of the huge tree that had been felled across the tracks, the train engineer slowed to a stop. But it was, David noticed with slight dismay, farther back than they had planned.

"Damn!" he hissed. "Now we will have to split up. I am going to run back through the wood and try to get onto the tender. God, I hope Leokadja can still hit that rear car with her bazooka."

As David ran unseen down the length of the train, Leokadja fired at two guards who had disembarked to look around. The rocket struck the front wheels of the car, knocking it from the rail but not effectively hurting any of the soldiers who were now scrambling out the other side and running for cover. David managed to capture the engineer and fireman, and Abraham disarmed the two forward guards who were taken by surprise by the explosion at the rear of the train.

Both of the guards were held fast by Abraham as David signaled to Leokadja to keep firing the bazooka to distract the rear soldiers while he opened the car doors.

It was evident by the frantic screams from inside the cars that they did not contain cattle. David struck at the lock lever with the butt of his submachine gun, pushing each door open as he ran from car to car.

"Come on!" he screamed as he ran. "Get out! Follow me!" David waved his gun over his head. "Get out! You can save yourselves!"

He signaled to Leokadja to keep firing the bazooka, but she motioned that she had fired her last rocket.

David opened two more boxcars then cast a quick glance over his shoulder. What he saw made him stop where he was and stare in horror.

No one had gotten off the train.

He saw them huddled in there, pressed back from the open door, ragged, frightened people staring at him with white, blank faces.

"Get out!" he screamed. "Get out and save yourselves! The Germans are going to execute you! They've lied! You go to your deaths! We have weapons for you! You can fight! You can be free!"

But they didn't move, didn't make a sound, and David Ryż, paralyzed with confusion and disbelief, stared aghast at the hollow faces peering down at him.

Suddenly he heard a scream behind him. He whirled and saw Leokadja being held by an SS officer who had a pistol at her head. Slowly the officer advanced toward David, holding fast to the girl. "Drop your gun, young man," said the German smoothly, calmly. "And you down there," he said to Abraham. "Drop your gun also."

Too stunned to move, David looked back up at the people huddled in the boxcar. And as he listened to the lonely echo of the forest silence all around, he realized what was happening.

The patient but stern voice of the SS officer spoke again. "Put down your guns, we don't wish to kill you. We are not barbarians." When he was even with the youth, David could see the terror in Leokadja's eyes.

"These people," continued the German, "have been starving in the Warszawa ghetto. We have promised them food and shelter and useful work. Why should they want to leave the train?"

David let his hands fall helplessly to his sides, his mind only barely registering the distant sounds of the tree trunk being rolled off the track. And above him, silent, unmoving, the ghostly Jewish faces bound for Auschwitz looking impassively at him.

"David," pleaded Leokadja. "You can shoot your way out! Don't worry about me. Save yourself!"

The young Jew continued to look at the people in the boxcar, pressing as far back from him as they could. And he heard his own voice say, "But you don't understand. . . ."

"Come now," said the SS officer, a trace of impatience in his voice. "We are behind schedule now. We don't want to kill you. Please drop your weapon."

Other soldiers now advanced through the trees, guns pointing at David and Abraham. One of them said, "It's useless for you to die in this lonely place. You can come with us and help build a new world."

David stood dumbly, the far-away voice of the German echoing in his brain, "It is useless for you to die in this lonely place. . . ."

Then he thought of Brunek Matuszek and Moisze Bromberg, how little dignity there had been to their deaths. He thought of what he had seen at the Auschwitz camp through his field glasses. He thought of bravery and of valor and of shooting his way out of this mess and dying in a blaze of glory and heroism.

Then he looked again at the starved, pathetic faces above him—his people—and felt the gun slip from his fingers.

"Excellent," said the officer, releasing the girl.

Hearing from very far away the slamming of box-car doors, David felt himself move forward and hoist himself up into the car. He drew Leokadja up inside and took her in his arms. Abraham was at their side, his face buried in his arms against the wall of the dark boxcar, weeping. David heard the door clang shut and plunged into night.

The train gave a lurch, then resumed its slow, relentless roll.

CHAPTER 21

It was a bitter cold night with April rains beating torrentially upon the Wisła Valley. There was a gray lifelessness to the world, as if all the warmth had been doused. The men and women of Sofia, particularly those who had had to help dig the mass grave of the fifty-two partisans, looked out upon the miserable weather in private contrition. The execution had shocked everyone, especially after word had spread how these fifty-two had so courageously fought the Nazis. It seemed only right, therefore, that Sofia should never see the sun again.

Of the five men now sitting late at night in Edmund Dolata's living room, four felt the weight of a troubled conscience, for these had personally known the partisans, had supplied them with food and had even, on one occasion, helped them transport German weapons away from a blown-up train.

"We are as guilty as they were," said Edmund Dolata, sitting as close to the fire as he could but still not getting warm. "We worked with them and helped them. We were as much a part of them as any of their group."

One of the other four, his head bowed in the dim light, spoke softly. "What are you saying, Edmund? That we should have died with them?"

"No, Jerzy. What I'm saying is they remained silent, even in the face of German submachine guns. Until the very last, they were questioned who in Sofia had helped them, and they kept their silence."

"What would it have served," said Jerzy, raising his head, "to name us? It wouldn't have saved their lives."

"I don't know, Jerzy." Dolata pushed away from

252

the fireplace and paced the room. "But it's important to me. They did not give our names to Schmidt."

A hush fell over the room, magnifying the crackle of the fire against a background of driving rain. Beyond the windows, Sofia slept uneasily beneath the spring storm. Many people were unable to erase the memory of the sight in the town square.

Dolata suddenly stopped where he was, faced the other four men and said quietly, "I feel we owe them something."

His companions looked at one another and then back at Dolata. In the half-light of the fireplace—for no other light burned in Dolata's flat—it was difficult to read each other's expressions, and yet the mood was sensed by all five. The overwhelming guilt that they had done nothing to help those fifty-two men and women.

"They were partisans," came a husky voice. This was Feliks Broninski, Sofia's postmaster and one-time member of Dolata's Town Council. "They knew the risks they ran. They knew the dangers."

"Yes," said Dolata in a bitter voice. "And we knew them, too. That's why they fought the Nazis and we didn't."

"Are you calling us cowards?"

Dolata stared at the four faces.

"Edmund," said Jerzy Krasinski, "it is not cowardly to want to survive. I have a wife and daughter to protect and I want to see them get through this war."

Dolata's voice rose. "Those men and women that were slaughtered in the town square were trying to regain Poland's freedom!"

"That's impossible. There is no power big enough to stop the Nazis."

"Jerzy," Edmund hurried around the sofa and sat upon it opposite Krasinski, his hands clasped on his knees. "I'm not saying the Resistance thinks it can drive the Nazis out of Poland. But, *psiakrew*, they can make life inconvenient for them! Those people who were massacred by Schmidt used to be our neighbors! You used to go to Jakoby's pharmacy for your hemorrhoid cream—"

"Edmund—"

"Listen to me! Those pathetic men and women were only trying to make life difficult for the Nazis until bigger powers could take over. Maybe the Russians won't lose to the Wehrmacht. Maybe they'll start pushing back. And maybe the Allies will reach us; the Americans, perhaps. All right, so our Underground can't defeat the Germans, but by the Holy Virgin, they can certainly slow them down till help arrives!"

The painful truth of his words stung each man as he exchanged troubled glances with the others. Dolata was right. The Nazis *were* being slowed down by the Resistance; their forces *were* being held up or set back by partisan attacks.

"Edmund," said Ludwig Rutkowski, Sofia's police chief, "why did you call us here tonight?"

The short, bald-headed man drew himself up before the four seated men, took a deep breath, and said solemnly, "I want to continue their fight."

Of the four, only one did not outwardly react. When Feliks and Ludwig and Jerzy Krasinski shot to their feet, saying, "You're not serious!" one man remained seated. He heard Dolata's voice continue calmly, "If the Nazis must be our overlords, then it will not be a comfortable life for them. That much we can do. We five have the power and the influence with the people to organize a new, more efficient Underground here in Sofia."

"But, Edmund," came Ludwig's voice, "aside from that execution, things haven't been so bad here in Sofia because of the typhus. Ever since the quarantine started, there have been few soldiers about and Schmidt is hardly ever seen. We have plenty of food now, because it isn't being taken away by the Germans."

"Yes, and when the quarantine lifts? We all know how desperately the Nazis need that munitions and repair depot. When the quarantine lifts there'll be more Germans in Sofia than we'd ever thought possible. Then how peaceful do you think it will be?"

"An epidemic of typhus can last a long time," came the quiet voice of the fifth man who had, so far, not spoken.

Dolata said, "I have confidence in the doctors of this town to bring it to an end as soon as possible."

The police chief suddenly growled, "If Szukalski was smart, he would just let the typhus continue so that the quarantine will last for as long as the war does!"

Jerzy spun about. "That's a hell of a thing to say, Ludwig! Holy Mary, wishing a disease like that on your own people! On your own *family,* for God's sake!"

"Gentlemen, gentlemen." Dolata held up his hand. "I'm sure Ludwig didn't mean it. Please sit down, my friends, and let us talk like reasonable men."

With Jerzy and Ludwig exchanging challenging glances, the four men resumed their seats. In the hour that they had spent here in Dolata's house, only one had so far not voiced his opinion. The other four looked expectantly at him.

Finally, Edmund Dolata said, "Tell us what you think, Jan."

Dr. Szukalski placed his palms on his knees and released a deep, troubled sigh. "I know I've been silent, my friends, but please don't think it's because I have no concern in this matter. Quite the contrary. It weighs so heavily upon me that I hardly know where to begin."

"Just a simple yes or no," said Ludwig flatly. "Do you fight with us or not?"

Seeing the friction, Dolata abruptly got to his feet and strode away from the couch. He walked to an armoire which stood against a dark wall, opened it, and produced five small glasses and a bottle. When he came back, he placed the glasses on the low table between the men and poured out the vodka. "It's a cold night," he murmured. "And possibly a long one."

The five drank down the vodka in one toss, and when the glasses were replaced on the table, Ludwig Rutkowski said, "Jan, you're a man whose opinion we respect. In fact, almost everyone in Sofia esteems you and values your judgment. That's why Edmund asked you to join us tonight. Now you've heard what he has to say and you've heard our feelings on the matter. All we want to know is what you think."

Jan's eyes were filled with sadness as he gazed across

the coffee table. And his voice was heavy as he said, "Ludwig, none of you was more stricken than I when the sun rose that morning and revealed what Dieter Schmidt had done in the square. I saw the bodies, Ludwig. And I'll tell you, my friends, as a doctor I have had more intimacy with death than any of you will ever know. I have seen it in all its forms, from its beauty and peace to the obscenity of those fifty-two executed by Schmidt. I have never been more profoundly affected by death that I was that morning."

"Then you'll want to fight!" said Feliks Broninski.

"Let Jan finish," said Jerzy Krasinski, reaching for the bottle and refilling the glasses.

Szukalski went on, measuring his words. "Yes, Feliks, I want to fight. But I have to tell you now, that I do not condone what you propose, nor do I ever intend to."

"Then you won't fight," said Ludwig angrily.

"I *want* to fight, my friends, and in fact I am doing so right now. Indeed, I have been fighting the Nazis for several months."

Four pairs of eyebrows went up in surprise.

Picking up his drink, Jan rose from the chair and went to stand by the fire, leaning on the mantel. Standing over the fireplace was an alabaster statue of the Blessed Virgin, and it was upon this that Jan now fixed his gaze as he spoke. "I knew from the moment I saw those bodies in the town square that sooner or later I would have to reveal my secret. I knew this because I saw the faces of other Sofians. The fury, the rage, the sudden lust to kill. Dieter Schmidt, by his theatrics, has created the need for revenge in many a man's heart in this town, men who, like yourselves, were trying to coexist peacefully with our Nazi overlords. For this reason, I have made the decision to let you four in on my secret."

"Secret?" he heard Dolata say.

Jan turned to regard them. "I had hoped never to reveal it because the fewer who know of it the better guarded it is. But now everything is different in Sofia. I cannot allow open warfare between Nazis and the civilians."

"Why not, Jan? What is this secret?"

Before the doctor could reply, Feliks Broninski said, "There must be warfare, Jan! It's time we fought! I for one will no longer be a sheep for Schmidt! I have my pride! For God's sake, *women* were in that group, Jan! Women who carried guns and risked their lives to give hell to the Nazis. While I slept peacefully in my bed. How am I supposed to feel!"

Jan's voice remained calm. "Violence is not the way, Feliks. It only breeds more violence. Look what it got those pathetic people. All their heroics and explosions and sneak attacks. Look what it got them."

Edmund Dolata stood up and said softly, "Jan, we do want revenge. If we risk our own lives, then we must. There is no other way."

Jan Szukalski smiled at him cryptically, sadly. "But you see, my friends, there *is* another way."

"What do you mean?"

"I told you I've been fighting the Nazis for several months now, that I had a secret. And in my fight I have shed no blood, taken no lives. And it is a large-scale fight, not just a mere inconvenience as you are suggesting."

"What is it?"

Szukalski stared at the drink in his hand, then brought it to his lips and drank it down in one gulp. Still looking into the glass, his face set in a troubled frown, Jan said, "There is no typhus epidemic in Sofia."

At first there was only silence, then one of the men asked in a hushed voice, "What?"

He looked at them. "I said, gentlemen, there is no typhus epidemic in Sofia."

Dolata frowned. "But the quarantine—"

"The quarantine is real, the disease is not."

"I don't understand," said Jerzy Krasinski.

Jan Szukalski stepped away from the fireplace and resumed his seat with the other four. Refilling all the glasses with more vodka, and drinking down his own, he said in a low, even tone, "My assistant, Maria Duszynska, and I found a way, back in December, to make blood samples appear as though they carried typhus when in fact they did not. I will not go into the technicalities with you, gentlemen, but be assured that the German authorities in Warszawa are convinced that we have a raging epidemic here."

"Jan," said Dolata, leaning forward, "am I understanding this correctly? You and Dr. Duszynska purposely faked an epidemic of typhus? But why?"

"For the very reason you said a moment ago. Quarantine." Jan turned to the police chief. "And for the reason you stated, Ludwig, a few minutes ago, to keep the Nazis away from us. You said you wished the quarantine would last for as long as the war."

Ludwig nodded dumbly, his face set in amazement.

"But my uncle," said Jerzy. "He was put in the hospital for it! He was in the isolation ward!"

Again the doctor shook his head. "We only told him he had typhus. All he really had was stomach gas from too much spice in his dinner."

"But there have been deaths! And there are health notices posted all over town. And my wife has been steaming. . . ." Feliks Broninski's voice drifted off. "Sweet Blessed Virgin . . . you can't mean that it's all a charade!"

"That's exactly what I mean."

"But it isn't possible!" cried Ludwig.

"But it is. We're quarantined, aren't we? And there are fewer Germans here now, aren't there? And we've kept them from being able to use their munitions and repair depot. And we've kept our own farm produce from being shipped out. And we've stopped troop trains from unloading here. So why do you insist it isn't possible?"

Edmund Dolata slowly rose and walked to the window. Drawing the heavy drape open a crack, he peered out at the rain. The street was dark; no pedestrians, no lights. The world was cold, wet, and formidable. He turned around and settled his gaze on Szukalski. "And there have been no deaths due to typhus?"

"Maria and I have faked all the death certificates."

The room was absolutely silent.

"Who else knows?" asked Dolata.

"In all, only five."

"Five!" blurted Feliks. "Five people managed to stage a widespread typhus epidemic? How long did you expect to keep it up?"

"For as long as we could. We never told anyone because we were afraid of the secret getting out."

"Then why have you told us now, Jan?" asked Dolata.

"Because I had to stop you from doing something rash. My anger was the same as yours when I saw those bodies; I knew what was in your heart. When you started talking about resistance and fighting—"

"Let us help you, Jan."

Szukalski looked at Ludwig Rutkowski and smiled. "I want your help, my friends, now. It's gotten too big, the epidemic, and the five of us have too much to handle."

"What can we do?"

"I'm afraid, gentlemen, that many other Sofians are going to try to continue the partisan fight. We can't allow that. They will only make the Nazis so angry that they'll do away with Sofia altogether. Your job will be to tell the people, those whom you think necessary, about the hoax. This way they will realize that there *is* a fight going on in Sofia and that they are indeed a part of the battle against the enemy."

Dolata pushed away from the window and took to pacing again. "You're right, Jan. We have to protect the quarantine. We can spread the word among those we trust—"

"Make sure there are no German sympathizers among them."

Dolata stopped behind the couch and smiled at the doctor. "I know who I can trust, Jan. Just as the rest of you know. The word will go out cautiously. It will be regulated and systematic, I assure you. If I know the people in this town, Jan, they'll rally to your fight. The Nazis will be surrounded by so many sick people they'll be desperate to keep away from us!"

Jan Szukalski nodded gratefully. When the doctor leaned forward and proceeded to refill all five glasses with the last of the vodka, Feliks Broninski said, "We've had three, Jan. That's my limit."

But Szukalski, raising his glass in a toast, said in all seriousness, "I was thinking of that old saying, my friends. The first glass is for myself, the second for my friends, the third for good humor, and the fourth glass," he smiled grimly, "is for my enemies."

The word went out slowly, methodically. Each member of Dolata's former Council organized a secret network of communications, informing small groups of people at a time. Within weeks Szukalski was no longer beleaguered with the problem of how to make the town look as sick as the lab reports indicated, for the Sofians took it upon themselves. Shops closed down with signs in the windows saying there was illness in the family. Women volunteered their services as nurses in the crowded hospital wards. Szukalski and Duszynska were called to homes to treat the "ill." And the town of Sofia gradually grew quiet and peaceful.

Two weeks after the execution of the partisans, four members of the Sofia detachment of the Gestapo stood silently outside the flat above the dry goods store. With their guns cocked and ready, moving quietly and furtively, they watched smugly as their leader took a step back from the door and with one thunderous kick with his heavy jackboot, burst the door open.

Sergei Vasilov, caught in the motion of rising from the living room couch, stared stupidly into the barrels of four cocked Ermas. He was searched roughly and obscenely by two of the men, and then marched out into the snow and the waiting Mercedes.

SS-Hauptsturmführer Dieter Schmidt greeted him with a smooth, frosty smile, instructing the bewildered Russian to remain standing behind the line that had been painted on the floor two meters from the desk. "It would be a sad thing for both of us, *Herr* Vasilov, if you were to infect me," said Schmidt in a surprisingly amiable tone.

Sergei regarded the formidable little man behind the desk helplessly, wondering what this was all about, if it had something to do with Lehman's disappearance of two weeks before.

"Tell me, my friend," said the Gestapo commandant unctuously. "Who are you?"

"Sergei Vasilov, *Herr Hauptsturmführer,*" he replied haltingly in German.

Schmidt's mouth snaked into a smile. "I know that. What I mean is, *who are you?*"

Sergei started to tremble. "I . . . I. . . ."

"A Russian deserter?" asked Dieter politely. "Is that it?"

"Oh no! *Herr . . . Hauptsturmführer. . . .*"

"I see. What was your relationship to Lehman Bruckner?"

Sergei's eyes yawned in confusion. "Was?" he said in a small voice.

Schmidt fixed his eyes on the Russian's face. "Surely you know he is dead."

All the color drained from the deserter's face, and when it appeared he might slump to the floor, an armed guard stepped forward and prodded him with a gun. Sergei saw the image of the commandant swim before his eyes.

"I didn't know. . . ." he whispered in Russian.

"Are you a Red Army deserter?" repeated Schmidt, the sweetness fading from his voice.

Sergei found a shred of voice to say, "No. . . ."

Schmidt laughed, and it was a cold, metallic sound. "Come now, you donkey! Do you see this file on my desk?" He slapped it with the tip of his swagger stick.

The Russian inclined himself forward and squinted at the folder. His name was printed in large letters across the front. "Yes."

"We know who you are, Vasilov! Look how much we have on you! About twenty pages worth! We know who you are, where you have come from, and why you are here! But we don't quite have everything! We need one more piece of information."

Sergei closed his eyes against the nightmare, obliterating, for the moment, the cruel voice of Dieter Schmidt. All that mattered in this painful minute was that Lehman was dead. . . .

"Look at me, swine!" shouted Schmidt.

When Sergei opened his eyes, a tear tumbled down his cheek.

"There is some information you have that we want. You can tell me now, or we can have my men question you for it. If you tell us the truth and cooperate, things will go much easier for you. Remember, Vasilov," Dieter tapped the folder again. "We already have more than enough information on you to hang you."

With a flick of the swagger stick, Schmidt had the stricken man dragged from his office. Immediately after, the efficient aide was at his commander's desk, picking up the file, removing the twenty blank pages, and tossing the folder into the waste basket.

The interrogation of Sergei Vasilov took several hours. He was a tough and hardened man and, as well, he had no idea of what it was Schmidt wanted out of him. That Bruckner had been an SD agent Sergei had not known, so that if Lehman had died with any valuable information, it was not known to his roommate.

After five hours of detailed torture until he was more dead than alive, Sergei Vasilov confessed to being a Red Army deserter, a homosexual rapist of a Nazi agent, and the cause through his perversion of Lehman Bruckner's suicide.

The following morning he was hanged as a spy.

With the break-up of the Wisła River came true spring, and still the typhus quarantine held. By the summer of that year, 432 people had died and several thousand had suffered agonizingly for many days. The fact that no one had really had the disease and that Jan Szukalski and Maria Duszynska were falsifying death certificates was a secret known to almost everyone except the Nazi commander and his men.

While they should have breathed a little more easily by this time, two of the five original conspirators could not.

One was the beautiful Maria Duszynska who, in the sweet, balmy spring air so kind to lovers everywhere, could only relive over and over again the precious memories of her days with Max Hartung in Warszawa.

The other was Father Wajda. His heart suffered from a deep, crippling affliction. Nights found him on his knees before the statue of the Virgin, his rosary clutched fearfully between his sweating fingers, his eyes gazing heavenward in a desperation that would have shocked anyone who might have come upon him thus. Yet because he was a man of the cloth and a man who was used to dealing with the conscience and the troubled soul, Father Wajda was, for the most part, able to disguise his torment. It was when he was alone and in his own company that the disguise was dropped, and he suffered the full thrust of his agony.

For a Catholic to be denied the Sacrament of the confessional meant also that he was denied the Eucharist, which meant he could not share in the Body of Jesus Christ, the very essence of his faith. But for a priest, the very man responsible for the transubstantiation of bread into the Body of Christ, it was a living hell.

His problem was this: He had committed a sin that could not be confessed.

As a consequence, he could not be granted purification in order to receive the Sacrament. While a layman could continue to survive without taking part in this most holy of Catholic rituals, a priest could not. He had to handle the Eucharist. He had to take it himself. If he was to administer it to others, if he was to hear the confession of others, then he himself had to be pure before God. But Father Wajda was not. And there was no possibility of absolution.

Father Wajda had killed a man. Lehman Bruckner.

And this he could not confess. He could not place in the hands of a fellow priest information that Dieter Schmidt would gladly torture to get. Piotr Wajda must carry the secret within himself, to protect his brothers, and because of this he had to suffer the eternal damnation of his soul.

And just how he suffered for it, no one could ever know.

With the summer came the banks of fog that filled the early morning Wisła Valley, enveloping Sofia in thin silence. And as in the spring, the typhus contagion continued. The number of victims dropped, but the quarantine remained.

The pressure on Dieter Schmidt from the High Command became too much for him to bear. The quarantine had caused a great deal of upheaval in the military movements of Wehrmacht troops along the Ukraine; their tanks should have been taken to Sofia for repair, the gasoline was needed, the soldiers should have been outfitted and disbursed from that point. But despite the strategic value of Sofia the Nazis dared not enter, for their fear of carrying the contagion to the front was too great.

However, there was little the Gestapo commandant could do, for the epidemic was too widespread, covered too large an area, and Sofia's doctors were trying their hardest to end the strife.

The heat of summer saw the opening of bowling lanes and the intrepid gatherings of a few Sofians. Those who had gone to the hospital in the previous months or who had been treated at home for the illness were now considered immune from the disease and could congregate in small numbers.

Every factory, every large firm that employed a sizable crew of people, owned a bowling lane. Set in a green lawn to the rear of the building, the wooden parquet alley was set up with its nine pins, its wooden bowling balls that had no holes, and its little boys who sat in small huts at the end of the lane to replace the fallen pins and shout out the scores. The Poles gathered on warm days, drank their potent beer, and challenged one another as if the only care they had in all the world was achieving the highest bowling score.

The Nazis, afraid of being contaminated, watched from a safe distance, and all that was left for Dieter Schmidt was to keep a keen watch for new Resistance activity.

The traditional Polish holidays came and went; All Saints' Day, Christmas, New Year's Day and Easter. With winter came a rise in typhus cases, all of which the Warszawa laboratory confirmed. The quarantine held. The Sofians, receiving periodic instructions from the members of Dolata's Council, continued to play their part.

It was in April of 1943, exactly one year and three months after the onset of the epidemic, that the peace ended.

The two men were enjoying a luncheon of sausage and sauerkraut and sharing a bottle of schnapps. It was so seldom they were able to get together that, when they did, they unfailingly had a good time.

Shaking his head, Fritz Müller, senior medical officer at the public health laboratory in Warszawa, said, "You lead an exciting life, my friend. And all those medals!" He shook his head and grinned admiringly at his friend's throat. Between the collar patches of rank hung the coveted Knight's Cross with Oak Leaves. "And now you command an *Einsatzgruppe!* I am impressed!"

The other man smiled modestly. The praise was, of course, flattering, but the achievements were not as laudable as the doctor claimed. "It is nice of you to say so, my old friend," he said in true humility, "but I still strive for higher honors. After all, the man who is without ambition is without life."

Dr. Müller nodded thoughtfully. "We must all continue to fight for something. As you say, what else is there?" He picked up his glass and held it over the table. "Here's to the Reich."

His friend, likewise picking up his glass, said, "To the Reich."

After the toast, they devoured a few more mouthfuls of their lunch, then the commander of the *Einsatzgruppe* said, "The way you speak of my life, Fritz, one would think that your own is very dull. After all, you are a Major in the SS, just like me."

Fritz Müller, a man in his early thirties, shrugged. "All is relative, my friend. I find laboratory work fascinating. It would probably put you to sleep. But once in a while a problem comes across my desk and I find myself embroiled in a real challenge."

"Like what?"

"Like a typhus epidemic."

The other man looked up, a dripping piece of sausage halfway to his mouth. "Oh?"

"There are always such things in these swinish countries, you know that," said Dr. Müller. "But this one requires particular notice. Never before have I encountered such a virulency. And I am thankful, believe me, that we quarantined the area when we did. Otherwise, who knows what would have happened to our troops on the eastern front if such a strain of typhus had reached them? I would estimate a thirty- to forty-percent mortality."

"Indeed!"

"Thank God we've confined it," said the doctor. "The commandant of the area has assured me that the disease will not spread beyond the limits we've imposed. But still. . . ." He cocked his head to one side and stared down at his half-eaten sausage. "It's my responsibility to see that it goes no further than that area."

"Where is this epidemic, Fritz?"

"In a region to the southeast of here. About two-thirds of the way between here and Krakow, but more toward the Ukraine. Its center is a town named Sofia."

SS-Sturmbannführer Maximilian Hartung brought his head up sharply.

CHAPTER 22

"Did you say *Sofia?*"

"Yes, why?"

"What a coincidence," said Max Hartung, his handsome face folding in a frown.

"What is it, Max?"

After another moment of thought, the striking, chiseled face of the *Sturmbannführer* brought itself back to Dr. Müller and broadened into a look of surprise. "You see, I was there just over a year ago, looking for partisans. There was no typhus there at the time."

Maximilian Hartung's voice faded again and his face took on an absent aspect, almost as if he had forgotten Müller's presence.

"Max, what is it?"

He replaced his glass with a thump, folded his hands under his chin and regarded the man opposite for another moment. Round-faced and round-eyed, Fritz Müller wore his pale blond hair cut so short to his scalp that he appeared from a scant distance to be completely bald. He was tall and lanky, but, unlike his SS friend who had won medals for his special raids and "liquidations," the physician was not what one would call an imposing man. While Max Hartung had the broad shoulders and muscular arms of one born to fight and to lead, Fritz Müller had the pale, smooth look of a man who never sees sunlight.

Although he studied his friend intently, it was none of these things that occupied Hartung's mind at the moment, for another face briefly sat opposite him across the table, and the voice that spoke to him was not that of the German-speaking doctor but the soft lilt of a young Polish woman. And she was saying, "He thought he had developed a new vaccine for typhus a while back, but he only found himself on the wrong track. If there's one thing he's determined to do, that's keep diseases like typhus out of Sofia."

She had been Maria Duszynska. *He,* Jan Szukalski.

Max Hartung dropped his eyes to his cold plate of sauerkraut. There was something else too. . . .

The last night they had spent together. He had been dozing in her bed, and he had thought she was asleep. And then, all of a sudden, she had blurted one word: typhus.

Talking in her sleep, she had said. Dreaming about a case she had seen that day. And yet such an odd way she had blurted it, almost as if it had just occurred to her. . . .

"Max?"

He brought his eyes back to the face of his long-time friend. "I'm sorry, Fritz. Sofia has been on my mind. I can't seem to put certain memories away. And now you have brought Sofia up again. Forgive me, I'm spoiling a pleasant meal."

"Forget it, Max. Let's order another bottle." Fritz raised an arm, snapped a finger at a passing waiter and gave his order for more schnapps. Then he turned back to his friend. "Who would have thought, Maxie, you a *Sturmbannführer* in the SS. And commander of an *Einsatzgruppe!* Purifying the land for the expansion of the Reich!"

Max displayed his modest smile again and waited while the waiter opened the new bottle and refilled their glasses. When the man was gone he said quietly, "It is in truth dirty work, Fritz. Shooting unarmed people into trenches. But it is necessary. The Reich cannot support subhumans. They serve no purpose. But still, where is the glory in it?"

"There are medals, Max."

"Medals, yes, but still I am only a Major in rank and haven't seen a promotion in two years."

"You want more?"

"Yes," he said quietly. "I want more."

Fritz Müller sat back in his chair and took a long draw on his drink. In the cold, predatory eyes of his friend, in the square aristocratic chin, and in the brutal handsomeness of the man, he recognized the ruthless determination that he had seen years ago in his childhood friend. All along he had known that Max Hartung would be not only a survivor, but also a leader. Just look at him in that black uniform, catching the eyes of all the ladies, walking with the pride of an eagle. And still he wants more. . . .

"Like what, Max?"

"I want *real power,* Fritz." Max leaned forward and a fire of blue ice flared in his eyes. "I want to command something more than an extermination group."

"Max—"

Hartung held up a hand. He didn't want to say any more. There were some things that he would always keep to himself, that he would never share, not even with as close a friend as Fritz Müller. Long ago, in the Hitler Youth, when the Nazis were inflaming the German people with a fresh new national pride, Maximilian Hartung had sworn himself to only one cause: the glory of the Reich and the glorification of himself. No, medals and ranks were not enough. He wanted recognition from men like Himmler and Goebbels, and even the *Führer* himself. Max Hartung had consigned himself long ago, to the exclusion of all else—even of love—to the single goal of making himself a very important man. And he had been able to, so far, move up that ladder of victory with little effort. But now he wanted more. He wanted to be *Reichsprotektor* of all Eastern Europe, and he planned to find a way to do it.

His thoughts returned to Sofia. Suddenly, another memory exploded in his brain. It was his visit to the Szukalski household more than a year ago; it had been Christmas night and Maria and he had taken some wine and pastries for a little celebration. Jan Szukalski had been coaxed to speak a little of partisanship and had, after a few Resistance words from Max, uttered the offhanded comment: "Sometimes I think I'd rather have an epidemic on my hands than this war. At least that way we could keep the Nazis out."

Max brought his focus back to Müller. "Tell me

something, Fritz. Is it possible to make an epidemic look worse than it really is?"

"I beg your pardon?"

The face of Maria Duszynska materialized fleetingly before his eyes and then just as quickly faded away. It had been easy, all these years, to sacrifice love and friendship for the attainment of his goals. Maximilian had never loved anyone. And he never would.

"Is it possible to take an area where there is typhus and make it appear to be much worse than it is?"

Fritz Müller's pale, almost transparent eyebrows rose up. "Why do you ask?"

Something else was now irritating the *SS-Sturmbann-führer*. He was recalling a report he had read just less than a year ago, the report of a Resistance group that had been found near Sofia and that had been executed by Dieter Schmidt. More than fifty people, Max now recalled, who had been plotting to blow up the munitions dump. It had infuriated Max at the time, that report, and today it infuriated him anew.

A year and a half ago Hartung had been sent to Sofia to sniff out partisan activity. He had ingratiated himself with certain key people in the town—finding his old girl friend Maria had been a stroke of luck—and had tried for several days to unearth evidence of an Underground.

But, having found nothing, Max had left Sofia under the mistaken impression that no Resistance existed there, until four months later he had read that startling report of Schmidt's brilliant success.

At the time, Hartung had been mildly rebuked by his superiors for not having uncovered those partisans and it had remained a thorny issue with him ever since.

"Just tell me, Fritz, is it possible to make the disease appear more widespread than it really is?"

"Well, I suppose so." The doctor hesitated. "I would have to think about it."

"In fact, Fritz, would it even be possible to make it appear there was an epidemic of typhus where there in fact *was not?*"

"That's an interesting question, Max. I suppose you

have some basis for posing it? All right, let me see. If I wanted to make it look as though a typhus epidemic appeared where there wasn't one, I suppose I would take serum from someone who had severe typhus, divide it up into several samples, label each with a different patient's name, then send those samples to the lab here in Warszawa for the Weil-Felix test."

Although his voice did not change, the irises of Max Hartung's eyes changed from blue slate to glowing Arctic seas. And Fritz recognized the sign; he had seen it many times before. So when his friend spoke, he listened earnestly.

"Fritz, I think there is something suspicious about the epidemic in Sofia. In fact, I don't think there is an epidemic there at all. Don't ask me why, it's just a feeling I have deep down in my tripes. I think that you and your lab are being played for fools by a bunch of Polish pigs!"

"Max. . . ." said the doctor quietly. Reaching for his glass, he drank the rest of the schnapps, slammed the glass back down on the table, and tipped his head to one side. "You can't be serious. It isn't possible."

"Why not? You yourself said—"

"I know what I myself said, Max, but you are forgetting one thing. The blood samples we are receiving from Sofia are showing extremely high titers. That is, a particularly virulent disease. If one patient's blood was being divided up into several samples, then the titers would be the same; at least many of them would be."

"Are you sure? Is there no way that could be rectified?"

Fritz felt himself held prisoner by the magnetism of Hartung. And when he said, "I suppose it can be done if someone is clever enough to take additional blood from anyone with a very high Weil-Felix titer and then—" he was not surprised that Max interrupted him with, "Then that's what they're doing!"

"Oh come now, Max, you have nothing to go by. A faked typhus epidemic? No one would be foolish enough to even attempt it. How could they expect to get away with it for long?"

"I don't know, Fritz, but I have a feeling—"

"Max," said the doctor, leaning forward with a grave expression, "it's not possible to fake an epidemic in a town of that size. And also to include the surrounding farms and villages. The people would know! There are communications. Telephones, letters. Somehow word would get out that there was no sickness in the town—"

"Unless, my friend," said Max slowly, drawing his thin mouth back in a wolfish smile, "the people are part of the hoax."

"What?" Again Müller's eyebrows shot up. He stared incredulously at his friend, his mouth open to speak.

"Would it be so difficult, Fritz? Listen, the High Command has been quite anxious for some time to find a way to clear up Sofia so the munitions and repair depot can be used again. No one has been able to come up with a solution so far, since no one has wanted to risk entering the quarantine area to investigate. Do you know what I'm going to do, Fritz? I'm going to *volunteer* to go to Sofia and try my damndest to get the troops using that installation again."

"You can't mean that! You can't enter that quarantine, Max—"

"And I want to take you with me, Fritz, because it will be your authority that will prove there is no disease in that town. We'll take lab technicians, equipment, and two companies of SS troops with some heavy artillery."

"But it's an infected area! You would expose us all to typhus!"

"No, Fritz." Max felt himself grow strangely calm. It was more than intuition that guided him now, it was *need*. The need to take revenge on the town that had made a fool of him. "We will expose them as nothing more than a nest of swinish resisters, which I am sure we will all be honored to liquidate for the Reich."

"And you intend for me to examine these filthy people?"

"No, Fritz. You won't have to look at anyone. Just take your own blood samples and test them right there.

You'll choose at random; pick several from a thousand. Jan Szukalski may be able to get a few people to pretend that they're ill, but there's no way he can make their blood look sick!"

Fritz Müller, not quite convinced, nodded uncertainly.

Suddenly filled with a comforting sense of purpose, Max Hartung sat back in his chair and smiled. He was thinking of the honors he would receive for uncovering the hoax and freeing the installation. For giving their staging area and repair depot back to them, the High Command would be very generous.

It could even take him up to the final rung of the ladder. *Reichsprotektor* of Eastern Europe.

"Dr. Szukalski?" came the timid, almost apologetic voice. "Dr. Szukalski? Excuse me?"

Jan looked up from the chart he was writing in and saw the bowed, submissive form of a hospital orderly named Bernard. "Yes, what is it?"

"May I speak with you, sir?" The old man glanced over either shoulder. "In private?"

An undertone of urgency in the man's voice brought Jan to say, "Certainly. I'll be in my office in a few minutes. Why don't you go there and make yourself comfortable."

"Yes, sir." And he ambled dutifully off.

Szukalski finished writing his orders and was walking through the door of his office exactly five minutes later. He found the old man standing nervously by the window, looking down at the sidewalk.

"What can I do for you, Bernard?" Szukalski came round his desk and took a seat.

The orderly wrung his hands as he spoke. "It's my wife, sir; she's found something and she said I should give it to you."

The panic on the man's face caused Jan to sit up. He felt himself grow tense. "What did she find, Bernard?"

"You know Nazi Headquarters, don't you, Doctor?"

"Yes, I do, Bernard."

"And you know my wife is one of the ladies who clean the place at night, you know, the offices and things like that, but she doesn't get paid for it."

"Yes, I know that, Bernard." Szukalski narrowed his eyes. The orderly's face had gone the color of a freshly peeled potato.

"Well, sir, we were told by someone about the . . . you know, sir, about the typhus."

Szukalski eyed him cautiously. "Yes, go on."

"Well, sir, it was in the trash, and my wife can read and she's, well, nosy, if you know what I mean, sir. She found this and said you should see it."

He thrust a meaty hand into the pocket of his white smock and produced a crumpled piece of yellow paper. Bernard handed it to Szukalski, quickly drawing his hand away as if it had been burnt. "She says it came off a machine."

"Yes, it did. . . ." Jan unfurled the paper between his hands and felt his eyebrows come together as he saw two lines of German. "It's called a teletype, Bernard."

"Well, my wife speaks German, you know, Doctor, because she's from Unisław. That's up in the west, you know, and when she saw this, Doctor, and thinking about what we'd been told about the typhus and all. . . ." The man's voice lost wind.

Szukalski felt his heart come to a complete standstill as he read the message:

SS-HAUPTSTURMFÜHRER DIETER SCHMIDT. SENDING CONTINGENT TO INVESTIGATE TYPHUS EPIDEMIC. WILL ARRIVE THIRTEEN MAY, 1943. GIVE FULL CO-OPERATION.

Jan read those few words over and over again and thought he was reading his own death sentence.

Bernard's humble voice drifted into his consciousness. "Everyone knows, sir, about the . . . and my wife, well, she got scared and—"

"Bernard," Szukalski was amazed at how calm his voice sounded. "Does anyone else know of this message?"

"No sir, Doctor. Just me and my wife."

"It's nothing to worry about, Bernard. There is absolutely no need to be frightened. It's just a small medical team. Just a routine check. And if any of your friends should ask you who they are, Bernard, you just tell them that they are doctors who have come to confirm the epidemic. Do you understand?"

"Yes sir, Doctor."

"Thank you, Bernard, you've been a great help."

When the orderly was gone, Szukalski lit a match and touched the corner of the yellow paper to the flame. He then dropped it into his ashtray. Watching it turn black and curl, Jan felt his mind race in all directions at once.

The inspection team would be here in two days.

Dieter Schmidt was elated at the thought of the important visitors coming to Sofia. And their purpose was even more heartening. In a year and a half, Schmidt had been powerless against the disease, and yet the High Command had continued to send their useless orders to free the installation.

Well! Now they were coming, and this nightmare would be brought to an end!

The brittle light from the naked bulbs that swung like party lanterns from the vaulted ceiling created eerie shadows on the stone walls. The five conspirators sat in a tight circle in the damp burial crypt of Saint Ambroż. Father Wajda, the last to arrive, settled himself into his folding chair and looked up at Jan Szukalski.

Szukalski cleared his throat and said quietly, "We have had seventeen months of good luck, my friends. No one of us can deny that we have been successful in what we had set out to accomplish. While Hitler's Final Solution continues to transport 'undesirables' to the death camps, the people of Sofia have lived in relative freedom. Now, however, it seems our luck has run out.

"I will admit to you, my friends," he went on, looking from face to face as he spoke, "that when I first read that teletype message my impulse was to take my family and run. The Germans will come tomorrow and find a clean town, discover that they have been hoaxed all this time, and then our lives will be worthless."

"Then why not run?" came Anna's small voice.

"There will be no running for us," said Maria, the halo of her hair and whiteness of her face making her appear like a ghost that dwelt in the crypt. "We have made it seem that the worst typhus epidemic ever to strike central Poland is raging right here in Sofia. If we run, the Germans will know at once that it was a hoax and they'll probably kill every single person in the town as retribution. But if we stay," she spread out her slender, white hands, "then we can hope the Nazis will be satisfied with punishing just us."

Jan Szukalski nodded down at her, his eyes full of admiration of her courage. But he could also see the patent fear on her face.

Anna, holding firmly onto Kepler's hand, spoke again. "But they wouldn't wipe out an entire town, would they? I mean, the *whole town?*"

The priest spoke up. "You have all heard of a man named Reinhard Heydrich, the man who once was Himmler's deputy and right hand. He was assassinated in June of last year in the streets of Prague by men who were believed to have come from the nearby village of Lidice. In retaliation, the SS forces swooped down and razed Lidice to the ground, killed all the men, dragged the women off to concentration camps, and distributed the children to *Lebensborn* families. That was a year ago. To this day, there remains no sign of the town that once stood on that spot."

"Oh my God. . . ."

"Maria is right," said Jan. "We have to stay. To pick up now and run would alert the Germans to something they might not yet know."

"What do you mean?"

"I mean they might not suspect a fake epidemic. After all, there was no mention of that on the message. They might not be coming here to investigate us at all. Remember, with the sealing of this whole area that munitions installation was also rendered inoperative. I'll wager they're coming here to see what can be done to free it up."

"All right. But what if, Jan," said Father Wajda, "they have somehow gotten on to the hoax?"

"Piotr, if the Germans suspect a staged epidemic, then they'll think we're doing it by dividing up blood samples from real typhus cases and putting other people's names on them. They don't know about Proteus, I'm sure of that. They are probably coming here fully intending to avoid the real typhus victims and draw blood from random cases and expect to come up with a lot of negative findings."

"But what if," said Kepler, "they *do* know about Proteus?"

"The only way they could know about our vaccine is if someone let the secret out by one means or another. And that I doubt, since everyone in Sofia still carries the memory of the partisans' execution in the town square. Our secret is safe, I'm certain."

"But if by some chance," said the priest, "the secret has gotten out, then we have no hope at all."

"Then we should run," said Anna again.

Dr. Szukalski shook his head. "We can't. We have a responsibility to this town now. We have involved them in something for which we alone must take the blame. We can't abandon them now, not after considering what happened to Lidice. What we can hope for is, if the Germans do indeed uncover our hoax, that they will take their anger out on just us five and let the town go."

"What about Dolata and his Council?" asked Father Wajda.

"I never gave anyone of them the details of our operation. They knew only that we had found a way to confuse the lab tests. If Edmund Dolata is questioned, he can't give the Germans any vital information."

Anna looked up at him with large, frightened eyes. "What are we going to do?"

Jan Szukalski measured the faces before him, marveling at their courage and wanting to do more for them than offer a bit of frail hope. Yet all he could do was say, "We are going to go along with the investigation as if we had nothing to fear. We are going to give the delegation our full cooperation."

"But how—"

He held up a silencing hand, and his eyes blazed up for a moment. "For what it is worth, my friends, I have a plan."

CHAPTER 23

Maximilian Hartung, *SS-Sturmbannführer,* had managed to assemble only fifty men for his inspection of Sofia, but he was not deterred; the new Panther tanks which had been rolling toward Lublin had been rerouted for Hartung's assignment, and it was these, more than the soldiers, that he had been counting heavily upon. For it was Hartung's plan, once the epidemic was exposed as a hoax, to use the tanks' new L/70 75 mm guns to raze the town of Sofia to the ground.

Dr. Fritz Müller faced the undertaking with considerably less determination. In fact, of the entire entourage, including the four other doctors and two lab technicians who were to conduct the examinations and tests and who now rode behind Hartung and Müller in open-topped cars, only Fritz Müller maintained his initial reservations about the wisdom of their task.

Three large military trucks followed the cars, pulling field guns and carrying the *Einsatzgruppe* troops, all of whom had served Max Hartung in the past and who now had complete and blind confidence in their leader; and were just as certain as he was that no typhus existed in the town and that a day of glory and spoils lay ahead of them.

Hartung had the charismatic ability to convince anyone of almost anything so that when he had approached his superiors with his suspicions, he had quickly received permission to first investigate, and then, if necessary, demolish the area. He had also secured, before embarking on his mission, their solemn promise to give full credit and recognition to him once the partisans were exposed.

Only one man was not totally convinced, and that man rode next to him in the automobile.

"I am still uneasy about this, Max, I must tell you." Dr. Fritz Müller, squinting at the bright countryside and at the occasional flashes of sunlight on the Wisła River, spoke quietly enough so that only his companion could hear. "You still have no evidence. You're going on a hunch."

"Yes, I am. But then, I am rarely wrong. And think of what you are doing for the Reich. Our superiors are quite pleased with us for coming up with a solution to give their munitions and repair depot back to the Wehrmacht. Think of the honor!"

"I know, Max, I know. But still . . . to risk unnecessary exposure to a disease like that. There's not a man among us who has any kind of immunity."

In response, Max only laughed.

The tanks had preceded the delegation by half an hour so that by the time Hartung's parade entered the town, the ten Panthers were already situated before the town square, their massive guns aimed directly at the church. The open-topped cars rolled up in front of Nazi Headquarters while the three transport trucks took up places behind the tanks.

It was a lazy, honey-sweet summer morning but few Sofians were out on this sad occasion, for word had rapidly spread the day before of the approaching delegation, and the townspeople remained indoors, peering in fear through their curtains. They had also heard of the fate of the Warszawa Ghetto.

Dieter Schmidt, standing at rigid attention on the steps of his headquarters, saluted his distinguished visitors with the Party salute. Returning it, *SS-Sturmbannführer* Hartung then introduced the commandant to the rest of the people in his group. Everything was polite, reserved and, Schmidt noted uneasily, extremely stilted.

Dr. Szukalski and Dr. Duszynska, having been summoned earlier that morning, were sitting in a room off to the side of Schmidt's office, their eyes fixed apprehensively on the door. Slightly ajar, it allowed them to see, one by one, the entry of the lofty guests, and when, slightly above the heads of all the others, one man was clearly visible, Maria gave a strangled cry.

"What is it?" whispered Szukalski, trying to see, in the small crowd, what had startled her.

"I don't believe it. . . ." she breathed, her hands fluttering to her breast.

Standing several inches above the shaven head of stocky Dieter Schmidt, his own head bare after having removed his hat, was Maximilian Hartung.

"Jan. . . ." Maria started to rise, her voice tremulous. *"Oh, Jan. . . ."*

"What is it?" He took a step toward the door and saw in the next instant the face of the man she beheld. "Why it's—"

"Max," she whispered hoarsely. Maria groped for Szukalski's hand and squeezed it. "Oh Jan, he's come with them! He's one of the group!" She turned her face to him, her eyes welling with tears and confusion.

Her dream of reuniting with her lover suddenly turned into a nightmare.

The crowd parted slightly and both doctors saw at the same time the black uniform Hartung wore.

Sudden and complete comprehension dawning on her, Maria spun about and collapsed onto the wooden bench, her throat giving out a strangely animal sound.

"Oh my God," murmured Jan Szukalski, still staring at the SS Major. "Sweet crucified Jesus, *he's one of them.*" He turned to look down at Duszynska. "Maria—"

But she couldn't hear him. She sat frozen on the bench, her face as white as marble, her mouth slightly open, her eyes staring like those of a doll.

"Maria," he said gently, sitting next to her and taking a hand. "We don't know for sure. He might be here to help us."

Although her body was rigid and her face like that of a corpse, she was still able to speak. "No, Jan. That uniform. I understand it all now. For the past seventeen months I've been writing to him and wondering why I never heard from him. And back at the university, when he suddenly disappeared without a word, showing up two years later with no notice. I understand it now. He *is* one of them. Oh Jan . . . he's one of *them*."

She would have liked to cry just then but was not given the chance. The door came all the way open and in it stood the magnificent, defiant Maximilian Hartung.

As they peered through a second-story window of the hospital, Father Wajda and Anna Krasinska could just barely see the front steps of Nazi Headquarters. It was very important to their plan that they see the German delegation as soon as it emerged from the building.

"If you would like to get the medication ready," said the priest, "I'll keep watch."

Anna nodded and turned away. Being the sole nurse on duty in the typhus ward at this hour, she was able to work in relative ease, unencumbered by shaking hands which she had been afraid might afflict her. For the task at hand, Anna needed steadiness.

Twenty milligrams of morphine sulfate to be drawn up into seven separate syringes, and then lined up in a towel ready for quick administration.

Twenty milligrams, a hefty dose, was not enough to be lethal but was enough to make an adult appear extremely obtunded.

As she worked she went over the checklist once more in her mind. The bed linen had not been changed in two days. The bedpans were all full and either sitting on the side tables or on the floor. Laundry hampers were full and overflowing with stained sheets. And the linoleum floor had been left unattended for two days, looking deplorable for a hospital usually clean and spotless.

It was an unholy sight, and the place smelled ghastly. Anna was satisfied. It was exactly the way she wanted it.

At the window, Father Wajda continued to watch, ready to move at the signal.

Barely a moment later, Hartung was joined in the doorway by a red-faced, blustering Schmidt. Without ceremony he blurted, "Szukalski! These men tell me that you have perpetrated a hoax! They say there is no typhus in this town! Is that correct? Goddammit, is that correct?"

Szukalski remained calm. His voice was steady and controlled. "I believe they are mistaken, *Herr Hauptsturmführer.*"

"Mistaken!" The commandant burst into the room and made as if to lunge at the doctor, but Hartung got in his way.

"Herr Hauptsturmführer," said Max with a smile, "the swine are obviously lying. They have to in a last effort to save their worthless skins. Now I suggest we approach this problem the way men of the SS are supposed to. Shall we?"

Schmidt first glared up at Hartung in undisguised hatred, and then flashed his furious gaze at Szukalski. For that one moment, Jan was glad Hartung was there.

The two officers were followed into the room by a third, pale-haired man who also wore a black SS uniform. Hartung made polite introductions and then all five of them took seats, with Schmidt kicking the door closed behind him. They faced one another guardedly.

"Dr. Szukalski," said Max nasally, "it is all over."

"What is all over?"

"Your typhus epidemic."

"Oh? Have you brought us a cure? Some DDT perhaps?"

"You know goddamn well what—" snarled Schmidt, who was once again silenced by the *Einsatzgruppe* commander.

Max turned his hard cold gaze to Maria and dragged the corners of his mouth up into a smile. "It was you who first gave me the idea, *liebchen,* when you spoke your few reckless words about typhus. And then you, *Herr Doktor,*" he turned to Szukalski, "words of an epidemic to keep the Nazis out. Christmas night. Do you remember?"

Maria remained silent. Since the moment of seeing him and realizing what he truly was, Maria had searched her memory for anything that might tell her why he was involved in this. And she had come up with their evening together at the White Eagle, and later, their last night in her bed. But Duszynska's memory was excellent. Neither she nor Szukalski, she was certain, had accidentally disclosed any important details to Hartung. The secret of Proteus was still safe.

"Anyway," said Max in amusement, enjoying the shock and pain on her face, "you can tell us all about it now, or you can make it very hard on yourselves."

"There is nothing to tell, *Herr Sturmbannführer,*" said Szukalski. His relaxed and confident manner made Dr. Müller shift uneasily in his chair. "You have arrived in the middle of the worst typhus epidemic I have ever seen. I hope that you are immune."

Hartung sneered. "You don't frighten us, pig."

"May I say something?"

Everyone turned to regard Fritz Müller. "You know me, don't you, Dr. Szukalski, Dr. Duszynska?"

"Of course we do, *Herr Doktor.* Your name has been on many of our test results. It's a pleasure to meet you."

"We have been told, *Herr Doktor,* that you do not have a real epidemic of typhus here in Sofia, but that you have been falsifying blood samples. Is that true?"

"How do you mean, falsifying?"

"By taking blood from a typhus victim and dividing it up into several samples, putting on them the names of healthy people."

Now Szukalski allowed himself a look of righteous indignation. "I beg your pardon, *Herr Doktor,* but I do not falsify records. Nor do I invent disease where none exists. You say you have brought other doctors with you. And lab technicians and equipment. May I make a suggestion? Let us go over to the hospital right now and I will show you typhus. I will show you my records." Szukalski permitted his voice to rise. "And I will show you that I have nothing whatsoever to hide. And if that is not enough, gentlemen, then you may choose a village or villages at random and we will all visit typhus victims together. You may examine anyone you wish and draw as many blood samples as will suit you. The hospital laboratory is at your disposal. You will see for yourselves the extent of our epidemic."

Müller cast a nervous glance at Hartung.

"Bluffing," said Max with his same smile. "Let's do just what he says. We'll visit his hospital and go to some farm or village, and I will show you gentlemen that this man is only bluffing."

He aimed his penetrating gaze at the immovable face of Szukalski and attempted, by sheer force of his predator's eyes, to disintegrate the smug exterior of the man.

But Szukalski was not to be daunted. Matching the *Einsatzgruppe* commander's stony gaze, he rose to his feet and said almost flippantly, "Shall we go then, gentlemen?"

Father Wajda watched intently as Jan Szukalski, the last of the group to exit Nazi Headquarters, stopped on the top step to pause and scratch his head. The priest murmured, "All right, Anna, there's the signal. They're on their way to the hospital."

Between the two of them they administered the morphine to seven selected patients.

It had been Szukalski's idea that they walk, and everyone was just as glad to have the opportunity to be out in the fresh air and sunshine. As the impressive group strolled down the quiet street, the troops in the tanks and leaning against the trucks laughed and murmured among themselves, many of them making wagers as to the length of time it would take to obliterate the town.

Szukalski, barely limping at all and at the head of the group of thirteen, kept up a constant banter with the doctors at his side, asking professional questions, and keeping up a perfect show of confidence. He stretched out the time in order to give the morphine a chance to work by pointing out the interesting architecture of Saint Ambroż, remarking on the quaintness of Sofia's cobblestone streets, and telling an amusing anecdote about the installation of the equestrian statue of Kosciuszko in the center of the town square.

As her colleague kept a small segment of the party involved, Maria Duszynska let her step fall back until she was even with Max, and after they had gone the length of a block, she said casually, "I see you have a new suit, *Herr Sturmbannführer*. Is this how the well-dressed Danzig businessman looks these days?"

"It is how the well-dressed Danzig businessman has dressed for the past three years, my dear Doctor."

"Very impressive, I must say. You remind me of a bantam cock. Although I don't recall you strutted quite so much."

"Take care, *liebchen*, I have no private war with you. This uniform and the Reich are my life. You were just a stepping stone."

"My memory fails me, *Herr Sturmbannführer*. I seem to recall that the last night we spent together in my bedroom you did more than *step on me*."

Hartung gave out a laugh. "You are not the first, *liebchen*, nor will you be the last. And as a matter of fact, you weren't the only one in Sofia the four days I was here."

Had he struck her, the blow would not have been as painful. Trying not to falter in her step, Maria kept her shoulders back and her chin tipped up. "You were very busy then, weren't you?"

"More so than you think. Do you remember the gypsy?"

Maria stopped short. "What?"

Taking hold of her arm, not gently, Max said, "Let's not hold up the group, shall we? Please keep walking, Doctor. I'll tell you about the gypsy. His story was true. All of it. And it was my group that exterminated his people. When you mentioned to me that one of them had escaped and was telling his story to everyone, I had to do something about it, didn't I?"

Maria forced her eyes forward, concentrating on the back of the lab technician who walked directly ahead of her. "What did you do?" she heard herself ask.

"I found a way to get into the hospital that night—remember when I went off for some champagne?—and then I sneaked into the ward and suffocated the man with his pillow. It was a good thing, too, for he recognized me."

"I see. . . ."

From here they continued to the hospital in silence. Dr. Szukalski glanced at his watch as they all stepped through the main entrance. He had managed to drag the walk out to fifteen minutes, more than enough time for the morphine to take effect.

He showed the inspection team first the crowded ground floor where the usual hospital cases lay separated from the contagious patients upstairs. Next they saw the kitchen and the laboratory.

He said, "I certainly admire your courage, gentlemen, coming into an epidemic area as you are. Merely on a suspicion. I assume you are all typhus-immune."

The doctors, for the past ten minutes extremely silent, answered him weakly, one by one. "I'm not."

"Nor I."

"Nor I."

He took a moment to regard them with elevated eyebrows. "Is this true? Then I am doubly impressed, gentlemen. I realize that you have your suspicions, but to expose yourselves to typhus merely to prove a point seems a little reckless to me."

Everyone looked at Max Hartung. His face remained impassive.

"Very well, then," said Szukalski. "Now I will show you the worst cases of typhus we have. Because of the epidemic we treat people in their homes; there just isn't enough hospital space. But these require constant care. Now, since it is foolish to expose all of you to the contagion, why don't you choose from among you someone to accompany me, and he can draw the blood samples for your lab tests?"

"It is a bluff," said Hartung. "We'll all go."

Müller, silent since leaving headquarters, spoke up. "It may be a bluff, Max, but I don't want to expose all my people to possible typhus just to prove your point. Two will be sufficient. Dr. Kraus, will you come with me? And you also," he said, pointing to one of the lab technicians. "The rest can stay here."

As the group ascended the stairs to the isolated ward, Father Wajda, having heard their approach, deliberately spilled a urinal on the floor.

Before they reached the top of the stairs Szukalski said, "Now I must warn you. Because of deaths due to the epidemic, our hospital has been sadly short-staffed. It is only because Dr. Duszynska and I have had typhus in the past that we are immune. Ah, here we are."

The entourage came to the top of the stairs and were at once visibly struck by the stench in the air. The first sight to meet their eyes, as they entered the ward, were the obtunded bodies breathing laboriously beneath soiled sheets, and the weary bent figure of a priest administering last rites to a hopeless patient.

"Be careful where you step," said Szukalski.

Slowly the six—Maria and Jan, Müller and his two assistants, and lastly Hartung, who had insisted upon coming along—moved between the two rows of beds.

Szukalski said, "Choose any patient you wish, Dr. Müller, and I will draw back the bedclothes for you to examine him. You will not want to touch the patient, of course, or come too close as it has not been possible to get rid of all the lice."

They pointed to one man, and when the bed sheets were drawn back, the two German doctors could not mask their dismay. Before them, on the moribund body of this poor victim, was the classic rash of typhus fever. Seeing their expressions, Szukalski made a brief mental prayer: Thank God for trichloracetic acid.

They proceeded to the next patient. This one was almost comatose, with ashen skin, and perspiring heavily.

In a voice unlike his own, Müller said to the technician, "Draw blood from this one, that one, and those five there. Now let's get out of this cesspool."

As they regrouped outside the hospital, breathing deeply of the warm summer air, Szukalski said, "Would you gentlemen like to visit one of our villages now? The choice is, of course, up to you."

All the visitors but one agreed they should go. Only Müller was silent.

Feeling his anger rise but not wishing to show it, he avoided looking at Hartung for fear he would lose his control. Reluctantly, he produced a little notebook from his coat pocket. Then he took a deep breath and said, "Our records show that you have an extremely high concentration of typhus in the region of a village called Slavsko."

Szukalski could not help but smile. "I see you have kept accurate statistics on our reports."

"You must understand, *Herr Doktor,* that as employees of the German central health labs, it is our business to keep track of the spread of disease. We kept such records on this area long before *Herr Sturmbannführer* informed us of his suspicions. We wish to go to Slavsko."

"Very well." Szukalski turned on his heel and led the way back to Nazi Headquarters, risking as he did so a quick glance up at the second-story window. This was his signal that the next part of their plan was to be put to work.

The choice of Slavsko was a good one and it pleased Szukalski. He knew that the delegation would not have let him choose a village, since they would have suspected him of "setting it up." But Slavsko was a particularly dirty, poverty-stricken village, and would certainly be an excellent backdrop against which to play his charade.

As they went down the steps, Müller left instructions with one of his own lab technicians to remain behind at the hospital and run stat tests on the blood samples just drawn from the typhus patients. Then he hurried to catch up with the rest of the group.

Having seen, from his place at the window, Jan Szukalski's signal, Father Wajda at once left the hospital by the rear door, and hurried off in the direction of the White Eagle.

The German lab technician cleared a working space for himself and set up his own rack of test tubes, being careful to measure the proper amount of saline into each. Fortunately he knew the trick of using tuberculin syringes and spinal needles so that the tedious measurement with pipettes was eliminated, thus speeding up his work. He quickly diluted the serum and saline and then added the small volume of Proteus X-19 suspension as the antigen.

He shook his head a moment later as he saw, half in wonder and half in irritation, all of the tubes from the 1:20 out to the 1:1280 dilutions show the classic settling out and clumping of the bacterial suspension.

"Donnerwetter!" he muttered in disbelief. "Positive to the highest dilution!"

Writing the results in his notebook and then cleaning up after himself and gathering his pieces of equipment into the carrying case, the German technician hastily departed from Sofia's hospital and headed for Nazi Headquarters as fast as his nervous legs would carry him.

The rotund owner of the White Eagle, having been told that Father Wajda wanted to see him, emerged from the steamy kitchen with a linen apron tied beneath his fat breasts. Wiping his greasy hands down the linen which was stained with pork blood and cabbage juice, he said, "Good day, Father. Have you come to bless my premises? I hope so; business hasn't been so good since the sickness."

Wajda removed his four-cornered hat and greeted the man with a handshake. They had known one another for twenty years. He had married this man and had performed baptisms and first Holy Communion for all his children. "Bolisław," he began quietly, looking around the empty hotel lobby; at this hour of the day little traffic was about, "I've come to ask you a favor."

"Me?" The man's porcine eyes grew big. "You want to ask a favor of *me?*" He belched out a great belly laugh. "After all these years of confessions—Bless me, Father, for I have sinned—you come to me. . . ." The innkeeper's voice drifted away when he saw the serious set of the priest's face.

"It's something only you can do, Bolisław," said Wajda quietly. "I need your help."

The fat man adopted the same serious attitude and

placed a hand on his sweaty chest. "Of course, Father. Anything you say. You know that. But first can I tell you something, Father? You look like you could use a glass of wine."

Now Piotr allowed himself the barest jerk of a smile. And he said softly, sadly, "What I need, Bolisław, is a banquet."

The car in front was ominously quiet, and it set the mood for those which followed. Since Hartung, Müller, and Szukalski had not uttered a single word from the moment they had left Nazi Headquarters, neither did any of the others following behind dare to speak. This was to be the moment of truth. What they had seen in the hospital could easily have been part of the hoax the *Sturmbannführer* had spoken of. But out here, in a village which Dr. Müller himself had chosen, they would see the real proof.

Father Wajda assumed something close to a military gait as he approached the man who appeared to be the commander of the Panther tank group lined up in front of the square. The priest lifted his face now and then to the hot, white sky, and appeared to be out for nothing more than a constitutional walk.

When, however, he sidled up to the Panther commander and greeted him with a disarming grin, a few of the soldiers felt their hands automatically reach for their guns.

"*Guten Tag, Herr Hauptmann,*" he called out in his perfect German.

The Captain turned to his aide and muttered, "Now what in hell do you suppose he wants?"

The *Unterfeldwebel,* who had joined his Captain for a cigarette while they awaited the return of *Sturmbannführer* Hartung, said with a snort, "Probably wants to know why you missed church last Sunday!"

The *Hauptmann,* grinding out his cigarette with his boot, stood up from the gray wall of the tank he had been leaning against and barked, "What do you want?"

"It's a beautiful day, isn't it, *Herr Hauptmann?*"

The two Germans exchanged glances.

"What I mean is, *Herr Hauptmann,* that it's such a shame for you all to be restricted to your vehicles like this. The sun is shining, God is smiling on all of us, and today is a holiday."

The tank Captain eyed the priest suspiciously. "What are you talking about?"

"What I am talking about, *Herr Hauptmann,* is the fact that I feel sorry for all of you. Oh yes, I'm a Pole and you are Nazis. But I am, after all, a man of the cloth. God is my ultimate superior. I take orders only from Him. Do you know what I mean?" He gave them his biggest grin. "The people of Sofia will be having a picnic today in the park by the church. Over there." He pointed over the men's shoulders and they both turned, squinting in the summer sunshine at the grassy lawn attached to Saint Ambroż. A team of Poles was setting up long wooden tables while women were busily spreading out table cloths and setting out plates. A wagon was pulling up loaded with steaming pots and brass urns. "What I have come to say, gentlemen, is that you are all invited."

The German Captain turned back to the priest and eyed him again with suspicion. He growled, "So we can all leave and then you can sabotage our vehicles?"

"Really, *Herr Hauptmann,* you disappoint me. I merely feel sorry for you. I am extending this invitation of my own volition. No one else is involved, I assure you. I just hate to see men standing around for hours without food. And we have so much—more than we can possibly eat. And you see, we'll be over there eating, right in front of your eyes, and here you are . . . well, you see how it would bother me, *Herr Hauptmann.*"

"You know why we're here, don't you?"

"Yes, I do, but I don't hold it against you. After all, you are acting under orders, aren't you? It's just that, as a priest, I cannot bear to be enjoying good food and schnapps and vodka in plenty while all of you must stand here and watch. It goes against my sense of humanity. I would like to have you join us, as my guests. And there will be pretty girls there, too, *Herr Hauptmann.*"

The Captain looked at his aide. "Is he serious?" he asked, jerking a rude thumb at the priest.

The aide shrugged his shoulders. "Sounds kind of nice to me, *Herr Hauptmann*. Schnapps and girls and who knows when the *Sturmbannführer* will be back."

"Well," said Wajda carelessly, "I was only extending the invitation. It's up to you, of course. You can send a few of your men, if you like, or send them in shifts. You will be able to see your tanks from over there. Or just yourself can come, *Herr Hauptmann*. It will be a long, hot day, and a boring one, I'll wager. Over there in the park, under the trees, we'll be having music and vodka and potato pancakes and fried sausage and hot bread with butter. Unless, of course, you're afraid of the typhus."

The Captain let out a dry laugh. "There is no typhus in this town, Father, that's why I'm here. What do you think these tanks are here for? To take blood samples? *Sturmbannführer* Hartung has assured us there is no disease in this town and that by tonight we'll be able to raze every building down to powder. What do you think of that, Father?"

Wajda shrugged, still smiling. "That is all in the hands of God. For today, we have a holiday here in Sofia and the people would be most willing to have you join them."

But the *Hauptmann* said only, "We're not the fools you take us for."

As the three-car caravan rolled into the village of Slavsko the doctors all looked at one another in disgust. Their first view of the place told them that this village must be one of the poorest and dirtiest they could have chosen.

And the ride from Sofia had been no more pleasant. Bouncing over potholed country lanes and through puddles left by the spring rains, they had at times become mired down in the mud, and the entire party had had to push and heave the cars free.

With mud covering their boots and clothing, the esteemed visitors were less than relieved to find Slavsko at the end of their journey.

A cluster of lime and straw bungalows with thatched roofs, Slavsko was no more than a medieval hamlet situated at the locus of about fifty farms. The peasants stood dumbly in the shade as the cars drove up, and chickens and mules had to be honked out of the way.

Szukalski said, "Do you want to pick randomly from the list of typhus victims or do you want me to save you the time and point out who has had the disease in the last few months?"

Dr. Müller adjusted his glasses and attempted to wipe off some of the mud from his uniform but only succeeded, to his annoyance, in rubbing it deeper into the fabric. "By all means, *Herr Doktor,* point them out to us. We'll draw blood and run Weil-Felix tests back at the hospital. As far as I'm concerned, this is an exercise in futility, but we must satisfy *Sturmbann-führer* Hartung. This is really his enterprise."

"Very well, then. I suggest we begin with that family over there." He pointed to his right and all heads turned. A rude dwelling rose out of a muddy field, its only sign of life the stream of smoke curling up from the chimney. "The whole family had typhus two months ago and one old uncle died of it. I am sure they are still Weil-Felix positive."

Szukalski stepped down into the mud, and as the others did so, they cast wary glances at one another. Max Hartung, firm in his belief that no disease existed here and that the hoax was soon to be exposed, was the first to march toward the hut.

Presently they were all gathered before the door, and as Szukalski knocked, again the German doctors exchanged glances. With each passing minute, their uneasiness increased.

A toothless old woman opened the door and grinned at once to see Dr. Szukalski. She immediately fell into a heavy country dialect of Polish that the Germans didn't understand, and which Szukalski right away translated. "She says that her son, to whom I administered protein therapy, is still very ill with typhus. But, of course, gentlemen, you will want to see for yourselves."

He removed his hat and ducked his head to step

through the door, explaining to the old woman as he did that these distinguished men would like to have a look at her son. And as the Germans stepped cautiously, one by one, over the dirt threshold, Szukalski said over his shoulder casually, "Be careful here, gentlemen, lice are frequently found in the cracks and thatching of these old shacks."

At once the doctors grouped closer together.

It was a room not unlike that of the Wilks farm— dirt floor, limestone walls, cooking pot over the fire— except there were fewer windows and no loft. This was a simple hut, inhabited by the old woman, her son, and two older male cousins. They slept in a corner, four in a row, on the same pile of straw. The only furniture was a roughly hewn table and one chair. Hanging from the ceiling was a smoked ham around which buzzed a few flies.

Szukalski and his party took up the entire room standing over the recumbent man on the hay.

Müller ordered the technician to draw some blood, a task the man gingerly and hastily performed, while one of the other doctors did as brief a physical examination of the patient as he could.

Meanwhile, in painful silence, Müller shifted his gaze from Szukalski to Hartung, back to Szukalski again. Seeing the unreadable faces of both men, he began to wonder just what was really going on here.

They all breathed deeply and with great relief as they stepped outside, and as Szukalski thanked the woman and closed the door behind him, Müller could not stop himself from blurting out, "My God, what squalor!"

Szukalski raised his eyebrows. "And what did you expect, *Herr Doktor?* This is a rural area. The people are savagely poor. Now you see what a public health problem we have here. Is it any wonder we have such a typhus epidemic?"

Müller's eyes flickered to Hartung. The SS man's facade of silence was beginning to raise his anger to the boiling point. Turning to the doctor who had performed the cursory examination, Müller said, "What is your opinion?"

He shrugged. "That is hard to say, *Herr Doktor*. The

man is definitely suffering from a serious illness. And his symptoms could be those of typhus. But to tell you the truth, I didn't want to get too close. . . ."

"Yes, I understand. The blood tests are really all we need, Dr. Kraus. The physical exams are really only a formality." He turned to Szukalski. "Shall we continue, *Herr Doktor?*"

"Whatever you wish. However, I must caution you that you are taking great risks being here."

"But *Sturmbannführer* Hartung assured me that there is no typhus and that we are safe."

Szukalski smiled. "Very well then, gentlemen. Shall we proceed?"

After the second hut proved to be as squalid as the first, Müller delegated only one doctor and a technician to accompany Szukalski into the others, and the rest of the group remained outside beneath the curious gaze of the villagers. A disquieting silence hung over the village. When the breeze shifted, the odor of human excrement and urine filled the air, and the doctors knew that the source of it was not far away. They could see garbage piled against the rear walls of several huts, where grunting pigs now foraged. The filth and the poverty of the hamlet became increasingly intolerable to the fastidious Germans who, when Szukalski emerged from the last dwelling, were more than anxious to leave the area.

In the whole time, Hartung had said not one word.

"Would you care to see more, gentlemen?" asked Szukalski as they walked toward the cars.

Müller looked at the displeased faces of his colleagues and said, "Are all the villages like this one?"

"I can take you to a hundred exactly like it. Oh, watch your step, Dr. Müller." Szukalski took the doctor's arm and steered him around a trench dug for drainage. "I only want you to satisfy yourselves that I am most assuredly not faking a typhus epidemic here. You are welcome to draw as many samples of blood from as many villages as you please."

Hartung, striding ahead of the group, had not heard Szukalski's warning about the drainage and so landed a heavy step right into the slop—a bog created by run-off from a nearby hog pen. He lost his footing, and fell backwards. Although able to keep himself from plunging totally into the mire, he could not save his coat and hands from the gooey combination of mud and pig feces.

As the *Sturmbannführer* quickly collected himself and looked about for somewhere to wipe off his hands, Szukalski turned abruptly about and said, "I must recommend, Dr. Müller, that you clean your clothes thoroughly when we return to Sofia. I cannot emphasize the degree of contamination you have been exposed to here. I need not point out the obvious to you gentlemen, that even breathing the dust in one of these cottages will occasionally result in typhus."

As Szukalski turned to climb into the first car and the others followed suit in the cars behind, Fritz Müller glared at Hartung, who was wiping his hands on some straw, and said quietly, "I cannot believe I let you talk me into this."

But the SS man was unperturbed. Calmly drawing his mucky fingers through the hay as if it were a dinner napkin, he said confidently, "There is no typhus here, Fritz, and we will soon have an end to this masquerade. Szukalski will bluff to the end. He's a stubborn, cunning man, he will fight to the last, even though he knows he's beaten. I also believe he's stalling for time, trying to think of some way out of this. He knows that once the blood tests are run and that they have negative results, my tanks will raze his precious town to the ground. It is an interesting game; I would expect him to play it no other way."

Before stepping up into the car, Müller regarded his friend in deadly earnest. Then, in a casual tone, Dr. Müller said, "Max, would you mind if I didn't ride back to Sofia in the lead car with you? I'm afraid you smell like pig shit."

The convoy arrived back in Sofia one hour later. When they drove up to Nazi Headquarters, they couldn't believe the sight that met their eyes.

CHAPTER 24

The feast had reached festival proportions.

Long tables covered with brightly colored cloths were laden with a great show of food, most of which had been brought by townspeople to supplement what was provided by the White Eagle. Women served and men helped themselves to platefuls of steaming vegetables, sweet ham, boiled potatoes, sauerkraut, sausages, hot thick soups, and mounds of fresh bread. The vodka and beer were flowing, and accordions and violins had appeared to add music to the festivities. The small green park off to the left of Saint Ambroż was alive and noisy with Sofians of all ages, laughing and eating, children and dogs romping on the grass, and everywhere, intermingled with the peasantry, were the Nazi soldiers who were under the command of *SS-Sturmbannführer* Maximilian Hartung.

The doctors, the technician, and Hartung himself all sat gaping in disbelief at the spectacle. By the time one of them thought to react, the lab technician who had stayed behind came running down the steps.

"Herr Doktor!" he called breathlessly, running to the second car where Fritz Müller sat gawking at the picnickers. *"Herr Doktor!* Here are the results of the hospital patients. All of the serum tests are strongly positive. Every last one of them. I didn't even bother to run them through the water bath, and they sure as hell don't need overnight refrigeration. There was immediate clumping. There's no doubt, *Herr Doktor,* that everyone we tested in the hospital has typhus."

His voice and face visibly controlled, Müller said evenly, "We have twenty more specimens. Take them over to the hospital and run tests at once. I want the two of you to work at the same time as quickly as you can, and then report to me back here."

"Yes, *Herr Doktor!*" Together the technicians hurried off down the street.

Müller stepped down to the sidewalk and walked stiffly to Hartung. "Those seven cases were positive," he said in a restrained voice. "All positive."

The *Sturmbannführer* barely heard his friend's words. His piercing eyes were fixed on the spectacle in the city park. He said calmly, quietly, "I am not surprised. Szukalski expected you to examine them. It is only reasonable to expect he would put the real typhus cases in the hospital. I assure you, Fritz, there is no way he can stage his hoax in all the villages and farms of this area. In a few minutes you will see that I have been right."

Müller glanced over at Szukalski who was engaged in idle talk with one of the other doctors. "He doesn't look troubled, Max. In fact, he looks quite confident. I'm worried. I don't like this. That village was incredible! Truly I can't believe I allowed myself to be led into such filth!"

Müller's face, drawn tight, turned in the direction Hartung was staring and, seeing the partying soldiers, hissed, "And just what the hell is *that* all about!"

"Excuse me a moment, Fritz," said Hartung quietly. "I'll go and see."

Dr. Müller felt every muscle and nerve in his body stretch to their limits as he watched the tall and arrogant form of Max Hartung stride across the street and over to where the tanks stood empty except for a few guards. When he heard a voice behind him he spun around.

It was Dieter Schmidt. "Well, *Herr Doktor?* What is your finding? Do we have a fat prize for the Reich?"

Müller's cold pale eyes studied the face of the Gestapo commandant, and as he did so, he felt a fist of cold steel slowly take hold of his stomach. There was something wrong in this town. Something terribly wrong.

They waited outside Nazi Headquarters until the test results came back. And when the two lab technicians, white and shaking, reported them to Fritz Müller, the German doctor felt his body snap. *"Hartung!"* he shrieked.

The *Einsatzgruppe* commander had been talking quietly with the *Panther Hauptmann* about the systematic way they would destroy the town, and when he looked up, he appeared surprised.

"Get over here!" shouted Müller.

Hartung's face darkened as he pushed away from the tank, and as he hurried across the street to join the group, the concern was evident in his eyes. "What is—"

"Positive!" screamed Müller. "You stupid swine! Every single case in that village is positive!"

Hartung's face went instantly white. "But that's not poss—"

"Goddamn you, Hartung!" shouted Müller, veins bulging in his neck. "You pompous ass! You shit-stinking, strutting, preening, insufferable popinjay! *Did you hear what I said?"*

The *Sturmbannführer* flicked his eyes over the faces around him. They all registered shock. "But that—"

"You and your goddamned delusions have exposed us all to typhus!"

"We can all go and steam our clothes in my office," whimpered Dieter Schmidt.

Dr. Müller, struggling to contain himself, found the composure to turn to Szukalski and say, "Have you any DDT?"

And Szukalski, his face masterfully hiding his elation, said, "It's all gone, *Herr Doktor*. The few shipments we received from Germany weren't in sufficient quantities to stop the spread of the disease."

"Hartung!" sputtered Müller. "It's over! You who had great plans to be *Reichsprotektor!* When I am through with my report on your stupid bungling—" Müller gasped and wrinkled his nose at the pig smell still clinging to Hartung, "they will create an office of *Scheissprotektor* for you, and station you on a dung heap!"

He swung around to his colleagues. "Do as the

Hauptsturmführer says, and get your clothes steamed! All of you!"

Then he returned to Hartung, shaking a finger. "And as for you—" Fritz Müller stopped before he could form the next word, his hand frozen in midair. "Oh my God. . . ." he breathed.

Someone said, "What is it, *Herr Doktor?*"

Müller was gazing across the town square at the park next to the church. And he whispered again. "Oh my dear God. . . ."

Before anyone else could make a move or utter a sound, the doctor was running across the road, waving his arms and shouting, *"Herr Hauptmann! Herr Hauptmann!"*

The tank commander, in the process of chewing, looked up in bewilderment at the man who descended upon him. He had a half-eaten sandwich in one hand and a bottle of beer in the other. "What is it, *Herr Doktor?* Time for the fun to begin?"

"Get your men out of here!" screamed Müller.

"Get my men out—"

"Now, Herr Hauptmann. Pull them back at once!"

"But why?" The tank commander shot a quick look over Müller's shoulder and saw Max Hartung standing dumbly by one of the cars, his face strangely blank. "What's the matter, *Herr Doktor?* My men are only having a little something to eat and drink before the artillery practice. The townspeople thought they could buy their lives with a bit of—"

"Those townspeople, *Herr Hauptmann,* are carrying typhus!"

"Carrying—" The Captain fell back a step. "But we were told there was no typhus epidemic here and that we were to level this town!"

"It appears there's been rather a serious error committed, *Herr Hauptmann,* and we have all been exposed to typhus." Müller looked over at the picknickers, at the women carving the hams, handling the breads, laughing over the soups. And he looked at the soldiers of the Reich putting everything into their mouths that was offered them.

Fritz Müller suddenly felt strangely ill.

In a considerably calmer tone he said, *"Herr Hauptmann,* we are in serious danger here. Please call your men out and have them form up in front of headquarters."

Dropping his sandwich and bottle to the ground, the Captain whistled to his Staff Sergeant to move the men out on the double.

The scene would have been comical had it not been so blackened with fear. The entire delegation stood totally nude in Dieter Schmidt's office while their clothing was being steamed. In tense silence they examined one another for lice, saying nothing, and deporting themselves with dignity as if this were something other than the humiliating spectacle it was.

The strange silence was broken when one of the doctors moaned, *"Gott im Himmel,* I found one," ferreting a louse from his pubic hair. "All I did was go behind one of those shacks and piss, and now I have lice!"

This prompted Müller, standing off to one side and having not spoken for a long time, to say slowly, "You are quiet, *Herr Sturmbannführer.* I've never seen you so silent. Usually one can't get you to stop talking."

All eyes turned to the SS man who held himself rigidly and whose face didn't acknowledge the address.

Müller went grimly on. "Have you nothing to say, Hartung? Or does your voice leave you when your fancy black uniform is removed? Do you know what you've done to us? You've exposed us all to a disease we stand a good chance to die of. All because of your ambition. You'd kill your own mother to further your career. But I'll tell you something. From this day forward, you are worthless! I'll see to it that. . . ."

Müller droned on, spilling out his anger and fear, voicing the dread of every man in that room, but Maximilian Hartung heard none of it. His trim muscular body held erect, the SS man fixed his gaze upon a sight that could just be glimpsed through the window of Schmidt's office. It was the stone gray roof of Sofia's hospital.

And as he held his eyes on it, appearing to the others

like a vengeful hawk, Maximilian Hartung made a silent, deadly vow.

Sofia returned to its former, peaceful existence. Jan Szukalski, refusing to take all the credit for their victory over the German delegation, explained to the people of Sofia. "It was not really we who made the hoax a success, but the Germans themselves. That is what I had been counting heavily upon, the fact that their fear of the disease would prevent them from examining the patients too closely. If they had not been so concerned about their own safety, Dr. Müller and his colleagues would have given closer examination to our so-called typhus victims and would have seen that they were doing an excellent job of acting. But instead, the cautious Germans were content to rely on the Weil-Felix test results, satisfied that if they drew the blood themselves and ran the tests themselves, then whatever the outcome, it had to be correct. So you see, my friends, it was ironically not we who saved ourselves from the Germans, but the Germans who saved us from them."

They returned to their regular routine as if no interruption had taken place. Maria and Jan continued to inject their Proteus vaccine and Hans and Anna continued to make up new batches in the crypt. Summer passed like a dream, tranquil and untroubled by the nightmares of war that were ravaging all the other towns and cities of Poland. Szukalski made his daily reports to Schmidt. The epidemic followed its expected course. And the people of Sofia continued to pretend they were in the grip of the worst typhus epidemic Poland had ever known.

Maximilian Hartung, shortly after his return to Warszawa, received transfer orders from his *Einsatzgruppe* command to the position of subcommandant at an extermination camp at Majdanek near Lublin.

He assumed the subcommand with characteristic dignity and soon found, to his grim satisfaction, that Majdanek was the perfect outlet for the anger and hate that had festered within him ever since his shameful defeat. It was not long, therefore, before his cruelty in the camp earned for him a name that he would carry with him till the day he died. The Devil Dog of Majdanek.

By the end of 1943 it was becoming obvious that his career with the Reich would terminate when the eastern front collapsed under the Russian advance. And so Max Hartung saw his only opportunity in the crematoria of Majdanek.

And it was from those who became ashes that he gathered and hoarded a trove of diamonds and gold.

Spring of 1944 brought to Poland the promise of new life as the Russian Army pushed the Germans farther out of their country. The Nazis were losing the war. Rumors flew through all the cities and towns of Poland that the end of the war might yet be in sight, and Sofia was one such town where the possibility of being liberated from the Germans rejuvenated the spirit and hope of its inhabitants.

Jan Szukalski stood at his office window looking out over the sun-washed buildings and at the new leaves on the trees, recalling a similar day of a year ago when he had ridden out to Slavsko with the German deputation. He recalled now the terror that had filled him then, and he marveled at the difference between this day and that.

Because today he could look back over the two and a half years that his "epidemic" had run, and he knew they had been victorious.

"I'm going to Krakow tomorrow," he said quietly to Maria Duszynska, who stood a few feet behind him. "That symposium on infectious diseases I told you about. Schmidt has given me a travel permit."

"I'm surprised."

"I'm not. I told him I was going there to look for a way to stop the epidemic."

"Will you be gone long?"

"I think not. Just the two days of the meeting. But I will need a ride to Sandomierz to catch the train. I don't know how long that will take. Father Wajda can drive me to the quarantine boundary. From there I can walk to the train."

Szukalski turned away from the window and smiled at Duszynska. He was feeling good today. "It's amazing, isn't it? When you think about it? Two and a half years of freedom from the Nazis."

Maria returned the smile. The pain of Maximilian Hartung had long since disappeared. She had even found, after his ignominious departure from Sofia, that knowing the truth about him had suddenly brought her a new joy in her life at the hospital, working with Szukalski. "Just don't get too confident, Jan. We can still be found out."

"Yes, I know. But these days, Maria, we don't stand the danger of losing the whole town as we did a year ago. The Nazis are falling back now; they're on the defensive. Hitler needs every available man on the two fronts he's fighting. I don't think he would spare manpower and artillery to bother wiping out an insignificant town. Not now."

"But *we're* still in danger."

"Of course we are. We always have been and possibly always will be. But that's a risk neither of us has allowed to cow us. That's what being a partisan is all about."

"You like that word, don't you? And you like the idea that you have been a partisan."

"No one will ever know how proud I am to have been able to fight for my country. It's done something for me in here." He tapped his chest.

"It's funny, you know. It will never be possible to share the experience of our battle. About the battle that was won without a single shot being fired."

"We saved thousands of lives, Maria, and that is all that matters."

He returned to staring out the window. He looked at the flowers that were blooming.

Father Wajda drove Szukalski to the edge of the quarantine area. At the checkpoint on the road Szukalski showed his travel permit to the guards on duty, and then patiently suffered the spraying of DDT into his pants and down his neck. His small suitcase was also opened and dusted.

Before starting down the road, Szukalski called to Wajda, "Meet me here at noon day after tomorrow."

Then he walked the four kilometers from the checkpoint to Sandomierz where, two hours later, he boarded the train to Krakow.

Krakow had changed.

Tanks and artillery were everywhere. The soldiers on the streets numbered more than the civilians. There was broken glass in the streets, evidence of Resistance fighting. Buildings were boarded up. Gardens went unattended. Angry graffiti disfigured the walls.

But it was not so much the physical character of the city that had altered, for in truth Krakow had been spared much of the devastation that had demolished other Polish cities. Rather it was the mood of the place that struck Szukalski. While those in peaceful Sofia had for the most part been able to continue with their normal lives, the people of Krakow had had to suffer the full weight of Nazi occupation.

Recalling his happy boyhood here, Szukalski walked solemnly past the Czartoryski Palace and remembered the college students who had strolled along these sidewalks playing their violins and accordions for a *groszy*. When he entered the Rynek, the large cobblestone square at the center of town, he didn't see the garrisoned soldiers or the mud-spattered tanks, but saw instead the banners and statues of the Apostles on Corpus Christi Day when he had knelt and prayed with his parents. When Szukalski's eyes scanned the imposing structure of the Cloth Hall, he did not see the red Nazi banners, but rather the flower market that had once stood here, and he pictured his mother as she stooped to choose a small bunch of flowers.

Szukalski turned away and continued walking. This was a different Krakow. The one where he had been born and raised no longer existed.

He came to the walls of the Kazimierz, streaked with the yellow paint and obscene damnations of anti-Semites. Barbed wire crowned this massive wall, and Szukalski recalled the days when he and his mother had strolled through the Jewish market, and how as a boy he had been fascinated by the figures in long black coats and fur hats and corkscrew curls over each ear. Those Jews were gone now, Jan knew. This ghetto was no longer crowded. In 1939, the last statistic he had heard, there were fifty thousand Jews crammed into this wretched ghetto. Today, because of the death camps and the Final Solution, only a handful remained.

Jan Szukalski headed toward the Jagellonian University where the meeting would take place the next day. Of course, since 1939 when all institutions of learning had been closed down, Krakow's illustrious university had also been closed, and all higher education for Poles ended. But this symposium was German-sponsored, attended mostly by Germans, and therefore one hall of the old school had been opened for the session.

When he saw the statue of Kosciuszko on Wawel Hill, more painful memories returned. How he had sat beneath the shade of the fourteenth-century walls to study his medical books. How he had sometimes skipped his classes to go skiing in the Tatras Mountains. How he had met Kataryna in the little cafe across the street the day after he had received his physician's certificate.

But it did no good, Szukalski knew, to dwell on those happy days. He was in Krakow for a very important reason, and could not afford the luxury of nostalgia.

As most of the hotels were either closed down or barred to Poles, Dr. Szukalski had to take a small room in a private home accepting lodgers for financial income. After paying the outrageous sum of three *zloty* to the woman of the house, who would have preferred *Deutschmarks,* Szukalski retired for the evening.

In the amphitheater where the symposium on infectious diseases was being held, Jan was at first pleased to see such a large turn-out. But closer inspection and the babble of so much German quickly told him that not many Poles or Czechs would be in attendance. Taking a seat at the rear of the room, he wondered about his colleagues from his Krakow days and where they were now.

He opened his program and read the list of papers that were to be read before the assembly. The fourth one listed caught his attention.

"Complement Fixation in Rickettsial Diseases."

After studying the title for a long time, Szukalski drew a pen out of his pocket and circled it. The paper was to be read by its author, a noted microbiologist from Berlin, at ten o'clock. Jan had two hours to wait.

He read the title once more and felt himself grow tense. Typhus was a rickettsial disease.

Szukalski read further down the list. He stopped again. "Rickettsial Agglutination Studies in Typhus Fever." To be read just before noon.

Jan looked around the room. Most of the seats were taken now, the audience was settling down, and the medical men were murmuring quietly among themselves.

He circled this second title and read down the rest of the list. The remainder of the program was made up of topics on typhoid fever, hepatitis, and cholera. But these didn't interest Szukalski as much as the two he had circled. They were the only reason he was here. To find out what changes were taking place in the world of infectious disease control.

The opening speeches started and Jan sat in quiet detachment half listening to the well-prepared dissertations. Szukalski was only too content to reminisce once again about the days when he had sat in this very amphitheater scratching out the desperate lecture notes of a freshman medical student.

At ten o'clock he brought his focus back to the dais below him, and leaned forward with interest as the German scientist took his place at the lectern. Reading his paper on the "Complement Fixation Test in Rickettsial Diseases," the man droned through several minutes of explanation of his method of study and the number of cases he had to report.

"The test is positive in nearly all clinical cases of typhus and correlates one hundred percent of the time with the Weil-Felix test in clinically positive cases of typhus. There have been no false positive results in my series."

The man finished his paper, stepped down, and Szukalski applauded with the rest of the audience. During the next two readings he did not let his mind wander as before, for now he had something far more important to mull over. Jan could hear over and over again the closing words of the microbiologist from Berlin. *"There have been no false positive results in my series."*

Finally the other scientist he had been waiting to hear stepped up to speak. Jan leaned forward, tense and rigid.

In the same manner of the previous speakers, this man first discoursed on his theories and methods of research, and, after what was an agonizing wait for Szukalski, concluded with what Jan was waiting to hear.

"The test is of great value in differentiating between murine and epidemic typhus. In both the rickettsial agglutination test and the complement fixation test specific rickettsiae are employed and the false positive results sometimes found with other tests can be eliminated."

Szukalski sank back in his chair. The room seemed deathly silent to him, even though all the members of the audience were applauding and turning to one another for comment. Jan Szukalski, upon hearing the last words of the speaker, was instantly deaf to all else.

". . . the false positive results sometimes found with other tests can be eliminated. . . ."

Jan felt himself rise to his feet and hurry to the nearest exit. In the empty corridor outside the amphitheater, he paused to lean against the wall as he digested those haunting words. This was it. This was what he had come to Krakow for.

The Weil-Felix test could now be checked. And any blood sample not coming from an actual typhus patient would inevitably be negative. The Germans now had the ability to see how Sofia's specimens had been tampered with. And they would uncover the hoax.

Jan would have left at once had it not been for one important question that remained unanswered, and as the answer to this question was the most crucial factor to his next plan of action, Szukalski knew he would have to remain here for just a while longer.

There was a luncheon during the midday break for all the attending doctors and, although it took some engineering, he was able to secure a place at the table where the two rickettsial experts were seated. It was during the amiable conversation that he found the opportunity to ask his question.

They were eating blintzes stuffed with sour cream, discussing recent advances in medical technology. Szukalski, who had taken a polite but minimal part in the exchange, leaned forward and addressed the two men.

"I was most interested in your studies, *Meine Herren*. Can you tell me, how soon do you think your agglutination test and the complement fixation test will be in general use?"

The microbiologist from Berlin replied, "I think within a few months. The tests have been somewhat tedious and expensive to run, but they certainly are accurate if there is any question of diagnosis."

Jan Szukalski dropped his hands below the table and squeezed them together. He tried to keep his voice light. "And can you tell me, gentlemen, how long these tests remain positive?"

Now the other scientist spoke, and he smiled as he said, "Here is a new advantage to our tests that the others don't have. You know, *Herr Doktor,* that the Weil-Felix titer usually disappears three months after the disease so that it is not valuable in analyzing the blood of a typhus patient six months later. However, with the complement fixation test a higher titer will be present for many months. Possibly years."

Szukalski stared at the two men. His hands were clenched so tightly that they hurt. *Possibly years.* To be able to go back to Sofia and recheck all those supposed typhus patients and find out that not one had really had the disease. . . .

"I would like to commend you on your studies," he

heard himself say, and was amazed that he had the ability to smile. "Very admirable indeed."

He did not stay for the rest of the symposium, and he left Krakow with a troubled mind and a heavy heart. He knew before coming here that he might learn something that would give him and Maria something to think about. But he had not been prepared for data quite so explosive.

Not only could the Weil-Felix now be double-checked and his artificially induced antigen discovered, but also past typhus patients could still be checked. With tests that were irrefutable.

"I think the tests will be in general use within a few months."

Although Szukalski left Krakow with a troubled mind, he also left thinking that none of his peers in the field had attended the symposium. But he was mistaken. One had attended; a man named Fritz Müller.

CHAPTER 25

The moment they had been expecting for two and a half years had finally arrived.

The conspirators sat in their familiar circle in the church crypt, gazing in the dim light at the faces they had come to love and respect. The risks they had faced together had created a unique bond among the five of them, so that they felt now as if they were joined together in a special brotherhood. And because this was the hour they had always known must eventually come, the sadness in their hearts matched the sadness in Szukalski's voice.

"So that's it, my friends. What I learned in Krakow. It seems that the miracles of science have come up with a way to expose our hoax. Using the new complement fixation test, the Germans will see that we have been deliberately creating false positives. And I don't think we have more than two months left before we will be found out."

The fear and uncertainty the news created was softened somewhat by Szukalski's report of conditions in Krakow and of conversations he had overheard concerning the concentration camps. While the rest of Poland had suffered terribly under the Nazis in these past two and a half years, Sofia had been spared the worst of it. This small consolation—the knowledge of their incalculable victory—helped them to face the defeat they knew lay ahead.

"What will we do now?" asked Hans.

Szukalski weighed his next words. Rising from the chair and turning away from the four faces turned up to him, he thought a moment before saying quietly, "We will have to make plans to escape."

Anna gasped.

"You mean leave Sofia?" said Father Wajda.

Jan turned around and smiled down at his friend. "You've known it all along, Piotr. Don't pretend to be surprised."

"Jan," said Piotr slowly, "we have always said that we would never abandon the town. Why speak of it now?"

"I'm not speaking of abandoning it, Piotr. I'm talking about ending the epidemic and then leaving. There's a difference. If we end the epidemic ourselves before the Germans discover our hoax, then chances are they'll never know about it. We could never leave before now because Sofia would then have been right back where it started with the Nazis taking all the food, carting off undesirables, and so on. But I don't think that will happen now. The Russians are getting closer every day and the Nazis are continually falling back. The day will come when the quarantine can be dropped and the town will still be safe. And I think that time is nearly upon us."

"But we can't just get up and leave—"

"No, Piotr, we can't. And we won't. Not all of us. And not all at once. First of all, we have to wind down the epidemic in a way not to arouse suspicion. Remember, we must take care to keep the Germans from trying the complement fixation test on our specimens, and I think the only reason they would do that is if their suspicions were aroused. I think that once the epidemic is made to look as if it has run its natural course and is ended, then the Germans will simply forget about us."

"Jan."

He looked at Maria. "Yes?"

"Then why must we leave? If the Nazis are pulling back, and if it appears as though the Russians will be, in a sense, liberating us, why leave at all? We can simply wind down the epidemic, and then the quarantine will be lifted, and we'll be safe from—"

Szukalski shook his head. "I had thought that at first, but then I got to thinking about certain people." Jan emphasized his thought by raising his right hand and pointing a finger toward the ceiling. "Dieter Schmidt is bent on revenge. I have known this a long time. He has been unhappy with Maria and me ever since the epidemic began, and I know he is only biding his time until he can get back at us for his miserable time here. He's waiting for the quarantine to lift, and for the day when we are no longer needed."

"You said *people*," murmured Father Wajda, already knowing what Szukalski was going to say.

"Maximilian Hartung. We all know that he left Sofia with revenge in his heart. Once it is safe for him to come back here, I think he will."

"But why?" asked Anna. "For all he knows, the epidemic was genuine."

"Yes. But I'm sure he holds us responsible for his humiliation. Perhaps I'm wrong, but I don't think I'd care to put my theory to the test. Anyway, my friends, I do believe it is time some of us left Sofia."

His words left the air ringing with an uneasy silence. All eyes stared in open apprehension. A slight hum from the incubator and electric lights seemed to fill the room, while the bishops in their coffins continued to sleep undisturbed through the night.

Finally, after a long, uncomfortable silence, Father Wajda said, "I must stay, Jan."

"Yes, I know that. And I will, too. We are necessary here, and our departure would arouse suspicion."

"I want to stay, too," whispered Maria.

But Szukalski shook his head. "You must go, Maria, and so must Hans and Anna."

When Kepler started to speak, Szukalski silenced him with a hand. "I've made the decision; there will be no discussing it. You and Anna are no longer needed here, Hans, since we have enough vaccine to last us until summer. After that, there will be no more epidemic. There will be nothing for you to do here. And Maria, you must go because this will be your only chance to get out without arousing suspicion. Now please, my friends, I now only want from you your full cooperation. We have worked so well together for two and a half years, how sad it would be to be torn now over such an issue."

He smiled wistfully at them all, wishing there was

something more he could say to each of them. "Think about what I have told you, and come back tomorrow night. Escape plans will have to be made."

Something had been bothering Fritz Müller ever since he had left the infectious disease symposium in Krakow.

Sitting in his office now in Warszawa at the Central Laboratory, he thought again about seeing Jan Szukalski leaving the symposium in a very agitated state.

Fritz had first espied Szukalski just before the lectures began in the amphitheater, and had made a mental note to approach him during the lunch break. As a physician of great personal esteem, Müller had for more than a year been disturbed by the debacle he had had the misfortune to take part in in Sofia, and had long wished he could personally voice to Szukalski his regret that it had taken place. While he was a German and a Nazi Party member, Fritz Müller was nonetheless a member of the fraternity of medical doctors, and held some small respect for Jan Szukalski, despite the fact that he was a Pole.

Fritz Müller might have dismissed the whole thing had Jan Szukalski stayed for the rest of the symposium, and had they had a chance to meet in an informal manner. But the Pole had disappeared after the luncheon and had not returned to the amphitheater.

Prior to the reading of the two papers on typhus, he noted that Jan Szukalski had been relaxed and calm. Afterward, he had joined the authors of those special dissertations for luncheon, his face and manners betraying a certain nervousness. And then, immediately after that, he had disappeared.

In his office now Fritz Müller read again the titles of those two papers, and understood the cause of Szukalski's distress. New and more definitive tests for typhus were now in existence.

Müller tapped his pen thoughtfully on the desk top. It could be his imagination. It could have been something altogether different that had upset Szukalski that day. But the senior doctor of the German-controlled Central Laboratory in Warszawa was going to find out for certain just what it had been to cause so abrupt a departure.

Unfortunately, Müller knew that it would be a good two months before he could get the equipment and reagents to run the complement fixation test. If he had thought he could make it through to Berlin right away, he would have personally gone to collect the necessary supplies for the tests. But since nothing could be done for the time being, he picked up the telephone and called down to the lab.

"I want you to save all of the specimens we get from the quarantined area of Sofia from now on. In about two months we will be running some special tests on them."

After he hung up, he thought about his old friend Maximilian Hartung, whom he hadn't seen or heard from since his transfer to Majdanek. And he suddenly felt like talking to him again.

The conspirators met the next night in the crypt of Saint Ambrož.

"Maria, I want you to be ready to leave by the end of the week. I am going to tell Schmidt that you have been found to have cancer, and that you have to go to Warszawa for treatment. I anticipate no problem getting you a travel permit."

She gazed up at him with a mingling of sorrow and regret. "I would rather stay," she said softly, "and see this through to the end. I'm not afraid."

"I know you're not. But you *have* seen it through to the end. We have saved thousands from dying, and now we must save ourselves. Warszawa is the best place to go for cancer treatment. Will you be ready by the end of the week?"

"Yes," she whispered.

"All right." Szukalski cleared his throat, and found himself reluctant to turn away from her wide, staring eyes. "Hans? Have you been able to come up with something?"

"Yes, Doctor." Kepler reached out and took hold of Anna's hand. "Anna and I have come up with a plan. We will go Saturday night."

"Good." Szukalski nodded thoughtfully. "Good. . . ." he said again.

Then he turned to Father Wajda, who sat abjectly, and said quietly, "Piotr?"

The priest said with a half-smile, "I know what my job is, Jan."

The two men gazed at one another for a long time.

Maximilian Hartung boiled with hatred and anger as he read Fritz Müller's letter.

SS-Sturmbannführer Maximilian Hartung; Majdanek KZ:

Dear Max,

I may owe you an apology after all for the way I treated you at Sofia and especially about being instrumental in getting you relieved of your *Einsatzgruppe* command. Recently I was in Krakow. . . .

In his dismal office in the stark hell that was Majdanek, Maximilian continued to stare down at the letter long after he had finished reading it. There was so much rage within his soul that, for a moment, it was difficult to think coherently.

He had suffered the degradation of Majdanek for one full year, personally responsible for sending fifty thousand Jews and others the Reich considered subhuman to their deaths. Through it all, he had relived over and over again that humiliating day in Sofia.

He wanted revenge.

After some time Hartung was able to gather himself together, and write a reply to Müller.

Dear Fritz,

If it should turn out as you suspect that the complement fixation tests on Sofian specimens will be negative, do not report this fact to Szukalski. Continue to report positive results to them so that they will not suspect we are on to their hoax.

I want personally to blow their brains onto the cobblestones of their quaint town square. Especially that miserable bastard Szukalski and his sanctimonious priest friend. I will expect to hear from you as soon as your suspicion is verified.

Max.

The five were trapped in a mood unlike any they had known before, and none of them, on this unhappy Saturday night, could have put into words just how they felt.

Szukalski looked at Maria as she stood before him in the crypt, a coat over one arm and a small valise under the other. She had had to make it appear as though she would be gone for only a week, as that was all Schmidt would allow her. Father Wajda was going to drive her to the northern quarantine checkpoint, from where it would be a short walk to the train that went to Warszawa.

Szukalski and Duszynska gazed at one another through the medieval light, unable, for the moment, to speak.

In the shadows, Hans Kepler shuffled uneasily.

"Dieter Schmidt suspects nothing," said Father Wajda comfortingly. "As far as he is concerned, everything is going on as usual. The Russians may only be three hundred kilometers away in the east, and the Allies are approaching from the west, but Schmidt remains confident that nothing is going to change. The man is either blind or deluded."

"Good-by, Jan," said Maria softly, her face so close to his she could feel his breath on her eyes.

He reached for her hand and grasped it warmly, then released it and said, "This is the moment we must begin our separate paths. I wish you safety and luck, Dr. Duszynska. And I wish I could give you a medal or—"

She forced a little laugh. "Just for now I'll be content to make it to the northern checkpoint."

"What will you do in Warszawa?"

"I don't know. I used to have many friends there. Some family. But who knows if they're still there? Or

even if the city is? From what I've heard, I'll be returning to a different Warszawa from the one I knew
five years ago."

"Is that all it's been? Five years?"

"Yes, Jan, five years since I first set foot in your
office, and you disapproved of me because I was a
woman."

His eyebrows rose.

"You think I didn't know. But never mind, Jan,
the past is gone. Right now we all have to find a future
that will hold us for a little while. If I make it to
Warszawa, I'll try to contact you somehow—"

"Don't, Maria. It's unsafe. Once you've been gone
longer than your permit, Dieter Schmidt will be asking
about you. Then he'll watch me like a hawk to see if I
hear from you. It's best that we don't communicate."

"But after the war ends. . . ."

"If it ends. We'll see, Maria. We'll see."

Surprised that the moment held such sadness for
him, Szukalski abruptly turned from Maria and cleared
his throat to address Kepler. "Hans, you look as though
you have decided to return to battle."

He stepped out of the shadow and into the light,
where the other four could see the gray uniform of
the *Waffen SS* he had arrived in. It was as fresh and
neat as the day he last removed it. "Yes, Doctor, my
own battle. Anna and I have decided to try to get out
through Rumania. We think that's our best chance."

"Across the mountains and forests," said Father
Wajda.

"Yes, Father, but it is springtime and Anna and I
might make it."

"How will you get out of Sofia?" asked Szukalski.

"Tonight I will requisition a motorcycle from Dieter
Schmidt."

"Requisition?"

"Requisition," he replied with a smile, holding up a
short length of lead pipe.

Szukalski slowly nodded, saying, "Yes . . ." and
recalling the morning he had walked into his office, and
had found an amazingly young and vulnerable soldier
standing there. In two and a half years Hans Kepler

had grown up. Clean shaven again, he was a handsome, striking young man with the wisdom of life in his eyes, and a new maturity in the squareness of his shoulders. "Yes . . ." said Szukalski again.

He took a moment to measure each face before him and said gently, "Perhaps no one outside this town will ever know about what we did here in Sofia these past two and half years. Only the Sofians themselves know how we saved them or from what. But I want you all to know how proud I am to have been able to stand by your side and fight for our people." His voice caught as he spoke, and he had to pause to regain control of it. "As with all good things, the beginning is difficult and uncertain, and the ending is painful. And from this point on it will be everyone for himself and God for us all."

They exchanged embraces, and wished each other good luck as one by one they left the crypt for their separate destinies.

SS-Rottenführer Hans Kepler stood in the shadow of the statue of Kosciuszko in the town square as he watched the guard in front of the entrance to the motor pool pace his beat back and forth in front of the locked gate. It was a small compound attached to Nazi Headquarters, formerly the garage and stable for the cars and horses belonging to the city of Sofia, but now a storage area for Schmidt's Mercedes and military equipment. At one o'clock in the morning there was little activity; all was peaceful and still.

At last what he was waiting for occurred. An outpost guard arrived on a sidecar motorcycle and pulled up to make his report. The other guard slowly rolled open the chain-link gate, and motioned the cyclist over to the gasoline pumps for refueling. After a few minutes of chatting with the gate guard while he refueled his cycle, the outpost guard went into headquarters.

The gate to the compound was still open and Kepler made his move. Shooting across the town square and dashing headlong into the compound, he motioned wildly to the startled guard to follow him, and at the same time he held a finger up to his mouth to indicate silence.

The gate guard was visibly stunned by the sudden appearance of a strange soldier in a *Waffen SS* uniform, and cocked his Erma submachine gun as he ran after the intruder.

Kepler ran directly into the maintenance shop, stopping only long enough to turn to the gate guard and whisper hoarsely, "Come on, man! There's a thief in here! Let's get him!"

Kepler plunged into the dark room and ducked immediately beside the door. As the gate guard entered, Hans swung the lead pipe with both hands into the man's throat. The guard fell, grasping at his fractured larynx. Kepler knocked his helmet off, and delivered a second blow to the back of his head, killing him instantly.

Kepler waited for a few seconds inside the deathly silent shop, conscious only of the thunderous pounding of his heart. Then, after quieting the tremble in his hands and making sure that no one's attention had been aroused, he stole quickly to the motorcycle, started the engine, and drove out through the gate.

At the northern checkpoint, after having shown her travel permit, Maria patiently withstood the DDT spraying. Then she walked across the line and paused long enough to wave good-by to Father Wajda.

He waved back, smiling sadly, and stood to watch as Dr. Duszynska started off down the road where she would eventually join the column of pathetic refugees moving aimlessly across Poland.

Hans Kepler did not drive the country lane alone. In the sidecar sat another *Waffen SS* soldier, also a *Rottenführer,* wearing a uniform exactly like his own. In fact, it was his own, the one spare uniform he had brought with him to Sofia, and it struck him as ironical, on this crisp morning as they drove through birch and aspen trees, that there had been a time when he had contemplated destroying both uniforms. Now they might very well save their lives. And the gray suited Anna's coloring very well.

The dawn was breaking into a beautiful clear morning as the spring sun rose above the crest of the Carpathian foothills, and despite his great fatigue, Hans was free and happy. They had traveled all night, and still had a long way to go before reaching the Rumanian border, but just being out of Sofia and beyond the quarantine boundary made him feel that their escape was assured.

"I think we had better start looking for a place to stop for the day," he said to the soldier in the sidecar. "I would like to avoid contact with anyone until we're out of Poland."

Traveling across fields and along dusty country lanes they had been able to avoid the checkpoints, and had not run into a single Nazi. But Hans knew that, entering the mountainous area, they would have to travel the main road if they intended to keep the motorcycle.

A grove of elm trees a kilometer off the lane looked as though it would offer good protection from passersby, and Kepler wheeled off the road across a broad sprawling meadow toward the trees. They parked the motorcycle beneath the trees and camouflaged it with branches. Then he and Anna took their few possessions into the thicket to find a place to rest.

A startled deer broke from its hiding place beneath the boughs and caused Kepler to reach for his Luger before he realized that they were in no danger. Spreading the blanket on the grass-padded ground, the two ate some sharp cheese and hard bread that they had brought along, and soon fell asleep in each other's arms.

They awoke about midmorning, and after another small snack wandered about the little wood, enjoying the beautiful day. Although their greatest dangers and trials lay before them, the young couple preferred not to think of anything other than the hour at hand. And when they came across a narrow stream gushing with icy water from the distant Carpathians, Hans waded in, and caught two fish with his bare hands.

They slept again in the afternoon and then risked a small campfire to cook the fish, extinguishing it before nightfall. When darkness finally set in, the two refugees loaded their few belongings into the sidecar of the motorcycle, and returned to the road that led eventually to the Rumanian border.

There were few other travelers on the road at this late hour and the full moon silhouetted the mountains against the sky. Large cloud banks gathered on the horizon, lending a feeling of impending doom to the air as Hans and Anna motored toward the last German checkpoint before the border.

Hans eyed the telephone wires and decided to risk taking time out to sever them. The final and most crucial step of their escape plan depended upon split-second timing and upon their ability to convince the border guards, if only for a moment, of the story they were going to tell them. So he stopped the cycle at what he estimated to be about five kilometers from the checkpoint, climbed the pole, and cut both telegraph and telephone lines.

Kepler's hands grew moist and his mouth felt like a dusty sponge as they approached the guard station with its drop arm blocking the passage through the gate. The station was situated in a narrow canyon to prevent any skirting around its barricade, and Kepler felt suddenly like a salmon caught in a fish trap, able only to move forward toward the submachine-gun-armed guards who had heard the approach of his cycle, and who now stood at the ready as he drew near.

Hans had anticipated this, and launched at once into his act. *"Heil Hitler!"* he called to the guards as he pulled his cycle off the road adjacent to the guardhouse.

The guards, both enlisted men in the regular army, were startled at the sight of two SS men, and briskly returned the salute. *"Heil Hitler!"*

"Come inside!" said Kepler officiously. He strode to the guardhouse as if he were in command.

The puzzled soldiers followed him into the small shack. Anna, saying nothing, got out of the sidecar but kept her back to the two guards and pretended to be unloading equipment from the cycle.

"We are relieving you of your duty here," said Hans authoritatively. "You are to report back immediately to your company. There is an organized retreat—or should I say regrouping—to the rear. The Russians have broken across the Zbrucz River, and will over-run this area within twenty-four hours. And they are not taking any prisoners."

A look of terror rose in the faces of the guards.

"The SS is charged with holding to the last man, so you two get out while there is still time."

"Yes, of course, *Herr Rottenführer.* I will get our motorcycle."

One of the guards ran out of the shack and into a barricade of brush, and started the engine of a cycle. The second guard saluted Kepler again and followed his partner. When Anna saw that both guards had left the guardhouse and were now getting ready to ride off, she ran into the shack to join Hans.

The two stood bent over the desk, studying the map pinned to its surface, waiting for the motorcycle to depart. The engine gunned and roared from its hiding place behind the brush.

Suddenly the door flew open, and the larger of the two Wehrmacht guards stood in the doorway, his submachine gun cocked and pointed directly at Kepler's chest.

"Put your hands up in the air, both of you!" he barked. Over his shoulder he called, "Okay, Karl, turn the motorcycle off! I have both of them together now!" The man grinned gloatingly at Hans and Anna. "How stupid did you think we were? Did you really think we couldn't spot two deserters when we saw them?"

CHAPTER 26

Maria Duszynska returned to a devastated and war-torn Warszawa. It shocked her to see how much the city had changed, how little of it remained from her childhood or even her university days. The destruction was incomprehensible. Entire blocks reduced to rubble. The ghetto entirely razed. On her first morning in the city, after stepping off the crowded train, she walked transfixed through sections that had once been familiar to her, along avenues that used to be her favorites; where now there was not a trace of the old romantic Warszawa she once knew.

She went first to her mother's house, where she learned that most of her family had left Warszawa. None of the neighbors could tell her where they had gone. Maria's one brother was presumed dead, having been arrested by the Gestapo one night and taken away, accused of being a partisan. Maria was certain of only one thing; the small amount of money Schmidt had allowed her to carry out of Sofia would not last very long.

Warszawa was a city of homeless, displaced persons, many of whom came from towns in the north and west where their property had been confiscated by the Nazis. They crowded into tenements, found menial work where they could, and lived a nameless, day-to-day existence.

Dr. Duszynska saw that for her own survival she must for now become one of these, and so found, after a morning of walking the city with her small suitcase, a boardinghouse where she could take a cramped and dirty room, no more than an attic, for a scandalous sum.

Once established there, she knew what her next step would be.

Her lodging was not far from the university hospital, and so she was able to walk to it. In the two and a half years of peace in Sofia, she had forgotten what it was like to see such a concentration of Nazis. They swarmed Warszawa like rodents, stopping her often to see her papers.

The university, of course, also had changed. Having been closed a few years before, it was now boarded up, adorned with graffiti and broken windows. Weeds had reclaimed the paths and walkways. But the hospital was still in operation, as she had known it would be, so she took up her place across the street. This was where she had trained, where she had received her doctor's degree, and so she had come here in hopes of finding someone known to her from those days.

Each day she watched the hospital entrance diligently, never remaining in one place for long, so as not to draw attention to herself, and each night returning to her oppressive attic.

She was at the point of despair when, four days later, at last, some one familiar appeared.

The young woman, an old friend who had been a technician in the laboratory where Maria had trained, recognized her at once, and was overjoyed to see her. They went straightaway to a tiny, smoky cafe where, after only a few moments of wondering how to begin, they were soon telling their separate stories.

After having lost her husband in street fighting, the young woman had carried on by herself at the Central Lab, and had been able to hold on to her small flat a kilometer from the hospital. Her story was very short and very simple; there was nothing else to say.

Maria's own tale was as brief: She had been forced to leave her home in the southeast because of the Russian advance, and now had nowhere to go. Of Dr. Szukalski, Sofia, and the epidemic she said nothing.

That evening Maria moved into the girl's flat, having come almost to the end of her money, and soon learned in the ensuing dark hours that the lab technician was involved in the Resistance. Maria was at first shocked that the girl should speak so openly of it, and to someone she hadn't seen in five years, but she soon realized how widespread and heavily supported the partisans were, and that in Warszawa the Resistance was a fact of life.

They talked all through the night over a plate of soup and a bottle of vodka, until Maria disclosed to her friend that she was not a refugee but that she was running away from something she couldn't talk about, and that her papers would soon be invalid. She added that it would not be wise for her to maintain her true identity, or to try to find work as a physician.

Without asking questions—for she had heard a thousand similar stories—the young woman said she would try to help. Maria would need a new identity and, to be given a food allotment, a job.

The speed and ease with which all this was accomplished amazed Maria. Her new papers were ready the next day, and she was given dye to change the color of her hair. She had to promise the girl that she would relinquish a certain amount of her first few paychecks to her, all of which would go into the partisan cause. Maria agreed to everything without hesitation.

With a new name, black hair, horn-rimmed glasses, and old clothes, she was transformed into a dowdy, spinsterish woman whose story was that she was a refugee who had fled from the path of the Russians.

Warszawa was a city of transients and of crowded conditions so that no one paid much attention to the addition of one more worker in the hospital lab. Because of the large number of military casualties packed into the hospital and the subsequent heavy work load in all departments, Maria achieved a safe degree of anonymity.

Jan Szukalski was growing more and more uneasy as the weeks passed, and he studied the daily reports from the Warszawa Laboratory carefully for any indication that either the complement fixation or the rickettsial agglutination tests were available. He knew that he would be in grave danger once they were in use and no positives resulted to correlate with the Weil-Felix.

It would be immediately evident to anyone who administered the new tests that the whole epidemic was a hoax after all, just as Hartung had suspected.

Szukalski had made up his mind that as soon as there was a hint that the new tests were in use, he would try to escape. Until that time he would continue to protect the people of Sofia with his Proteus vaccine.

Unfortunately, Szukalski had no way of knowing about the directive from Max Hartung to Fritz Müller to continue to report positives even if negative results were found. If he had known, his plans would have changed considerably.

It did not take Maria Duszynska long to learn her way around the large, busy laboratory, and to come eventually upon the area where technicians performed the Weil-Felix test on the many blood samples sent in from Eastern and Central Poland. After establishing a pattern of moving about the lab and making surface acquaintances with the other workers, she was able, without fear of arousing suspicion, to walk casually by the logbook where all the test results were recorded, and glance down its daily list.

Sofia was frequently recorded here, and the name Szukalski appeared beside it. The number of cases he was reporting was declining in exactly the way he had said it would. And it gave her some small comfort to know he was still alive.

The word had spread through the officer corps at Majdanek that it might soon be necessary to abandon the camp because of the persistent advance of the Russians. Until the last minute, however, the death camp was to operate at full capacity.

Maximilian Hartung hated his job at Majdanek, not because of the killing, but because he had been forgotten by the High Command. He was a cast-off who knew that soon he would have to scramble for his life. Germany was losing the war, and it was doubtful that the Allies would understand the necessity of the extermination. He knew he must not be taken prisoner. No one would go easy on the SS.

And yet it was not so much this that disturbed Hartung as the unbearable silence from Fritz Müller in Warszawa. What had happened since their exchange of letters? How far away now were those special tests that Fritz had mentioned? When would the day come when he would know for sure?

While he pondered this, Max Hartung went over and over again in his mind, giving full rein to his cruel streak, the names of those in Sofia whom he planned to visit once more. Dr. Jan Szukalski. Dr. Maria Duszynska. Father Piotr Wajda. And others? If there were others helping them, Hartung would find out the name of every last one of them. And with the finer arts of torture he had learned in his year at Majdanek, Maximilian Hartung knew he could reduce them to anything he wanted.

Maria continued to work in the laboratory in Warszawa, careful to avoid contact with anyone she had known when she had worked as a doctor in the same hospital. But that had been nearly five years ago, and almost all of the faces were new. Most of the Poles were gone, except for those in the subservient positions, and had all been replaced by Germans. Once, she had caught sight of Fritz Müller making one of his infrequent inspections of the lab, but she had kept her distance, and he hadn't recognized her.

It was at the end of May that Maria noticed some new apparatus being set up at the other end of the long laboratory, and casual inquiry told her that the new complement fixation tests were now going to be run to correlate results with the day's run of Weil-Felix tests.

Her heart froze at hearing the news. She knew it would only be a matter of a few days now before it was discovered that something was wrong—very wrong—with the blood samples from Sofia.

Trying to appear as though she was still tending to her own heavy task of cross-matching blood for surgery, Maria found her attention riveted to the hum of activity at the other end of the room.

Before too long, word raced around the laboratory that the new complement fixation test was more accurate than the previously relied-upon Weil-Felix, and that, so far, all specimens that had been Weil-Felix positive correlated perfectly with positive results from the complement fixation.

Later in the day, however, the mood at the other end of the room changed from one of mild confusion to utter disbelief when all but one of the blood samples from Sofia were Weil-Felix positive but complement fixation negative.

Then Maria heard one of the technicians call for Dr. Müller.

She watched as, a few minutes later, the tall and pale doctor was looking over the new equipment and reagents, and checking for himself these astounding results. Even from where she stood, Maria could see the flush of scarlet creep from his shirt collar and eventually cover his entire head. And she could see the controlled fury in his eyes.

Unfortunately, his words did not reach her, but she could tell, from his actions and gestures, that the mystery of Sofia was solved.

Her hands began to shake. Pushing away from the counter where she had been working and ducking behind a row of cabinets, Maria leaned against a wall and breathed heavily. From her hiding place, she could see the astonished expressions of the lab technicians. Then her eyes fell upon the logbook where all results were tallied. It would be picked up later this afternoon, and the results teletyped to the various Nazi Headquarters in the areas where the blood samples had originated. Then, those results would be distributed to the individual doctors concerned.

It was not long before the commotion subsided and Dr. Müller stormed from the laboratory. The technicians, shaking their heads, returned to work. Eventually the lab quieted down and was back to its normal routine.

Maria decided to take a stroll.

She reached the other end of the room a couple of

minutes later and, exchanging a few pleasantries with the other technicians, managed to look at the logbook. What she saw made her body go numb.

Dr. Müller had reported only the Weil-Felix tests; *no complement fixation results.*

She didn't know how long she stood there staring stupidly down at the book, but when she finally tore herself away, and wound her way back to her place at the cross-matching counter, Maria's mind was electrified.

Fritz Müller was not reporting complement fixation results to Sofia for only one reason: to keep Szukalski there in order to give them time to arrest him.

Her mind raced in all directions at once. While her hands went through the mechanics of cross-matching, Maria rapidly explored every alternative available to her.

All communications—telephone, telegraph—were out of the question. She had been gone from Sofia for two months; Dieter Schmidt would be watching and waiting for her to communicate with Szukalski.

How—how on earth to find a way to alert him?

Then it came to her.

Maria Duszynska would let the Nazis send her message.

At the desk where the logbooks were kept, she drew out the one for blood counts and dutifully recorded her own work for the day. Then, carefully and slowly, she made her way to the logbook for all the various agglutination test results.

The last one entered, with the patient's last name first, read:

Czarnecka, Danuzsa. WF+

Drawing a pen out of her white smock, Maria casually bent forward, and added one last entry to the list that would be teletyped to Sofia that evening:

Totenkopf, Jan. CF+

Maximilian Hartung listened in grim silence as Fritz Müller, his voice strained and choking, made his report. The connection was bad, but the apology came over the telephone exceptionally clear. Then, when his friend was through, Hartung felt himself smile as he told Müller what they were going to do.

Jan Szukalski glanced down the routine list of test results that had just been sent over from Nazi Headquarters. He had been reading such lists almost every day for nearly two and a half years, but this one was shorter than the rest. And he knew the next one would be shorter yet, and so on and so on until he had the epidemic wound down. By which time he hoped to be out of Sofia before the Nazis found out what had happened here.

It was a sultry, hazy day, portending the hot summer that lay ahead. Jan sat back in his chair, his eyes running down the list—all positive, of course—letting his mind wander and ramble. The names on the list fell out of focus as he daydreamed.

He brought himself back, however, when his eye caught on the error on the last line. Instead of WF+, the teletypist had accidentally written CF+.

Ah well, thought Jan with a shrug, maybe the man thought it was a cerebrospinal fluid test.

Then he saw the name that preceded it. Jan Totenkopf.

He scratched his head. There was no familiarity here. A name totally new to him. Szukalski had several patients with German names, but no Totenkopf, and certainly he would have remembered someone with the same first name as his.

He got up from his desk, and walked to the first-floor ward to start his morning rounds. The nurses stayed with him as he went from bed to bed checking each patient's condition, and discussing their projected treatment.

That last entry continued to bother him.

Finishing his rounds, he stepped back into his office, and once more scrutinized the last name on the list. Then he read the name out loud, trying to recall it, trying to remember when he had ever treated someone by that name. And as he read it out loud, "Totenkopf, Jan. CF+," it suddenly struck him that what he was reading was *not a name, but a sentence.*

And what he was reading was this:

Death's Head, Jan. Complement Fixation positive.

And it could mean only one thing. That the SS now had the complement fixation test. Someone in Warszawa was warning him, and Jan knew that that someone could only be Maria.

Dr. Szukalski, for the first time since the inspection team had come to Sofia a year ago, felt the terror of the damned creep over him.

He had to act quickly.

Father Wajda nodded gravely as he read the teletype list Jan had shown him, and said in a deep voice, "I'm afraid you're right. It can't mean anything else. Maria has somehow gotten in the lab and is warning you. Jan, it looks as though you won't be able to finish the epidemic here as you had originally planned. You'll have to get out."

"Piotr," said Szukalski in a strained voice, pacing in and out of the shadows of the crypt, "I don't know what to do. I am torn between running to save myself and my responsibility to all my patients in the hospital. It's Alex and Kataryna I'm worried about. If only there were some way I could get them out—"

"Not without you, Jan, and you know that. They'd be as good as dead if they tried to escape on their own, and whom do you know who would smuggle them out of Sofia? If not for yourself, Jan, then for those two. Run!"

Szukalski intertwined his fingers, and brought them up to his mouth. "Piotr—" he choked.

"Listen to me!" The priest was on his feet and placing a firm hand on his friend's shoulder. "You don't have much time. You know that Maria sent you that message to warn you of imminent danger, and not just to satisfy your curiosity. And if Müller now has the complement fixation test, you know you have no time left. Get your family together, Jan. You are dead if you stay. And so are your wife and child. How easy do you think Schmidt will go with Kataryna when—"

"But to run!" cried Szukalski spinning around. "To leave my patients!"

"They'll be cared for. The nurses are still here. The Russians aren't far away now. Who knows what will happen when they arrive?"

"And what about you, Piotr? Suppose they find out about your part in all this?"

Wajda managed a smile. "And who's to tell them? There is no one left who can inform on me, Jan. I'm safe. So you see, my good friend, you have to get out if only to save *my* neck. You're too big a risk to me, you see. They'll torture you to find out who else—"

"All right!" whispered Szukalski.

"Go home at once, don't stop back at the hospital, and get ready to leave. Don't tell Kataryna anything. Just tell her—"

"Kataryna won't question it, Piotr. If I tell her we have to leave, she'll trust me."

"I'll get your car from the hospital and pick you up."

Dieter Schmidt, having just finished his dinner, walked out onto the steps of the Town Hall and looked across the square. So quiet, he thought. So dull and quiet. The spring evening was warm and dusky and filled with the pungency of a thousand blossoms. He wished he could loosen his tie. His uniform was getting tight, and as he looked down at his protruding abdomen with disgust, he thought: Nothing to do but sit around and eat. Three years in the same shitty little town and the Russians almost within the Polish border.

The Gestapo commandant was wallowing in a mood of self-pity when the communications Sergeant ran down to him with a teletyped message.

COMMANDANT, SOFIA. *SS-HAUPTSTURMFÜHRER* DIETER SCHMIDT:
ARREST AND DETAIN FOR QUESTIONING DR. JAN SZUKALSKI AND DR. MARIA DUSZYNSKA. WILL ARRIVE TOMORROW A.M.
    SS-STURMBANNFÜHRER M. HARTUNG

CHAPTER 27

The last time Dieter Schmidt had known such total satisfaction and joy was when he had received a promotion in rank and the commendation of his superiors at Gestapo Headquarters in Berlin for his excellent work. But even that was pale compared to how he felt upon reading that message from Hartung.

It was the most delicious moment of Dieter Schmidt's life.

He nearly cried out with happiness as he bolted up the steps of his headquarters, and as he barked out orders to muster his men, the squat commandant began to fantasize about the punishment he would inflict upon Szukalski.

Maximilian Hartung took emergency leave from his duty at Majdanek, explaining that he had an unfinished extermination problem to take care of in Sofia.

Driving directly to Warszawa, he arrived at midnight and, after picking up Fritz Müller and two enlisted men, headed at once for Sofia. Visions of revenge burned sweetly in his brain.

At 2:00 A.M. Dieter Schmidt strutted out of Nazi Headquarters and entered his waiting Mercedes. Upon receiving the teletype, he had posted men to watch all angles of Szukalski's house, and he had alerted his men that there were arrests to be made that night. A contingent was armed and waiting behind the staff car. The full moon of the spring night lit the town square just brightly enough to give a sinister cast to the assembled group.

At his order the entourage rolled away from the building, and drove solemnly to the home of Szukalski.

Schmidt was so excited with the thought of getting the doctor in his grasp that he could hardly contain himself.

The small convoy stopped in the middle of the narrow street in front of the house and gunned their engines. The neighbors, awakened by the dissonant sounds, cautiously peeked out through their curtains.

"Cover the back," snapped Schmidt to part of the group. The rest of them lined up in front of the house, their Ermas ready to strafe at the slightest sign of trouble.

Schmidt himself went to the door flanked by two of his largest men. He rapped loudly on the door with the handle of his swagger stick.

"Szukalski, open up! This is Commandant Dieter Schmidt! If you do not open this door, I will smash it in and then crush your skull in front of your family and all these cowering swine watching from their windows!"

Schmidt's voice sailed away on the night silence.

"*Verflucht!*" he hissed under his breath.

Dieter banged once again on the door, and this time struck it so hard that the handle of the swagger stick broke off and flew into the street.

"All right!" he shouted, retreating down the steps. To the two waiting SS men he blurted, "Shoot the door open!"

They opened fire with their submachine guns and then kicked the door down.

"Drag him out here!" cried Schmidt. "I want him crawling in the street!" He motioned for six men to go inside and ordered them to tear the house apart if it was necessary.

SS-Hauptsturmführer Dieter Schmidt stood in the street, and listened impatiently as his men smashed furniture, tore open cabinets, broke glassware, and ripped down drapery. To his dismay, there came no screams of discovered victims.

"Get the axes and tear the house apart!" he shrieked, already knowing in his heart that Szukalski had won.

After a full hour of standing and watching and listening to the destruction of the house with no fruitful results, he ordered it to be set afire. From here they went to the apartment of Maria Duszynska, which he had also had watched since receiving the telegram, but Schmidt knew this was a futile search, for he himself had given her a travel permit two months ago, and she had never returned. After a useless search of the hospital, Schmidt and his disheartened men returned to Nazi Headquarters to await the arrival of *SS-Sturmbannführer* Maximilian Hartung.

"What do you mean, they are gone!" shouted Hartung, straining the sinews of his neck.

Fritz Müller, exhausted and soul weary, sat in Schmidt's office looking for all the world as if he had walked the full two hundred kilometers from Warszawa. He sat shaking his head while the two men argued.

"He's nowhere to be found, *Herr Sturmbannführer*," said Schmidt timidly, backing away from the man. "Duszynska left town two months ago and was supposed to be gone for only a week. She had cancer and—"

"God! What incompetence! No wonder they were able to fool you for so long! You don't even know when they come and go!" All the rage and fury of hell poured out of Hartung as he screamed at Schmidt. "I can't believe you let this happen!"

Schmidt shrank beneath the onslaught, keeping his mouth and eyes closed against the obscene expletives Hartung blasted at him. And when the *Sturmbannführer* was through, he said in a low, dangerous voice, "All right, Schmidt. One last chance to redeem yourself. There is still one person in this town who knows where Szukalski is. That white-sepulchered son-of-a-bitch priest Wajda. Get some men out here and let's find him, now!"

A small group—Hartung, Schmidt, Müller, and six enlisted men with submachine guns—burst open the main door of Saint Ambroż, and fanned out across the back expecting an attack from some secret partisan group from within the vaulted structure.

Father Wajda, hearing the commotion, slowly rose from his desk, smoothed down his cassock, steadied the gold crucifix that glittered on his chest, and walked out to the chancel where he stood adjacent to the altar.

"Are you looking for someone, *Herr Hauptsturm-führer?*" he called out, his voice ringing throughout the empty church.

The grim assembly moved warily down the center aisle and approached the altar.

"And you, *Herr Doktor,* and even the glorious *Sturm-bannführer!*" said Wajda from his place on the last step before the altar. "All of you! What a pleasant surprise! I expected you, of course, but not quite so soon."

"Bastard!" seethed Hartung. "Where is Szukalski? And Duszynska? Where are they and who else was in on your charade?"

"Charade?"

"You know goddamned well what I'm talking about, you fork-tongued swine! I'm talking about your stinking fake typhus epidemic!"

The priest surveyed the group of men below him. "You don't have to shout, *Herr Sturmbannführer.* And there is no need to intimidate me. I fully intend to cooperate with you. And how right you are! It *was* a faked epidemic!"

Hartung and Müller exchanged glances.

"And you, *Herr Doktor,*" said Wajda smoothly. "Would you like to know how we carried it out? It was a vaccine, you know. That's all. A simple vaccine that made the Weil-Felix test positive."

Müller stared up at the priest with a mingling of disbelief and admiration. "A vaccine. . . ."

"Yes, indeed, and something not known to Germans. Would you like to see where the vaccine was made up and how we did it? And you, *Herr Haupt-sturmführer,* would you like to know what went on right under your very nose for two and a half years? And you, *Herr Sturmbannführer,* would you like to know who laughed behind your back a year ago and where they are now?" He smiled angelically. "Come with me and I'll show you."

Wajda turned away and started for the rear of the apse. When one of the armed soldiers raised his gun to shoot, Hartung said softly, "Wait. Let's go with him."

The little group followed the priest as he walked to the recessed doorway and turned the key in the great iron lock, revealing the spiral stairway leading down to the crypt. He snapped a switch that turned the lights on, and slowly descended the stairs, saying, "See, gentlemen? Even electric lights."

"What is this place?" whispered one of them as they followed him, single file, down the stone stairway.

Finally they reached the bottom, and nine pairs of eyes grew wide.

"Ah. Here we are. This, gentlemen, is our laboratory."

Wajda strode across the small chamber and situated himself on the other side of the equipment-filled table. He addressed his visitors. "I can tell you everything now, gentlemen, because I know that Sofia is beyond your devices. The Russians are too close, and you must think of your own safety. Myself and the others who perpetrated the fraud, well," he shrugged, "we always were prepared for the consequences. But the town, I had to make certain first that it would be safe."

Father Wajda then launched into a detailed explanation of how the vaccine had been discovered, how it had been prepared, why it worked to confuse the Weil-Felix test, and how the "epidemic" was engineered.

When the priest was through, Fritz Müller said, "That is absolutely incredible."

"Incredible, yes," said Hartung darkly, "but you have left something out of your interesting story."

"Have I?"

"The small fact of who your fellow conspirators were and where they are now."

"Now here I shall have to disappoint you gentlemen, for you see, they are all safely out of Poland by now and I am the only one left."

"But you do know where they are, don't you?"

Father Wajda looked squarely at the cold, slate eyes of Hartung. "As I have said, they are out of Poland. They are beyond your reach."

"I can *make* you tell us, priest."

Father Wajda smiled and slowly shook his head. "I don't think so. And I think, *Herr Sturmbannführer,* that you know deep in your heart that nothing you do to me will ever get me to talk."

Hartung glared for another moment into the calm eyes of the priest, then he suddenly exploded, shouting orders at the top of his lungs to the men around him. The explosion of submachine guns filled the air as the bullets tore apart Piotr Wajda's body. And as the roar echoed off the surrounding stone coffins, Maximilian Hartung saw with a mingling of horror and fury that Father Piotr Wajda had died with a serene smile on his lips.

NEW YORK CITY—
THE PRESENT

"Maria . . ." he whispered. "So it's you. And you're alive."

"Yes, Jan." Her voice trembled and she could hardly keep from crying.

They had been sitting in his office for only a few minutes, studying one another across the desk, feeling the years and decades roll away until, recognition and realization dawning, Dr. John Sukhov had put his hands to his face for a long moment.

"I've been looking for you," she said quietly. "I have always harbored the hope that you were alive and that you got out of Poland somehow."

"My God, I can't believe this . . . seeing you again. . . ."

"How did you escape, Jan?"

"Ironically, it was easy for us. Father Wajda drove Kataryna and Alex and me to the village of Dobra where we lived in hiding for eight months until the Russians had liberated Poland as far as Auschwitz. We had originally planned to go back to Sofia, but the Russian treatment of Poles was so harsh that we joined the masses falling back to Germany, and from there, two years later, were able to emigrate to America. We changed our names—as I see you did, too—and have lived here in New York ever since. But, Maria, you! What happened to you? I had thought you dead all these years!"

"Then you got my message from the lab—"

"Yes, I did! It was confusing at first, but when I finally deciphered it, I wasted no time in getting out. But tell me about you!"

"I became involved in the Resistance, Jan, and was an active part of the August uprising. After that, I was just one of the hundreds of thousands without homes or identities. Changing my name and my profession, I was able to make my way to England, and that is where I have been all these years as a hospital administrator. But you know, Jan, I had heard indirectly from other refugees that you had somehow gotten out of Poland, and there was a rumor that you were in the United States, still working as an infectious disease specialist. I've looked for you and looked for you. I've been to so many doctors. . . ."

Jan let his eyes drift down to the photograph on the front page of the *Buenos Aires Herald*. The face, though older, was unmistakably that of their erstwhile friend Maximilian Hartung. "We changed our names because of him, didn't we?"

"Yes, I suppose so. Somehow, I always knew Max would survive the war and would get away. And I have always felt that he would keep looking for us to the ends of the earth. I knew you must have changed your name. That's why it has been so difficult searching for you. But once . . . once I saw this," she tapped the newspaper, "then I was impelled to find you, to seek you out after all these years. He's dead, Jan. We don't have to fear him anymore."

Dr. Szukalski picked up the paper, and scanned again the column describing the jeweler's death. "How ironical. He died not only from a gunshot but also from a large dog bite on his neck. That's justice for you. The Devil Dog dies in the jaws of a dog."

They lingered over that thought for a moment, then Jan looked again at the face across the desk. Thirty-six years older now, the face of an old woman, but still the distinctly beautiful face of Maria Duszynska. "And Father Wajda? Do you know—"

"He was a martyr, Jan. Max did get one of us after all. I was able to learn something of the incident from rumors going around the lab after Müller returned. Oh, yes, I see you're surprised. Müller went back to Sofia. You didn't know that. And Hartung, too. In fact, they went back looking for us and were shocked to find we'd already escaped. Apparently they missed you by hours."

"Sweet crucified Jesus," he murmured in Polish.

"And the story goes that they were sure they were going to get their confession from Father Wajda. But of course he would not submit and they killed him in the crypt, in a glorious blaze of gunfire. Isn't it what he wanted after all, Jan?

"Hartung never did return to Majdanek," Maria went on without waiting for his answer. "He and Müller planned to escape to South America together, but Müller was killed in the August uprising in Warszawa. Hartung, as you know, got out, bought his way out with gold taken from the teeth of dead Jews. He established himself in South America as a jewelry manufacturer, always keeping a low profile since he was a war criminal and he knew the Israelis were after him."

"I guess they found him."

"Yes, Jan, they did."

"What about Anna and Kepler? Were you ever able to learn anything about them?"

Now she smiled broadly. "I've been in touch with them, Jan. They live in Essen in West Germany and have a family. It seems they were able to make good their escape through Rumania, although they told me a rather extraordinary tale about being held at gunpoint by the border guards. Hans had told them some story about the Russians being very close when quite by coincidence a contingent of Russian troops suddenly showed up. So it turned out that the border guards ran into Rumania with them! After the war, Hans was reunited with his parents and his grandmother. Believe it or not, Hans Kepler is now a supervisor at the Krupp Steelworks."

Jan was relaxing back in his chair now, his mouth faintly smiling. "Did you ever learn what happened to Dieter Schmidt?"

"Dead. Two weeks after Father Wajda's death and Hartung's return to Warszawa, Schmidt went on a rampage around the countryside, arresting and interrogating people about the epidemic, determined to get the answers that would make him a hero. From what I heard, the man went quite mad. And while he was in one of the outlying villages, Jan, Dieter Schmidt actually contracted typhus and died from it. I saw the result myself of his complement fixation test in the lab."

"My God . . . Maria, Maria. . . ." Jan Szukalski got up from his desk and walked to the window. He stared down at the life and movement in Central Park, seeing for the moment the cobblestone street of a time long past. "How long ago it all was. And yet . . . I remember it all as if it had happened yesterday. I haven't thought much about it these past few years, you know, but, my God, Maria, how you've brought it all back to me. . . ."

She also rose and went to stand by him.

His voice went quietly on. "There we were, fighting our battle. Five partisans. . . ."

"Perhaps we should include two others."

"Two others?"

"Yes, Weil and Felix. Weil was a Czech and Felix was a Pole. And did you know, Jan," her voice fell to a whisper, "that they were also Jews?"

Szukalski gave a little laugh. "Do you think they would have approved of the way we used their famous test?"

And Maria replied softly, "I think they would have been proud of us."